This Time

By Amy Reece

This Time

Copyright © 2018 by Amy Reece.
All rights reserved.
First Print Edition: June 2018

Limitless Publishing, LLC
Kailua, HI 96734
www.limitlesspublishing.com

Formatting: Limitless Publishing

ISBN-13: 978-1-64034-391-7
ISBN-10: 1-64034-391-1

Dedication

For the first responders who risk their lives on a daily basis. Also, for parents who adopt. Your giant hearts are a blessing and an inspiration.

Chapter One

Seamus

Late again. Seamus pulled his t-shirt over his head and ran his hands through his hair, setting it on end, then brushed it back into something approximating a style. He and Sloane hadn't been on time for the weekly family dinner in over six months and they certainly wouldn't be today. His siblings would razz him mercilessly, of course, but neither of his parents would bring any word of reproach. They would simply claim they were happy he was there, no matter how late. He'd prefer an ass-chewing; the unmistakable look of disappointment in their eyes was hard to swallow. *Why do I let her do this to me every week?* He would arrange to pick her up with plenty of time to spare—and lately he'd padded the time in an attempt to circumvent her chronic tardiness—but she was never ready. This afternoon he'd arrived at her apartment a full hour before they needed to leave, but she was still in bed when he let himself in.

"Don't be mad, hon. I was up all night working on the spring lineup." She was a buyer for Macy's, currently in charge of junior women's fashion. Then she smiled in that sultry, seductive way she had and flipped the covers back to reveal her warm, naked body. *"Join me."*

His irritation slipped away as other, more primal emotions took over. His big brain ceased to function as his little brain grabbed control of the situation and ordered him to get naked as fast as humanly possible. Within seconds he was pulling Sloane's gorgeous body against his own and moaning into her mouth.

Forty-five minutes later, he was cursing himself for his inability to resist her. She was now in the shower, which he knew from experience also meant at least an hour extra while she blow-dried her long, blonde hair and applied a crap-ton of makeup. The sex had been great, as always, but was it worth disappointing his family yet again? He used to think so, but lately he wasn't sure. He sighed and grabbed the remote. *I might as well catch part of the game while I wait.*

An hour and fifteen minutes later, she finally reappeared from the bathroom, perfectly coiffed, her full lips glistening. "Why don't I choose a shirt for you from the ones you keep here?" Sloane spritzed perfume as she asked.

"This one's fine. You ready?" He clicked the television off and stood.

"It'll just take me a second to get you a different one." She was already headed toward her closet.

Here we go again. "No, Sloane. The one I'm wearing is perfectly fine." But she wasn't listening.

"Here." She reappeared, a long-sleeved dress shirt in her hands. "This one makes your eyes look so blue."

"My eyes *are* blue." He was not in the mood for this right now. "And I'm wearing this shirt to my parents' house." He pointed to his t-shirt, emblazoned with the logo of the Albuquerque Fire Department. "I like it. It's soft."

She frowned, reaching out to finger the hem. "But it's getting really ratty, babe. It's not something you want to wear out in public."

"It's not public! It's my parents' house! My folks don't give a shit what I wear, Sloane! We're over an hour late, so can we please just go?"

"Fine, Seamus!" She flung the shirt on the bed and crossed her arms. "I guess you don't care how you present yourself to the world, but have you ever thought about how your appearance reflects upon me?"

He laughed, unable to help himself. "What are you talking about? How does me wearing a t-shirt to my parents' house for a barbecue reflect on you in any way?"

"In my career, I need to look good all the time. I also need my boyfriend to look good."

"I wasn't aware your boss would be there today at our family dinner." He was so sick of this argument and the variants of it they'd been having for the past few months.

She apparently didn't care for his snarky comeback. "Well, maybe I should stay home."

He sighed and tried hard not to roll his eyes. "Could we not do this right now? Let's just go to the barbecue, okay?" How did they go from heating up the sheets to a stupid fight in just over an hour?

She stared at him through narrowed eyes for a long moment. "Fine. Wear whatever you want." She turned and stalked out of the bedroom, anger oozing out of every pore.

***

"So, what crawled up the fair Sloane's ass?" Finn appeared at his elbow and handed him a bottle of beer.

"Thanks." Seamus glanced to where Sloane was standing—arms crossed and a sour look on her beautiful face—with his sisters and sisters-in-law. The other women were all chatting amiably, laughing and touching Mel's burgeoning belly, obviously comparing it to Izzy's smaller baby bump. Mel was due in about a month, Izzy sometime around Christmas. The DeLuca family had gained three new members in the last year alone: Mel, Finn's wife; Chris, Hugh's wife; and Mac, Izzy's husband and the father of their five-year-old daughter, Janey. Seamus liked all his siblings' new spouses—although at first, he'd deeply mistrusted Mac, who had been conspicuously absent for the first five years of Janey's life—but he was slightly horrified at how fast things were changing for the DeLuca family. How long would it be before Cara got married? Surely she was next. "Sloane doesn't like my shirt.

4

We had a fight about it earlier." He twisted the top off his beer and took a deep, much-needed pull.

"Is that why you were so late?"

He choked slightly and coughed to cover it up. "Yeah, pretty much."

"Why doesn't she like your shirt? It looks exactly like what you always wear."

"Apparently it's 'getting really ratty.' I'm making her look bad." He took another swig and wished Finn would drop it.

"Nothing could make Sloane look bad." Finn took a pull from his own beer. "But she does look pissed. Better you than me, bro."

Seamus grunted and set his beer on the table. "Whatever. You up for some bocce?"

***

"Are you coming in?" Sloane directed the words to the passenger side window, refusing to look his direction. She'd stayed angry throughout the afternoon, making everyone uncomfortable, until he'd finally decided he should take her home.

He shook his head but realized she couldn't see him in the dark. "I don't think so. It's probably better if I don't stay."

She was silent for a moment. "Fine." She sniffed and finally turned back to him. "I leave for Chicago in the morning."

"I know. I'll be here in time to take you to the airport."

"Don't bother. I'll take an Uber."

He sighed and ran his hand through his hair.

"You don't have to do that, Sloane."

She laughed harshly and wiped her eyes. "I want to."

"How long will you be gone?"

"Um, I'm not really sure. I may stay for a while." She turned to stare out the window again. "I think we need some time apart, Seamus. I love you, but all we ever do is fight these days."

He knew she was right but didn't know how to feel about it. She'd been vocal about saying she loved him for months, and although he'd said it back a few times, he wasn't so sure anymore. What was 'love,' anyway? He loved his family, of course, but loving a woman was obviously different. He'd initially been attracted to her beauty and was thrilled when she gave him her phone number after they were introduced at a friend's party. When they started dating, he'd loved spending time with her and they quickly became exclusive. She'd invited him into her bed a lot sooner than he'd expected, but he certainly hadn't objected. Lately, though, there was more arguing than enjoyment. She constantly harped on what he should wear, what he should eat, where he should spend his free time, etcetera. She resented how much time he spent with his family; she'd rather they went to a club or a bar. "Time apart. Yeah, okay." He stared out the windshield, not seeing anything. "I'll walk you to your door."

"No need. I'll be fine." She opened her door and got out.

He met her at the front of the car. "I'm walking you to your door, Sloane. I don't care how mad we are at each other."

She said nothing until they were on her doorstep. Then she turned to face him. "Thanks. You're always such a gentleman." She reached her hands to his shoulders and stood on tip-toe to kiss him softly, her lips barely brushing his. "I'll see you in a few weeks, okay?"

He nodded, but when she started to step away, he pulled her back and kissed her thoroughly, his tongue sweeping in to meet hers. She complied, but he sensed she wasn't into it. "Bye, Sloane. Call me when you get back." He waited until he heard the deadbolt engage, then turned to leave, wondering if their relationship had a future.

***

He was woken before nine the next morning by his phone buzzing insistently on the nightstand. He reached for it, groggy, thinking it must be Sloane wanting to talk before she left town. But the screen showed his brother's name. Alarm shot through his body as he realized Finn wouldn't call so early on his day off for something innocuous. "What's wrong?" He didn't bother with a greeting. "Is it Sloane?"

"No. It's Neal."

Seamus sat up and rubbed his hand over his eyes, trying to understand what his brother was saying. Why would Finn know anything about Neal Braden, his best friend from high school? Before the question could even finish in his mind, the horrible realization of why Finn would be involved hit him, causing him to gasp for breath. "What happened? Is Neal hurt? Is he okay?"

"He's dead."

***

Nina

"No, David, I don't understand. I'm tired of understanding. And I don't think Lily and Iris are going to understand why you can't be at their birthday party, either. Dammit, David! This is by far the shittiest thing you've done yet!" *Besides leaving me and our daughters for another woman.* Nina rubbed her temple, behind which a mammoth headache was building. Talking on the phone with her ex-husband was always an ordeal.

"Christ, Nina! You're making a federal case out of this. The girls don't care if I'm at their little party. I'll make it up to them later."

They would be heartbroken; they adored David and missed him terribly. He would undoubtedly attempt to make it up to them, bringing them extravagant, unnecessary gifts rather than giving them the time and attention they deserved. "Fine, David. Do whatever you want." He would anyway, no matter how much she nagged or complained; he always did. She never used to consider herself a nag, but she didn't always recognize the woman she'd become since the divorce. She didn't always like her, either. The knock on her office door was a welcome reprieve from the irritating conversation. "I have to go. It would be nice if you could make the time to call sometime on Sunday and wish the girls happy birthday." She hung up before he could find an excuse for not calling. "Come in." She glanced up, expecting one of her students; she was shocked to see Finn DeLuca at the door. She hadn't seen any of the DeLucas for over five years. "Finn? Oh, my God! What in the world are you doing here?" She was halfway to him when she saw he wasn't alone. She stopped in her tracks. His younger brother, Seamus, was with him. Seamus DeLuca, her twin brother's best friend all through high school and the focus of the most intense crush she'd ever had. Neal and Seamus had drifted apart when they went to different colleges but had reconnected over the last few years. Neal had told her about Seamus, but she hadn't seen him since graduation. He'd always been good-looking, but he'd matured into an extremely handsome man, with slightly curly brown hair and muscular arms showing beneath the sleeves of his t-shirt. She cringed to remember the ridiculous things she'd done to attract his attention, all to no avail. He'd never shown the slightest interest.

"Nina, hey," Finn said, looking serious. "I'm afraid I have some bad news."

Her entire body went cold as she realized a state police detective standing at her office door with bad news meant someone she loved was injured or dead. Names and faces ran through her mind: Lily, Iris, Mom, Dad...Neal. *Oh, God!* The only reason Seamus would be here was if something had happened to Neal. She crossed the small room to stand in front of them. "Tell me."

"It's Neal. He's dead. He was found early this morning in his office. I'm so sorry, Nina," Finn said, his demeanor professional, yet sympathetic.

Her knees buckled, and she crumpled to the floor. "No."

Seamus stepped forward and gently lifted her to her feet. He guided her toward the sofa across from her desk and sat next to her. "God, Nina. I'm so sorry."

She looked into his handsome, ravaged face and frowned. "I just talked to him yesterday. He can't be..." She couldn't say the detestable word. "What happened?"

Finn pulled a chair up and sat. "He was discovered early this morning in his office by one of his employees."

She barely heard his words through the buzzing in her head. "What do you mean?" She stared between the two men, perplexed and horrified.

Finn sighed heavily. "At this point, it looks like suicide. I'm sorry."

"Suicide? No, that's not possible." Her head shook from side to side and she didn't seem able to control it. Her hands began to shake, and Seamus reached his over to cover them. "Oh, God, oh, God." She realized she was whimpering, but she couldn't stop. She began to rock back and forth, but Seamus slipped his strong arm around her and pulled her against his warmth. She stopped rocking as the sobs racked her body. She had no idea how much time passed, but she finally felt a wad of tissues being stuffed into her hand and saw Finn place a glass of water on the table in front of her.

"Thank you." She sat up, wiped her face, and reached for the water. "Please, Finn. Tell me what happened."

"The call came in around eight this morning from security at RiskCom." He referred to the computer security company Neal and his business partner, Gordon Sanderson, had started three years before. "Neal's secretary arrived at her normal time and was surprised to see Neal's car already in the parking lot. She said he was in his office when she got to her desk, but his door was locked, and he didn't answer when she knocked. Apparently, he'd been known to spend the night on his couch, so she left him alone. But when he still hadn't appeared an hour later and didn't respond to her knocks or calls, she had security open the door." Finn stood and ran his hands through his hair. "He was slumped over his desk, dead. It looks like he shot himself. He left a note. We tried to contact your parents, but we couldn't reach them."

"They're on a cruise," she said numbly. "I can't believe this. Seamus? Neal would never...oh, God!" She took a moment to gather her composure, breathing deeply and clearing her throat. She could fall apart later, when she was alone. "Do I need to go somewhere and, I don't know, identify him or anything?" She'd never had to deal with death before and had no idea what to do.

"No. Seamus took care of that."

She leaned into his warmth again. "I'm sorry. That must have been awful." She felt him nod and swallow hard, and knew this had to be horrible for him too. She slipped her small hand into his much

11

larger, rough palm and squeezed. "Why? Why would Neal do this? I thought he was happy."

"I don't know, Nina. I just saw him last week and he seemed fine. If I'd known…ah, Jesus!" He swallowed convulsively, and she knew he was struggling against his own tears.

Finn coughed and stood. "I'm gonna head out. Seamus, can you—"

"Yeah, of course. I got this."

Finn told her he'd be in touch soon and left, closing her office door quietly behind him.

She and Seamus sat, arms around each other, for endless moments. Finally, she spoke. "I can't believe this is happening. Please say this isn't real."

"I wish it wasn't." He stood and grabbed a handful of tissues for himself. "When will your parents be back from their cruise?"

"Sunday. I guess I need to call the cruise line and see if I can get in touch with them. Does Kira know yet? What about Gordy?" Kira was Neal's fiancée; Gordy was his business partner.

"We came here first, but Finn will notify them."

"Okay. Oh, God, this is going to destroy Kira! They were planning their wedding!" The tears began again.

"Shh. I know, I know. Listen, let me drive you home. I know you have a lot of phone calls to make, and you'll feel better once you're home. Where are the girls?"

"They're at school. Half-day kindergarten. Then they'll be at the babysitter's until I get off around five. How do I tell them? They loved their Uncle Neal so much!" Her twin daughters, Lily and Iris—

adopted two years ago from Uganda—had formed a special attachment to their uncle, especially after David moved out.

"I'll help you. Do you need to do anything here? Cancel classes or something?"

She shook her head; how did you deal with the mundane when your world had just been knocked off course? "No. I only have office hours this afternoon. I already taught two classes this morning." She was an associate professor of history at the University of New Mexico in Albuquerque. She had completed and passed her dissertation last spring from the university and had been hired to teach the 101-level classes the other professors abhorred. It was fine by her; she got paid no matter what she taught and was able to begin her post-grad work. She had managed to snag one upper level class, anyway, and thoroughly enjoyed it. "I need to talk to my department head about cancelling classes tomorrow, though." She stood and crossed to her desk to send the emails. "Seamus, you don't have to stay. I know you must have things you need to do."

"I'm staying, Nina. Period. I'm not scheduled to work until Wednesday." He crossed to where she was seated and stood behind her, massaging her shoulders, the way he'd done so many times in the distant past when they were kids. "You don't have to do this on your own."

The tears sprang to her eyes again. She felt like she'd been on her own, working, raising two adorable, yet precocious daughters, for so long. Her parents were wonderful, of course, offering to babysit at least once a week, but she hated to burden them. These were their golden years and they should be free to take the cruises and tours they'd never been able to before when they had a houseful of children. She and Neal had two older brothers who lived out of state. Neal helped out whenever he could, but starting a business took nearly all his spare time; his fiancée demanded the rest. Kira was understanding about Nina's situation, but she rightfully expected a fair amount of Neal's time; Nina was reluctant to ask the two of them to watch her children simply so she could have a social life. She reached her hand up to touch Seamus's. "Thank you. I can't tell you what this means to me."

"Of course. Come on. Let's get you home."

Chapter Two

Seamus

"Okay, Nick. Yeah, love you too. See you soon." Nina set her cell phone on the table and leaned her head into her hands.

Seamus placed the mug of tea in front of her and rubbed her tight shoulders.

She sat up and sipped the tea he'd liberally laced with honey. "Thanks."

"When is Nick coming?"

"He's going to check the airlines and get the soonest flight he can." She sighed heavily and sipped the tea before reaching for her cell again. "I need to call Nathan, and then try the cruise line once more." She'd been able to get hold of her oldest brother right away, but the other brother hadn't answered, and the cruise line had given her the run-around, telling her she needed to call their customer service line, which had stated her wait time was forty-five minutes.

"What time do the girls get home?"

"Around five." Her first phone call had been to her afternoon babysitter to arrange for them to be driven home so she wouldn't have to leave to pick them up. Seamus had volunteered to go get them, but since he'd never met them she declined, saying it would freak them out to be picked up by a strange man.

"Is there any way I could convince you to lie down for a little while? I can call the cruise line. I promise I'll wake you up if I get through to your parents." He continued to rub her slim shoulders. This had to be one of the worst days of her life and she was holding up like a champ, but he could tell she was emotionally exhausted and he wanted to help.

She glanced up at him, her eyes hollow and haunted. "Maybe. I'll try to get through to Nathan again first. Thanks, Seamus. I don't think I could do this alone."

"Sure. Of course. Call Nathan while I make you a sandwich or something." He gave her shoulders a final squeeze, then retreated to the kitchen to see what he could find that she might like. The refrigerator was covered with crayon and watercolor artwork from her daughters, along with brightly colored alphabet magnets spelling words such as 'cat,' 'dog,' and 'poop.' He smiled at the last word as he searched inside, finding the makings for turkey and cheese sandwiches. He made one for Nina and two for himself; he hadn't eaten anything all day and his stomach was growling, although he had no desire to do something as mundane as eat a meal. His best friend was dead, had apparently shot

16

himself. If Seamus lived to be a hundred, he'd never forget the sight of Neal Braden slumped over his desk, a gun in his left hand, blood and brain matter pooling around his body and dripping from the walls. As a firefighter, Seamus was used to accident scenes with plenty of blood and gore, but it was different seeing it on someone he knew. He'd taken one look and rushed for the adjacent bathroom to vomit repeatedly into the toilet. Finn had asked him to come to identify the body, which Seamus was glad to do. No family member should have to see something like that, and as the only one currently in town, it would have been Nina.

He grabbed a couple sodas from the fridge and carried the plate of sandwiches to the dining room, where Nina was sitting at the table, talking on her cell phone, tears streaming down her face.

"I know, Nate. Yeah, me too. I'll let you know when I get the funeral scheduled."

Seamus set the plate near her and waited while she finished the tough conversation with her brother.

She hung up and wiped the tears away. "Oh, God."

"Here." He slid the plate and soda toward her. "See if you can eat a little bit."

She took a half sandwich and bit into it unenthusiastically. "Nate's wife is pregnant and due in a few days, so he can't leave right now. He'll be here for the funeral, though, if it's at all possible."

He watched her take a sip of the soda, noting her hand was shaking. He made no comment as he reached for one of the sandwiches and ate it in two

17

bites, needing the food even though it tasted like sawdust. She was handling this like a trooper; he couldn't begin to imagine the level of sorrow she was going through. His older brother, Finn, had been seriously wounded the year before in a hit-and-run and had been in a coma for two weeks. The entire DeLuca family had gone through hell during those long days, but Finn had recovered and now had only a slight limp as evidence of all he'd endured. Neal was dead and would never be restored to the Bradens. Family was everything and theirs had just been ripped apart.

She ate only a few bites before pushing the plate away. "I think I'll lie down for a while, if you don't mind."

"Good idea. I'll keep trying to get through to your parents."

She stood and moved to stand behind him, then leaned down and hugged him from behind. "Thank you."

While she slept, he cleaned up the few dishes from lunch, throwing the unwanted remains of the sandwiches in the trash, before he attempted to call the cruise line again. He was finally connected to someone who could help, and hung up after being promised a return call as soon as they located Neal's parents. He wandered around Nina's living room, unable to settle down. He examined the many books on the shelves; Nina had always been such a brain, even back in high school. Neal was no slouch in the grades department, but Nina had always been a straight-A student and had earned a full academic scholarship to some Ivy League college he'd never heard of. Neal had been so proud of his twin sister and her achievements, including graduating summa cum laude with her master's degree in history and completing her doctorate two years later. Neal hadn't been as thrilled when she married David Schaeler, one of her professors from graduate school. Seamus had never met the guy, but Neal said he was an arrogant idiot and Nina could do so much better. He'd dragged her off to Africa about a year later for some sort of research for a new book he was writing and decided they needed to adopt an orphan. Neal said Nina had let it slip that she wasn't too thrilled with the idea, but David insisted. He'd managed to push through an adoption in record time—Neal was sure he'd bribed the officials—and ended up with three-year-old twins, Lily and Iris. The marriage hadn't lasted, and Nina ended up with full custody of the girls; Neal suspected David hadn't contested it because he'd already found another woman whom he'd gotten pregnant and moved in with. The only thing Neal had approved of was David's new position here in Albuquerque that caused Nina to move back. Seamus didn't think he'd handle it as well if someone had treated one of his sisters that way.

He continued to roam the living room, noting the many photographs of family members and of Nina and the girls. He picked up a glossy photo of the three of them taken near a pool, probably the one in her parents' backyard. The girls were cute in their glittery swimsuits, laughing with their mother; Nina was gorgeous in a pair of shorts and a red tank top. He smiled crookedly at the photo and set it back on

19

the mantle. Yeah, he'd always thought Nina Braden was beautiful and would have loved to ask her out, but Neal wouldn't hear of it.

"No way, man! You are not allowed to date my sister! I know what kind of guy you are. My sister is a sweet girl and I'm not about to let her go out with a horn dog like you. Forget it."

So, he had. He knew she'd nursed a bit of a crush on him—he wasn't blind, deaf, and dumb—but he never acted on it. Neal was right: Seamus was more interested in girls he could sweet-talk into sex than his best friend's brainy sister. But he'd always thought she was pretty. There *had* been one memorable kiss, but—

"That was taken in June. Neal took it," she said from behind him, causing him to jump guiltily.

"Sorry. I didn't mean to snoop."

She reached past him and took the photograph. "You're not. Pictures are made to look at. We had such fun that day. Lily had just lost her front tooth that morning."

Seamus looked at the girls and noticed the one in the blue swimsuit had a gap in her smile. "How can you tell them apart?" The girls looked identical to him, apart from the missing tooth, which was temporary.

She glanced up at him, her green eyes wide. "I don't know. I've always been able to tell the difference. David had trouble, though. Did you get through to the cruise line?"

"Yeah. They'll call as soon as they locate your

folks. Did you sleep?"

"A bit." She turned as the front door opened and two small girls ran in, shedding colorful backpacks as they entered.

"Momma! Why didn't you pick us up?" One of the girls ran straight to Nina and flung her arms around her legs.

"Are you sick, Momma?" The other little girl stopped as she caught sight of Seamus. "Who's he?"

Seamus watched as Nina took a huge breath and knelt down to hug and kiss her daughters. Both girls had short, black hair and dark, chocolate-hued skin. He was surprised at how good their English was; Neal had said they'd learned it quickly, but they didn't have any trace of an accent as far he could tell.

"This is Seamus. He's Uncle Neal's best friend. Girls, I have some bad news."

***

Nina

"I don't understand, Momma. Why did Uncle Neal die?" Lily's eyes filled with tears again as she looked into her mother's face.

Iris was still huddled against her, head butted hard against Nina's chest as she sobbed.

Nina looked helplessly at Seamus, seated on the other end of the sofa. She had simply told them their uncle had died earlier that day, without going into any of the details. She didn't want to tell them anything about gunshots or suicide. It wasn't something a six-year-old needed to know. "We don't really know yet, sweetie," Nina said, hedging.

"But I don't want him to die!"

Nina pulled Lily close and kissed her head, inhaling the comforting fragrance of her little girl. She hadn't been ready to be a mother when David manipulated her into agreeing to the adoption— she'd only been twenty-three years old, after all— but she'd fallen completely in love with these two angels the moment they met. She'd held her breath through the appearance in front of the judge in the courthouse in downtown Kampala, even though she knew for a fact David had paid him off to expedite their case. He'd also paid off the officials at the orphanage, who were amenable to the bribes as long as David and Nina were willing to adopt the two sisters together. They'd brought the little girls home and had been amazed by how fast they adapted to life in the United States and how quickly they learned English. Both parents regretted the girls' loss of their native Swahili, but neither David nor Nina spoke much beyond the most basic of greetings. It was quite different than what Nina had envisioned for her life as she finished her master's degree and began working on her PhD in history, but she loved it. David, however, was soon bored by the structure required to successfully raise two young children; he eventually told Nina he was having an affair with a grad assistant and wanted a divorce. She wasn't terribly surprised. After all— and to her everlasting shame—she'd been the one he'd left his first wife for. "I know, baby. I know."

She hugged the girls, sniffing and swallowing hard to control her own tears.

"Listen, I know everyone's sad, but you girls have got to be hungry. What if I order a pizza?" Seamus asked quietly.

Nina smiled gratefully over the top of Lily's head.

Iris peeked up at her. "I'm hungry, Momma. Can we have pizza?" It would be a special treat since she was usually careful to serve more nutritious food, so Nina nodded.

Lily sat up and glanced at her twin. "I'm hungry too. Can we have pepperoni pizza?" She was typically the more outspoken of the two girls, but Iris was more often the leader.

Nina took the opportunity while the girls were distracted by the thought of food to ask about their day at school and get them started on their homework sheets. Soon, they were seated at the kitchen table with a box of crayons, practicing their letters. She'd needed to tell them right away, but she didn't want them dwelling on their uncle's death too long. There would be days and weeks ahead filled with the myriad issues that accompanied a death in the family. Seamus seemed willing to handle all the details associated with the evening meal, so she concentrated on listening to the girls practice their reading and helped them with their math problems, which they both hated. When a glass of wine appeared in front of her, she could have kissed him. She sipped the red blend he'd found in her pantry and remembered a time—long ago—when she had.

"How do I look?"

Her best friend, Ashley, stared at her critically. "You look fucking hot! Seamus DeLuca is an idiot if he doesn't sweep you into his arms and make mad, passionate love to you on the spot!"

Nina laughed self-consciously and turned back to her reflection. She smoothed her boring brown hair, teased impossibly high for the occasion, and added another layer of gloss on top of the dark red lipstick. Ashley had made up her eyes with lots of black eyeliner and dark eyeshadow, telling her it made her look sexy and sophisticated. Against her oh-so-pale skin, Nina feared it made her look dead. She'd borrowed the short, tight skirt, low-cut blouse, and push-up bra from Ashley; she didn't begin to own anything designed to seduce a guy. And that was the purpose of tonight's adventure: she was planning to seduce her brother's best friend. Neal was out of town for the weekend, on a college visit with their parents, and she was finally going to make her move on the guy she'd been dreaming about for six years, ever since they were in sixth grade. She had no experience whatsoever in seduction, of course—she'd never even been kissed—but Seamus undoubtedly had plenty. She figured if she could get him to kiss her, he could handle the rest. She was seventeen years old and ready for this. Maybe. Probably. Oh, God. She knew everyone considered her a brainy nerd and she'd fostered the reputation, happy to spend her time dreaming of Seamus; the real world of boys scared the crap out of her. She had spent her adolescence fantasizing about a time when he would look at her and finally realize they were soul mates. *"Hopefully not on the spot. I don't really fancy such a public deflowering, thanks."*

"Deflowering? You read way too many Regency romances. We need to get going, Nina! We want to make sure we get there before he hooks up with some slutty girl."

"Some other slutty girl, you mean?" Nina adjusted the push-up bra. *"Are my nipples supposed to be poking out?"*

Ashley pulled the blouse up slightly. *"There. All your goodies are tucked in. For now. I'm sure Seamus will love unwrapping his present."* She wiggled her eyebrows up and down.

By the time they arrived, the party was in full swing. Nina had never attended one of the parties her brother and Seamus frequented; Neal never allowed it. She would have sneaked out and gone, but it would be stupid when he would just rat her out to their parents. Besides, she wasn't interested in parties. She was only interested in Seamus. She spotted him soon after they walked in. He was sitting with a group of his friends, laughing and drinking a beer. One of them spied Ashley and Nina as they helped themselves to drinks and tapped Seamus, motioning to them with his red plastic cup.

Seamus choked on his beer, set it on the table, and walked to her slowly. *"Nina?"* He looked her up and down, narrowing his eyes as he took in her breasts oozing out of her top. *"What the hell, Nina? Why are you here? You never come to these parties. You hate them."*

"No, I don't." She already did. The music was

too loud, there were far too many people, and it smelled like sour beer. Ashley melted away with a wave; Nina was on her own. "Neal never lets me come. But he's out of town this weekend, so what he doesn't know won't hurt him."

"Unless I tell him." Seamus took the beer from her. "You're drinking now?"

"Why not? You and Neal do. Why shouldn't I have fun like you guys? I'm sick of staying home every goddamned weekend while you two are out painting the town, getting drunk, and sleeping with any girl who will have you. Well, tonight I'm going to get drunk and get laid. It's my turn." She had no intention of doing either of those things; she hated the taste of beer and she planned to make love with Seamus, not get laid. There had to be a difference. Surely there did.

"Oh, it is, huh? And you think I'm gonna stand by and let my best friend's little sister go wild at a party?"

She stepped forward and poked him hard in the chest, fury infusing her at his over-protective reaction. He was supposed to take one look at her and realize he'd always wanted her. What was happening to all her plans? "We're twins, asshole! I'm not his little sister! And I'm sick to death of missing out on everything because I'm too nerdy and ugly for anyone to want to fuck!" She ended on a sob as her visions of how the evening was supposed to go evaporated. God, what a fool she was!

He grabbed her hand and pulled her close. "Okay, okay. Shh. You're causing a big scene, sweetheart. Come on." He led her to the family room, where several couples were dancing. "Let's dance. You can tell me what's going on and why you decided to suddenly dress like a hooker."

She pulled her hand away and punched him as hard as she could in the stomach. "I hate you, Seamus DeLuca!" She turned to leave. This had been an epically bad idea.

"Ow! God, girl! That hurt!"

"Yeah, well, you and Neal taught me how to hit, so it's your fault." She spit the words over her shoulder.

He grabbed her arm and pulled her back. "I'm sorry. I shouldn't have said that. You don't look like a hooker. You just...I've never seen you like this." He reached to button her blouse.

She swatted his hand away. "I like the way I look." She hated it. "And I'm going to find someone who appreciates it more than you. Goodbye, Seamus. Have a lovely time tonight with your slut du jour. I'm sure you'll rat me out to Neal, but there's nothing he can do at the moment, so you can both suck it!"

He laughed and grabbed her hand again. "Come on. I said I'm sorry. I'm not about to let you loose looking all sexy and illegal in that getup, but you can stay for a little while if you stick close to me. Deal? I won't tell Neal."

She narrowed her eyes and frowned.

"Come on. Let's dance." He pulled her into his arms as the music changed to something slow.

She'd dreamed of this moment for almost seven years. She put her arms around his neck and laid

27

her head against his chest. She wanted to bottle his smell. She could feel his hard muscles pressed against her breasts and it did funny things to her nether regions. Oh, goodness!

"You have quite a mouth on you. I had no idea."

"I've been saving up for a rainy day."

"Apparently," he said with a chuckle. "What's this really about, Nina? This isn't like you."

She shrugged, unsure of her reasons any longer. It was hard to remember when he was holding her so close. God, he felt and smelled so good. "Maybe I just want to see what I'm missing."

"I don't think you're missing anything. You're smart and beautiful and sweet. You don't need to hang out at a party like this."

He thought she was beautiful? Her heart sang as they danced. When the song was finished, he led her to the kitchen for a soda and some snacks. She wasn't sure she could eat in the tight skirt, but she accepted a bowl of chips. She stayed at his side for the next hour or so as they made their way through the crowded house. It wasn't like the party scenes from movies. These people were obviously veteran partiers and contained themselves to drinking, smoking, and talking loudly. No one was trashing the house or vomiting on the carpet. Seamus shook his head when she asked about what was going on upstairs. She'd seen people disappear, some couples, some singles, and figured the hard partying happened up there.

"You don't need to see upstairs, sweetheart. We'll stick to the first floor tonight."

"Is that where the sex and drugs are?"

28

Seamus choked on his beer. *"Yeah. Something like that."*

She leaned close and whispered, *"Is that pot?"* She pointed to a group on the sofa who were passing around a small, white, cigarette-type object.

"Yes."

"I've never tried marijuana," she mused.

"And you're not going to try it tonight. Not on my watch." He steered her toward the door. *"Okay. You've had your party experience. Time to get Cinderella home from the ball."*

They drove in silence. She stared out the window as she wiped the ridiculous red lipstick off with a tissue. Tonight had been a disaster. Yeah, she'd gotten Seamus's attention, but he still treated her like a sister and nothing more. It was humiliating.

"You okay?"

"I'm fine." She didn't turn to look at him as they pulled in front of her house. *"Just drop me at the curb."*

He cut the engine and opened his door. *"No."*

She sighed and got out. Would this God-forsaken, miserable mistake of a night never end? She trudged up the walk to her front door as he followed behind. She fished in her bag for her key, swallowing the tears that were fighting their way out. *"Thank you. This was stupid. Sorry I ruined the party for you."*

"You didn't ruin anything, Nina. Are you going to be okay?"

She nodded and squeezed her eyes shut as a tear leaked out, streaking through her makeup.

Seamus wiped it away with his thumb. "I like you better without all this crap on your face."

Sure he did. That's why all the girls he dated looked like they'd just stepped out of a Sephora makeover. She laughed shakily. "I just wanted to see what it was like to be one of your crowd for a night. I wanted a little excitement."

"Was it exciting?" He smiled crookedly, a look of doubt on his face.

She shook her head. "It was embarrassing." She looked down at her borrowed clothes. "I look ridiculous."

"You look hot. But you don't need all this. Just be yourself, Nina."

"I'm sick of being myself! All I do is study and sit around reading books! I've never even been kissed! Guys don't like me, Seamus."

"Guys are intimidated by you because they know you're smarter than they are." He wiped away another tear. "Never been kissed, huh? Well, we can't have that." He bent his head and laid his lips softly on hers.

She stood, stunned, as his arms slid around her waist. He was kissing her! Seamus DeLuca was actually kissing her! It was over before she could make up her mind what to do.

"There. Now you can't say you've never been kissed." His hands rested loosely on her hips.

She stared up into his achingly handsome face and bit her lip. "Could you do it again? Please? I was so shocked I didn't have a chance to enjoy it."

He raised his eyebrows as if surprised by her honesty. "Sure. No problem." Then he bent and kissed her again.

This time she was ready for him. She reached her arms around his neck to play with the dark brown curls at his nape. God, his hair was so soft! She didn't know what exactly to do with her mouth, but she'd read a lot of kisses and tried softening her lips under his, moving them slightly to match what he did. It seemed to work, because he made a soft groaning sound and she felt his tongue lick her bottom lip, as if seeking entrance to her mouth. She knew what French kissing was and was eager to try. She opened her lips a bit and was thrilled when his tongue swept inside. Then she stopped thinking and analyzing and simply felt. Oh, God, it was good. He backed her against the screen door and let his hands wander to curve around her bottom, pulling her tight against him. Then his other hand slipped up to tease her breast, flicking lightly against the nipple poking through her blouse. Her heart pounded so hard she was sure he could feel it, but she had no intention of stopping him. He tasted so good and his touch set her on fire. She met his tongue stroke for stroke, her hands slipping down to his strong shoulders.

He pulled away with a groan and rested his head against hers, panting. "I didn't mean to get so carried away. Sorry, Nina."

"I don't mind. I liked it. Do you want to come inside?" She would gladly continue this on her couch and see it to its logical conclusion.

"No!" He stepped away quickly and stuffed his hands in his jeans pockets. "I've gotta go. You get inside and lock up. I'll wait. Go on!" His voice was

rough.

She blinked at his sudden change of mood. "Oh. Okay. Well, thanks for...everything. Good night." She turned and fumbled to unlock the door.

"Good night, Nina."

She went in and locked up, then watched through the glass as he drove away.

"Done! Momma, can we watch cartoons 'til the pizza comes?" Iris tapped her arm impatiently.

She shook herself out of her ill-timed reverie and smiled. "Of course, Angel. Put all your papers in your homework folders first." She supervised the organization of their backpacks and sent them to watch television. She glanced at Seamus as he prepared a salad at the counter. Why, on the day her brother died, was she remembering her teenage folly? Then he turned and smiled at her and she knew.

Chapter Three

Seamus

He awoke to the smell of coffee and a painful crick in his neck from sleeping on Nina's sofa. It would have been a better idea to go home, but once she'd put the girls to bed she'd needed to talk. It was past midnight when she'd finally felt like she could sleep, and she'd asked him to stay. He could hear her now in the kitchen, so he folded the afghan and spent a few minutes in the bathroom, splashing his face with cold water and finger-combing his hair into some semblance of order. He grimaced at the dark whiskers covering his jaw, but he didn't have a razor, so it would have to do.

Nina was at the stove, scrambling eggs. She turned as he reached to pour himself a cup of coffee. "Hey. Did you get any sleep?"

He took in her pale face, red eyes, and drooping shoulders. "Some. Looks like you didn't get much."

She smiled wanly as she shrugged. "Not really." She turned back to the stove. "The girls will be up

33

in a few minutes."

He watched as she stirred the eggs, her petite, slim figure wrapped in a black knit robe. *God, this is the worst day of her life and yet she has to carry on, fixing breakfast and taking care of her kids. She shouldn't have to do this by herself.* He admired her strength while at the same time his heart ached for her. "Here. Let me do that." He gently took the spatula from her hands and took over at the stove. "You go take care of the girls."

She smiled gratefully and padded out of the kitchen, her bare feet making no sound on the tile.

Seamus stirred the eggs, then turned to pop some bread in the toaster. By the time Nina reappeared with the two sleepy girls in tow, he had the table set for four. The girls eyed him warily and he knew they had to be confused by his sudden appearance in their lives. "Good morning, girls. Your mom made you some eggs; I just finished them up. Here you go, Iris." He set the plate in front of one of the girls and prayed he'd got it right. "And for you, Lily." The girls looked at their mother, eyes wide, so he figured he'd remembered correctly. "I hope it's okay that I slept on your couch last night. Your mom and I stayed up pretty late talking, so she said I could sleep there." Although he knew they were too young to know much about it, he wanted to make it clear he hadn't taken advantage of Nina.

"Momma's sad about Uncle Neal." Lily spoke through a mouthful of eggs. "Are you sad too?"

He set his mug on the table and nodded. "Yeah. He was my best friend all through middle and high school." When Neal had moved back to

Albuquerque after college and started his own business, Seamus had welcomed the chance to reconnect. They met up every couple weeks for a beer and had introduced their girlfriends to each other. Sloane hadn't clicked with Kira, though, so they'd never repeated it.

He offered to clean up while Nina got the girls ready for school. He had no idea how one woman managed to do all that was involved with taking care of two small girls, keeping her house fairly clean, and working full time. He hoped she had some sort of help occasionally. He also hoped her ex-husband was generous with the alimony and child support. The guy had written some book that turned out to be a best seller or something, so he could afford it.

Finn had arranged for Nina's Subaru to be brought home from her office, so they buckled the girls into their car seats and dropped them off at school before heading to Seamus's apartment so he could grab a shower, shave, and change clothes before they set to work seeing to all the funeral arrangements. They were scheduled to meet Kira at the funeral home in a little over an hour. He left Nina sitting on the couch with the TV remote while he headed to his bedroom to clean up.

Once back in the SUV, she cleared her throat. "Seamus, I can't tell you how much I appreciate all your help." She stared out the passenger side window as she spoke, so he wasn't able to see her expression. "But I know you probably have a million other things you'd rather do on your day off."

35

"Yeah, I'd rather do anything except help arrange my best friend's funeral, but I'm sure it's not at the top of your list, either."

"No, it's not." She whispered the words then turned to him suddenly. "What about your girlfriend? Sloane, isn't it?"

"What about her?" Guilt made him wince as he spoke. He hadn't thought much about Sloane since Finn's phone call the day before. "She's out of town on business right now."

Nina stared at him for a long moment before turning back to the window. "Oh."

He glanced at her as he drove, noting the graceful curve of her slender neck. She'd pulled her hair back into a low ponytail, and he could see where her neck met her shoulder, the skin creamy and soft. He felt the pull of desire low in his gut and quickly turned his gaze toward the road. *Seriously? On a day like today? Don't be a dick! Plus, remember you have a girlfriend.*

Her cell phone dinged with a text message. "Nick's flight gets in at five."

"I can pick him up."

She smiled at him, but it didn't quite reach her eyes. "Thanks. I'll tell him to look for you."

She'd finally been able to talk to her parents late the night before and Seamus had held her for a long time after she'd hung up. They were making arrangements to catch a flight home from their next port of call, Barbados, the following day. He knew once she had her family with her he would need to clear out, but he was determined to stick close until she had them here. He pulled into the parking lot of the funeral home.

She sighed heavily but opened her door.

Kira was waiting for them. She wore jeans and an oversized sweatshirt, but Seamus noted she'd still made up her face with lots of eyeliner and lipstick. She was one of those high maintenance types, much like Sloane. Nina had barely taken time to change out of her pajamas and it didn't look like she wore any makeup, yet he thought her natural beauty and grace much more suited to the occasion. Kira and Nina shared a brief hug, then held hands as they were shown to the reception room where they would have to choose a coffin for Neal and make other decisions regarding his funeral service. Seamus had never been closely involved in a death before and hated every second they spent in the funeral home. He'd attended funerals, of course, but he'd never seen all the decisions that went into them beforehand.

Once they'd chosen the casket—a simple, dark cherry-finish with smooth lines—the director sat them down around a small table. "I spoke with the coroner's office this morning about when your brother's body will be released, but they weren't able to give me an exact day."

"What does that mean?" Seamus asked the question as Kira and Nina frowned at each other.

The funeral director smiled sympathetically. "In cases like this, there has to be an investigation. It shouldn't take more than a few days. I'll call you as soon as I hear from them and we can make arrangements for a specific day and time for the funeral."

They decided on the type of service and filled out the paperwork, including the payment options, which Nina insisted the family would take care of. Kira argued softly, but briefly, and Seamus felt sure she was relieved. When there was nothing else to be done, they left and walked to the parking lot together. The bright, sunny day mocked the darkness each was feeling as they stood beside Nina's SUV, shielding their eyes, and talked.

"Nick will be in tonight," Nina said. "Why don't you come over?"

Kira nodded. "Sure. Should I bring anything?"

"No. I'll take care of dinner." She sighed. "I hate this. Have you talked to Gordy, yet?"

"Briefly. He's keeping the office closed for a few days until Neal's office can be cleaned." She finished on a sob and Nina pulled her into her arms, rubbing her back as she cried. At length they finally separated, and Kira bid them goodbye.

Seamus and Nina sat in the SUV with the air conditioner on full blast for a few moments, collecting their thoughts. Finally, Seamus spoke. "Finn texted. He wants us to stop by the precinct for a few minutes."

Nina turned to him, smiling softly. "Okay."

He put the car in reverse and backed out. "Listen, I was thinking maybe I could take the girls for a while tonight, so you and your brother and Kira can talk freely about what happened. I can take them over to Mom and Dad's to swim and have dinner."

"Oh, Seamus! You don't have to do that. We can wait until they go to bed. I'm sure babysitting is the last thing you want to do tonight."

"Let me help, Nina. The girls don't need to be around all this sorrow. Let them come with me and have some fun. I'll wear them out so they'll sleep good tonight. Maybe I can get Izzy to bring Janey over. She's in kindergarten too, and I bet they'll all get along great." He pulled up to a red light and turned to her. "Come on, Nina. I'm a firefighter, trained in CPR and advanced first-aid, so I'm about the safest babysitter you'll ever find. Plus, my mom will love them."

"Well, if you're sure, it would be a great help. Thanks." She reached for his hand and squeezed it briefly.

Finn wasn't at his desk when they arrived at the state police precinct, but Chris, Seamus's sister-in-law and Finn's partner, introduced herself to Nina and showed them to a small conference room. "Finn just stepped out for a few minutes, but he'll be right back. I'm so sorry for your loss, Ms. Braden."

"Thank you. Call me Nina, please. You're Hugh's wife, right?"

Chris smiled and nodded. "We've been married nearly a year."

"Congratulations. He's a nice guy."

Seamus stepped out to call his mom while Nina and Chris chatted. She was, as expected, thrilled to host an impromptu swim party later that evening and said she would make sure Janey was there. He thanked her and hung up as Finn rounded the corner.

"Sorry. I was in a meeting with some Border Patrol agents. Let me grab the file. How's Nina today?"

"She's okay. She's holding it together better than Neal's fiancée." Seamus put his phone away and followed his brother to his desk.

"Yeah, we talked to her yesterday. I'm glad you're there to help Nina get through this." Finn clapped him on the shoulder and led the way to the conference room.

Seamus claimed the empty chair beside Nina and held her hand as Finn handed her a copy of the note they'd found on Neal's desk. She held it so he could read at the same time. It was typed except for the signature.

My Darling Kira,
I'm so sorry, but I just can't live like this any longer. The pain of living every day, trying to put on a smile and pretend it's all going to get better is too hard. Tell Nina I'm sorry.

Love,

Neal

***

Nina

Oh, God! This is rough! Neal, why? Why didn't you talk to me? I had no clue you were so desperately unhappy! She sniffed, determined not to cry. She needed to keep it together here at the police station so she could get information about Neal's death. She could fall apart later, and no doubt would, when Nick arrived. For now, there was serious business to attend to. "May I keep this?"

Finn nodded. "Of course. We have to retain the original, but you can take this copy." He pushed a box of tissue closer as he spoke. "We need to ask you some questions, Nina. I know this is hard, but we want to find out what happened. Okay?"

"Yeah. Yes, of course. Go ahead." She reached for Seamus's hand again. She needed his strength to get through this.

"Can you tell us about Neal's state of mind in the days preceding his death? How was he acting?" Chris opened a small notebook as she spoke.

"Um, he was fine, as far as I could tell. I saw him on Saturday when he came over to the house. He and Kira came for dinner. He seemed fine! God, why didn't he tell me?"

"What about you?" Finn addressed the question to Seamus. "When was the last time you saw or heard from Neal?"

"We met up for a beer on Thursday. He talked about his wedding. He said he and Kira had finally set a date and she was getting all into looking at dresses. We laughed about it. Nina," he said as he turned to her, "he was fine. I would swear he was fine. Why did he do this?"

She shook her head, the tears escaping from her eyes against her will. "I don't know."

Chris took over. "Were you aware he was taking a prescription medication for depression?"

"What?" Seamus and Nina spoke at the same time.

41

Chris reached into a box beside her chair and pulled out a plastic baggy containing a prescription bottle. She placed it on the table between Seamus and Nina.

Neal M. Braden. Paxil (paroxetine) 30 mg. Take one tablet by mouth daily.

"This doesn't make any sense." Nina smoothed the plastic over the pill bottle. "Paxil is an antidepressant, isn't it? Why wouldn't he tell me he was depressed?"

"Did Neal own a gun?" Chris scratched notes in her notepad as she asked.

Nina nodded, still staring at the prescription bottle. "He had several, I believe. My dad and brothers were big into hunting, so I'm sure Neal had guns."

"Was it unusual for him to go into the office on a weekend? His secretary found him early Monday morning and we have a time of death between 10 p.m. and 2 a.m."

"It was his company—his and Gordy's—so they worked a lot. Nights, weekends, it didn't matter. It was only this year that they've been able to afford to hire office help."

"And how was the company doing financially?"

Nina looked up. "It was doing fairly well. He said they'd cleared a decent profit in the last few months and he felt like it was finally going someplace. I don't know the exact figures; Neal only talked about it in generalities."

"What about you, Seamus?" Finn asked. "What

did he tell you about his financial situation?"

Seamus scrubbed his hands through his hair, setting it on end. "Not much. I would usually ask him how business was and he'd say 'oh, it's great,' and then we'd talk about sports. I don't know anything about computer cyber security or whatever it was he did. God, I don't understand this! Neal was the last guy on earth I would have thought would kill himself! He had everything going for him! Why?"

Nina reached her hand to squeeze his arm. She was eternally grateful he was here with her—she didn't think she'd have been able to get through it on her own—but she knew it had to be killing him. She turned back to the detectives. "When will they release his body? The funeral director didn't know, and I'd like to be able to set a date for the service."

Chris and Finn looked at each other, as if trying to decide who would field the question. Finn finally spoke. "We're not sure. The Office of the Medical Investigator is requiring a full autopsy—"

"Why?" Nina was shocked. "What does that mean? I don't understand."

"Suicides are reportable deaths, meaning we are required to report them to the OMI, who investigates and eventually issues the death certificate. Neal's body can't be released to your family until they have determined the cause of death."

Nina frowned. "But it was a gunshot, wasn't it?"

Chris closed her notebook and stood, signaling an end to the questioning. "That's for the OMI to determine. I'm sure we'll hear from them in a few days and then you'll be able to make the final arrangements. I know this is a difficult time for your family, Nina." She suddenly switched from her professional demeanor. "Please let Hugh and I know if there's anything we can do."

"Thanks, Chris. You too, Finn." She attempted a weak smile. "My brother, Nick, is coming later today. Nathan can't leave his wife right now, and my parents won't be able to get here for a few more days, so maybe this delay is a good thing."

Seamus led her from the precinct and they sat in her SUV for a few minutes, both emotionally exhausted by the morning. "We need to eat, but I don't think I can take sitting in a restaurant right now. What if we grab a couple sandwiches and find a park?"

They stopped at a nearby deli and then found a picnic table under a tree at a park where Nina frequently took the girls to play. She picked at her sandwich unenthusiastically. "This is surreal, Seamus. An autopsy? This doesn't happen to people like us. What's going on?"

"I don't know. All those questions made me realize there's a lot about Neal I never knew. Depressed? Do you think it had anything to do with his headaches?" Neal had suffered from migraines since he was a kid.

Nina shrugged. "Maybe. I know they still bothered him, but he never made a big deal out of it. He said Kira gave him something that helped more than anything he'd ever used, but he never said what it was. Maybe she got one of her doctor friends to prescribe something." Kira was an ICU nurse at one of the local hospitals. "And I never asked. God! I never asked him anything! He rarely mentioned his headaches to me anymore, so I assumed they'd gotten better."

They both nibbled at their lunch for a while, then decided to head back to Nina's. She needed to clean up the house and get some work done. They would both be returning to work the next day, Seamus for a twenty-four-hour shift. He volunteered to run the vacuum and dust, saying he needed to stay busy. She gratefully accepted his offer, glad for the extra time it provided her.

Nina sat at her computer and planned for the next day's classes, but her heart wasn't in it. She usually loved creating PowerPoint presentations to go along with her lectures, attempting to make history as fascinating to her students as it was to her, but today she was going through the motions. She also needed to spend time on her article for *The Western Historical Quarterly*—publish or perish, after all— but found herself researching paroxetine instead. The lengthy list of possible side effects was horrifying, including suicidal thoughts or tendencies. Was this what had happened to Neal? Had this medication, designed to help him deal with depression, caused him to want to kill himself instead? Her doctor had wanted to prescribe an antidepressant in the wake of her divorce, but Nina had refused after looking into the side effects. Perhaps Neal hadn't researched the side effects. Another website told her the off-label uses for paroxetine included premature ejaculation, migraine relief, and diabetic neuropathy. *Migraine relief.*

Perhaps this was what Kira had somehow acquired for him to help with his headaches. Nina tried to remember if she'd seen a doctor's name on the pill bottle but couldn't.

Seamus's car was still parked at her house, so he was able to go to the airport to pick up Nick while she drove to get the girls from the after-school babysitter. She hoped they would be amenable to going with Seamus for the evening, but worried they would be shy around him since they'd only met him the day before. They tended to be clingy around strangers.

She needn't have worried. He mentioned swimming and they were putty in his hands, racing to put on their suits and find beach towels. She handed him her keys, saying it was easier than moving the car seats to his sports car. Nick was drinking a beer and talking about ordering in, so she finished packing the girls' towels and a change of clothes for after swimming, then kissed them goodbye, watching as the SUV pulled out of the driveway. She turned to her older brother. "You want to see the note?"

They talked for two hours, crying and cursing, as they tried to process the tragedy of the day before. Nick and Neal had been close, and he couldn't begin to understand his little brother's suicide. "What does Kira say? They were living together. Did she see any signs of depression?"

"I haven't had a chance to talk to her yet. She's coming over later. Maybe she can shed some light on what was going on with Neal." She chose not to mention her suspicions about the medication until she'd had a chance to ask Kira.

Kira finally arrived, and Nina suggested they order Chinese food. She was starving, having had little appetite at breakfast and lunch. It seemed awful to be thinking about food when her twin brother was dead, but her body was demanding sustenance. As they waited for the delivery, she handed Nick another beer and poured a glass of wine for Kira. "When did Neal start taking meds for depression?"

Kira sipped slowly before answering. "About two months ago. He was ashamed of it, Nina. He didn't want anyone to know. He thought it made him weak. I'm so sorry, but he made me swear I wouldn't tell you."

"But why was he depressed? I thought everything was going so well in his life right now."

Kira shook her head. "Depression is often unrelated to life events. It's a mental illness and has biological causes. I tried to get him to understand this, but he wouldn't listen. I was glad when he agreed to go on the medication. I thought it was helping." She didn't seem to want to meet Nina's eyes.

Nina frowned, sensing Kira wasn't being completely honest. "I read online that it sometimes causes suicidal thoughts. Did he say anything about that recently?"

Kira shook her head again. "He never said anything, but I noticed he was more withdrawn recently. I should have said something! God, if I had made him talk to me, maybe this wouldn't have happened!" Tears streaked from her eyes, tracking through her black mascara. "What am I going to do without him?"

Nina tried to comfort her brother's fiancée, wondering the whole time how she could have missed his escalating depression. And how could she, herself, not known her own twin was going through such severe depression? She suspected Kira had gotten him the paroxetine to treat his headaches and possibly depression, though she was now worried the side effects had caused his suicidal ideation. But Kira was obviously heart-broken over his death and Nina couldn't bring herself to voice her suspicions so soon.

Chapter Four

Seamus

"Are we going to your house?" Lily asked.

Seamus glanced in the rearview mirror, catching Iris's somewhat unnerving stare. She didn't say much, but he noticed she listened carefully to everything going on around her. Lily was much more bubbly and talkative, but he realized he would have to win over Iris in order to be fully trusted by either of them. She strongly reminded him of Nina in so many ways. "No. We're going to my mom and dad's house. I used to live there, but I have my own apartment now."

"Can we see your apartment?"

"Hmm, maybe sometime. It's not very exciting, though. For tonight we'll stick with my parents' house because they have a pool. So, I guess you two like to swim, huh?" He flashed a smile at Iris, but she simply looked at her twin without reciprocating. *Yikes. Tough crowd.* He turned his attention back to the road. "I hope you both are hungry because my

49

mom is a great cook."

"We're starving!" Lily exclaimed. She seemed to be the designated spokesperson for the twins.

"Good. My niece, Janey, will be there too. She's in kindergarten like you guys, so maybe you could all be friends."

"Okay."

He smiled at her easy acceptance. They drove in silence for the remainder of the trip save for the soft jazz music from the radio station Nina obviously favored. He wondered how the meeting with Nick and Kira was going, and hoped Nina would be able to eat something. She'd only picked at her sandwich at lunch, as he had, but his own stomach was now grumbling loudly, and he hoped his mom would have some sort of appetizers waiting. He worried for a moment about how shallow he was to be thinking about food when his best friend had died the day before, but then realized Neal wouldn't care. He could almost hear him now. *What, you don't get to be hungry anymore just because I'm dead? Don't be such a putz, DeLuca!* That was Neal's favorite derogatory term: putz. Seamus used to tease him that he sounded like an old man whenever he said it, but he'd give an awful lot to hear it again now. *Shit, Neal! Why did you do it? Why did you kill yourself? You could have talked to me about whatever was bothering you! I would have done anything to help you. I thought you knew that. Damn it, Neal! I'm so fucking mad at you right now!* The tears welling up were more anger than sorrow, and he squeezed his eyes shut as he pulled to the curb in front of his parents' house to quash them. He caught Iris's eyes in the rearview mirror again and knew she noticed. *Jeez, she sees everything! It's spooky!* If anyone had told him even a few days ago that he'd have offered to babysit his best friend's nieces, he would have scoffed. He knew nothing about kids, nor had he ever been interested in learning about them. But life had a way of smacking you in the face every once in a while, and here he was, babysitting of his own volition. *Son of a bitch.* He shook his head as he exited the SUV.

The girls had already unbuckled their seatbelts and extricated themselves from their car seats by the time he opened the back door. He grabbed their pink duffle bag and led them up the walkway. Janey waited on the front porch but ran to meet them as they neared the house.

"Uncle Seamus!"

He scooped her into his free arm and kissed her cheek. "Hey, Munchkin. I want you to meet some friends of mine." He set her on the ground and turned to the other girls. "This is Iris, and this is Lily." He gestured to each one in turn. Was it only yesterday he had trouble telling them apart? Now they were such distinct personalities he knew he'd never mistake them again. "Girls, this is my niece, Janey."

Janey hugged his leg tightly, shy as always around strangers, but she smiled at them.

Iris said nothing, but Lily obviously had no problem meeting new people. "I like your hair."

Janey melted at the compliment and reached to twine her fingers through her bouncy, brown ponytail. "Thanks. I like yours too. I have twins in my class, but they're *boys*." She managed to imbue such disgust into the term Seamus had to chuckle.

"Eww," Iris said softly.

"Come meet my Grammy." Janey turned and led the way into the house.

Seamus followed, finding his mother in the kitchen prepping dinner. His brother-in-law, Mac, was setting a plate of small sandwiches on the counter. "Hey, Mac," Seamus said as he reached for one and stuffed it in his mouth.

"Hey. Sorry about your friend, man. That's rough." He turned back to the refrigerator. "Here." He handed Seamus a beer.

"Thanks." Although they'd had a rather rough start to their relationship when Izzy had introduced him as Janey's long-absent father months before, Seamus had since come to deeply appreciate the former Green Beret his oldest sister had married. "How's Izzy feeling?"

Mac grinned. "She's doing a lot better now that the morning sickness is finally gone. She was glad to have a few hours to herself tonight."

"I'll bet. Thanks for bringing Janey over."

"Daddy!" Janey inserted herself between the two men. "These are my new friends, Iris and Lily. Can we go swimming now?"

"Hi, girls. It's nice to meet you." Mac dropped to one knee as he scooped Janey against him. "Yes, we can go swimming, Princess. Let's go get your suit on. Lily, Iris, if you want to come with us, I'll show you where you can leave your clothes."

Seamus ate another sandwich as he watched

52

them go.

"Oh, my boy." His mom slipped her arms around him from behind. "I'm so sorry."

He turned and folded her into his embrace, gladly accepting the comfort. God, nothing was better than a hug from your mother at times like this. "Thanks, Mom." His throat closed and he rested his head atop hers.

She pulled back and looked into his face, one palm cupped against his cheek. "How is Nina?"

"She's so strong. I don't know how she's managing to keep it together so well."

"She's a mother. We have to be strong, even when we think we can't. But remember, son, how hard this is for her. She's lost her twin and in the most horrible way possible. She needs you, Seamus. Be there for her. That no good son of a—" She closed her eyes briefly and shook her head. "Sorry. I mean that ex-husband of hers left her high and dry to deal with those little girls and all of this sorrow. It doesn't matter how strong she is; she still needs help and support, and you've been placed in her life at this crucial moment. Don't let her down."

Her words caused a physical pang in his stomach. "I won't. I swear it."

She smiled up at him. "You're a good man, Seamus Liam. I'm very proud of you." She stood on tip-toe and kissed his cheek, then turned back to attend to dinner.

Seamus stood in the middle of his mother's kitchen, vainly attempting to pull himself together. *Too many emotions! I can't take much more! Shit!* He sniffed and cleared his throat, determined to deserve the words his mother had spoken. "I'm gonna go find a swim suit. Thanks, Mom."

She smiled at him over her shoulder.

The girls were splashing and laughing in the shallow end of the pool when he joined them in the backyard, and he was glad he'd brought them. They needed a break from all the gloom and sadness left in the wake of their uncle's death. Mac stood guard at the point where the pool sloped into the deep end, his arms crossed and an amused expression on his face, the water lapping around his waist. He had multiple tattoos on his muscular chest and arms, not surprising for an ex-military guy. Seamus had several, as well, including a rather embarrassing tribal design encircling his left bicep that he'd thought was a good idea on his twenty-first birthday. Heavy drinking and walk-in tattoo parlors turned out to be a terrible combination. His brothers, of course, never missed an opportunity to razz him about it.

He piled the towels he'd brought outside on a deck chair and headed to the diving board. He always preferred to dive into the pool, getting the initial shock over with quickly. He dove and swam underwater to the shallow end, easily locating Janey's legs next to the twins' dark brown ones, and grabbed her ankle. He surfaced next to them as Janey squealed.

"Uncle Seamus! You scared me!" She splashed him in the face.

He laughed and picked her up. "You love it. Admit it!" He held her above the water and made it clear he would drop her.

"No!" She giggled madly as she squirmed in his arms.

"Admit it!" He dipped her closer to the water. She was already wet, of course, but it was a game they'd played ever since she was old enough to swim. The twins watched avidly, Lily with a half-grin, and Iris with a typical frown.

"Help me, Daddy!"

Mac chuckled but made no move to help his daughter. "You're on your own, Princess."

Janey continued laughing as Seamus dropped her, catching her just before she hit the water. Lily crept closer as they continued, but Iris remained at the far side of the shallow end by the steps. He finally let Janey slip into the water as Lily grabbed his arm.

"My turn, Seamus! Please?"

He grinned and scooped the little girl up above his head as she giggled and squirmed.

Janey swam over to Iris and tugged on her hand to pull her over to where the rest of them were. "Come play, Iris!"

Seamus watched out of the corner of his eye as his niece coaxed the reticent girl to participate in the game the rest of the group was playing. Iris might be quiet and reserved, but she was no match for Janey's infectious sense of fun. He lowered Lily into the water and engaged them all in a water war, making sure to involve Mac as his ally. By the time Big Tony came out to tell them dinner was in fifteen minutes, the girls were exhausted. Mac helped him wrap them in beach towels before sending them in to change back to their clothes.

Moira had prepared Chicken Marsala, one of his all-time favorites, and both the twins seemed to enjoy it as well, although Lily ate only a small bit of her chicken and Iris pushed all her mushrooms to the side of her plate. His mother asked the girls about school and what they liked to do in their free time while Big Tony watched, inserting frequent questions of his own. The girls were well-mannered, and Seamus thought Nina would be pleased by their behavior. Moira served sorbet and fresh fruit for dessert, then Janey led the girls to the family room to watch a movie while the adults cleared the table and enjoyed a cup of coffee and some adult conversation.

"Has Nina decided when the funeral will be held?" Big Tony asked.

Seamus sipped his coffee and shook his head. "They haven't released the body yet." *Body.* He hated thinking about his best friend as nothing more than a body. The delicious dinner his mother had prepared churned in his stomach. "Everything's on hold until that happens."

"When will her parents be getting back?" Moira reached to cover his hand with hers as she asked.

"They should be here day after tomorrow at the latest. This has been too hard on Nina with the rest of her family scattered all over the place."

"I'm glad she has you to help out. It was a good idea to bring the girls over here for some fun. It can't be good for them to be around all that sadness," Big Tony said, echoing his wife's earlier comments.

Seamus turned his hand over and squeezed his

mother's gently. "That's what I thought. And I'm more than happy to help out, but I have to go back to work tomorrow and will be unavailable to her for the next twenty-four hours."

"Well, I'll give her a call and see if I can do anything." Moira stood and fetched the coffee pot to refill the mugs in front of each of them. "What does Sloane think about all this?"

He grimaced as he reached for the small pitcher of cream. "I have no idea. She's out of town for a while. We're...taking a bit of a break from each other."

"Oh? I hope everything's all right."

Seamus rolled his eyes as he stirred his coffee. He knew his mom and sisters didn't care for his girlfriend; they were all terrible at faking any sort of liking for Sloane. It was none of their business, however, and he didn't appreciate their nosiness. "Everything's fine. We're both just super busy right now. Her career is really taking off."

"Well, that's wonderful, of course, dear," Moira said with a sniff, clearly annoyed she wouldn't be hearing any juicy details.

Across the table, Mac tried unsuccessfully to smother a chuckle. Seamus shot him a dirty look. "Careful, Mac. I'm pretty sure I could talk Izzy into hosting a slumber party at your house soon."

His brother-in-law snorted, clearly amused rather than threatened. "Sounds like fun. I'm game if Izzy agrees."

***

Nina

The sesame chicken had congealed in an unappetizing glob on her plate. She'd managed to eat nearly half, but the smell of the leftovers caused her stomach to roil. She stood to clear the dishes, noting that Nick had also only eaten half of his beef broccoli. Kira had done nothing more than pick at her fried rice, and Nina decided to pack it in a plastic container for her to take home. She scraped the rest of the cold food into the trash can, then stacked the plates in the dishwasher. She filled the kettle, deciding tea would settle her stomach better than another glass of wine. She braced her arms on the counter and took a deep breath while she waited for the water to heat. *God, what I wouldn't give for a few hours by myself.* That was a luxury she couldn't afford right now, however. She had to be present for the rest of the family, including her twin's fiancée, but she was physically and emotionally drained. *I wish I could just be quiet and alone for a little while. Seamus could be there, though. He's such a restful person.* She wrenched her thoughts away from her selfish wishes and watched her brother and Kira across the kitchen counter as they sat in the family room. One of the main reasons she'd chosen this house over the more luxurious ones David had favored was the open floor plan with the kitchen melding into the family room. She didn't want to miss out on what the girls were doing when she was busy in the kitchen.

Kira flipped her long blonde hair away from her face and reached to pour herself another glass of wine, something Nina doubted the wisdom of, given Kira was drinking on a nearly empty stomach. Nina couldn't remember if it was her third or fourth, and would make sure she got home safely, even if she had to call her an Uber. Kira was beautiful in a high maintenance sort of way, always perfectly made up and well-dressed, something Nina never seemed able to get a handle on. She watched as Kira reached to softly pat Nick's arm and Nina regretted her mean-spirited, jealous thought. The woman had made Neal happy for the past two years and was clearly mourning his death. The fact that Nina had never cared much for her, had thought her brother could do better, was exceptionally inappropriate at the moment and Nina was ashamed of herself. She left the kettle to heat and grabbed a bottle of water from the refrigerator.

"Kira, why don't you stay here tonight?" Nina handed her the water, knowing she'd have a raging headache the next day if she didn't hydrate. "You too, Nick. I've got plenty of room."

Nick stood and stretched. "I know, but you've got your hands full with the girls. You don't need to be fussing over house guests."

"I'm fine," Kira said as she fumbled with the lid to her water bottle.

Nick met Nina's eyes and winked. "I'll run her home on my way to Mom and Dad's." Seamus had taken him to pick up a car from their house on the way back from the airport. "We can get your car tomorrow, Kira. Come on." He held out his hand and helped her to her feet. "Let's get you home. I'll bet you didn't get any sleep last night."

Seamus and the girls came in as Kira and Nick gathered their belongings. He immediately volunteered to drive Kira home, but Nick waved his offer away as the girls objected.

"I got it, Seamus. Thanks."

"We want you to stay until we go to bed. Please, Seamus?" Lily begged.

"Please, Seamus?" Iris echoed her sister softly.

Nina, noting his exhausted face, hushed the girls and told them to go get in the shower.

"I'll stay. Maybe I can read you a story before bedtime, okay?"

"*We* can read a story to *you*!" Lily called as she and Iris retreated to the bathroom.

Nina shook her head as she told him to relax on the sofa. "You want a beer while they get ready for bed?"

"Nah. I'll take some water, though." He reached past her to the refrigerator, clearly ignoring her suggestion to take it easy. "I don't need you to wait on me, Nina."

"Fine." She waved her hand and returned to wiping her counters down. "I can see you're in a stubborn mood."

Kira stumbled back into the family room at that moment, followed closely by Nick. "I almost forgot! Here, Nina." She fished in her oversized bag and pulled out a slim silver laptop. "This is Neal's computer. I know he'd want you to have it since you were his silent partner."

"Oh." Nina dried her hands and crossed the room to take it from her. "Um, sure."

"He told me you'd know the password."

What? I have no idea what his password is. "When did he say that?"

Kira rubbed her temple and shrugged. "I don't know. Maybe a few days ago."

"You can figure it out later," Nick said as he took Kira's arm. "We're all too exhausted right now to make much sense of anything."

Kira nodded tiredly and allowed herself to be led from the house.

Nina stared at the computer, wondering what Neal had been thinking.

"What's up with that?" Seamus gestured with his water bottle.

"I don't know."

"What did she mean by 'silent partner'?"

She set the laptop on her desk in the corner of the room, not ready to deal with any of her brother's possessions yet. "I loaned him some money a few years ago when he was starting the company with Gordy. I never thought of myself as any sort of partner, though."

"How much did you give him?"

She named an amount, which made Seamus whistle. She was saved from further comment, however, by the return of the girls, hair wet and pajamas on.

"We brought some for you to choose, Seamus. Here." Iris dumped a stack of picture books on his lap and plopped onto the sofa next to him. Lily hopped up on his other side and snuggled close.

Nina watched, amused, as Seamus settled on a book called *Dragons Love Tacos*, and the girls took turns reading. Iris was a better reader, but Lily was more animated. Seamus was patient, helping them sound out the difficult words and laughing at the antics of the dragons who loved salsa but breathed fire when they ate it. She knew the girls were hungry for a father-figure since David was rarely around to give them any substantive attention, but worried they were growing fond of Seamus too quickly. She had no expectation of him staying once the funeral was over and didn't want them disappointed yet again.

"Do you like tacos, Seamus?" Lily turned the page as she asked.

"Of course, but I'm not a big fan of fish tacos."

"Eww, gross! We hate fish! I like chicken tacos." Iris looked up at Seamus. It was so typical for the girls to speak collectively as "we" then turn around and use "I" in the next sentence. As a twin herself, Nina knew it was sometimes difficult to differentiate, and thought it must be even tougher for identical twins. "I don't like salsa, though. Do you?"

"I love salsa! The hotter, the better."

"I like salsa," Lily added. "I'm not afraid of spicy stuff! Pick another book!"

"Lily," Nina warned.

"Sorry, Momma." Lily bit her lip. "Please," she added belatedly.

Seamus met Nina's eyes and winked. "If it's okay with your mom. How about this one? It's Janey's favorite."

"Momma, can we go to Janey's house? Please?" Iris asked. "She's really nice and she has a kitten."

"Well," Nina hedged, "we'll see. I'll have to

check with her mom. It's almost bed time, so read that book to Seamus and then go brush your teeth."

"Okay, Momma," they said in unison.

Nina packed the girl's lunches as she listened to them read another story to Seamus. He must have been beyond exhausted and wanted nothing more than to return to his apartment, but he exhibited endless patience as they plodded through the story. *I could get used to this.* She shook her head at the thought. *God, how desperate am I? Pathetic! Snap out of it!*

"Can Seamus tuck us in?" Iris asked.

"I'm sure he needs to go home, sweetheart." She slid the last sandwich into a plastic baggy and set it atop the container of baby carrots in Lily's *Moana* lunchbox. "I'll tuck you both in."

Seamus stood and stretched. "I don't mind, Nina. I'm happy to tuck them in. Come on, girls. Who wants a piggyback ride?"

"I do! I do!" Lily clambered onto the arm of the sofa—Nina had lost count of the number of times she'd reprimanded her for it—and leapt on Seamus's back.

"Oof!" But he laughed as he said it and scooped a giggling Iris into his arms. "All right. Your mom said you need to brush your teeth, so let's get that done first."

Nina smiled at their retreating figures and turned to stack the lunch boxes in the refrigerator. The kettle was still hot and she figured Seamus might appreciate some herbal tea to wind down after this hideous day. She found a tray and used her good mugs rather than the mismatched thrift store mugs she'd never gotten rid of and used every day. She added a small plate of cookies, knowing she was fussing—foolish girl—but was unable to stop herself.

"They fell asleep almost as soon as their heads hit their pillows." He chuckled as he resumed his seat on the sofa.

"Swimming always wears them out. Here." She set the tray on the coffee table and sat next to him. "I thought tea would be nice. Unless you'd prefer a glass of wine or something?"

"Tea is fine." He accepted the mug and sipped. "You have amazing kids, Nina."

She handed him the plate of cookies. "Thanks. I agree, of course." She sipped her own tea for a long moment. "I can't tell you how much I appreciate all your help tonight, Seamus."

"I'm happy to help. How did the talk with Nick and Kira go?"

She shrugged. "Okay. Kira said Neal started taking the meds for depression two months ago. She said he was ashamed of it. How could I not have known my own brother was depressed? We're twins, for God's sake!" The tears started again, and she tried to blink them away. *I'm sick of crying!* She wasn't sure she totally believed Kira, but hesitated to mention her suspicions to Seamus.

"Hey." He set his mug and half-eaten cookie on the coffee table and slid next to her. He put his arm around her shoulders and pulled her close. "It's okay, Nina. Listen, you've been busy raising your kids by yourself for the last year. That's a lot to deal with."

She sniffed and allowed herself to melt against his warm body. *Just for a minute.* "I should have known."

"I should have too, but I didn't have a clue. Blaming ourselves isn't going to help, though. Your family needs you to be strong, hon. Kira is a mess, and I'm sure your parents aren't going to be a whole lot better."

"Maybe I don't want to be the strong one." She whispered the words, knowing what she wanted made no difference at the moment.

He squeezed her gently. "I know. It sucks, but you can do it. And I'll help any way I can."

She forced herself to pull away and reached for a tissue from the box on the table, which she'd placed there earlier in the evening and had utilized liberally, along with Nick and Kira. "You've already done so much. Thanks again for taking care of the girls tonight. I can't tell you how much it helped."

"Of course. It was no problem. You don't have to do everything by yourself, Nina." He reached for her hand. "You want me to stay here tonight?"

Yes. "No, that's not necessary. You have to work tomorrow, and you need a good night's sleep in your own bed."

"Are you sure? I don't mind."

Please stay. Please don't listen to my words; listen to my heart. "I'm sure. Go home and get some rest."

He smiled and squeezed her hand. "All right, but I'll keep my phone next to the bed. Call if you need anything or even if you just want to talk. Promise?"

"Promise." She wouldn't call of course; she wouldn't dream of waking him.

"My shift is twenty-four hours, but then I have forty-eight off and I can help with whatever you need." He reached for the door knob. "Let me know when you find out about your parents' arrival, okay?"

"I will. Goodnight, Seamus. Thanks." She locked up after him, then leaned against the front door as loneliness swamped her, taking her breath away. *I don't have time for this! I've been doing fine all by myself for well over a year and I'll continue to deal with it.* She straightened and walked through the house, turning off lights as she made her way to her bedroom.

Chapter Five

Seamus

"Davis and Greerson have bathrooms; DeLuca and Baca, you've got KP. Last shift had a call and wasn't able to restock, so you two will have to make a Costco run. That's it. Let's get to work." Captain Diaz closed his laptop and rose. Technically, they'd all been at work for two hours already, washing the engines and checking their personal gear carefully, making any necessary small repairs and requisitioning new items as needed. It was the first thing they did at the beginning of each shift to be ready for a call at any moment. Clean bathrooms and a well-stocked kitchen were nice, but definitely secondary in importance.

"Well, it's better than scrubbing toilets." Jon Baca lightly punched Seamus's shoulder. He turned to Shella Greerson and Brandon Davis. "Suckers!" He laughed good-naturedly as Shella flashed him her middle finger.

"True. Let's make a list and head out before we

get a call." Seamus much preferred kitchen duty to bathroom cleaning; if his fellow firefighters could actually manage to piss *in* the toilet instead of around it and all over the floor, it might not be so bad. "We'll have to squeeze in our workout after lunch." Each firefighter was required to spend an hour of each twenty-four shift in the station gym, unless they were hammered with calls that would prevent them from working out.

"Sounds like a plan." Jon fell into step beside him as they made their way from the conference room to the kitchen. "You doing okay, man?"

Seamus had called Jon the day before to let him know what had happened with Neal. He and Jon had planned to hang out in the evening, but Seamus hadn't wanted to leave Nina, so he'd cancelled all his social plans. He sighed and ran his hand through his hair. "I don't know. I guess I'm managing. Nina's having a rough time, though."

"That's his sister, right?" Jon had met Neal on a few occasions and the two had gotten along pretty well, but he'd never had a chance to meet Nina.

"Yeah. They're twins."

"That sucks. I'm really sorry, Seamus. Is there anything I can do?"

He glanced down at his friend with a crooked smile. He and Jon had gone through the academy together, bonding over the rigorous mental and physical challenges of learning to be a firefighter. They'd become good friends and lucked out when they were assigned to the same station. They frequently managed to pull the same shifts, and Captain Diaz was usually happy to team them up for station chores since they worked so well together. They used to spend more of their free time together, but Jon had recently become a father and now—understandably—devoted most of his off-duty time to his wife and new baby. Seamus was happy for his friend, but as a result, had found himself spending more time with Neal since Jon's daughter had been born. His other best friend, his younger brother Tony, was also recently unavailable to hang out, since he'd graduated with his bachelor's degree last May and then shocked everyone by announcing he had been accepted to veterinary school at Eastern New Mexico University in Portales, four hours east of Albuquerque. The entire family had assumed Tony would eventually scrape through college and go to work for their older brother, Hugh, in the family construction business. The little asshole hadn't bothered to mention to anyone that not only was he not majoring in business, but he was doing a whole lot better than 'scraping by.' It wasn't until the family were all seated in the Pit—as the university basketball arena was lovingly known—and they searched through the many columns of names in the program for Tony's, that they'd seen the italicized words beside his name: B.S. Biology *magna cum laude*.

"That little shit." Hugh chuckled to his right. "He didn't tell you?"

Seamus shook his head. "Nope." But he hadn't asked, either. He should have known, though. Tony had spent way more time studying than any of them expected and Seamus had noticed all the massive science textbooks lying around Tony's apartment. But he'd never bothered to ask deep questions about his little brother's education, assuming he was fully living up to his playboy reputation.

Tony had dropped the bomb later that day at his graduation party: he would be moving to Portales in a few weeks to start veterinary school, and had qualified for an internship which paid tuition and even some living expenses.

So, Seamus had, within a few months of each other, lost regular access to two of his best friends and found himself a bit adrift. He was a naturally social person and didn't care to spend much time alone. The two main people left in his social circle were Sloane and Neal, and lately spending time with Sloane was more frustrating than anything else. So, he'd turned to Neal and the two of them had recovered much of their earlier friendship, remembering why they'd been such good friends throughout middle school and high school. *I thought I knew him, especially lately. How could I have missed his depression?* He'd been asking himself the same question for days, ever since Finn had woken him with the awful news of Neal's death.

"Which do you want, Seamus?"

He pulled himself back to the present, realizing he'd missed what Jon had asked him. "Sorry, what?"

"It's okay. You want to write the list or check the cabinets and fridge?"

Seamus hated the sympathetic look on his friend's face; he shrugged his shoulders and squared his jaw. *Enough. Focus on doing your job right now.* "You write. I'll do the inventory." They'd made it to the kitchen and Seamus began looking through the various cabinets, pantry, and refrigerator, calling out items they needed to Jon. It had been more than a week since any of the shifts had managed to make a full Costco run, so the list was lengthy. Seamus was glad for the mundane chore; it required a certain level of concentration as they decided what needed to be restocked and what ingredients they would purchase for lunch and dinner. Each shift tried to eat at least one meal together if they weren't out on a call. These guys—and girl, since Shella had joined their station last year—were more than colleagues. They were a sort of family, and eating together was an important family ritual. Seamus actually liked kitchen duty and was a fair, though limited, cook. He enjoyed cooking for his friends and girlfriend, but Sloane preferred to go out and usually insisted eating somewhere pricey with the kind of fancy-schmancy gourmet food Seamus hated. They'd fought about it a few times—they seemed to fight about everything lately—since Seamus had some old-fashioned notions about who should pay for the meal when they were on a date. Sloane made a hell of a lot more money than he did, though, and had no problem taking care of the check, often laughing about how old-fashioned he was. He knew he should be more enlightened in this day and age, but it went against the grain to let a woman pay for his meal.

"Check the milk."

Seamus did and told Jon to add two gallons to

the list. "That should do it. Let's get going and hope we can get the shopping done before we get called out. They took Jon's pickup and were soon loading a large orange cart full of food at Costco. The appreciative looks from the female shoppers merely amused him after five years on the job. He knew two fit, muscular guys in fire department t-shirts tended to draw some attention, especially since Jon was—according to his sister, Cara—really hot. She assured Seamus he was too, but he'd simply rolled his eyes. He knew he was decent-looking, but Finn was the handsome one in their family. The rest of the boys were merely average in comparison. They managed to finish and get back to the station in under an hour and had the groceries unloaded—his least favorite part of the job—and lunch on the table by noon.

It was a quiet afternoon and Seamus was glad to be back to the structure and familiarity of the station after the past few days of grief and chaos. He and Jon spent a punishing hour in the gym after lunch, then showered and did paperwork for a few hours. He was glad for the down time so he could put the finishing touches on his application to arson training, something he'd wanted to do ever since he studied fire science in college. He had finished the requisite five years on the job last month and had lost no time downloading the information and application. He loved being a regular firefighter, but he knew he belonged on the arson investigation team. He hoped to make it in his first time applying, but had determined he would continue to apply every year until he did. He took a few minutes to send a quick text message to Nina, just to see how she was faring her first day back at work. She didn't respond right away. It was nearly thirty minutes later when she sent back a brief reply, assuring him she was fine and relieved to be busy. She hoped he would stop by on his day off. He smiled as he shoved the phone into his back pocket and turned his attention back to his application. They had a short call mid-afternoon for a brush fire along the Bosque—most likely started by one of the many homeless people who camped in the forest area next to the Rio Grande River, but were back at the station in under two hours. He and Jon had decided to fix pasta for dinner—always a favorite around the station—and were soon setting the huge bowl of spaghetti, hot garlic bread, and a big salad on the long, Formica-topped table.

"God, Seamus! Your marinara is to die for!" Shella spoke through a mouthful of pasta. "I'll marry you right now if you swear to do all the cooking!"

He reached for the salad and piled it on his plate as he answered her. "Tempting, Shel, but I'm afraid your husband might kick my ass."

"Yeah, well, I'm sure he'd understand if he tasted this. We could probably work something out. Sloane is one lucky bitch!"

"Sloane doesn't eat carbs." He helped himself to more pasta.

The look of disgust on Shella's face was priceless. "Ugh! What does she eat? Lettuce?"

"Pretty much." He desperately wanted to turn the conversation away from his troubled relationship.

73

"Anyone up for some pool after dinner?" They'd had a pool table donated to the station and found it helped pass the long evening hours when there were no emergencies that called them away. "Loser buys a round next time we're out for beers."

"You're on." Captain Diaz forked a huge mouthful of pasta into his mouth. "This really is great sauce. Any chance you'd give my wife the recipe?"

"My grandmother's secret marinara recipe that she smuggled out of Italy right under the nose of General Franco in 1941?"

"You are so full of shit, DeLuca, and you suck at history! Franco was in Spain, not Italy. I think you mean Mussolini. You probably got it out of your Betty Crocker cookbook!" Brandon Davis laughed and reached for more bread.

"Be nice or you'll never know. Sure, Captain, I'll give your wife the recipe, but it's not the same if an Italian doesn't make it."

"I'm sure it's not, but I appreciate the gesture anyway."

He and Jon cleaned up the kitchen then joined the rest of the crew in the rec room for a few hours of television and pool, enjoying the relative relaxation that came with few calls throughout the shift. They headed to bed around eleven and Seamus hoped he would be able to catch up on some of the sleep he'd missed the past few nights since Neal's death. He should have known better. The alarm rang at 1:30, jarring them all out of sleep. The loudspeaker announced a multiple-alarm fire at an apartment complex as Seamus and the rest of his crew hastened to don their pants and boots before sliding down the pole and grabbing the rest of their equipment. Seamus swung himself up into the engine and took his seat behind the engineer, trying to rub the sleep from his eyes and clear his head for the job ahead. The adrenaline was starting to kick in and would hopefully keep him going through the night.

When their engines pulled into the parking lot of the apartment complex, his stomach clenched in horror at the sight in front of him.

"Oh, shit," Jon murmured beside him. "The whole place is on fire!"

Seamus grimaced as he followed his friend out of the engine. Jon was right: the entire complex was ablaze, and Seamus knew they had a long, hard fight in front of them. The parking lot was full of engines, paramedic units, and people in pajamas milling around, many crying, some holding shaking pets; all looked lost and confused. He and Jon fastened their oxygen masks in place and headed into the complex to check for residents who hadn't been able to get out. He prayed they wouldn't find any bodies.

Three hours later, they pulled off their masks and sat on the curb, gulping water from the bottles they kept in the truck. His entire body was soaked with sweat and he had a nasty burn on his left forearm where a ceiling beam had crashed down, narrowly missing his head. It had burned through his outer coat and caused a painful, three-inch long welt.

"You should have Shella look at that before we leave."

"It can wait until we get back to the station." He took another long pull from his water bottle, then poured the rest over his head. "She's still swamped with smoke inhalation vics." He looked across the lot to where Shella and Brandon, the two paramedics attached to their station, were working over patients. They rested for a few more minutes before finally heaving to their feet and walking back to see if they could help the rest of their crew as they dealt with the smoldering remains of what was once an apartment complex.

***

Nina

"Remember to read the Turner thesis by next Monday. And don't forget about the midterm next Wednesday." A wave of groans greeted her words as the students rose from their seats in the classroom. "The thesis is only ninety pages, people. Stop whining." Soft laughter followed.

"Sorry, Dr. Braden. It's like we're hard-wired to complain about homework." Greg was the type of student who always sat in the front and raised his hand to ask questions at least ten times per lecture. He usually managed to work the word "trope" into at least fifty percent of his comments. The pretentious little ass drove Nina crazy.

"Hey, nobody's forcing you to take this class." She gathered the stack of papers the class had turned in as she spoke. She glanced up at the awkward silence and noticed the remaining students staring at her wide-eyed. They dropped their eyes and shuffled nervously as she watched. *Crap. I guess I was a bit harsh.* She shrugged and finished packing her belongings. "Sorry, guys. It's been a rough couple of days. I'll see you all Friday." She left them standing at the front of the room and knew good and well they would be gossiping about her as soon as the door shut behind her. *I am definitely off my game today.* She stopped by the student union building food court for a cup of coffee and a bagel, hoping the caffeine and food would help clear her head. She ate as she walked across the open area between the SUB and Mesa Vista Hall, the crappiest and least updated building on campus and the home of the history department. Nina's office had almost certainly begun life as a broom closet; some days she could swear she still smelled the cleaning products. The building itself was a relic of the 1940s, with grimy windows and anemic heating and cooling. Nina loved every square inch of it. She'd scarcely dreamed of securing a teaching post at the same institution where she'd done her doctoral work, but David had used his connections and status as a best-selling author to make it happen. It went against the grain for Nina, but David had, as always, down-played her concerns, certain he knew better than she. He could be such an insufferable asshole at times.

But he'd been sophisticated and charming once, a long time ago when Nina was a first-year grad student. She'd taken his anthropology seminar because she'd needed an elective and thought it sounded interesting. He'd asked her out for drinks a few weeks into the semester and proceeded to sweep her off her feet with his larger-than-life grand gestures and expensive tastes. She'd recently broken up with her long-term college boyfriend and was stupidly susceptible to the charms of the much older man. She'd let herself be talked into sleeping with him before they'd been dating a full month and had found out a week later that he was married. He'd claimed they were separated and he was planning to file for a divorce, and she let herself believe him. *God, I was such an idiot.*

She fished her laptop out of her bag and set it up on her desk, along with the coffee and remainder of the bagel. She sipped the gourmet dark brew while she checked her email, noting a time change for the weekly faculty meeting and several student drops from her U.S. History survey course. She reached for the remote for her iPod and clicked it on. As the soft classical music filled the small space, she took another bite of the bagel and chewed, enjoying it more than anything she'd tried to eat since Seamus and Finn had showed up here Monday morning. She glanced around at the overflowing bookshelves, her eyes pausing lovingly on several of her favorites: *Blood and Thunder, Bury My Heart at Wounded Knee, Virgin Land.* The shelf above was entirely devoted to Annie Oakley and Calamity Jane. Nina got a kick out of shelving the two together: one so prim and proper and the other anything but. Although she wouldn't say no to an office with a window, she adored this room and knew she was surrounded by friends—book friends that never expected her to dress up and go to fancy cocktail parties to schmooze with publishers and agents. She finished her bagel and settled in to work on a new article for a few hours until her next class. She read what she'd written so far and felt the tension and stress of the last few days melting away as she focused on the words she'd crafted detailing Annie Oakley's life and career, and how she embodied the myth and spirit of the wild west. She'd proposed the article to *True West* magazine six months before on a whim, hoping to use a small portion of what she'd researched so deeply for her dissertation as a pathway to a wider audience. She'd been shocked when they offered her a feature article. She knew her colleagues in the history department would sneer at her writing for a popular, non-scholarly publication, but she was thrilled with the thought that regular people—rather than rarified academics—might read about a topic so near and dear to Nina's heart. For a precious hour, she lost herself in writing, surrounded by the scent of books old and new with the faint overtone of her rapidly cooling coffee.

The buzz of her cell phone alarm jolted her out of the old west, reminding her she had a class in thirty minutes. She turned it off, noticing she'd missed a text message from Seamus.

Seamus: Hey, how's your first day back going?

She smiled and composed her response.

Nina: Rough start, but good now that I'm here and focused. Be safe. Come by when you have a

day off if you can.

She stood and stretched, trying to decide if she wanted to grab a quick sandwich before her afternoon classes. She opted for a protein bar from her desk drawer instead and ate it while she went over her lecture notes. Her cell phone buzzed insistently, pulling her away yet again from her comforting, academic focus. She grabbed it without checking the caller ID.

"Hey, Nina. It's Gordy. Sorry I haven't called yet. How, uh, how are you doing?"

Oh, God. She rubbed her forehead as she grimaced. She'd been dreading this conversation. Gordy and Neal had been college roommates and continued their partnership after college when they started their cyber security business. They'd started small, just the two of them in a tiny back room in Gordy's uncle's spare office space. Gordy was the computer genius of the pair and had written what would eventually become a highly sought-after program to detect cyber hacking attempts. Neal was the business side of the partnership. Gordon Sanderson was a great guy, but he'd followed Nina around like a puppy dog whenever Neal had brought him home for the weekend during college when Nina also happened to be home. She and Neal had each been awarded academic scholarships, he at New Mexico State in Las Cruces, and she at Davidson College in North Carolina. Being separated from her twin had been hard at first, but both had decided it was for the best if they were ever to develop their own identities. When she'd first met Gordy, she knew immediately he liked her and, although he wasn't bad-looking, he didn't hold a candle to Seamus or Ben, the guy she'd recently begun dating in North Carolina. Ben had been her first real relationship and the first guy she'd ever slept with. They'd dated all through college and she figured they'd get married eventually, but he got accepted to a grad program in Washington, D.C., and she'd gone to the University of Nebraska for her master's degree. Long distance proved to be too much, and they'd drifted apart and eventually broke up. She'd met David soon afterward, clearly while she was still on the rebound from Ben.

"Nina? Are you there?"

"Sorry, Gordy. Yeah. Of course. How are you holding up?" Guilt crashed through her; she should have called.

"Um, I guess I'm okay. I opened the office today since the police are finished in Neal's…" His voice faded, and he coughed softly. "Anyway, I thought I'd give you a call and see how you're doing. I'm so sorry, Nina."

"Oh, Gordy." She squeezed her eyes shut against the sudden tears. There had been too many tears in the last few days and she couldn't handle anymore at the moment. *Why did he have to call and disrupt the only peace I've managed to find?* Irrational anger burned through her and she fought to sound civil. "Listen, I have a class in a few minutes, so I need to go."

"Sure, of course. Listen, I was wondering if I could swing by for a few minutes later this evening?"

Crap. That's the last thing I want to deal with right now. But she knew he had to be hurting nearly as much as she. "That would be nice. Why don't you come for dinner? I know the girls would love to see you." She didn't know any such thing, of course. Neither Lily nor Iris had ever seemed terribly interested in their uncle's business partner.

"Oh. Okay. Yeah, that would be great. Can I bring anything?"

She assured him he didn't need to bring a thing and hastily said goodbye. If she didn't hurry, she'd be late for her afternoon class.

***

"Do you remember the time you visited us in Las Cruces and we drove down to Juarez? God, we used to have some great times, huh?"

Nina smiled weakly over her glass. She remembered that Gordy had assumed he was welcome to tag along the whole weekend when she had wanted to spend some time with her brother. She also remembered the vast amount of tequila they had all consumed and certainly didn't want to share her drunken college exploits with her small daughters. She also seemed to remember a lapse in judgment that led to a slow dance and a rather lingering kiss with Gordy. *Yikes, Gordy. Don't you dare bring that up now!* It hadn't been terrible, but she had nothing in common with him except her brother, and she hadn't been at all interested in pursuing a relationship with him. "We had some times, that's for sure. Lily, aren't you going to finish your chicken?"

Lily shook her head and looked at her twin. "May we be excused?"

"Don't you want dessert?" Nina was not a proponent of the 'clean plate' club. As long as the girls tried a little of everything, she was satisfied. Against her instructions, Gordy had arrived with a cherry pie and vanilla ice cream.

Both girls shook their heads and slipped out of their chairs. Iris sidled close to Nina and whispered in her ear. "When is Seamus coming over?"

"He's at work, sweetie. Remember, I told you he has to work really long shifts as a fireman?"

Iris nodded and turned to follow her sister out of the dining room.

"Sweet kids," Gordy murmured and reached for another helping of the roast chicken Nina had prepared.

"Yes, they are." They'd been quiet during dinner, though, and Nina missed the giggles and chatter they usually brought to the table. Gordy insisted on talking about Neal almost constantly and she knew it upset the girls. They shouldn't have to deal with this kind of issue at such a young age and Nina was relieved they had left the room.

"So, Nina. I've been thinking. I'd like to buy out Neal's half of the business."

She forced herself to swallow the chicken, which had suddenly gone bone dry. *Jesus, Gordy. We haven't even buried him yet!* "I'm not really ready to think about all that right now, okay? Could we just focus on getting through the next few weeks before we make any business decisions, please?"

She could feel the pressure building behind her eyes and wanted nothing more than to get rid of her unwanted guest and spend the rest of the evening with her girls.

"Sure, sure. Sorry. It's just that we're at a crucial point with the new program and I can't afford to lose momentum."

"I know. I just need some time to figure things out." She wondered if he was aware that she, not Neal, had controlling interest in the business, due to the loan she'd given him. She'd had no intention of getting involved and was content to let Neal pay her back over the next few years. But now she would have to decide what she wanted to do, and if she was willing to stay in contact with Gordy in order to keep her interest, or if she wanted to sell to him outright. She had no idea how he would come up with the money to purchase her half if she decided to offer it to him. She stood to clear the plates. "Are you ready for pie?"

He took the hint. "I guess I'll take a rain check on dessert, if you don't mind."

Her relief was palpable, but she tried not to let it show on her face. "I understand." She saw him to the door, trying vainly to contain her impatience to have him gone.

He turned on the front step and put his hand against the door before it closed completely. "Maybe we could get together again, Nina. Just the two of us?"

Shit. Could your timing be any worse, Gordon? Like I could possibly be romantically interested in anyone just days after my brother died? Against her will, Seamus's face flashed across her mind, but she shoved it aside impatiently. "I don't know, Gordy. I can't think about that right now, okay?"

"Yeah, of course. Sorry. I'll, uh, I'll call you soon. Bye." He waved tentatively as he walked toward his car.

She shut the door and turned the deadbolt, then leaned her forehead against the wood. *I so did not need this! Seamus, I wish you could come tonight. I never feel stressed around you.* She turned to find the girls.

Chapter Six

Seamus

The hot water stung his burned arm and he figured he would have to get Shella to give him some more ointment before he left the station. The shower felt amazing, though, rinsing away the dried sweat and soot from the fire. By the time he dried off and changed into clean jeans and the ever-present fire department t-shirt that made up the bulk of his wardrobe, the second shift had arrived and was setting out breakfast items for their exhausted colleagues. Seamus grabbed a packet of Pop-Tarts and leaned against the counter to wolf them down along with a huge glass of milk as he joined the general conversation about the apartment fire. Shella redressed his burn and covered it with a bandage.

"It would be great if you didn't get it wet again for a couple days, Seamus. You really don't want an infection."

He grinned and offered half his second pastry.

"Aw, don't be mad, Shel. I promise I'll keep it dry from now on. It stings like a bitch, you know."

"I can imagine. It's pretty damn nasty. You're going to have one hell of a scar, DeLuca. Might even interfere with your photoshoot for the firemen's beefcake calendar."

"There goes my dream of a modeling career." He spoke around the mouthful of Pop-Tart Shella had refused. He'd actually been approached several years ago about modeling for the calendar, but had stated unequivocally that he would not even consider it. "I heard they're doing a female version of it this year. I nominated you, of course."

"I will if you will." She tweaked his nose and walked away.

"So much sass, Shel." One by one the rest of his shift wandered away, all of them obviously feeling the afterburn of the adrenaline from the fire. It was difficult to come down after such an intense experience and he knew he'd never be able to get to sleep, although he'd only gotten a few hours the night before. He finally took his leave of the station but didn't want to go back to his apartment. He checked his phone and noticed several text messages from Sloane, which he ignored. He wasn't ready to talk to her yet. The break from her constant nagging was nice. He had a flash of guilt, but shoved it aside as he unlocked his car. He planned to take a long drive to calm his nerves but found himself driving to Nina's house before he even realized where he was going. It wasn't quite seven o'clock, but he figured she'd already be up and getting the girls ready for school. He skirted around to the side yard and peered in the kitchen window, hoping none of the neighbors would call the cops and report a peeping Tom. She was measuring grounds into the coffee maker. Her long brown hair fell messily around her face and she wore a baggy t-shirt with a kitten on it and plaid shorts. She looked tired, and Seamus worried she hadn't slept well. He rapped softly at the window, hoping he didn't scare her to death.

She jumped slightly, but didn't appear too startled. She hurried to open the side door for him. "Hey. What are you doing here? Did you just get off work?"

"Yeah. I thought I'd stop by before I head home. Sorry about the skulking. I didn't want to wake anyone."

She finished preparing the coffee and pushed the start button. Within seconds, the fragrant aroma of fresh brew filled the kitchen. "We can have some coffee before I need to wake the girls." She narrowed her green eyes at him for a long moment. "What's wrong? And what did you do to your arm?" She gestured to the bandage.

He shrugged and fiddled with the edge of a placemat. "It's just a little burn. We had a fire last night—this morning really—and I guess I was too keyed up to head home yet. I thought I'd swing by and see if I could do anything for you."

She smiled and pushed her hair behind her ear. "You're sweet, Seamus. Stay for breakfast?" She stood and poured them each a cup of coffee, then turned to the refrigerator for the creamer.

"On one condition." He sipped the steaming

beverage, which was ten times better than the station coffee.

She raised an eyebrow as she sipped her own coffee. "Condition?"

He grinned. "Yeah, condition. I'll cook while you get the girls ready." He raised his own eyebrow, daring her to disagree.

She waved her hand. "Fine. If you think I'm going to turn down the chance to not cook a meal, you're crazy." She sipped, then set her mug down and covered his hand with hers. "Thanks, Seamus."

He turned his hand over and squeezed her fingers lightly, enjoying the soft warmth too much. He pulled his hand away and stood. "No problem." He opened the fridge and perused the contents. "Do the girls like pancakes? You do have flour, right?"

"Yes, to both." She was silent for a moment. "My parents should be back in town this afternoon."

He closed the fridge and opened cabinets until he found her flour canister. "Are you taking the day off?"

She shook her head. "No. I may leave work a bit early, but I need to go in to teach my classes. I hate canceling."

He found a large bowl and measuring cups and began mixing up a batch of pancake batter. "I'll bet you do. What's the plan for tonight? Do you think they'll expect to gather here?"

"I imagine they'll want to be home, so I'll take the girls over there. I'll probably take something for dinner, so we don't have to order in."

Seamus stirred and wondered why Nick couldn't handle dinner duty. He didn't have a job to go to since he was visiting from out of town. Why did everything seem to fall on Nina's shoulders? "Do you mind if I tag along? Or would I be intruding? You can be honest, Nina."

"Of course I don't mind. You're like family. But are you sure you want to spend your day off hanging around us? You've got to be exhausted, and it's not going to be pleasant. My parents are undoubtedly freaking out."

He had been like family once, but he hadn't spent much time with Neal's parents since he'd graduated from high school. He had no great desire to see them under these circumstances, but Nina needed him, and he was determined to be there to support her through this. "I'm sure. I'll go home and grab a few hours of sleep this afternoon, so don't worry about me." He set the bowl aside and searched in the cabinet under her stove top for a griddle. He set it on the burner to heat and turned to her. "Listen, what if I see about the girls spending a few hours at Janey's house tonight while we're at your folks'? Your parents are going to want to talk about the details of Neal's death and the girls don't need to hear it."

She bit her lip and frowned. "I've been worried about that too, but I hate to impose on your sister. Why don't I call a babysitter?"

"I think they'd be more distracted if they got to play with Janey. Let me call Izzy and see if she can do it; if she can't, we can get a babysitter. Okay?"

"I guess." She rubbed her hands on her arms as if she were cold. "I hate this, Seamus."

He stepped behind her and massaged her neck

gently, pushing her soft hair over one shoulder. "I know. One day at a time. It will get better, eventually."

She groaned softly, a sound that went straight to his gut—and places further south, if he were totally honest. "I hope so. I can't tell you how glad I am that you're here. I don't think I could do this without you."

He leaned down and kissed the top of her head, then decided the conversation had waded into deep enough waters for this early in the morning. "I am pretty great, huh?" He stepped away and returned to the stove. "Go wake the girls. The first batch will be up in five."

A few minutes later, Lily and Iris stumbled into the kitchen, each clutching a ragged stuffed animal. Lily caught sight of him and stopped in her tracks. "Seamus!" She ran to him, animated now, and hugged him, her arms not quite reaching around his thighs.

"Hey, Squirt." He hugged her back with one arm as he flipped the last of the pancakes in the first batch. "Hey, Iris." The other girl smiled at him but said nothing as she took a seat at the table and set her stuffed bunny beside her plate. She might not be as effusive as Lily, but it was better than the last time he'd fixed them breakfast, when her glare could have singed the hair on his head. He'd take what he could get at this point. While the girls ate, he made another batch of pancakes for himself and Nina, then made sure she ate what he placed in front of her. Nina insisted on stacking the dishes in the dishwasher while Seamus cooked up the rest of the huge batch of batter he'd mixed.

"What in the world?" Nina stood, hands on her hips, watching him as he cooked.

"You can keep them in the freezer for quick breakfasts. What?" he asked as she shook her head.

"Nothing," she said with a laugh. "I'm just wondering when all this domesticity occurred."

"Shut up." He turned back to the stove with a chuckle. "I like to cook. It beats eating out of a box all the time."

"I'm sure it does." She shooed the girls out of the kitchen, telling them they needed to hurry and get ready for school. Then she turned back to Seamus. "How long does it usually take you to come down from the adrenaline high?"

He shrugged and searched through her drawers until he found her freezer bags. "Depends. This was a bad one, so it may take a few hours."

"Did anyone die?"

He focused on fitting the pancakes in the plastic baggies for a moment before he answered. "Yeah. An elderly couple who lived on the third floor. They couldn't make it down the stairs. They died of smoke inhalation." He spoke in short, choppy sentences; it was the only way to keep control of his emotions. Slim, warm arms slipped around his waist.

"I'm so sorry, Seamus."

He fought it for several seconds until he couldn't hold it in any longer. He choked out a harsh breath and turned to pull her against his chest, holding tightly and breathing in her sweet fragrance, a lifeline to sanity in this moment. "Shit." He murmured the words against her hair. "Jon and I found them when we were sweeping the complex. God, Nina, they were lying together on their bed, holding hands."

She said nothing, but held him tighter, rubbing her hands up and down his back.

He held her as long as he dared, then took a deep breath and stepped away. "I'll finish up in here. You go get ready for work."

She stared up into his face, a small frown line between her eyes. "Okay. I hope you're able to get some rest later."

"I will. Don't worry about me." He saw tragedies on a near-daily basis in his line of work, but the old couple's death had been so poignant and heart-breaking, the two of them lying next to each other in their pajamas, untouched by any flames, but suffocated by the smoke filling their apartment. "Listen, I'll take care of dinner tonight."

She turned at the doorway. "No way. You have done enough already."

"You need to let me do this, Nina. I sponged more meals off your folks than I can remember. Plus, I have all day to cook and you have to work until five. What time should I be here? I can catch a ride with you and the girls, can't I?"

"Well, yes, but—"

"Good." He turned back to the counter, smiling as he heard her sputter.

"You're impossible. Fine. That would actually be a huge help. Be here around five. And let me know if Izzy is okay with watching the girls."

***

Nina

"Yeah, Mom. Love you too. Give Daddy a kiss for me. See you this evening. Bye." Nina ended the call and set her cell phone on her desk. Her mother had called from the airport in Miami, where they were waiting to board the plane back to Albuquerque. They would arrive around 5:30, and Nina had assured them she and Nick would be there to meet them. She neglected to mention the girls would not be there. Her mother would fuss and insist she needed to see her granddaughters, but Nina knew Seamus was right; they needed a break from the horrors of Neal's death. He had secured Izzy's approval to take the girls over to play with Janey for the evening and they were beside themselves with excitement, jumping up and down as if they were going to a party. *Party? Oh, crap. Crap, crap, crap!* She had completely forgotten about their birthday party this weekend! The invitations had already gone out and she was expecting ten little girls at her house Sunday afternoon. *I need to cancel. I can't possibly get a party together before then! Lily and Iris will understand.* They would, of course. But they would have that look in their eyes, the one they'd had when she met them for the first time at the orphanage in Kampala. It was much too adult a look for three-year-old children, as if they'd seen too much in their short lives. The officials at the orphanage had little information about the girls, except that they had been part of a family displaced from the Democratic Republic of the Congo by Joseph Kony's Lord's Restoration Army. The family had found refuge in one of the many camps set up for war refugees, but the parents had contracted cholera and died. Their six children had been sent to various orphanages across the region and the infant twins ended up in Kampala, where they stayed for two and a half years because the nuns at the orphanage were reluctant to adopt them out separately. It was one of the reasons David had been able to secure the adoption so quickly: he and Nina were the only ones who had been willing to adopt two children at once. Nina had sworn on the spot she would do whatever it took to erase that haunted look from their eyes and give them a happy childhood. *And that includes birthday parties. It's not that big a deal. You just need a cake and some favors. And games. And ice cream. Oh, God.* Single motherhood really sucked sometimes, and she regularly wanted to hang her ex by his testicles. Not that she wanted him back—God, no!—but he'd gotten her into this situation, insisting they adopt, then philandered his way into another woman's arms and knocked her up. *But how surprised were you, Nina? Isn't that exactly what he did with you, except for the pregnancy?* It was a good thing he had a lot of money from his family and his books, because he was supporting four children now and two ex-wives. *How could I have been so naïve?* She shook off the glum, non-productive thoughts and decided she'd use her lunch hour to order a cake.

She was halfway through her emails when the

phone rang again.

"Ms. Braden? Yes, this is Donald Mason at French's Mortuary. We just received word that your brother's body will be released this afternoon. Has your family decided on a date for the funeral?"

Nina's stomach flopped unpleasantly. She'd been expecting this phone call, but it brought reality back suddenly. "Oh. Um, we haven't yet. I'm so sorry. My parents will arrive this afternoon and we'll discuss it this evening. What are your available slots for next week?" She cringed as she realized she'd described her brother as a 'slot.'

"We have Monday at 2:30, Wednesday at 10:00 a.m., or Thursday at 1:00 p.m. If none of those are convenient, we'll have to look at the following week."

She rubbed ineffectually at the headache building behind her eyes. "Let's schedule for Wednesday at 10:00." She was fairly sure it would work for the rest of the family with the possible exception of Nate, but she couldn't really wait to schedule around him.

"I'll put it on the calendar. Would you be able to come in on Monday to discuss the arrangements?"

They agreed on a time and Nina hung up. She continued to massage her temples, trying to ease the pain. She stood, deciding a brief walk around campus would clear her head. She had several hours before her next class and she knew she wouldn't be able to concentrate on grading or writing at the moment. It was a gloriously sunny day and she headed toward the duck pond, a place that usually never failed to cheer her up. She paused on the wooden bridge for several moments, watching the ducks race toward the bank whenever someone threw them a few breadcrumbs, as she attempted to rein in her racing thoughts. *Why, Neal? Why? Why did you do it?* She'd read enough about grief after her divorce—she'd been grieving the loss of her marriage, or at least the notion of an ideal marriage—to know she was still in the early denial stage. Anger would come next, if she believed what the books said, and she thought she might welcome it at this point. The constant questioning and disbelief that her beloved twin brother could take his own life was futile and depressing. Wait, wasn't depression one of the later stages? Crap, it seemed she couldn't even get that right. Kira had said Neal was depressed and the prescription seemed to support her claim, but how could his sister and best friend not know? Gordy too, had said he wasn't surprised to hear Neal was suffering from depression, claiming he had seemed withdrawn and moody over the last few months. *But he was never that way around me. Why did he feel the need to hide it from his twin sister? I would have understood. I would have talked to him about it! Shit!* Okay, there was some anger. Maybe she was making progress after all. The drive to do something productive made her pull out her cell and dial Finn's private number; he'd told her to call if she had any questions or concerns.

"This is DeLuca."

She winced slightly at his brusque greeting and hoped she hadn't interrupted anything important. "Finn, it's Nina. I wondered if you might have a few minutes?"

"Sure, Nina. What's up?"

"Well, I've been thinking a lot about what you said about Neal's depression, and I have some questions. Do you think I could get the doctor's name from the prescription? I don't remember seeing one on the bottle."

He hesitated. "Uh, listen, Nina. I don't think that's a good idea. Doctor-patient confidentiality doesn't end at death. We would have to get a court order to get that information, and there doesn't seem to be any compelling reason in this case. I'm sorry."

She squeezed her eyes shut. She'd expected his answer, but had hoped for more. "I'm having a really hard time believing Neal was suffering from such severe depression, when I wasn't aware of it. Please, Finn. I just need the name. There should have been a doctor's name on the label, right?"

His exasperated sigh was perfectly audible over the phone. "I'll tell you what. How about a compromise? I'll call the pharmacy and see if I can squeeze any details out of them, okay?"

She ran her free hand through her hair as she watched a family of ducks swim under the bridge. "Fine. I'm sorry to be so pushy, but this isn't sitting right with me. I can't believe Neal would kill himself."

"I know, Nina. It's tough, but the evidence is pretty clear." He was silent for another long moment. "Do you have any reason to believe it wasn't a suicide?"

What was he implying? What was she thinking?

Of course it was a suicide. He'd been found in his locked office with a gun in his hand. It couldn't be anything else. "No, of course not. But…" *But what?*

"Listen, I know this is rough right now. Have your parents gotten back yet?"

"This afternoon. We're all going to meet over there for dinner. Seamus is bringing the food. God, he's been such a huge help."

"Good. I know Neal meant the world to him. I'm glad he's here for you. Listen, I gotta go, Nina. I'll call you if I hear anything from the pharmacy, okay?" He paused for a beat. "Try to think about starting to move on. Neal wouldn't want you to be so upset."

"Then he shouldn't have fucking killed himself!" She glanced around, hoping no one had heard her outburst. "Sorry, Finn. I just…" She turned and leaned her forearms against the bridge railing.

"It's okay. I understand."

She said goodbye and slipped the phone back in her pocket, then pulled it out again to call Kira. If she had somehow arranged for Neal to get the paroxetine, for whatever reason, she would know the name of the doctor who had prescribed it. But Kira didn't answer, a sure sign she was on duty at the hospital. Nina sent a text and hoped Kira would call back later. *Okay. Time to get back to work. You need to stop obsessing over this.* She squared her shoulders and finished her circuit around campus, stopping by the SUB for a cup of dark roast before heading back to her office.

***

"Seamus, this is lovely." Nancy Braden set the bottle of wine she'd chosen on the table next to the sizzling pan of fajita beef and peppers Seamus had prepared. He'd also made a beautiful green salad and warmed a stack of flour tortillas. "Thank you so much." Nina's parents had arrived home thirty minutes late and were clearly exhausted from their long day of traveling.

"It's my pleasure, Mrs. Braden."

"Where did you learn to cook so well? The meat is so tender." Mr. Braden helped himself to seconds as he spoke.

"I have an extremely limited repertoire. You've tasted about fifty percent of it tonight. I guess I'm going to need to check out some new recipes soon." He laughed and poured Nina another glass of wine.

Nina was glad her parents and brother were enjoying it, although Seamus seemed a bit embarrassed by their praise. He obviously didn't realize what a help it was to not have to prepare a meal or even order in. And, yeah, where the heck did he learn to cook like this? Talk about your hidden talents! She and Nick had left him at their parents' house so he could prepare the meal while they drove to the airport to pick Mr. and Mrs. Braden up. The older couple had arrived tired and hungry, saying their layover in Dallas hadn't been long enough to hit the food court. Nina was pleased to see they both had apparently regained their appetites, although neither looked like they'd slept much in the last few days. How did a parent ever get over losing a child? Parents were supposed to go first, when they were old and gray, and when their kids were pushing sixty or so. It wasn't supposed to happen when the kids were in the prime of their life and just starting their career, or—God forbid—when they were five years old. She had a moment of panic and nearly pushed away from the table to call Izzy and check on Lily and Iris. Seamus must have sensed her mood because he reached under the table and gently squeezed her hand. She glanced at him, smiling crookedly at his concerned look. *Pull yourself together! They're fine. Right now, your mom and dad need you.* "So, I talked to the funeral director today and tentatively scheduled Neal's service for Wednesday morning, if that works for everyone? Seamus? Are you scheduled to work?"

"I'm off. I'll be there." He stood to start clearing the plates.

Nina started to rise to help him, but he shook his head slightly and looked at her parents. She got the message and let him clean up while she, Nick, and her parents planned the funeral service. They called Nate and made sure he could be there as well. His wife wasn't due for another week, and she insisted he go to his brother's funeral, so he said he'd book a flight. As sad as the conversation was, having something tangible to focus on seemed to help them all. By the time Nina and Seamus left to pick the girls up from Izzy and Mac's, they'd cried and laughed and tried to begin to deal with the reality of Neal's death. She knew there would be other bad days ahead, but it was enough for now.

***

Wednesday dawned clear and bright—not surprising for Albuquerque, of course—but today especially it seemed designed to piss her off. It was doing a great job. The day they buried her twin brother should be dark and dreary; the brilliant sunshine beating down on the mourners gathered at the graveside service was an offense. Seamus stood beside her, handsome and grim in his navy suit, the muscle in his jaw flexing spasmodically as he tried to keep his emotions in check. He lost the battle when the minister closed the service with a final prayer and a soloist began singing "Amazing Grace," Neal's flower-draped coffin sinking slowly out of sight as the lowering device creaked and groaned. She swallowed a hysterical gurgle as she thought about slipping forward and dripping W-D 40 over the gears. *Why am I thinking about such inappropriate things during my brother's funeral?* She shook her head to clear her thoughts, forcing them back to the final moments of the service.

The luncheon reception in the church social hall was interminable. She pushed the remains of some unnamed casserole around on her paper plate, then reached for the Styrofoam cup of too-hot coffee. She sipped, then grimaced at the bitter taste.

"It's not Starbuck's, that's for sure." Seamus joined her with his own cup of the foul brew.

"Definitely not." She pushed the plate away and stirred another packet of sugar into her coffee. "How are you holding up?"

He blew out a breath and ran his hand through his hair. "I'm dealing with it. You?"

"Today won't make my top ten list, that's for

sure. I need this to be over, Seamus."

He reached for her hand. "I know. Are all these people family friends?" He gestured to the crowded room.

"Friends of my parents, mostly." She saw Kira sitting at a nearby table, her hands lying limp in her lap. "I should go talk to her." But Gordy reached her first and Nina couldn't bring herself to rise out of her chair. "I'm so tired."

"Let's get out of here."

Yes, please. "I wish I could." She sighed and reached for her cup again. "But I need to stay for my parents."

"Okay, but just say the word when you're ready to split. Just a sec." He reached into his jacket for his phone and glanced at the screen, frowning. "It's my mom. She knows I'm at the funeral and she wouldn't call unless it was important. Excuse me."

She watched him step out into the hallway, a sinking feeling in the pit of her stomach. *Oh, please, God. Don't let it be anything else bad! We can't handle it!* When he stepped back into the social hall several minutes later, his face was pale, and his expression preoccupied. "What's wrong?"

"It's Mel. She's in labor."

"That's great—"

"Something's wrong with the baby. They're taking her into surgery now. I have to go."

Chapter Seven

Seamus

"Cara! Hey, wait!" He jogged to catch up with his sister, who was struggling to balance a cardboard tray of coffee cups while simultaneously trying to punch the button on the elevator. "Here, give me that." He took the tray of coffees out of her hand. "How's Mel?"

"They just took her in to surgery."

The elevator doors opened, and Seamus ushered his sister in ahead of him. "What happened?"

Cara slumped against the back panel of the elevator. "Finn said she went into labor early this morning. He drove her here to the hospital about an hour ago and I guess things went downhill pretty fast. The baby is breech, so they have to do a C-section. I guess the heartbeat dropped suddenly and they rushed Mel away. Finn's freaking out."

"Shit. I can imagine." He loosened his tie with his free hand. "Is everyone else here?"

She nodded. "Sorry we had to call you away from the funeral, but Mom figured you would want to know."

"Yeah, of course. The funeral was already over, anyway."

"How's Nina doing?"

"She's a rock; she's so strong, but this is really rough on her." The elevator dinged to a stop and opened. He followed Cara down the hall to the surgical waiting room, where the rest of his family waited. Cara handed the coffee around, then sat beside Finn.

Seamus found his oldest brother, Hugh, standing across the room. "I thought they let the dads be there during C-sections these days." He muttered the words under his breath, so Finn, whose face had lost nearly all color, couldn't hear.

Hugh turned toward him, his back to the rest of the room. "That's only when the mother is awake; they had to put Mel under. Finn's a wreck."

They both turned to glance at their brother. Finn's hand was shaking so hard he couldn't manage the coffee. Cara took it gently from him and put her arm around him, rubbing his back as he leaned forward to rest his elbows on his thighs.

Moira approached and pulled Seamus close for a hug. "I'm sorry I had to pull you away from the funeral."

He inhaled the comforting fragrance of his mother's perfume and held her tighter than he had in years. "Please tell me she's gonna be okay." He didn't think he could take any more bad news this week.

"Well, of course she is, and the baby too." She spoke confidently, but the uncertainty in her eyes as she pulled away sent a chill down his spine.

He glanced around at the rest of his family; they all had the same bleak, scared faces. Only Mac was absent—undoubtedly at home with Janey—and Tony, who was away at school. His phone buzzed in his pocket and he pulled it out to see Sloane's face and number on the screen. He knew he needed to talk to her, but her timing sucked. "I gotta take this." He stepped into the hallway. "Hey, Sloane."

"Seamus! I've been trying to call all week. How come you never called back?" She sounded pissed.

Christ. He pinched the bridge of his nose. *I was really hoping talking to my girlfriend would make me feel better.* "Listen, babe. I'm sorry. It's been a hell of a week."

"What happened?"

He huffed out a harsh sigh and leaned against the wall. "Neal's dead."

"Neal Braden? Your friend? Oh, my God! How? Car accident?"

God, why did I think this would make me feel better? Rehashing everything wasn't going to help. "Uh, no. He, uh, it was suicide."

"Oh my God! Oh, Seamus! I'm so sorry! Listen, I can wrap this up in the next few days and then I'll get a flight home. I can be home by this weekend."

The headache that had been plaguing him all week came back with a vengeance. He knew he should want her to come back and when he'd seen her beautiful face on the screen he'd felt relief, but the feeling was short-lived. "No. Don't do that."

Lengthy silence followed on the other end before she spoke at last. "So, you're still mad at me? We're still fighting?" Her voice was pinched.

When did this become about her? I don't have time for this. "No, that's not it. It's just…listen I gotta go. I'm at the hospital right now. Mel's having her baby and there's been a few complications. She's in surgery right now."

"Oh." More silence. "I'm sorry. I'll, uh…call me when you can, okay?"

"Yeah." He took a deep breath. "Take care, Sloane. Bye."

"I love you, Seamus."

"You too." He couldn't say the words she wanted to hear. He clicked off before she could say anything else. *I can't deal with her right now, that's all.* Sloane tended to be dramatic about everything and it was likely to push him over the edge if she came home now. The phone buzzed in his hand and he grabbed it up, prepared to tell Sloane he needed some space. But it was Nina's number with no picture because he didn't have one of her. "Hey."

"Hey."

He felt the relief flow through his body at the sound of her voice. "Are you home yet?"

"Yeah. The girls are in the bath. How's Mel?"

"She's still in surgery."

"How's Finn?"

"He's a wreck."

"How are you doing?"

He smiled crookedly. It was so like her to be concerned about him when she'd just gone through what had to be one of the worst days of her life. "I'm fine. This isn't about me. Listen, I should go." He wanted nothing more than to stay in the hallway and listen to her voice.

"Yeah. Can you call or text when you have news?"

"Sure. Try to get some rest. Say goodnight to the girls for me, okay?" He waited until she hung up, then pocketed his phone and returned to the waiting room.

It was nearly an hour later when the nurse finally came for Finn. He spoke with her in the doorway for a moment, then turned to his family. "She's okay. It's a girl. Mel's in recovery. They're both okay." Then he rushed to follow the nurse.

"Oh, thank God." Moira spoke for the entire family.

More waiting ensued, but Finn finally returned, a huge grin replacing his earlier pallor. "They're moving Mel to a room. She says to tell everyone she's fine and she's sorry for causing such a fuss."

"That sounds like Mel," Cara said. "When can we see your daughter?"

"Soon. They're taking her to the nursery so Mel can get some sleep."

After a general round of congratulations, hugs from his mom and sisters, and back-slapping from his father and brothers, Finn led them to the nursery, where they were able to view the newest member of the DeLuca family sleeping in her Lucite bassinet, a tuft of dark fluff crowning her red face.

"What's her name?" Big Tony whispered the words although the thick glass between them and the babies rendered it unnecessary.

"I don't know." Finn hadn't stopped grinning.

"What do you mean you don't know?" Cara demanded. "You've had nine months to think of a name!"

"Mel and I haven't decided. We were sure she'd be a boy."

They let Finn return to his wife then, saying they would be back later. Big Tony suggested they all grab a bite to eat at a nearby restaurant and come back in an hour or so. Seamus filled them in on the funeral, accepting their expressions of sympathy and offers to help Nina's family.

"I'll take some casseroles over to her parents tomorrow."

"Thanks, Mom. That would be great." He was sure the Bradens' freezer would be well-stocked thanks to his mom and the church ladies he'd met at the funeral.

***

Nina met him at the door, stepping aside to let him in. He'd texted her earlier and she'd suggested he stop by on his way home if he wasn't too tired. He was exhausted, both physically and emotionally, but he'd jumped at the chance.

"Did you get to see Mel and the baby?"

He smiled and reached for his phone. "Yes, to both. Meet Ava Sophia DeLuca." He handed her the photograph of Mel holding her small daughter, Finn gazing down on both of them, an expression of utter devotion on his face.

She took the phone from his hand. "Oh, wow. She's so beautiful!" She glanced up at Seamus, her eyes shining slightly.

He nodded and followed her to the living room. "She sure is." He'd never thought babies were anything near beautiful before—he'd actually never thought much about them, at all—but this was different. This was a DeLuca baby. He remembered thinking Janey was cute, but he'd been barely twenty when his first niece was born and had been somewhat ambivalent. But holding his tiny newborn niece had been different this time. He'd looked into the wrinkled little face and fallen in love. He'd FaceTimed Tony while the family was still in Mel's hospital room and was thrilled his brother planned to come home the following weekend to see the new baby.

Nina smiled radiantly up at him and handed his phone back. "You want a beer?"

"God, yes. This has been the world's longest day."

"Agreed." She pointed him toward the sofa as she headed toward the kitchen, returning seconds later with an ice-cold beer apiece. "Cheers."

"Cheers." He took a deep pull and let the events of the day—good and bad—seep away. "Are the girls already asleep?"

"Yeah." She sipped her own beer. "They crashed right after their bath. They were so good at the funeral, huh? I was proud of them."

"Me too." He was getting attached to Nina's daughters, something he never would have imagined a week ago, when he had nothing more serious to worry about than a fight with his gorgeous girlfriend. Life had a funny way of smacking you in the face every so often. *Son of a bitch.* He chuckled as he took another long pull on his beer.

"Care to share with the class? I could sure use a laugh."

He glanced at her, smiling wryly at her small figure tucked into the opposite corner of her couch. She'd changed out of her funeral dress into a pair of khaki shorts and a red tank top partially covered by a grey zippered hoodie. The fuzzy socks covering her feet were somehow endearing, almost distracting him from the smooth, pale skin of her legs. Nothing could distract him from noticing she didn't wear a bra. *Stop looking, dickhead!* He fondly remembered the time he'd briefly caressed one of those small, delicate breasts. She was so petite; Seamus doubted she weighed more than a hundred pounds soaking wet. Neal had been fairly short for a guy, but he'd been stocky. Nina, on the other hand, was slim and barely over five feet tall. "Sorry. It wasn't funny. I was just thinking about how a week ago all I was worried about was a stupid fight with my girlfriend. What a difference a week makes, huh?"

"God, that's for sure." She fiddled with the moist label on her beer bottle, tearing it off in strips. "You had a fight with Sloane?"

"Yeah. It doesn't seem very important now."

"What was it about?" She didn't look at him until he sighed. "Sorry. It's none of my business."

"No, it's fine. Sloane has a tough time with punctuality. And I'm fashion-challenged, at least in her view. It was stupid."

"Oh."

"Yeah." He tipped back the last dregs of beer and rose. "I should probably get out of here and let you get some rest." The purple shadows beneath her eyes seemed to have taken up permanent residence.

"Don't go." She stood and took the empty bottle from him. "Unless you're tired, of course. But I could use the company. I promise I won't ask about Sloane."

He reached to take his bottle from her and walked it to the trash can. "I'd like to stay for a while." The thought of returning to his stark, empty apartment was depressing. "Maybe we could watch a movie or something?"

She smiled. "Sounds great, as long as it's something mindless. You mind if we switch to wine?" He was amenable, so she gathered glasses and a bottle of red while he chose something on Netflix. She poured them each a glass and curled up in her corner again. "Thanks again for helping with the party Sunday."

When he'd discovered Nina was on the hook for the twins' birthday party on Sunday, he'd rearranged his work schedule so he could help. She shouldn't have to do everything by herself, for Christ's sake! So, he'd set up tables and chairs in the backyard, drawn and painted a dinosaur on poster board for Pin the Horn on the Triceratops, and served plate after plate of pink frosted cake and bubble gum ice cream. "Any time, and I mean that literally." To his utter dismay, she set her wine glass on the coffee table and burst into tears, her face buried in her hands. *Well, shit.* He set his own glass on a side table and reached to pull her into his arms.

***

Nina

The tears surprised her. She'd been doing so well holding it together all day. She'd been determined not to lose it, especially in front of the girls, who didn't understand what was happening and why their beloved uncle had been taken away. But it had bubbled up suddenly—all the grief and confusion of the last week—and she was powerless to stop it.

"Hey, come here." Seamus's strong arms pulled her against his warm body.

So warm, so solid. She burrowed against him, the sobs shaking her body. She didn't want to wake the girls, but she couldn't catch her breath.

"Breathe, Nina. It's okay. I'm here." He crooned an endless stream of nonsense until she achieved a small measure of control.

"Sorry." The words were a harsh whisper, but her tears had slowed. She glanced up at his face and was devastated to see tears streaming down his cheeks.

"I know. Me too." He laid his head atop hers and stroked his hands down her hair.

They remained like that for more than ten minutes, until Nina sat up and reached for a tissue. She handed one to Seamus. When she made to move away, however, he pulled her back. She went willingly and leaned against his warmth while he grabbed the remote and turned on the movie. He'd chosen a thriller she'd been wanting to see, but she couldn't keep her eyes open as she finally relaxed against Seamus's intoxicating warmth. *Why does he have to smell so good?* It was her last clear thought until the early morning sun creeping through the blinds woke her. Her head was pillowed on Seamus's lap and he'd pulled the afghan off the back of the couch and spread it over her sometime during the night. His feet were propped on the coffee table and he'd shoved a pillow behind his head; he was still asleep. She managed to get up without waking him and, after answering nature's pressing call, she crept into the kitchen and started the coffee.

"Hey." He appeared a few minutes later, rubbing his hand across his jaw, now scruffy with brown whiskers.

"Hey. Sorry about falling asleep on you. You should have woken me. Your neck must be killing you." She handed him a mug of fresh-brewed coffee.

"Ah, this is great. Thanks." He sipped, looking at her over the rim. "It's fine. I wasn't about to wake you. I know you haven't been sleeping well. Besides." He grinned and winked. "I was out cold."

"You don't have a shift today?"

"Nope. What about you? Are you going in to work?"

She shook her head and sipped her own coffee. "Not yet. I thought it best if I took a day to myself. A day without any funeral arrangements or conversations with police officers."

He smiled. "I think it's a great idea. You want to

hang out? Unless you want some time alone. I won't be offended."

She had planned to spend the day alone, but the opportunity to be with Seamus was too good to pass up. "I'd love to hang out."

"Cool. Would you mind if we run by the hospital to visit Mel?"

"I'd love to."

"Great. Maybe we could swing by my place so I can grab a shower and fresh clothes before we head to the hospital. This 'walk of shame' look doesn't do a lot for me."

She choked on her coffee as she laughed.

"Seamus!" Lily ran into the kitchen and clambered into his lap. Iris followed, a hesitant smile on her little face. Seamus reached out a hand to her, inviting her to join Lily. Iris considered for a moment, then took his hand and climbed up next to her sister. And Nina's heart melted.

***

Seamus dropped her off with an hour to spare before she needed to pick up the girls from school. They'd had a pleasant, low-key day, enjoying a late lunch after visiting Mel, Finn, and baby Ava at the hospital. Neither of them was inclined to spend any more time with other people and opted for eating Subway sandwiches at a picnic table at a park near Nina's house. He was so restful, and she was glad she'd taken him up on his offer to spend the day together. She was very much afraid she was getting too attached, but pushed aside the unwelcome thought along with the rather inconvenient reality of his absent girlfriend. *When Sloane comes back, everything will change.*

She stood, irritated at herself for her thoughts. *Sloane will be back, so don't get any ideas.* She was tempted to take a short nap, but feared an hour wouldn't begin to be enough, so she took the opportunity to pick up a bit, aware that housework had gone by the wayside over the past week and a half. She hadn't done much when she spied the laptop on her desk in the living room, where she'd stashed it a few nights previously. She frowned, trying to remember what her brother's fiancée had said about it. *He told me you'd know the password.* She took the random shoes she held to the girl's room—why couldn't they ever manage to put them away?—and returned to pick up the computer. She took it to the kitchen table and lifted the silver cover, wondering if it had any battery power left. How long had it been since her brother last used it? The glossy screen blinked to life, with Neal's name and an empty box beneath. *What could his password be?* The guy owned a cyber security business, so it wouldn't be something easy. He'd tried to teach her how to create strong passwords, but Nina always fell back on her old favorites. He'd stopped by after work one day a year or so earlier to help her figure out how to install something—she couldn't remember what—on her laptop and had taken the opportunity to give her the third degree about her passwords.

"Nina! You can't use LilyIris18 as your

password! It's way too vulnerable!" Neal rolled his eyes at his sister.

"No one wants to break into my computer. Who wants to read a bunch of history stuff?"

He closed his eyes and shook his head. *"How can you be so smart and yet so dumb? Every credit card and bank account you've ever used to buy anything or pay a bill online is here in your computer, not to mention your tax returns."*

"Shut up!" She angled her computer away from him. *"No one asked you. I hate having to remember a bunch of different passwords and you told me not to write them down. What am I supposed to do?"*

"Okay, look." He softened his tone. *"I'm going to teach you a simple system to create strong passwords that are easy to remember, okay?"*

She sighed dramatically. *"Fine, but it better be really easy."*

"Don't be such a baby! All right, here's what you do: the basic password should describe the name of the site, like Facebook or Amazon, but find a symbol or two to substitute for some of the letters." At her blank look he continued. *"Like use a dollar sign or ampersand instead of an s. But be consistent with those symbols across your passwords. And don't forget to capitalize at least one of the letters."*

"Okay, like this?" She wrote 'AmaZ@n' on a notepad and showed it to him.

"Yeah, exactly, but never write them down. It's a memory system."

"Okay, got it." She tore up the piece of paper.

"We're not done. You need to figure out four

numbers that mean something to you, but aren't well-known to others, and use them at the beginning and end of your passwords. Those numbers stay the same across all your passwords. Like this." He took the notepad from her and scrawled 36AmaZ@n24.

"What's 36-24?"

He grinned and tore the paper into small pieces. "Kira's bust and waist measurements."

"Seriously? You're a pig, Neal." She grimaced as she realized if she used a similar system for her own measurements, the numbers would be a lot closer together and a lot closer to the smaller one.

Her brother grinned. "Yeah, well, now you know my secret. I better not catch you shopping from my Amazon account."

She smiled as she remembered their conversation and his resulting exasperation with her lack of interest in securing her computer and internet browsing. She'd tried to implement his system, but found it too complicated and a general pain in the ass. She'd quickly gone back to her old favs: the girls' names, her former pets' names, etcetera. But she'd always felt a bit guilty about it. *All right.* She pulled the computer closer and set her hands on the keyboard. *Let's see if Neal followed his own advice.* She typed in 36 then stared at the keyboard. "What did you call your computer? Hmm." She tried LapT@p followed by 24. It jiggled back and forth. "Shit." She tried 36LapT0p24, but the damn machine simply mocked her by jiggling again. "Ugh!" She tried several more combinations, all to no avail. *I have no idea why he told Kira I would know the password. And why on earth would he even bring it up to her?* The thought that perhaps he had been planning to kill himself for days and they'd all somehow missed the hints and clues haunted her. *If he said that to Kira, what had he said to me and why was I so oblivious to his pain?* But she'd never in a million years have expected him to do anything like this. Neal had always been so grounded, so sure of himself. Sure, he wasn't always jolly or up about everything, but neither was she. Her brother had been the extroverted one, always pushing her to get out more, to have more fun. Of the two of them, she was much more likely to have been depressed, or at least she'd always thought so. *Maybe he just hid it better than me.* She glanced at her cell and cringed. It was time to stop this nonsense and go pick up the girls. She snapped the laptop closed and carried it to the living room, where she stashed it on a bookshelf, determined to forget about cryptic clues and unfathomable passwords. What possible good could it do now anyway?

***

By two a.m., she realized sleep was an elusive little bastard. The old conversation with Neal and Kira's recent drunken comments kept swarming through her mind until she knew she had to have another go at the damned computer. She donned a sweatshirt against the chilly, high desert night and peeked in at her sleeping daughters. Lily had thrown her covers off, as usual, so Nina pulled them up, tucking them snugly around the little body and kissed her forehead. Iris was still covered and curled into a tight ball in the middle of her twin bed. Although it was a four-bedroom house, the girls were more comfortable sharing a room. Nina picked up Iris's stuffed elephant from the floor and tucked it back under the girl's arm. She kissed her also and left their door open a crack before tip-toeing to the kitchen. She filled her electric kettle and found a box of chamomile tea. While the tea steeped, she searched for her charging cord and hoped it would work in Neal's computer. He'd helped her choose hers, so she hoped he'd recommended the same thing he used. She was in luck and soon had his laptop plugged into her charger. She tried a few more iterations of her earlier password attempts, then stood to stare out the window while she racked her brain for any other possibilities. *Would he really call his laptop 'Laptop'? Wouldn't he choose something a bit more specific or personal?* She sat again and typed in 36NealsL@pT0p24. The box jiggled. *Dammit.* She tried a few more times and was nearly ready to give up and go back to bed when a memory flashed across her mind. *NealzRoom. KEEP OUT.* He'd hand-lettered and decorated the sign for his bedroom door to keep his nosey sister from prying into his business. *As if I'd ever had any desire to poke around his smelly, teenage bedroom!* She sat up straighter and typed 36NealzL@pT0p24 and held her breath as she hit enter. It jiggled. *Goddammit!* She tried a few more times with no success. She stared at the keyboard, willing it to give up its secrets, until the letters blurred. She felt in her bones she was on to something, but couldn't figure out which symbols he'd used. Then she spied the little arrow thingy on top of the number six. She frowned as she realized it reminded her of a capital A. *Maybe.* She typed 36NealzL^pT0p24 and pressed enter. The screen went black for a split second and then his desktop loaded. *Oh, my God! Okay, now what?*

She browsed through his Finder, noting he had organized all his files neatly with many folders and subfolders. *It's like looking for an unknown object in a giant digital haystack. What am I supposed to be looking for?* She figured it depended on what it was Neal thought she might need, if he'd really told Kira that Nina would know his password. It was entirely possible—probable even—that Kira had misconstrued his comment. *Well, I have controlling interest in RiskCom now, so maybe I should see if Neal kept any of the financial records on his personal laptop.* She found a folder on the desktop labeled 'Accounts' and opened it to find multiple subfolders for the three years RiskCom had been in existence. Each year had its own subfolder for the various months and Nina spent nearly an hour looking through them. *I have no idea what I'm looking at.* She knew Seamus's older sister, Izzy, was an accountant and wondered if she might help her make sense of all this sometime. *But not right now.* She yawned and shut down the computer then took her empty mug to the sink. As she crawled in her bed, she wondered if she ought to forget about poking through Neal's computer. She didn't much like the way it made her feel, as if she *had* broken into his bedroom and searched for illicit items. *I should just let it go. He's gone, and nothing is going to bring him back. I'll just drive myself nuts.*

Chapter Eight

Seamus

He let himself in his apartment door, juggling the two bags of groceries he'd stopped to pick up on his way home from the station. It had been a fairly quiet shift, so he'd been able to get nearly six hours of sleep and was looking forward to getting some work done around his apartment and washing his car. He'd bought the Dodge Charger, his first new car, last year. He'd shopped around and had nearly decided on a Mustang until he took a test drive in the shiny black Charger. God, the speed and power had been such a rush! He'd struggled to maintain his poker face while he negotiated with the salesman. Cara had scoffed when he showed it off proudly at the weekly family dinner, snidely adding her opinion that he must be compensating for something. *Brat.*

He put his few groceries away, wondering why he'd never bothered to stock his kitchen with more than the absolute bare minimum of dishes, pots, and pans. He wasn't a great cook, but he enjoyed it and was a hell of a lot better than Sloane, who could barely boil water. She rarely wanted to eat in and tended to pout if he insisted, so he hadn't had much practice beyond what he did at the fire station. But his mother's comment about taking a few casseroles over to the Bradens had made him wonder if anyone had bothered to take food to Nina. She had two little kids with no husband to help, and she'd had to handle nearly all the funeral arrangements by herself. So, he'd spent an hour the night before at the station—it had been *really* quiet—looking for a few recipes online that seemed within his skill set. He'd picked up a couple of those foil pans his mom always used to take food to people and headed home to cook some things for Nina and the girls.

Two hours later, he had three casseroles stacked in the fridge, ready to deliver to her later that afternoon when she got home from work. His stove and sink were full of dirty dishes and he spent the next half hour cleaning his kitchen. He was still in the zone, so used his excess energy to clean up the rest of the apartment, pausing only to run back and forth to the tiny laundry room tucked behind his bedroom to put his whites in the dryer and his colors in the wash. *When did I turn in to such a domestic god?* He chuckled and decided to just go with it. It felt good to get his environment in order. He grabbed a burger on his way to the self-serve car wash and spent a couple hours washing and waxing his Charger, enjoying the way the sun glinted off the chrome.

When he judged Nina had had sufficient time to

pick up the girls and get home, he sent a text, basically inviting himself for dinner. He knew it would be wiser to stay away that evening, to put some space between him and his best friend's sister, but couldn't make himself take his own advice. Spending time with Nina and her girls was enjoyable and made him feel useful, needed even. If Nina was sick of him hanging around, she'd have to be the one to push him away. His phone dinged and he grabbed it, wondering what she'd say.

Nina: Of course. We'd love to have you. I have not been to the grocery store, though. Maybe we can order a pizza.

He grinned and typed:

I'm bringing dinner.

Nina: Oh, Seamus.

He was amused, but not surprised at her excellent grammar, even in a text message. He never would have thought to use a comma after the 'Oh' and would normally have said 'o' with no capitalization.

Seamus: Oh, Seamus what? BTW your college professor-ness is showing.

Nina: What can I say? It's hard to compartmentalize. C U 2nite. There. Happy?

He laughed aloud and sent a clapping hands emoji. Then he got in his shiny, clean car and drove home.

***

"Three plus seven equals...ten!" Lily smiled across the kitchen table at Seamus.

"Very good. Your turn, Iris."

She shook her head. "We're not supposed to count on our fingers, Lily. Teacher said we had to amember it by heart." Her words sounded sorrowful, rather than accusatory.

Seamus fought valiantly to hide a smile. "Okay, Miss Lily. Let's try it again, this time with your hands on the table."

Lily frowned but dragged her hands out of her lap and spread them on the table. "I hate math."

"Aww, don't say that, Lils. Math can be pretty fun when you get to use it for interesting stuff."

"Like what?" She sounded suspicious.

"I use math all the time at my job. I have to calculate tank volume and pressure, flame height and wind speed, stuff like that. But Iris and your teacher are right: you have to memorize your basic facts. It will make the rest of it a whole lot easier. Trust me."

Lily seemed unimpressed. "Fine," she said sulkily.

He continued to quiz the girls on their addition facts while the chicken and rice casserole he'd assembled earlier baked in the oven, sending delicious aromas wafting through the kitchen.

"I'm hungry, Momma. Can we eat yet?" Iris spoke quietly, as always.

Nina turned from where she was slicing a cucumber for the salad. "Soon, sweetie. It smells great, Seamus. You're spoiling us."

He glanced up at her slim figure as she stood at the counter, not failing to notice how lovely her breasts looked in the strappy little top she wore—what did his sisters call them? A cami. Yeah. Nina's was a soft red—she obviously favored that color—and it was driving Seamus crazy. *You definitely shouldn't be thinking about her that way, asshole!* He dragged his eyes back to the stack of flashcards on the table in front of him. "You deserve to be spoiled. Okay, Iris. Four plus eight."

The casserole was a hit, although Lily picked out the chicken and left it in a pile on the side of her plate. He made a note to chop the pieces smaller for her next time. He remembered she'd done the same thing at his parents' house the week before with his mother's Chicken Marsala, eating very little of the meat. When the meal was finished, Nina stood to clean up and Seamus knew she would send the girls to get their bath.

"Why don't the girls and I do the dishes? It won't take long, and I'll bet you could use a few minutes to yourself." He took the dirty plate out of her hands as he spoke. "What do you say, girls? You wanna help?"

They slid from their chairs and took their plates across to the sink. They weren't quite tall enough, so Seamus grabbed a chair and slid it next to the cabinet. Iris rinsed, and Lily stacked the plates in the dishwasher.

"See? We got this. Go." He shooed Nina from the room, then searched for her Tupperware so he could put the leftovers away. "Great job, girls. Now, one of you needs to wipe the table and the other can wipe the counter. I'll wash the knives and the cutting board." They finished cleaning up the kitchen and Seamus sent them off to get their bath. He found the bottle of wine he and Nina had opened the other night and poured them each a glass, wondering if she'd be angry with him for interfering.

"Thanks." She accepted the glass and sipped. "How did it go in there?"

"Good. You're not mad?"

"For interfering in my parenting? Hmm. I guess not." She sipped again and reached to click off the television. "It took me by surprise, that's all. Do you think I'm too soft on them?"

"Not at all. I've just never seen them do any chores around here. Kids need responsibility. It's good for them. What?"

She was chuckling. "You always surprise me, Seamus. Never in my wildest dreams would I have pictured Seamus DeLuca making casseroles and helping little girls do the dinner dishes. Huh." She appeared surprised and turned back to her wine.

"Maybe you've been underestimating me." He tried not to be offended by her comment.

"Clearly." She was quiet for a long moment. "So, you're good at math. How are you with computers?"

"I'm okay, I guess, in that I know how to use one

fairly well. Why? Is yours giving you trouble?"

She shook her head. "Not mine. Neal's."

"The one Kira brought over?"

"That's the one. I managed to get in, but I have no idea what I'm looking for."

He frowned, wondering what she was trying to say. "What do you mean? Why would you be looking for anything? We've already seen the sui— the note." He didn't want to say the word aloud and ruin their evening. She seemed so much better than she had a few nights before, after the funeral, and he didn't want to spoil it.

She pulled the afghan from the back of the sofa and tucked it around her bare feet. "I don't know. But he told Kira to give it to me if anything happened to him and—"

"Wait." He put his hand up to stop her. "Did Kira say that? I don't remember her saying that."

"Well, it was something along those lines." She waved her hand dismissively, as if it didn't matter.

His stomach tightened as he took in her tired eyes with the purple shadows beneath them. He knew she wasn't sleeping well yet, but if she was staying up late to dig through her brother's laptop...crap. "No, it matters, Nina. Kira said *she knew he'd want you to have it*. That's a lot different than telling her to give it to you if anything ever happened to him. A lot."

"I'm not so sure." She sat up and leaned toward him, imploring him to understand. "What if there's something on that computer, something that might help explain—"

"Explain what?" He grabbed her hand and put it

between his palms, trying to rub some warmth into her soft skin. "Nina, sweetheart. Neal took his own life. We'll probably never understand the reasons, but we need to accept it and start to move on. It's not healthy for you to…to obsess over it like this."

She withdrew her hand and glared at him. "I'm not obsessing! I just need—"

But the girls trooped back into the living room at that moment with a stack of books. Seamus knew Nina well enough to know she would regroup and give him an earful as soon as Lily and Iris were asleep. How could he make her understand this wasn't healthy? She was going to drive herself crazy if she kept this up.

They listened as each of the girls read them a story, then Seamus scooped them up under his arms and carried them, giggling madly, to bed. He tucked them in and made sure their nightlight was on before returning to the living room.

Nina had refilled their glasses and was sitting, cross-legged, with a small silver computer on her lap. "I'm *not* obsessing, Seamus. I just want to be sure there isn't something somewhere in all his files that Neal wanted me to know. At the very least, I need to know what was going on with the business. Maybe he was in debt or something and didn't want to tell anyone."

Seamus considered her suggestion. "That doesn't sound like Neal."

She patted the cushion next to her. "I agree, but I need to know what was going on. Please, Seamus." She put her hand on his arm and looked up from under her dark lashes.

He swallowed past the sudden awareness her touch caused. "I'm worried about you. I don't think it's healthy to…spend a lot of time on this." He brushed the pad of his thumb gently under her eye. "You look tired. You're still not sleeping?"

"Some," she said with a shrug. "But it's hard to shut my mind off. Will you please just take a look?" She slid the laptop over to him.

He sighed and pulled it on his lap. "How did you even figure out the password?" He clicked open folders as he asked.

She scooted closer to him and pulled the afghan higher on her lap. "It took a lot of trial and error, but he tried to teach me how to create strong, super-secret passwords a year or so ago. It didn't sink in for me, but I was finally able to figure out what Neal had used."

"Yeah, he tried to teach me the same shit, but I glazed over within a couple of minutes. God, Neal sure could rant, huh?" He chuckled and looked at her. "You figured it out, though? Jeez, Nina. I knew you were smart, but this is impressive."

"Thanks. I found a bunch of financial records, but I'm not sure how to read them." She pointed to the file folder icon on the desktop and waited while he opened it. "Do you think Izzy might be willing to take look? I'd pay her, of course."

"I'm sure she will, and she won't take any money for it." He squinted at the spreadsheets and frowned. "Yeah, I don't know how to read accounting ledgers, either. I'll talk to Izzy." He closed the laptop and set it on the coffee table. "Will you promise me to stop spending your nights

131

searching through this until after she's had a chance to check the spreadsheets out?"

"Seamus," she objected. "Don't ask me to do that. Please." She implored him with those big, green eyes. "It's not a big deal."

"If it's keeping you from sleeping, it's a huge deal." He pulled her legs onto his lap and reached beneath the afghan; her bare feet were icy, so he took turns warming each between his palms. "Have you thought about talking to a doctor or a counselor?"

She shook her head and crossed her arms. "I don't want to take sleeping pills. I need to be able to hear the girls in the middle of the night, and I won't if I'm drugged up."

"Hey." He continued to rub her cold feet. "That's not what I meant." At her disbelieving glare, he rolled his eyes. "Okay, that's not *all* I meant. I get that sleeping pills aren't the best idea for you, but talking to a counselor couldn't hurt, could it?"

She stared at him for several long moments, but he refused to look away. "Ugh. Fine. Yeah, I'll talk to someone, if you insist." She reached for her wine. "I'm not crazy."

"Going to a counselor doesn't mean you're crazy, Nina."

"I need to know why Neal did it," she whispered. "I can't accept that I wouldn't have known how he was feeling."

His heart broke for her, but he worried her obsession—which is exactly what it seemed like to him—would stop her from properly grieving her brother's death.

***

Nina

Mental and Behavioral Health Benefits:

Behavioral health treatment, such as psychotherapy and counseling

Mental and behavioral health inpatient services

Substance use/abuse disorder treatment

Nina scrolled farther down the web page for the details. *At least the university provides decent insurance coverage. I'll give in to Seamus's ridiculous demands that I see a counselor, but only if I don't have to pay out-of-pocket.* Further investigation revealed she had eight counseling visits on the house to figure out whether or not she was clinically depressed, or obsessed, or whatever. She blew out a resigned breath and did a Google search for local counseling centers. The university had one, but she had no intention of using it in case she was seen going in or out. Her parents had suggested counseling after her divorce, but she'd been much too busy finishing her dissertation and wrapping her head around single motherhood to even think about adding one more thing on her plate. Neal had also thought it would be a good idea. Had he been seeing a counselor or a psychiatrist? Is that who prescribed the antidepressants to him? And what kind of crappy counselor couldn't tell their patient was suicidal? She remembered all the warnings she'd researched and wondered again if that's what happened to Neal. *Maybe I should call a lawyer instead of a counselor.*

The buzzing of her cell phone interrupted her thoughts and she glanced at it, surprised to see Chris Hart's name and number. She'd exchanged numbers with both detectives, but had only spoken with Finn so far. "Hi, Chris. What can I do for you?"

"Nina, hi. Sorry to bother you at work, but I need you to come down to the precinct."

Chills crept down her spine at the tone of Chris's voice. "What's wrong? What's happened? Is it Seamus?" *Oh, God, please let him be okay.*

"No, nothing like that." Chris sounded confused. "But you might want to bring him with you. Listen, Nina, we've got more information about Neal's death, but it would be better if we talked in person. Can you get away?"

"Of course. I'll be there as soon as I can." She hung up, heart pounding, and found Seamus's number in her contacts. *Please let him answer.* She didn't care to analyze why she needed him so badly; she simply knew she did.

"Nina, hey." He sounded sleepy.

"I woke you up. I'm so sorry."

"No, it's not a problem. Don't worry about it. What's up? You sound weird."

She huffed a brief laugh. "Yeah. Chris just called and said I need to go down to the state police precinct. She said they've got more information on Neal's death. She suggested you come too. Please, Seamus. Can you go with me?" She wasn't above begging, if that's what it took.

"Of course. Why don't I meet you there?"

"Thanks." She ran her hand through her hair distractedly. "I really appreciate it. What do you think they've found?"

He sighed and she could hear him moving around his bedroom. "I have no idea. Let's just wait 'til we get there. Speculation isn't going to help." He paused. "Drive carefully, okay? You don't need to speed or anything to get there. Promise me?"

"Yeah, okay. I wish you'd stop worrying about me." But she doubted the veracity of her own words; she kind of liked having someone worry about her.

"I don't think that's possible. I'm gonna grab a lightning-quick shower and then I'll head out. Meet you there in about twenty minutes. Okay?"

"Okay."

***

He was leaning against his shiny black sports car when she pulled into the parking lot twenty-five minutes later. It had taken longer than she liked to cancel her afternoon classes and let her department head know she would be missing the afternoon faculty meeting. Seamus's dark brown curls glistened, still wet from his shower. He straightened as she parked next to him and exited her SUV. "Hey." His smile was warm—the most comforting thing she'd seen in a long time.

Without conscious thought, she walked straight into his arms and inhaled his clean, male fragrance. It should be illegal to smell so good. "I'm so glad you're here." She had a bad feeling about what was coming, a sort of sixth sense.

He held her close for a moment. "Of course. Any time." He gently extricated himself. "So, let's do this?"

She nodded and walked beside him to the precinct doors. They checked in at the front desk. The receptionist picked up the phone to call for Chris, who promptly came to meet them.

"Hi, guys. Thanks for coming so quickly. Your parents arrived a few minutes ago, Nina."

Nina met Seamus's frown. *It must be serious if she called my parents in too.*

"Is Finn still out on paternity leave?" Seamus asked as they followed Chris into the bowels of the precinct.

"Yeah. He took a full two weeks off since Mel had to have a C-section. Little Ava sure is a cutie, huh?"

"She's a doll. Hard to believe Finn's a father, though."

They're chatting about babies? Seriously? But maybe it indicated this—dragging Nina and her parents down to the precinct in the middle of the day—wasn't as serious an issue as she feared. Or maybe it was simply an indication of Chris's ability to separate work and family issues.

She led them to a small, private conference room and Nina wondered if it was normally used to interrogate suspects. The Bradens were seated at the Formica-topped table, drinking coffee from Styrofoam cups.

Nina greeted them each with a quick hug and

joined them at the table. Seamus opted to stand in the back of the room, behind the table, his arms crossed over his chest as he frowned at Chris.

Chris took the empty chair at the head of the table and pulled a file folder toward her. "Thank you all for getting here so quickly." She opened the folder and pulled out a piece of paper. "I'm sorry to be so dramatic and mysterious, but I didn't want to tell you any of this over the phone." She sighed. "The coroner's report with the final autopsy results finally came back and they've discovered some discrepancies."

"What does that mean?" Mr. Braden set his coffee cup aside and leaned forward. "What sort of discrepancies?"

Chris glanced down at the report in front of her. "Apparently the angle of the gunshot is not consistent with a self-inflicted wound. There's more." She held up her hand as several of the others started to interrupt. "Although they found gunpowder residue on Neal's hand, the amount is also not consistent with a self-inflicted wound."

"What? Oh, my God!" Nina exclaimed. She stared at her parents, who appeared to be in shock.

Chris nodded. "I don't want to get too technical, but the void of gunpowder residue on his left hand, the one the gun was in, is indicative of another hand on top of his when the gun was fired. Because of these discrepancies, the OMI—that's the Office of the Medical Investigator—did a much more thorough autopsy and investigation than normal. They ran an extended tox screen and found high levels of ketamine in his system."

"What is ketamine? Why would Neal take it?" Mrs. Braden asked.

Chris shook her head. "Ketamine is a tranquilizer, often used to get high, but the amount Neal had in his system was fatal and it's highly doubtful he took it willingly. It was most likely injected, although the coroner was unable to find evidence of this."

"Neal was murdered." Seamus's voice was hollow as his hands squeezed Nina's shoulders.

Chris continued to nod. "We are now investigating his death as a homicide. I'm so sorry."

Mrs. Braden was now crying softly. "I don't understand."

Nina shook her head, trying vainly to stop the buzzing. She reached for Seamus's hand, her one tenuous hold on reality in that moment. "Who?" She cleared her suddenly parched throat. "Do you have any suspects?"

Now Chris's expression went carefully blank and Nina knew she wasn't about to tell them anything close to the truth. "We already have several leads, which we're actively following up, but I'm afraid I can't say anything more at this time." She closed the folder and stood. "I promise to keep you all updated as soon as we know more. We'll need to talk more about this to each of you, but I realize you're all in shock right now." She crossed to the door and held it open, a clear indication the conference was at an end.

The four of them walked together to the parking lot in silence. Mrs. Braden turned to Nina as she reached her car. "I don't even know what to say. Do you want to come to the house, Nina? We could talk about it there."

Panic set in as she thought about having to deal with her parents' suppositions and continued grief. *I just can't deal with that right now.* "Um, I don't...I don't think I can handle it right now, Mom. Could we meet up a little later?"

Mrs. Braden pulled her daughter into her arms and kissed her forehead. "Of course, dear. I know this is hard for you. It's hard for us all. Why don't you go home and get some rest and come over later this evening?"

Nina nodded and stepped away carefully. "Okay, yeah. I'll see if I can get a babysitter or something. I don't want the girls to know about this yet."

"All right." Her mother smoothed Nina's hair back from her forehead as she had so many times when Nina was growing up, then turned to Seamus. "Thank you for coming. Will you make sure Nina gets home safely?"

He nodded and gave Mrs. Braden a quick hug. "Of course."

Nina watched her parents drive away, then sighed. "I just couldn't deal with them right now. Does that make me a horrible person?"

He put his arm around her shoulders and steered her toward their vehicles. "Not even close. Parents can be intense." They reached her car and he turned her to face him. "What do you need from me right now, Nina?"

She dropped her gaze and shrugged. *So much. I don't even know what I need from you.* "Is there any way we could grab some coffee or something?"

He smiled crookedly and reached for her hand. "Sounds good. Let's take my car."

She nodded and followed him to his sports car. He held the passenger door open for her and she lowered herself into the black leather seat, noting how clean the interior was. It still smelled new. She sat back and prepared to enjoy the ride, determined to push the awful things Chris had just told them away for a few precious minutes.

Seamus glanced sideways at her before he started the engine. "You okay?"

She nodded and closed her eyes. "I need some time to process. Do you like to drive fast? Is there any way you could take us for a short drive before we find that coffee?"

He chuckled and backed out of his parking space. "I love to drive fast and I know the perfect place, not too far from here."

She kept her eyes closed as he drove; she may have drifted off for a few minutes, but the smooth feel of the road beneath them soothed her. His fancy car had better suspension than her SUV. She'd always gone for the practical option, the one with the highest safety rating for carting her children around town; this brief escape in a sexy sports car was fun and surprisingly good for her sanity. When she finally opened her eyes, she was shocked to see they weren't in Albuquerque. Tall pine trees towered over the small parking lot of Katrinah's East Mountain Grill. "Where are we?"

"Edgewood." It was a small town in the mountains just east of Albuquerque. "I figured it would do you good to get out of town for a bit. Are you okay with that? I can take you back, if you want."

She smiled sleepily and reached for the door handle. "This is perfect."

Seamus held the glass door of the restaurant for her and the delicious aroma of coffee and cooking meat greeted them.

"It smells great."

"Sure does. Let's have lunch." He winked at her.

She rolled her eyes. "Yes, Mother. You're worried about me not eating enough now?" She told the hostess it would be two for lunch.

He pulled her chair out with a chuckle. "Maybe. I happen to know you only picked at your dinner last night."

"It was delicious, Seamus." She put her hand on his forearm, enjoying the hard lines of muscle under a colorful tattoo. "It's not that I didn't like it. You're a great cook."

He put his hand on top of hers. "I'm not insulted, Nina. But I do want to make sure you eat properly."

The waitress approached, glanced at their clasped hands, and flashed them an indulgent smile. Seamus and Nina quickly let go and sat back in their chairs. "Hi. My name's Anna and I'll be your server." She handed them each a menu. "What would you like to drink?"

Nina buried her head in the menu as she felt a blush creeping up her neck. "Coffee, please."

Seamus ordered the same and waited until the waitress had retreated. "What's wrong?"

"She thinks we're together. Together-together."

He stared at her, eyebrows raised. "So? Who

cares? Relax, Nina. We don't even know anyone here." He set his menu on the edge of the table. "Can we talk about what Chris said, or would you rather wait until after we eat?"

She set her menu on top of his. "We can talk about it now."

"You promise you'll eat, though?"

"Yes! Stop fussing."

"I rarely fuss." He held his hand toward her, the little finger crooked. "Pinky swear?"

"What are we—twelve?" But she linked her pinky with his. "Pinky swear." *He's so good for me. I don't think I could handle this by myself.* She swallowed and forced herself to bring up the horrible topic. "Did Chris really just tell us Neal was murdered?"

Chapter Nine

Seamus

"She did. The police are investigating Neal's death as a homicide." He kept her hand in his as they lowered them to the scarred wooden tabletop. He needed to hold on to her, to have physical contact as they discussed this unbelievable revelation. Ordinary people, people you knew, weren't murdered, and Neal was the most normal guy he'd ever known! The waitress returned with their coffee and Seamus reluctantly let go of Nina's hand as they placed their food order and put sugar and cream in their coffee.

"Who on earth would want to murder my brother?" she said, echoing his thoughts. "Did Neal have any enemies?"

He sipped his coffee, a wonderfully strong, dark roast, and shook his head. "Not that I know of, but he and I didn't exactly move in the same circles. I really don't know any of his other friends any more. We kind of drifted apart during college and only really started meeting up again for beers fairly recently. We met more often over the past few months since Tony moved to Portales."

She reached for his hand again. "You miss him, don't you? Tony, I mean."

He rubbed his thumb over her soft palm. "You are incredibly sweet to worry about me, Nina. Yeah, I miss him, especially since the idiot didn't bother to tell me he was planning to go to grad school four hours away. But it was good to have a reason to spend more time with Neal. It was too short-lived." His throat closed, and he reached for his coffee, needing a moment to compose himself. "What about you? Did Neal ever talk about anyone he was having problems with?"

She shook her head. "Not at all. The police are going to ask us all this, aren't they?"

"I'm sure they will." He squeezed her hand. "I need to apologize, Nina."

She frowned. "For what?"

"For doubting you, for pressuring you to see a counselor, for saying you needed to grieve your brother and get on with your life." He pushed his coffee away and ran his free hand through his hair. "I was way out of line."

"Stop." She grabbed his other hand and pulled, forcing him to lean toward her. "Don't be so hard on yourself. We had no idea he was murdered."

"You did." At her disbelieving look he shook his head. "You knew he didn't kill himself."

"I didn't believe he had. I couldn't believe it."

He squeezed her hands gently, then pulled his away and leaned back. "I should have believed in you. I'm sorry. I won't make the same mistake again."

She smiled crookedly and set her elbow on the table, her little finger crooked toward him. "Pinky swear?"

He managed a half-grin and linked his pinky with hers again. "Yeah. Pinky swear."

They broke apart again as their food was delivered, a cheeseburger for Seamus and a spinach salad for Nina. The food was good and they devoted several uninterrupted minutes to eating.

He watched her carefully, making sure she ate enough. He was inordinately proud of her, of how she was holding up in the face of all this. She'd never stopped believing in her brother, had never believed he was capable of taking his own life. "So, what about the antidepressant prescription? Do you think that was legit?"

She chewed carefully and washed it down with a sip of water. "Well, Kira seemed to think so. She said he was depressed and was seeing a doctor for it."

He considered carefully before responding. "Do you trust Kira?"

She set her fork down and stared at him. "What do you mean?"

He ate another French fry, chewing slowly before answering. He wasn't sure what he meant; the question had popped out without a conscious decision on his part. "I don't know," he said finally. "How well do you know her?"

Nina picked up her fork and took a small bite, obviously considering her answer carefully. "Not terribly well. She and Neal have been together for more than two years, though. She's been at nearly every family gathering in that time, although there's not many of those. Not on the DeLuca scale, at any rate."

He chuckled, amazed they could find humor in anything today. "Yeah, my family can be…intense. Where did they meet?"

"I'm surprised you and Neal never talked about any of this."

He raised an eyebrow. "Um, guys don't really talk about stuff like that. At least, not on purpose."

She smiled resignedly. "I probably don't want to know what guys *do* talk about. They met through a mutual friend."

"Who was this mutual friend?"

"His business partner, Gordon Sanderson. Have you met him?"

"Sure, but I don't know him well. They were college roommates, right?"

"Yeah, but not until their junior year. Gordy is the computer expert and genius behind their business and Neal is…was…shit, sorry. Neal *was* the business side of things."

"Hey." He reached for her hand again. "It's still hard to think about him in the past tense, isn't it?"

She reclaimed her hand and pushed her bowl away. "You have no idea. Well, I guess you do, actually."

The waitress stopped by to refill their coffee mugs and Nina wrapped both hands around hers, as if trying to warm herself. "Murder is what happens on television, not to people you know and certainly not to family members. I'm having a hard time processing this."

He wanted to scold her for not finishing her lunch, but figured it was no use. She'd probably just skewer him with that green gaze and continue drinking her coffee. His own cheeseburger was less appetizing than it had been a few minutes before, so he totally understood. He didn't have a response for her, though; he'd been thinking the same thing.

"And if it does happen, it should be in a dark alley or something when someone is trying to mug you or carjack you. Who gets murdered in their office, for God's sake?"

"I don't know, hon." The endearment slipped out, but she didn't seem to notice. "Do you want me to stay with the girls tonight while you're at your parents' house?" He knew—and completely agreed—they shouldn't be told about the murder. Shit like that could give them nightmares.

"Um, I was actually hoping you'd come with me. I know it's selfish, but I dread having the conversation with them by myself." She looked down into her mug. "I understand if you'd rather skip it, though. It's going to suck, big time."

He knew it would; Mrs. Braden was not a calm, rational person. She would, no doubt, engage in a fair amount of crying and wailing while Mr. Braden sat quietly and let his wife emote. It had always been that way, even back in high school, and it often made Seamus, whose own mother would never do something like that, uncomfortable. It probably also helped explain why both Nina and Neal had been rather serious and quiet, although

Neal could cut loose when he wanted. Seamus wasn't sure if Nina knew how to loosen up and let herself have fun. "Of course I'll go. We're in this together, Nina." He wanted to reach for her hand again but thought better of it. He was starting to enjoy and crave those little touches entirely too much. *Remember your girlfriend, dumbass!* The little voice in his head could be such a nag. But he'd never cheated on a woman, and he didn't intend to start now. Nina and Sloane both deserved better than that. And he had no idea whether or not Nina still carried a torch for him. There'd been a whole lot of water under the bridge since that high school crush and she'd no doubt have gotten past it by now. They'd been thrown together by Neal's death and it was messing with their emotions. That's all this was. "Will you be able to get a babysitter this late?"

She nodded. "I'm sure I will. I'll see if their after-school nanny can keep them for a few extra hours." She fiddled with her paper napkin, tearing it into a small pile of shreds. "I appreciate all you've done for me, Seamus, during this…" she faded off, not seeming to know how to express the awfulness of Neal's death.

"I think 'clusterfuck' might be the word you're going for." This time he shoved the annoying voice in his head into a dark corner and reached for her small hand. It was still cold, even though she'd had it on her mug.

She chuckled and clutched his hand, as if it was her lifeline. "That sounds about right. And 'appreciate' isn't the right word, either, but I don't

148

know what is."

"Me neither. I'm not doing it to get any thanks or appreciation, though. Neal was my best friend, even though we hadn't been close for a long time. I can't understand what happened any more than you, but I need to try to figure it out. I loved the guy, you know? And I love you too." He hoped she knew he meant as a sister. He hoped he really meant it only that way. "We're in this together, Nina," he reiterated, "until you get sick of me."

"I don't think that's likely to happen," she whispered. "I need you, Seamus. I'm so glad you're here."

"Me too. And it's not a one-way street, you know. I need you just as much, if not more. This whole thing—"

"The clusterfuck, you mean?"

He grinned, grateful she'd lightened the suddenly somber mood. "Yeah, that. It's messing with my head. I can think better, clearer when you're near." His phone, which he'd placed on the table near his plate, lit up suddenly, displaying Sloane's gorgeous face above the accept and reject buttons. He saw Nina glance at it, then pull her hands from his and lean back in her seat.

"You'd better take that."

He wanted to reject her call; he was actually angry at the interruption. But he'd rejected too many of her calls lately and he needed to remind himself, to declare it publicly to Nina, that he still had a girlfriend. He'd been far too guilty of the old "out of sight, out of mind" paradigm since Sloane had left. He grabbed his phone as he stood. "Yeah.

Be right back." He stepped outside to take the call. "Sloane. Hey." He hoped his greeting didn't sound as anemic as he felt.

"Hey, yourself. You're off today, aren't you?"

"Yeah. What's up?"

She paused, as if taken aback at his abruptness. "Well, I wanted to see how you're doing. I know this situation with Neal has been really rough for you."

Situation? Rough? Fuck. He closed his eyes and pinched the bridge of his nose, trying to keep his anger in check. She was trying to sympathize, after all. But he found himself reluctant to tell her about the murder. *I don't want to be stuck out here explaining all the details to her while Nina waits.* He almost believed his rationalization. "Yeah, it is. Listen, Sloane. I'm kind of in the middle of something right now with Neal's...family. Can I call you back later tonight?"

She was silent again, and Seamus could tell she was annoyed. "Sure."

"Okay. Great. I'll, uh, I'll talk to you later." Only later did he realize neither had said "I love you."

Nina was signing a credit card slip when he returned to the table. "Everything all right?"

He frowned as he watched her slide the white slip of paper in the black folder. "Yeah. Tell me you didn't just pay for our meals."

"All right. I won't." She stood and looped her purse over her shoulder.

He sighed. "Nina. You didn't have to do that."

"I know, but I wanted to." She put a hand on her hip. "Are you about to object to me paying the tab based upon some antiquated notion of proper gender roles?"

"I have no idea what you just said, Professor Braden." He did, of course. He'd minored in sociology in college and even wrote a paper on gender role stereotypes. She was so damn cute when she was bossy. "But I have a hard time allowing a woman to pay for my lunch."

"Don't be a Neanderthal, Seamus. Come on." She slipped her arm through his. "I'll let you buy me ice cream."

Her hand was finally warm on his bare arm. "You're a trip, Nina. Fine. I guess I can force my emasculated self to buy you dessert."

They walked next door to the ice cream shop, where he bought them each a cone. They walked back to the car slowly, enjoying the warmth of the late September day and the fresh mountain air.

***

Nina

"Don't worry about it, Dad. I'm serious." Nina waved away the two twenties her father tried to hand her for the pizzas she and Seamus had picked up.

"All right. Thanks, baby. Your mom didn't feel like cooking tonight."

"Of course, Daddy." She led the way to the kitchen, where her mother was setting paper plates on the table. She walked into her mother's outstretched arms and held tightly. She'd hugged her mother more in the last week than in the previous ten years.

Seamus set the boxes on the table and accepted a hug in turn from her mom.

"Oh, I'm so glad you could come, Seamus." Mrs. Braden turned to Nina. "Kira should be here soon."

Nina and Seamus shared a swift glance as they remembered their earlier conversation about Neal's fiancée. Seamus didn't seem to trust her, but Nina wasn't sure. Neal had been so happy with Kira and beyond excited when she'd agreed to marry him. She'd spent every Thanksgiving, Christmas, and family birthday with them for the past two years; surely Nina would have picked up on something if she weren't trustworthy. Sure, she'd never really thought Kira was good enough for her twin, but then, Neal had never thought David was good enough for her. *But he'd been spot-on about that, hadn't he?* She still wondered what the truth was regarding the anti-depressant prescription, but it hardly mattered now that they'd learned Neal was murdered.

"Nina?" Her father had apparently asked a question.

"Sorry." She shook her head slightly. "What?"

"What would you like to drink? We have wine, beer—"

"Wine, please. Red, if you have it."

He poured a glass of merlot and handed it to her. "Seamus?"

"A beer would be great, thanks."

Kira came in as they were sitting down to eat, looking flustered as she accepted a glass of wine and waved away the offer of food.

"Well, that detective was certainly in a hurry to get rid of us this morning, wasn't she?" Mrs. Braden sipped her wine as she spoke.

Nina felt Seamus bristle at the criticism of his sister-in-law. "Mom, I think she just didn't want to spend time speculating about who murdered Neal. She said they've barely started the investigation."

"Well, I think it would have been nice to be able to ask a few questions. My son was murdered, after all, and that woman just shut us down!"

"Nancy," Mr. Braden warned. "Calm down, please. Let's talk about this in a rational manner."

Nina glanced at Seamus and noted the way his jaw flexed as if trying to keep his temper in check. "Mom, Chris is married to Seamus's brother, Hugh, so it would be great if you wouldn't blame this all on her." She saw no reason to sugar-coat it for her mother, who could be difficult at times. They were all reeling from the shock of finding out Neal had been murdered and her mother's form of coping wasn't helping anyone.

"Well, I'm sorry, but—"

"Have you been asked to go in for more questioning?" Norm Braden interrupted his wife, clearly used to intervening between her and Nina, as he had so often during Nina's teen years, when the two women couldn't seem to be in the same room without arguing.

Seamus reached for Nina's hand under the table and gave it a gentle squeeze. "Yeah. We're going in the morning. What about you all?"

Mr. Braden nodded. "We have an appointment

tomorrow afternoon. What about you, Kira?"

Kira jumped and knocked her wine glass over. Rivulets of merlot ran across the table top and trickled into her lap. "Shit! Sorry!" She waved her hands helplessly.

Nina stood and crossed the room to fetch paper towels. "Here." She handed a wad to Kira, then used the rest to mop the table. She glanced at Seamus as she wiped, noting his raised eyebrow and frown toward Kira, who was doing more damage than good to her cream-colored slacks. "Are you okay, Kira?"

"Not really." She slapped the soggy, red paper towels on the table and reached for her wine glass, which Norman had righted and refilled. Her hands trembled so much Nina thought she would spill it again. "Detective Hart asked me to come in early tomorrow morning before my shift at the hospital. I'm sorry." She set the glass aside and jumped from her seat.

They all watched her exit quickly to the bathroom, then turned back to stare at each other uncomfortably.

"Should I check on her?" Nancy Braden started to rise.

Norm reached a hand to rest on her shoulder. "Let her be, Nance. She probably needs a few minutes to herself. As hard as this is on the rest of us, poor Kira lost her future husband."

Always the peacemaker, Dad. "Did Neal ever talk to you guys about work?" Nina gathered up the wet paper towels and threw them away.

Her parents looked at each other and shrugged.

"Not very often," her mother said. "I think he assumed we were too old to understand the whole cyber security thing."

Nina smiled; Neal had said as much to her, that their parents were hopeless Luddites when it came to anything technological. "But did he ever talk about the people at work? Like, did he have problems with any of them?"

Her father frowned. "Sweetheart, you sound like the detective." He paused to top off her wine. "I'm not sure it's wise to speculate about all that."

Nina barely refrained from the eye-roll that comment so richly deserved.

"Yes," her mother agreed. "I may not have appreciated her rudeness, but I'm sure the detective is much better equipped than you to investigate Neal's case, especially when your brother returns." She addressed her final words to Seamus. "How is Finn's new baby? It was a girl, wasn't it?"

Seamus winked at Nina and turned to answer her mother. "Yes, ma'am. Ava Sophia. Would you like to see a picture?"

Kira returned as Mrs. Braden was admiring Seamus's new niece. "I'm so sorry for all this." She gestured to the table Nina had wiped. "I think I better go. I guess I'm just not ready to talk about it right now."

Mrs. Braden clucked her tongue and handed the phone back to Seamus. "Of course, dear." She rose and ushered Kira out of the kitchen, murmuring soft assurances the whole way.

Nina stood and began to clear the table, more than ready to leave the stressful get together and return home to her girls. *I just want to curl up with them and watch cartoons and forget about things like murder and suicide and police investigations. Mom is right: Finn and Chris are much better equipped to figure out what happened to Neal.*

Seamus took the hint and stood to help her clean up. By the time Mrs. Braden returned from seeing Kira out, they were finished. Nina's mother insisted they take the leftover pizza—no one had been very hungry, so there was quite a lot—with them for the girls.

"Thanks, Mom." Nina kissed her mother's cheek. They had a difficult relationship, but at the end of the day she was still her mom. "Maybe I can bring them over this weekend. I know you've missed them."

"Oh, yes! That's a wonderful idea! Perhaps we could take them for the day. Why don't they spend the night Saturday?"

"Sounds perfect." Although they'd expressed dismay when Nina told them she and David were adopting an orphan from Uganda—then shock when they'd brought home two—her parents had always been amazing grandparents, frequently taking the girls for the night so Nina could have some time to herself. Lately they'd begun hinting she should use the time to date someone new. *Ugh. As if I have the time or energy for that right now.* Her gaze drifted involuntarily toward Seamus and she mentally shook herself. *Forget it. It's neither the time nor the place. And he has a girlfriend.* She'd never met Sloane, but the glimpse of her picture on Seamus's cell phone earlier that afternoon had revealed she was gorgeous, and sexy, and everything Nina had never been. *The one time you tried for him, back in high school, was a complete and utter disaster! Remember that.*

They picked the girls up from the babysitter and took them home. They'd finished their small bit of homework already, so they were each allowed to have a slice of pizza and watch an hour of television.

"Thanks for coming with me. Sorry it was so awkward." Nina leaned her head against the back of the sofa and closed her eyes against the pressure building in her head. She'd half expected him to leave as soon as they returned, but was grateful he'd followed her in.

He angled his body toward hers and reached for her arm. "Here. Turn around." He pulled her gently until her back was to him. He rubbed her shoulders, massaging up and down her neck with his thumbs, smoothing her tight muscles.

She groaned in appreciation. His hands were wonderfully large and strong, the calluses a sharp counterpoint to her soft skin. "That feels amazing."

"Good." She could hear the smile in his voice. "Don't apologize for your parents. I'm used to them. Thanks for sticking up for Chris, though."

"Of course. My mom can be...well, I'm sure you understand. Mmm." She dropped her chin to her chest to give him greater access to her neck. He focused gentle pressure on the base, where her head and neck met. "You have magic hands." She cringed as she realized the possible innuendo in her words. "Sorry."

He chuckled. "No problem. Is it just me or did Kira seem...nervous tonight?"

She wondered at his hesitation. "Yeah. She's a wreck." She opened her eyes and glanced at the twins, relieved to see they were completely engrossed in their pizza and television show, some Disney offering that looked like *The Lion King,* but wasn't. "Today's news seems to have pushed her over the edge, which I don't quite understand. I mean, it's awful, of course, but it makes me feel a little better somehow. Is that selfish?"

"I don't think so. I get it. I mean, when we thought it was—" he stopped and glanced swiftly at the girls, "—the other thing, it was something he did to himself. This was something done to him. There's a big difference, at least to those of us left behind."

She nodded, appreciating both his insight and his attempt to keep the words "murder" and "suicide" out of the conversation when the girls were around. The program ended, and she sent the girls to stack their plates in the dishwasher while she filled the tub for their bath. Seamus promised them he'd stay for story time. She winked at him and handed him the remote.

Forty-five minutes later, the girls were tucked in and the house was quiet. Nina loved this time of day when she could relax and gather her thoughts. It was even better when Seamus was waiting for her in the living room. *Don't get attached! He's only here because of Neal.*

"How's the headache?" He poured her a glass of wine as he spoke.

"Better. Thanks." She sipped and leaned against him. *Might as well enjoy it while I can.* "You were right, what you said before. It's somehow easier to accept someone killed him than accept he could have killed himself. I think I feel guilty for feeling so much better about it. But he's still dead, and that sucks." It was the understatement of the year.

"Indeed."

"I really hope Chris and Finn can figure out who did it soon." She sat up and turned to face him. "They will be able to figure it out, won't they? I don't think any of us could take it if they don't."

"Hey, don't." He set his glass aside and cupped her face in his rough palm. "You don't need one more thing to stress about, okay? They're pros and will find out who did it."

She looked up through her lashes at his achingly handsome face, then allowed her gaze to drift to his full lips. She'd always loved his lips. She realized she was leaning toward him, but couldn't, wouldn't stop. She lifted her face and pressed her lips to his.

He froze, and his hands went to grasp her shoulders, undoubtedly to push her away. But then he groaned and softened his mouth against hers. His hands slipped around her back as he pulled her closer.

Yes. Oh, God, yes. She closed her mind to inconvenient thoughts about his girlfriend and concentrated all her efforts on making this the best, most memorable kiss she could. Who knew when or if it would ever be repeated? She parted her lips slightly, letting him know she welcomed any deepening of the kiss he might share to explore. He swiftly accepted, his hot tongue sliding in to tangle with hers. He tasted of wine and his own special flavor, one she'd craved since their last kiss almost a decade before. She slid one hand from his shoulder to tangle in the crisp hair at the nape of his neck as he moved from her lips to kiss along her jaw line, causing delicious shivers to chase down her spine. "Seamus," she moaned and slipped her other hand to feather over the vee of warm skin at the top of his shirt.

He wrenched his mouth from hers and sat back, his eyes wide as he stared at her in horror. "I'm so sorry, Nina. I shouldn't have done that."

She slumped as disappointment flowed through her. *You knew this would happen. Get over it.* She squared her shoulders and tried to smile. "You have nothing to apologize for. I'm the one who kissed you. Sorry about that. It's been awhile, that's all. I know you're taken."

He closed his eyes and sighed. "You may have started it, but I certainly didn't back away." He scrubbed his hands over his face. "Shit." He stood. "I should go."

"Yeah. I *am* sorry. I shouldn't have done it. I don't want to ruin anything. I'm so glad you're here and I don't want you to feel like you have to stay away and—"

"Shh." He placed his finger over her lips. "You haven't ruined anything. I just need to go before I do something stupid." He walked to the front door as she followed. "I'll pick you up tomorrow around eight, okay?"

She wondered if she should offer to drive herself

to the state police precinct but couldn't seem to work up the gumption. "Sure. Good night, Seamus."

"Night, Nina. Lock up, after I leave."

She watched him walk to his car. He didn't look back. *Just once, I'd like to kiss Seamus DeLuca without him pulling away. Just once.*

Chapter Ten

Seamus

He waited to make sure her door shut before he drove away, trying his dead-level best not to crash into the neighbor's mailbox. He drove carefully around the block and pulled to the curb. *Damn. Damn, damn, damn.* Then, when that wasn't strong enough: *fuck. What was she thinking? What was I thinking?* But he knew the answer to the last question: he hadn't been thinking, not once he'd felt her soft body plastered against his. *God, the woman can kiss.* Their first kiss, so long ago, had been sweet, but she'd been completely inexperienced. She'd certainly learned a thing or two since then. He'd been a hair's breadth from pushing her back into the cushions and reaching for the hem of her t-shirt. Only her soft whisper—his name—had forced his mind back to a slightly more rational state. He leaned his head back against the black leather and huffed out a harsh chuckle. *Oh, God. What am I going to do? I have a girlfriend! But I'm wildly attracted to Nina.* The problem was he knew he always had been, ever since he'd been old enough to start noticing girls. He could probably brush it off as a momentary lapse—pretty girl, girlfriend out of town, things happen. *But what about Sloane? She deserves better than you groping on the couch with another woman.* He'd never in his life cheated on a woman, at least he hadn't once they'd declared exclusivity with one another. He could count on one hand the times that exclusivity had happened—and have fingers left over. Sloane was his first serious relationship; he'd always favored a much more casual arrangement before he'd met her. But he hadn't dated or kissed—and certainly hadn't slept with—any other woman in the last three years. *But are you truly happy with Sloane?* He growled low in his throat and put the car back in gear. Now was not the time to think about ending a three-year relationship. *But I've been thinking about it for a while now, haven't I?* He shut down those thoughts and navigated to the freeway, where he accelerated well past the speed limit and purposefully passed his exit, needing an extended, fast drive to keep his mind off of things he couldn't have. *No matter how badly I might want them. Her.*

***

He slept well, which surprised him when the alarm screeched the following morning. He'd been expecting to toss and turn half the night, but he'd dropped off fairly quickly once he finally went to bed. He hated himself a bit for the outrageously sexy dreams he'd had about Nina, dreams in which he didn't back away from her kiss and he did reach for the hem of her shirt. He threw back the comforter, ignoring the insistent erection tenting his boxers as he headed toward the shower. For the first time in several years, he was glad Sloane wasn't there. She'd undoubtedly be happy to help him take care of it, but he was well aware making love to one woman while fantasizing about another was a shitty thing to do. He turned the nozzle to the right and stepped under the icy spray, knowing he couldn't afford to get rid of it any other way—not when he was due to pick up Nina in less than an hour. He wouldn't be able to look her in the eye if he'd done what he wanted. By the time he'd shaved and dried off, he'd calmed down enough to face the day—and Nina. He could smell the coffee brewing, glad he'd remembered to set it the night before. He'd wandered all over his apartment when he'd returned from Nina's house, upset with himself and too restless to sleep for several hours. He leaned against the counter, drinking a second cup of coffee and eating a bowl of cornflakes while he wondered how awkward it would be to see her again. He tried to remember if it had been awkward the last time he'd kissed her when they were still in high school, but he had a nasty feeling he hadn't even bothered to check how she was the day after the party. *Nice, Seamus. You're a real prince.*

He rinsed his bowl and set it in the dishwasher, then couldn't find any other excuses to delay, so he grabbed his keys and headed to Nina's house. He'd leave his car there so they could drop the girls at school on the way to the precinct; he had a cowardly moment and wished they'd agreed to meet there instead.

There was a strange car in the driveway and Seamus frowned as he parked at the curb. *Who's visiting her so damn early?*

She opened the door to his knock but didn't quite meet his gaze. "Hey." She stepped aside to let him in.

"Hey. Who's here?"

"Oh, Gordy stopped by a few minutes ago."

He was seated at the table, drinking a cup of coffee. "Seamus. What's up?"

"Uh, not much. What brings you here so bright and early, Gordy?" He'd seen Neal's business partner a few times when the three of them met after work for a beer, but Seamus hadn't clicked with the guy, finding they had nothing in common with each other save their friendship with Neal. He was not thrilled to find the man hovering around Nina now.

"I heard about the mur—"

"Gordy!" Nina turned from the counter, where she was packing lunches for the girls.

"Sorry! I forgot." He glanced uneasily toward the door to the hallway. "Anyway, I decided to stop by and see how Nina's doing."

Nina smiled at him before turning back to the lunches.

Seamus frowned again, not caring for the unspoken message in her smile or the smarmy grin on Gordy's stupid face. "Uh huh. Well, we don't want to keep you." He reached into the cabinet for a mug and poured himself an unwanted cup of coffee.

He did want the other man to be aware that he, Seamus, had been in Nina's kitchen often enough to know where she kept things. "We'll need to be heading out pretty soon."

A small smile hovered around Gordy's mouth as he raised his cup to his lips. He looked about to speak when the twins burst into the room.

"Seamus!" Lily threw her arms around his thighs.

Iris was more restrained, as always, but she at least came closer than she had at first.

"Hey, Munchkin." He hugged Lily and reached to gently ruffle Iris's short hair. "Hey, other Munchkin."

It was clear Nina had shared the morning's itinerary with them because they took his presence for granted.

"Are you going to cook tonight, Seamus?" Lily asked.

Seamus had not planned to hang around after the visit to the precinct, but that was before he found freaking Gordy sitting at Nina's table at seven thirty in the morning. "Sure." He hoped Nina wouldn't contradict him until they were alone. "What would you like me to make?"

Lily shrugged, but Iris grabbed his hand. "Can you make macaroni and cheese?"

"Is that your favorite?"

She nodded, and Seamus determined he'd be there to make it, no matter how weird things were between him and Nina.

"I'll see what I can do, okay? If your mom says it's okay, that's what I'll make. Are you and your sister ready for school?"

She nodded again, and he volunteered to take them out to the SUV while Nina locked up. *Time to leave, Gordon.* He jingled his keys until the other man took the hint.

"Let me know if there's anything else I can do, Nina, okay?" Gordy set his cup in the sink and slipped an arm around her shoulders. "You don't have to go through this alone."

She's not, jackass! Seamus rolled his eyes and shooed the girls out to the car. He waited until they'd dropped them at their nearby elementary school to ask the question that had been churning in his gut for the last half hour. "So, when did you and Gordy become such BFFs?"

She looked at him quickly, then turned her face back to the front of the car. "We're not. He just stopped by to see how I was doing."

"So he said." He stared out the passenger side window for a long moment, telling himself he wouldn't ask the next question. "Are you going out with him?" *Crap.*

This time she merely shifted her eyes his direction. "Hardly. I'm not going out with anyone right now. It's not really the right time to be thinking about romance, you know."

Then why did you kiss me? He managed to keep the question to himself, at least for the time being. "Okay." *Good.* "So, I kind of invited myself over tonight. Is that going to be a problem?"

"I think Lily actually invited you." She sighed and glanced at him again. "It's not going to be a problem, Seamus. I'm so sorry about last night. I shouldn't have done that. Is there any way we could just forget it ever happened?"

Forget that kiss? Not bloody likely! "Sure. For what it's worth, I'm sorry too." He winced as he realized how she might misconstrue his words.

She shrugged but didn't look at him and they finished the short drive in silence.

Once inside the state police precinct, Chris took Nina away while another detective took Seamus to a small room for questioning. Chris had told him the day before she wouldn't be able to take his statement or talk to him about the case again until he was cleared as a suspect since she was his sister-in-law. He'd freaked out, of course, at hearing he was considered a suspect, but she assured him it was simply routine procedure. The new detective introduced himself as Shawn Wilson and offered Seamus coffee or water. He chose water, deciding he was already jumpy enough from the extra cup he'd had at Nina's.

Detective Wilson left Seamus in the room for a few moments, then returned with a cold bottle of water and informed Seamus he would be recording their conversation. "Mr. DeLuca, would you please state your full name, address, and age?"

"Seamus Liam DeLuca, 26." He rattled off his address, then took a drink, hoping to quell the slight wobble in his voice. Being questioned formally by someone other than his brother or sister-in-law was nerve-racking.

"And what was your relationship to Mr. Braden?" The detective didn't look up from his notepad as he asked.

"He was my best friend."

"And how long have the two of you been friends?"

"Since we were in middle school. We kind of drifted apart in college, but we started hanging out again a couple years ago."

Detective Wilson glanced up. "And why did you drift apart? Did you have a fight?"

Seamus shook his head. "Nothing like that. Neal went to New Mexico State and I went to UNM. He didn't come home very often and made new friends down in Las Cruces. He came back to Albuquerque to get his MBA, but I was just starting at the fire station, so we didn't see each other more than once a month or so."

"But you still consider him your best friend?"

"Yeah, of course. Lately we'd started getting together a lot more, maybe once a week or so. We'd meet up after work for a few beers, play some pool."

"Why lately? What changed?"

Seamus took another drink and searched for an answer. "I guess the biggest change was my little brother, Tony, going away for vet school. He and I used to hang out a lot. I guess I have more free time now."

Detective Wilson scratched his pen across the yellow legal pad for a moment before speaking again. "Where were you on the day of Neal's death? That would be the Sunday before last in the late afternoon and early evening."

"Uh, I was at my girlfriend's apartment, then we went over to my parents' house for dinner."

"What time did you arrive at your girlfriend's apartment?"

"Around four." He remembered showing up an hour early, knowing she wouldn't be ready.

"And what time did you leave for your parents'? You said it was for dinner, right?" Wilson glanced up sharply, as if questioning Seamus's time line. "Why did you go to pick her up so early?"

Dude, seriously? Have you never had a girlfriend? Maybe I should show him a picture of Sloane. He probably wouldn't ask such a stupid question if he saw her. "Well, Sloane is perpetually late, so I usually try to get there really early so I can make sure she's ready to go."

"And was she ready?"

"Not even close. She was still in bed when I got there. We didn't leave for my parents' house until close to six o'clock." He felt it was better to skip over all the details of what had occurred between four and six.

"Your girlfriend was still in bed at four o'clock in the afternoon?"

"Apparently she'd stayed up all night working on the spring clothing line. She's a buyer for Macy's."

"And it took her two hours to get ready? What did you do during that time?"

Seamus felt himself flushing. "It took her a little over an hour to get ready. I watched the game while I waited."

"What about the other hour?"

Seamus coughed and reached for the water again. "When I let myself in, Sloane was still in

170

bed, like I said. So I joined her. We had sex, Detective Wilson. That's what you tend to do when you have a beautiful girlfriend. We had sex twice and then she went to take a shower and get ready." He stared at the other man, hoping he would look down in embarrassment.

He didn't seem fazed by Seamus's irritation. "And how long was she in the shower?"

"I don't know." He shrugged. "Maybe twenty minutes or so."

"And what is her address? I'll need her full name and phone number too." He slid another legal pad and a pen across the table to Seamus. He waited until he had the notepad back to continue. "And then you went to your parents' house? Did you stop anywhere along the way?"

Seamus told him they'd gone straight to his parents' house and had stayed there until close to ten o'clock. "We went straight home. I dropped her off and then I went back to my place."

"You didn't go in with her?" Detective Wilson raised his eyebrows, a blank look on his face.

I really hate this guy. "No. We had an argument and I just wanted to be by myself."

"What did you fight about?"

Seamus sighed and reached for his bottle of water. He wanted to tell the detective to go screw himself, that it was none of his business, but knew it wasn't a good idea. "What we always fight about: her lateness and my lack of interest in appearances."

"And did you go straight home after you dropped her off? Did you stop anywhere first?"

Seamus shrugged and crossed his arms. "I

stopped by a Circle K for a six pack. Then I went home and drank it." He hated fighting with Sloane, but it seemed to happen more and more often lately. He'd needed the oblivion of alcohol and had welcomed the buzz.

"You don't happen to have your receipt from the Circle K, do you?"

"I don't know. It might be somewhere in my car. I can look."

"That would be good. Do you have any roommates, Mr. DeLuca? Is there anyone who could vouch for your whereabouts from ten o'clock on?"

He shook his head and swallowed hard. "So, am I a suspect?"

Wilson looked up and smiled slightly. "I'm simply getting as much information as possible, Mr. DeLuca. We have barely begun our investigation into Mr. Braden's death. At this point, we don't consider anyone a suspect. We're just trying to nail down everyone's movements on the day in question." He scrawled a few more lines. "How was your relationship with Mr. Braden? You said you were best friends, but did the two of you ever argue? Had you argued with him lately?"

"No, we never argued. There was nothing to argue about. We just hung out, blew off steam, you know?"

"Did Neal ever mention enemies or people he was having trouble with? Did he ever talk about having to fire anyone at work?"

He was already shaking his head before the detective finished speaking. "Never, as far as I can remember. We kept it pretty light. I never really understood what he did for a living. He was always interested in what I did, though, in what it was like to be a firefighter." He gulped against the sudden, unexpected emotion. *I should have tried harder. I should have cared more about what he did all day, every day. I was kind of a crappy friend.* He glanced at his watch, although he had no pressing engagements. "How much longer will this take?"

"We're almost done, Mr. DeLuca." He consulted his notes. "Are you acquainted with Mr. Braden's business partner, Gordon Sanderson?"

Seamus hoped his dislike of the man didn't show on his face; it really had nothing to do with Neal, after all. "I've met him a few times." He shrugged. "Neal seemed to like him, so that's all that matters, right? I didn't have to work with him."

"So, he didn't tag along when you and Mr. Braden were 'hanging out'?" The air quotes were perfectly audible.

"I guess he did a couple times, but I liked it better when it was just Neal and me."

"So, you don't like Gordon." It was a statement rather than a question.

"He's okay. We don't have a lot in common." Except a fondness for Nina, apparently.

"And what about Mr. Braden's fiancée, Kira Karlsson?"

Seamus was fed up with the whole interrogation thing and wanted to punch Detective Wilson in the face. "What about her?"

The detective smiled an unpleasant smile, as if he could read Seamus's mind. "Do you like her?"

"I don't see why that matters." It was one thing to casually ask Nina if she trusted the woman, but another entirely to bring it up for discussion with the police.

"Why don't you let me decide what matters and what doesn't? Now, it's a simple question: do you like Kira?"

Seamus sneered slightly as he answered; he was so done with this. "She's okay, I guess. She's nice. I don't know what else you want from me."

"Were she and Mr. Braden fighting recently?"

"No idea. We never talked about our relationships, Detective."

"Hmm." He continued to scrawl on the notepad. "And what about Mr. Braden's sister, Nina?"

Seamus told himself to calm down, that getting arrested for assaulting a police officer would upset Nina, not to mention his mother. "Nina Braden had nothing to do with her brother's death." He ground the words out between clenched teeth. "She's the sweetest person in the world and she loved Neal."

"Thank you, Mr. DeLuca. Just one more question, for now. Who do you think killed your friend?"

***

Nina

"Can I get you some coffee, Nina? Or water? I could make you a cup of tea if you prefer. I've got some really nice herbal tea in my desk; Hugh brought it to me last week."

"Tea would be great, thanks." She followed Chris to her work station, noting the small photograph of Hugh and Chris by her computer monitor. They were on an overlook above the ocean and the love in their eyes as they gazed at each other was obvious. "That's a great picture."

"Thanks." She rifled through her top drawer as she spoke. "I wanted one of him alone, but he flat-out refused. I don't think those DeLuca boys realize how cute they are. Well, maybe Finn does. How could he not, right?"

Nina smiled, but didn't respond. Finn was gorgeous, of course, but she'd always thought Seamus was cuter. Chris obviously felt the same about Hugh.

"Got it." She held up the small, green box. She led the way back to the small coffee alcove, where she found each of them a clean mug. She handed one to Nina and they set about preparing their drinks.

"Okay, Nina," Chris said once they were seated in a small office across from the alcove. "We'll be more comfortable here than in one of the interrogation rooms." She gestured to the sofa and took a seat in the nearby armchair. "I don't want you to be nervous about this, all right? I just need to get your formal statement since we're now investigating Neal's death as a homicide." She paused for a moment. "I'm so sorry you and your family have to go through all this."

Nina smiled gratefully. "Thanks, Chris. It's been really tough, but believe it or not, it's a little easier now." She sipped her tea, then looked up. "Does that make me a horrible person?'"

Chris shook her head as she set her mug on the side table and reached for a legal pad. "Not at all. I'm sure it's easier to accept that someone killed him rather than he killed himself. It seems pretty normal to me."

"Thanks. I'm not sure how I'm supposed to feel anymore."

"Why don't we get started? I know you're anxious to be done with all this. So, let's get the formal stuff out of the way first, okay? You're okay with me recording this interview? Good." She clicked on the small digital recorder. "Go ahead and state your full name, age, and address so we have it on record with the recording."

"Nina Delaney Braden; 26; 2753 Calle Vista Avenue Northeast, Albuquerque, New Mexico." She blew out a breath. "This is kind of nerve-wracking."

Chris smiled. "I understand. Try to relax. Do you remember where you were and what you were doing the day of Neal's death? That would be the Sunday before last, in the late afternoon into early evening."

"Um, I was at home most of the day with the girls. We went to my parents' house to take the newspaper in and water the plants. They were still on their cruise, you know. The rest of the day we just stayed at the house. They had a play date with a couple friends from school in the afternoon and the moms dropped them off. They stayed for about three hours."

"Okay, great. I'll need the names and numbers of

those moms, okay?"

Nina nodded and took the steno notebook from Chris. "You're checking my alibi, aren't you?"

Chris reached to touch Nina's hand. "It's a formality, Nina. You're not a suspect."

"What about Seamus? Is that why you aren't allowed to question him?"

"We're simply trying to make sure this investigation is aboveboard. Right now, we're making sure we know where everyone was and what they were doing so we can start eliminating people as suspects."

Nina nodded and grabbed her cell phone so she could find the contact information for the little girls who had played at her house the Sunday her brother was killed. Only later, when she rewound the conversation in her head, did she realize Chris hadn't truly answered her question about Seamus being a suspect. She handed the pad back to Chris.

"Nina, did Neal ever talk to you about people he might have been having trouble with?"

She frowned as she thought back to all the conversations she'd had with her brother. "No one specific I can remember. He occasionally talked about how much harder it was to be the boss than he'd ever expected."

"What about his business? Was it successful?"

"I think so. He never said anything to make *me* think otherwise."

Chris raised her head sharply. "What do you mean? Why did you say 'me' in that way?"

Nina shrugged and wrapped her hands around the warm mug, trying to soak up the heat. She couldn't seem to get warm and wished she had chosen a heavier cardigan that morning. "It's just something Kira said when we all thought it was suicide. She said he'd been depressed about a bunch of stuff, including the company. That's why he was seeing a therapist and taking the anti-depressants. I didn't believe her."

"Tell me about your relationship with Neal. You're twins, right? Who's older?"

Nina chuckled softly. "Me. By about five minutes. I, of course, never let him forget it while we were growing up." She sniffed and looked around for a tissue. "He was a really good friend. I can't believe he's gone."

Chris stood and found a box of Kleenex for her. "Tell me about the money you loaned him."

Nina was shocked they already knew about that. "Wow. You guys are good. When he and Gordy decided to start RiskCom, they weren't able to get as much from the bank as they needed. They each had to come up with an additional amount. I don't know where Gordy got his. Neal asked me for advice on how he could acquire the extra funds and I offered to make him a personal loan." She named the amount and watched Chris's eyes widen.

"Where did you get that kind of money? I thought you were an underpaid college professor."

Nina smiled. "I am, but my ex has a lot of money and he's always been very generous. I was still married at the time Neal was starting his business and it was actually David who suggested the loan."

"Where did David's money come from? Isn't he also a college professor?"

178

"He is, but in addition to family money, he's written a couple books that have done well." It was a bit of an understatement; David was a good writer and had managed to find a way to bridge the gap between academia and popular writing. He wrote about some lesser-known anthropological phenomena that found a huge audience with the general populous. And he had a great publicist.

"And did Neal ever pay you back?"

"Yes, for the most part. He had a few more payments to make, but he always made sure to pay every month on the dot."

"And how did David feel about the loan? You said it was his idea, but did he ever change his mind?"

"No. David gave me the money, and then I'm sure he totally forgot about it. We never argued over money, Chris. David continues to generously support me and the girls." She sipped her tea and sighed. "Money was never our problem."

Chris smiled and continued scratching copious notes on her legal pad. "Okay. What do you know about Gordon, Neal's business partner? Do you know him well?"

"Not really. They met when they were in college in Las Cruces. I went out of state, so I never really spent much time with Gordy until recently. "

"And they were good friends? Did Neal ever say anything about them disagreeing about the direction the business should go in?"

"He never said anything. I think they got along really well."

"Okay. What about Neal's fiancée, Kira? How

long have they been together?"

"Just over two years. They've been engaged for about six months."

Chris wrote for a moment. "And how would you describe their relationship?"

"Well, they decided to get married, so I guess it was pretty good."

"Was it a volatile relationship?"

"No, not at all. Neal is…was…such an easygoing guy. We never even fought much when we were growing up." She felt her eyes get misty as she remembered. "He and Kira always seemed happy. Neal was so excited about the wedding."

Chris paused. "What about Kira?"

"Excuse me?" She frowned at Chris, not understanding her question.

"You said 'Neal was so excited about the wedding.' What about Kira? Was she excited?"

Nina shrugged. "I mean, yeah, of course. Why wouldn't she be? I don't really know her very well, either. Why do you ask?"

Chris smiled, but continued to write. "I'm trying to get a clear picture of Neal's life, that's all. Tell me more about Kira."

"Didn't you already talk to her this morning? She said she had an early appointment with you."

"She did, but I'd like to hear your opinion of her."

Nina grimaced as she realized Chris had certainly asked Kira about Nina. *I wonder if they're asking Seamus about me? I bet he's next on Chris's list.* "This is awful, Chris. I feel like I'm betraying all Neal's friends."

Chris patted her hand sympathetically. "I know, sweetie, but I need you to keep going. We're going to do our best to find Neal's killer. Just tell me what you've observed about Kira. I promise you're not betraying anyone."

Nina shrugged and sipped her tea again; it all felt so wrong. "Kira is nice," she said carefully.

"But?" Chris looked up from her notes. "Come on, Nina. There's a huge 'but' in there. Tell me."

She sighed and leaned forward to set her mug on the table. "No, there's really not. It's simply a case of his twin sister not thinking anyone is good enough for her brother. Kira's fine. For someone else."

Chris nodded sagely. "I have a little sister, so I get it. Can you try to explain, though? What was it that made you feel that way?"

Nina leaned back against the cushions and closed her eyes. *I'm so tired. I want this to be over.* "Nothing specific; not really. How do I say this? She's just not special enough for Neal. She's never done anything wrong, though." She wondered if she should mention how nervous Kira had seemed the evening before but decided against it. *I certainly don't want to prejudice the police against her in any way.*

"All right. That's fine, Nina." She took a deep breath and looked straight into Nina's face. "What about Seamus? I have to ask."

Nina frowned, although she'd known it was coming. "I don't know what you want me to say. Seamus is wonderful, and he's always been a good friend to Neal, even though they drifted apart some

181

during college, but that was simply due to them going to different universities. I don't know how I would be dealing with this without him. Please don't ask me to trash talk him."

"Is there anything to trash talk about?" Chris raised her eyebrows at her.

Nina squared her jaw and stared back. "Absolutely not."

Chris smiled and wrote. "Good. And I'm glad he's been around to help you out. Hugh would probably kick his ass if he didn't. Nina, do you know if Neal had a life insurance policy?"

Nina grimaced. "Yeah, he did. And before you ask, I'll tell you I'm the beneficiary. He wanted to make sure I'd get my money back for the loan if anything happened to him."

Chris nodded in a manner that told Nina she'd already known. "Now, do me a favor. Close your eyes." She waited until Nina did as directed. "I'm going to ask you a question and I don't want you to think about it. I just want you to say the first thing that comes to your mind, okay? Who do you think killed your brother?"

How can I not think about that? She tried, but no name magically surfaced. She shook her head. "I'm sorry. I don't have any idea. I wish I did."

Chris asked a few more questions then stood, indicating their session was at an end. Nina breathed a sigh of relief and reached for her mug.

"I'll get that, Nina. I know you want to get out of here."

Nina made her escape and found the ladies' room, hoping she wouldn't throw up. She ran cool water over her wrists and splashed her face, which seemed to suffice to calm her down. By the time she made her way to the bleak waiting area, Seamus was there.

He stood as she appeared around the corner. "Let's get out of here." He held out his hand.

She grabbed it, needing the connection to sanity. "Please." She glanced up at his face as they walked to the parking lot, noting how grim he looked. "That bad, huh?"

"It fucking sucked. I've never wanted to punch someone so bad in my life." He squeezed her hand. "How was yours?"

"Well, I didn't want to punch Chris, but it was a toss-up as to whether I would cry or throw up." She tried to laugh, but it was a strangled, weak sound.

They reached her SUV and she fished blindly in her purse with her free hand for her keys. As she clicked the button to unlock it, Seamus tugged her gently around and backed her against the vehicle.

"Hey." He dropped the hand he still held and brushed her hair back from her face. "Which did you go with?"

She looked up at him—he was so much taller than her—and smiled crookedly. "Neither, thank God. I splashed some water on my face in the bathroom. I felt like such a rat, Seamus. She asked me to talk about everyone and how well they got along with Neal."

He wiped a stray droplet of water from her cheek as he nodded. "Yeah, same here. She asked about me, I assume?"

Nina nodded. "Did your guy ask about me?"

He grinned. "Yep. It's a hell of a job they have, huh?"

"Ugh. I'll happily stick with teaching history. Speaking of which, I need to get to work." She turned to the car, grateful when he stepped away. *It's too hard to be so close if I have to keep my hands to myself.* She swallowed a giggle—vastly inappropriate to the time and occasion—and opened her door. "I'll drop you back at my house so you can pick up your car."

"Listen, since I'm coming over later anyway, why don't I just drop you at work? If you'll consider lending me a house key, I can run by the grocery store and get started on dinner before I come pick you and the girls up."

How am I supposed to forget about kissing him when he insists on being so sweet and thoughtful? Would he have pushed me away last night if Sloane wasn't in the picture? The thought of his girlfriend was sobering, however, serving to remind her exactly how far out of his league she was. "Sure. You can have my key for now and I'll grab you a spare when we get home later."

"Great." He smiled at her from across the car. "Since you don't have to take me all the way home right now, you have time to stop somewhere for lunch."

"Oh, I don't—"

"Come on, Nina. You have to eat. It might as well be with me."

Chapter Eleven

Seamus

"So, we're still on for Saturday night, right?" Jon tossed him a dry sponge as he asked. He and Seamus were assigned to wash the smaller engine and were gathering the supplies.

Seamus had a moment of panic as he tried to remember what Jon could be referring to. "Uh, sure." He closed his eyes and shook his head. "Sorry. I have no idea what you're talking about. It's been a crazy couple of weeks. What did I agree to?"

"It's okay, man. I understand. Saturday is the ball, remember?"

Oh, shit. The Annual Fireman's—now called *Firefighter's*—Ball. He and Jon had asked for the night off months ago and made plans to double date. They'd already purchased their tickets and reserved tuxedos. "Yeah. Listen, Jon, I don't—"

"Don't say you're bailing on me! Come on, man! I haven't been able to get Lisa to leave the baby for more than an hour and I'm desperate. I'll beg if I need to! Her parents are watching Louisa, and Lisa promised she would go. She bought a new dress, Seamus!"

He ran his hands through his hair and sighed. "Yeah, yeah, I know. But Sloane's still out of town, so…"

"Don't you have two sisters? Drag one of them along. I need this night out, dude, and Lisa will back out if she knows you're not going."

"Okay, fine. I'll figure something out." He stuck his bucket under the utility faucet and watched as the soap bubbles began to rise. "You don't think it's gonna get confusing to have a daughter named Louisa and a wife named Lisa? Did you really think that one through?"

Jon chuckled and grabbed the chrome polish. "It was Lisa's grandmother's name. I couldn't say no. You just wait, Seamus, 'til your wife pops out a kid. You'll see what it's like."

"Well, since I don't have a wife, I doubt it, at least for a long, long time."

"What about you and Sloane? I thought you two were solid? Why don't you marry her?"

He cringed inwardly as he realized how little he'd thought of his girlfriend over the past few weeks. He and Nina hadn't repeated the kiss, although they'd been together every night he wasn't working. It somehow felt natural to head over to her house or to use the key she'd insisted he keep to let himself in and start dinner before she got home with the girls. He'd never realized before how much he liked preparing a meal for people he cared about—

and he knew he cared about the three of them much more than he had any right to. Marry Sloane? The idea held little attraction any more, if it ever had. He'd enjoyed Sloane, enjoyed spending time with her, and definitely enjoyed sleeping with her, but he'd never planned to marry her. Marriage hadn't even been on his radar—still wasn't. But Nina's beautiful face came to mind, all the same. *Damn it. Not good.* He laughed off Jon's question and hoped it didn't come across as pathetic as it sounded in his own ears.

He decided to ask Cara since Izzy was nearly six months pregnant and probably didn't care to find a maternity evening gown.

"This Saturday?" He'd caught her on her lunch break. "Sorry, but no can-do. I'm going to be out of town with a friend for a spa weekend up at Ten Thousand Waves."

"Can't you reschedule? I need a date and Sloane is out of town."

"I would, but it's a prepaid package deal. Did you ask Nina?"

"I can't ask her."

"Why not? Is she not pretty enough for you to show off to all your fireman friends?" Her voice dripped ice.

"Shut up," he sighed. "That's not it at all. Nina's beautiful and I'd be happy to show her off to anybody, but she's not my girlfriend. It wouldn't be appropriate."

"That's total bullshit. You guys are friends and there's nothing wrong with taking a friend to a fancy-schmancy ball if you want to. What, are you afraid Sloane will be jealous if she finds out?" She was clearly taunting him.

He knew better than to rise to the bait, but Cara had always been able to goad him. "No. It's none of Sloane's business. Nina and I are just friends."

"Great. So, you'll ask her?"

Shit. Why do I always fall into her trap? "Yeah, okay. I'll ask her."

"God, Seamus! You make it sound like a death sentence! I'm sure you'll have a great time."

That's what I'm afraid of. "Yeah, yeah. Don't you have to get back to torturing teenagers?"

She laughed and hung up.

***

"They were asleep before their heads hit the pillow." Nina chuckled and sat beside him on the sofa. "I need you to wear them out more often."

He'd taken them all for a short hike in the foothills so they could enjoy the cool fall evening. It would be too cold before long and Seamus knew he would miss the chance to get out on the trails. They'd stopped to pick up Subway sandwiches on the way and ate dinner at the top of the trail, sitting on a huge, flat boulder. The girls had proved to be great little hikers, scrambling over the rocks with a natural agility he couldn't help but admire. "I think the fresh air was good for all of us." He'd tried vainly not to notice how pretty she was with her pale cheeks still flushed from the exercise. "Here." He handed her a glass of wine. "I thought white would be good for such a warm evening." He'd never drank as much wine as he had since he started spending time with Nina. Sloane was more of a gin and tonic fan and he preferred beer, but he'd discovered it was extremely pleasant to share a glass or two of wine with Nina after the girls had been tucked in and before he went home to his apartment. They never seemed to run out of things to talk about. He was fascinated by her work at the university and loved the funny stories she told about her students and the other professors. She always wanted to hear every detail of his shift at the station, and the worried look on her face as he described the calls they responded to was endearing. He stared at her, realizing Cara was right; they were friends—really good friends—and he could certainly ask her to go to the damned ball with him. So why was he more nervous than he'd ever been in high school to ask a girl to a dance?

"What?" She wiped her hand across her mouth. "Do I have mustard or something on my face?"

"No. You're fine. I, uh, I have a favor to ask."

She looked blank. "Sure, of course. Whatever you need, Seamus."

He set his wine glass on the end table and turned toward her. "You can say no. I'll totally understand."

She frowned. "Sounds ominous."

"Yeah, a bit. So, this Saturday night is the annual Firefighter's Ball. And I promised my friend, Jon, we'd double. His wife just had a baby and it'll be the first time he's been able to pry her away from the kid since it was born."

"And with Sloane out of town, you need a date,

huh?"

"Yeah. I asked Cara, because I thought it might be, you know, awkward with us, since, well, you know, but she has a spa day or something and I—"

She laughed softly and held out her hand to stop him. "I'll go. It's fine. We're friends, right? We have no reason to feel awkward around each other."

He wondered if she believed that any more than he did, but thought it unwise to disagree, especially when he needed a date. "Right. Thanks a million, Nina. It's, uh, a formal thing."

"I think I can manage," she said with a smirk.

"Oh, well, that's, uh, that's good. Great." *Shit. Why am I so nervous?*

"It sounds like fun. It'll be like the prom I never had." She reached for her wine.

Wait. What? "You didn't go to prom?" Where had he been? Why hadn't he noticed? Oh, yeah. He'd pre-gamed it with Neal and a few other friends and had been plastered before they'd even picked up their dates in the limo. He'd never stopped to ask whether or not his friend's twin sister would be there. He'd studiously avoided her ever since their kiss on her front porch. "Why not?"

She took a rather large gulp of wine. "For the usual reason, Seamus. No one asked me." She sounded distinctly irritated.

Well, crap. "I'm sorry. Nina." He had no idea why none of the guys at their school had asked her. She'd been a cute little thing back in high school, but she'd never dated. She'd admitted he'd been her first kiss, but he'd never stopped to think about whether she had a date to prom. He'd been too busy planning how he was going to seduce his own prom date and talk her into going upstairs with him to the room he'd rented in the hotel where the dance was held. It turned out he didn't have to do much talking; she'd been nearly as drunk as him and more than willing to end the night in a sweaty jumble on the king-size bed. *I was quite the prize back in high school.*

"Why on earth should you be sorry? It wasn't your fault."

No, it wasn't, but if he'd bothered to spare her a thought, he could have gotten one of his friends to ask her. No, not one of his friends; they were all complete horn dogs who were only interested in girls they could screw. "Maybe not, but I still feel bad about it."

"There's no need. I got over it."

He had a nasty feeling girls never quite got over something like that, but he kept his mouth shut. "So, I'll pick you up at seven? Do you need me to ask Izzy if she can watch the girls that night?"

She shook her head. "I'll see if my parents can watch them. They haven't spent the night over there in a while. It'll probably be good for them to get their minds off Neal for a night."

"Oh. Good. That's, uh, great." He picked up his wine and sipped in the awkward silence that followed.

She finally sighed and turned back to him. "Seamus, I hate to ask this, but what about Sloane?"

He frowned, not wanting to have this conversation. "What about her?"

"Don't be dense. Where is she? When is she

coming back? What will she think about you taking another woman to the Firefighter's Ball? I assume you were originally planning to take her, right?"

Why did women have to be so damned perceptive? He coughed, stalling for time. "Sloane's in Chicago on a business trip. I don't really know when she's coming back. We had an argument and decided to take a break from each other. And I have to assume she wouldn't be thrilled with me taking another woman who is not my sister to the dance. Anything else?"

"God, don't be such a crank." She patted his knee. "I just need to know, okay? I don't want to be caught by surprise if she shows up on my doorstep to fight me for trying to steal her boyfriend." She laughed softly.

He knew she meant it as a joke, that she was trying to keep it light, but it hit home with him. *What am I doing asking another woman out? This is going to cross a line somehow.* "I highly doubt she would ever show up on your doorstep. It's not her style."

Nina reached for the wine bottle and topped each of their glasses, as if she thought they needed fortification for what she was about to say. "Look, Seamus, I know you and I are just friends, okay? I get that. I mean, I've seen Sloane's picture and, wow. She's stunning. I know I made a mistake when I kissed you and I won't do it again. But, where are you with Sloane? It might not be any of my business, but I've been in the middle of someone else's relationship before and I swore I'd never be the cause of someone cheating again." She laughed again. "I know it's hard to imagine me, of all people, as a femme fatale, but…"

He grabbed her hand and squeezed. "No, it's not." He took a deep breath. "Is that what happened with David?"

She nodded as she sipped her wine, a faraway look on her face. "He was married. They had a little boy, only four years old. He told me they were separated, but it wasn't true. They were still living together. God, Seamus. I slept with a married man."

"Hey." He took her hand again. "He lied. You didn't know."

"But I should have. I should have checked, or asked, or something! I wanted it to be true, so I let myself believe what he was saying. I was such an idiot." She sniffed and blinked away what looked like tears. "Once I found out, I let myself believe his marriage was empty and they were only staying together for their son. Idiot."

"Haven't we all been idiots at one time or another? Neal said David basically did the same thing to you."

"Yes. It was very similar. I suspected he was having an affair; he didn't deny it when I confronted him. I was surprised to learn his new girlfriend was pregnant, however. He'd told me he didn't believe in bringing any more children into the world when there were already so many orphans. That's why we adopted Lily and Iris. We hadn't even had them for a full year when he knocked up his girlfriend."

His heart broke as he listened to the sordid story of betrayal. *God, I'd love to meet up with David in a*

193

dark alley some night. "You weren't the cause of him cheating, either with his first wife or with you. The man is a cheater, period. You're not. And except for our kiss a couple weeks ago, I'm not either. I won't cheat on Sloane." He knew what it meant but shoved the thoughts aside until he had time to process them more fully.

She smiled weakly. "Good. It's not terribly pleasant for the one being cheated on. I still feel horribly guilty about David's first wife, Anna." She sipped her wine. "And yet, for all that, David is a wonderful father, when he's around. He's always been extremely generous with the girls."

Seamus didn't think that qualified the man as a 'wonderful father' but deemed it wise to keep his thoughts to himself. He also deemed it wise to bring the enlightening, yet depressing evening to a close. He had a lot to think about and needed some quiet time alone.

It wasn't to be, however. When he pulled into the driveway of his apartment, half of an old adobe house that had been split into a duplex arrangement, he noticed a car parked at the curb in front. Sloane's car. *Well, shit.* He killed the engine and scrubbed his hands over his face. He wasn't anywhere near ready to have the conversation they needed to have, but his time was up. *I guess there's no time like the present. Man-up and get it over with.* He locked his car and let himself into the apartment.

Sloane was curled up on the couch, a mug of tea in her hands. "Hi." Her voice was soft and uncertain.

"Hi." He took a seat in the armchair next to the

sofa.

She smiled sadly as she noticed his choice of seat. "I guess we need to talk."

"I guess so." He leaned forward and braced his arms on his knees. "When did you get back in town?"

"A few hours ago. I came straight here. I was hoping you'd be home."

He ignored the implicit question. They needed to have this conversation regardless of where and with whom he'd been. "Sloane, I—"

"I know." She kicked off her shoes and crossed her legs under her. "I've known since I left. I just didn't want to believe it. I still love you, Seamus."

He smiled crookedly at her, looking so beautiful as she sat on his couch. "I still love you too, Sloane. But."

"Yeah. But." She actually laughed softly. "It's not enough anymore, is it?"

He shook his head. "I think we want different things from life, hon. I'm never gonna be the designer guy you want me to be. I'm never gonna match."

She nodded and sipped her tea. "I think I finally get that. But you're so goddamn gorgeous!"

He raised his eyebrows. "Thanks? I guess I just prefer jeans and ratty t-shirts to fancy button-ups."

"And beer and football to cocktail parties."

"Uh, yeah. Sorry about that."

She waved her hand dismissively. "I should have seen it a whole lot sooner, that's all." She sniffed, blinking away tears, then smiled at him. "I've been offered a promotion."

He sat up and smiled, relieved at the change in direction. "Really? Here?"

She shook her head. "Chicago. If I impress them, I may be on my way to New York."

It had long been her dream to escape the backwater of Albuquerque and move to where fashion was happening. He'd known it throughout their relationship and it was one of their repeated arguments: he loved Albuquerque and never wanted to leave his family. She wanted to get out as soon as possible. "Congratulations. You deserve it, and I know you've dreamed of it for a long time."

"Thanks. When I got the news, I couldn't wait to tell you, to try to convince you to go with me." She took a sip of the tea. "I even brought home the paperwork for you to apply to the Chicago Fire Department." She pointed to the stack of papers on the coffee table in front of them. "But I guess I knew you wouldn't, and I don't think we could survive a long-distance relationship."

"Probably not."

"Yeah." She finished her tea and stood, slipping her feet back into her shoes. "I should go. I really don't want to get my stuff right now if that's okay."

"Not a problem. I can get it together tomorrow." He stood and took her hand. "I'll drop it by your place and leave the key." She'd never left much more than a toothbrush and a few blouses. He would have more to pack up at her place since that's where they usually spent the night. He had several sets of clothing and some bathroom items he would need to get.

She reached into her pocket. "That will work.

196

Here." She placed his house key in his hand. It was clear she'd removed it from her keyring earlier in the evening in preparation for this break-up conversation. "There's no rush." She stood on tip-toe to brush her lips across his cheek. "Goodbye, Seamus. I'm sorry."

"Me too."

Once she'd left, he took her empty mug to the sink, then wandered restlessly around the apartment, not quite knowing how he should feel. There was relief, certainly, but there was also an unexpected sense of loss and sadness. She'd been his first serious girlfriend and they'd dated for more than three years. He knew his family—his sisters at least—would be thrilled. He wasn't blind, and knew they'd never loved Sloane. *I wonder what they'll think about Nina?* But he knew it was way too soon to be thinking about starting a new relationship. *Your timing sucks, dude! You literally just broke up with your girlfriend and Nina's still trying to come to terms with the death of her twin brother.* She was too important to be simply a rebound relationship. He sighed as he turned off the lights and locked the front door. It was late, and he had to work the next morning.

***

Nina

"Hey, Barb." Nina hoped she sounded casual as she slid into the seat next to her colleague in the small break room. "Where do you get your hair done?" In truth, she'd been lying in wait for the other woman, who always looked sleek and well-groomed. Nina hadn't been to a beauty shop in over two years, but knew she needed some maintenance before the ball Saturday night. *What I really need is a fairy godmother.*

"I go to this great little place in Nob Hill." She searched through her phone. "I'm sending you the number."

"Oh, thanks." Her shoulders slumped in relief. "I haven't been in way too long; I didn't even know where to begin."

Barb, the history department's resident expert in Latin America, smirked, but not unkindly. "What's the occasion? Big date?"

"Oh, no. Well, sort of, I guess. But we're just friends." At Barb's disbelieving look she rushed to continue. "I'm going to the Firefighter's Ball with my friend, Seamus."

"Ooh. Spending the entire evening with a roomful of hot firemen? Nice! Way to go, girl! I hope this Seamus is the hottest of them all!"

Nina giggled, then clapped her hand over her mouth, looking around in horror lest any of the other professors witness her immaturity. "Oh, my God! It's like I'm back in high school. Seamus is incredibly handsome, but we really are just friends. Unfortunately, he has a girlfriend."

"Hmm. Well, let's see what we can do about making him forget about this girlfriend. Now, I'm going to call my stylist, Melinda, and get you an appointment. You'll need hair, nails, and a Brazilian wax." She dialed the phone as she talked.

"I don't need a wax of any sort, Barb! That's not going to come up, I promise you!"

"Shh." Barb held up a finger. She spoke into her cell phone for several moments, then hung up and grinned at Nina. "Good news. Melinda has an opening tomorrow afternoon, so I booked you an appointment with her for hair, and with Greta for a Brazilian wax, and with Cho for your mani/pedi."

Nina wondered how she'd gone from tentatively asking where to get her hair done to having a full salon treatment package booked for the following afternoon. *I don't even want to think about how much this is going to cost!* But she didn't tell Barb to cancel it. She wanted to look her best, even if it was wasted on Seamus. "Thanks. I'm probably crazy to be fussing like this, but…"

"Hey, nothing ventured, nothing gained. Am I right? You're a beautiful woman, Nina. Go for it. If you want this guy, go get him."

"If only it were that easy. But I appreciate your help. Who knows? Maybe I'll find some other hot fireman there who doesn't have an inconvenient girlfriend."

"That's the spirit!" Barb raised her cup, as if to cheer Nina on. "Now, what are you wearing?"

"Well, I have a dress I bought for one of David's fancy cocktail parties. I only wore it once."

"What does it look like? If it's frumpy, we're going shopping."

Nina laughed. "It's not frumpy. It's black and skimpy. I was actually thinking of getting something a little less—"

"It sounds perfect! Make sure this guy—Seamus,

right?—knows what he's missing out on. Make sure you wear some sexy underwear, a thong, preferably."

"It won't matter if I wear granny panties, Barb. Seamus won't be seeing them."

"Sexy underwear isn't for our guy—well, it isn't *only* for our guy. It's for making *us* feel sexy and confident. You should definitely make a quick trip to Victoria's Secret."

"I'm sure I have something that will work." She didn't know any such thing. While she didn't buy true granny panties, nothing currently residing in her lingerie drawer could be considered remotely sexy.

Barb pushed her plate away and leaned forward. "Nina, sweetie, I know it's difficult to get back in the game." She patted her hand as she smiled sympathetically. Barb had divorced her second husband six months before. "But this is your golden opportunity to rip the bandage off and dip your toe into the dating world. It's not the time for chickenshit crap like wearing your ratty, old cotton panties under a slinky dress. You owe it to yourself to dress to the nines and wow this guy!"

Nina raised her eyebrows and tried to find the message buried under all Barb's euphemistic verbiage. "I don't even know if Seamus is interested in anything more than friendship. He was my brother's best friend, you know." She had no idea why she'd added that last bit.

"Oh, sweetie." Barb squeezed her hand. "I'm so sorry for all you've been through. Are you doing okay?"

Nina nodded as she stared at the tray of condiments in the center of the table. "I'm getting there. Seamus has been a huge help through all of it." She reached for her nearly-cold cup of coffee. "I had a massive crush on him when we were kids."

"Sounds like you still do."

Nina shrugged and nodded. "His girlfriend is beyond gorgeous. I don't think I have much of a chance."

"Well, not with that attitude. You've got to bring your A-Game, babe. Play to your strengths. You are really pretty and super slim—I hate you for that— but you could do a little more with color and maybe wear things that accentuate your figure, rather than hide it."

Nina glanced down at her office uniform: blue jeans, a lavender t-shirt, and a gray, baggy cardigan sweater. "I like comfortable clothes."

"Do you also like spending every night alone?"

"That's so harsh, Barb. Jeez. Is it really that bad?" Why had no one ever said anything?

Barb shook her head. "No, I didn't mean it to sound so dire." She sat straighter and looked Nina up and down carefully, clearly assessing her more fully. "You do have the female version of the rumpled professor going on, however. It's cute, but you're seriously down-playing your natural assets.

"Why do I feel an 80's shopping montage coming on?"

Barb clapped her hands delightedly. "Yes! Let's stop by your place to check out the dress first. You don't have any classes this afternoon, right?"

Nina sighed, but nodded her acquiescence. *Looks*

like I got my fairy godmother after all.

***

She was almost late picking the girls up from the sitter's house. Barb had dragged her to the mall, one of her least favorite places in the entire world, and then forced her to try on countless outfits, including dresses for the ball. Barb had advised against wearing the dress Nina already owned, saying that while it was okay, she thought they could find something more flattering and more Nina's style. *The problem is I don't have a style. Or at least I didn't.* Barb had helped her find not only a silky dress in a beautiful deep purple, but she'd also insisted she try on a new office look she promised had endless options for variety yet showed more of Nina's naturally slim figure rather than hiding it beneath the baggy jeans she favored. Her new basic look included several pairs of slim fit slacks, a few leggings, colorful silky blouses, and a pair of short boots in a soft calf-skin leather Nina had fallen in love with. Barb had made her promise to go home and weed out ninety percent of her jeans and t-shirts, saying they could only be worn now on weekends. Nina had promised to do it immediately after dinner, knowing if she didn't, if there were another option, she'd find herself reverting to her familiar wardrobe. But she'd liked the way she looked in the new clothes: sophisticated and confident, rather than mousy and small. Barb had promised to look for a few hairstyles and color ideas and bring them the next day. Nina had balked at the thought of coloring her hair, but Barb had cut her off, saying a few lowlights would make a world of difference.

"Do you think all those gorgeous women out there go *au natural?* Hell no, sweetie. We all need a little help. I'd bet a million dollars that Seamus's girlfriend is high maintenance when it comes to her beauty routine." And then Barb had dragged her to Sephora for a mini-makeover.

Nina had been surprised and pleased to discover what a little bronzer, mascara, and lip gloss could do. It was still natural, but not the I've-been-dry-camping-for-three-days look. She wouldn't see Seamus until he came to pick her up for the ball— he'd had to work an extra-long shift in order to get Saturday night off—and she hoped she could pull her new look together by then. *But I don't think I'm doing this only for him anymore. It makes me feel good too. Maybe I* will *find a hot fireman at that silly ball. Why should I wait around for someone who doesn't want me?*

The lofty sentiments carried her through Friday and nearly through Saturday. They began to falter as she got ready for her date. *It's not a date. It's two friends attending a work function. Yeah.* But her hands trembled as she applied the scented lotion after her shower. She blow-dried her hair, appreciating how the expensive cut fell into place like it never had before. It was only slightly shorter, but the layers and highlights brought it to life and it no longer hung against her neck like a dead possum. Her nails were short, but glossy, and her secret places, only somewhat hidden by the tiny scrap of lace Barb called a thong, were smooth and touchable. Nina closed her eyes and took a deep breath at the delicious image of Seamus touching her there. *Slow down, girl! Remember it's not really a date!*

By the time he let himself in with the key she'd insisted he keep, she was slipping into the black heels she hoped she could manage to walk in. "I'm back here, Seamus. I'm almost ready." She grabbed her shawl and tentatively stepped into the hallway.

He was seated on the sofa, remote control in his hand. "You really were almost read—wow." He lowered the remote and stared. "Wow times a thousand." He tossed it on the couch and stood. "You look incredible." His eyes roved appreciatively up and down her body.

She grinned, pleased at his assessment. "You clean up well too." He looked amazing in his tux, his broad shoulders filling out the coat to perfection. "I hope there's food. This," she gestured to herself, "took forever and I forgot to eat lunch. I'm starving."

"It's a dinner, so don't worry. I can't have my gorgeous date passing out on me." He grinned and took her hand to spin her around. "You really do look amazing, Nina."

She bit her lip and looked up at him. *Better to get it out in the open now.* "Did you tell Sloane you were taking me to the ball?"

He winced. "Not exactly."

"Seamus, I don't know how I feel about—"

"Shh." He squeezed her hand lightly. "We broke up."

"What? When?" She tried in vain to calm the sudden thumping of her heart. *He's free.*

"A few nights ago, right after I left here, actually. She was waiting at my place. I didn't even know she was back in town." He sat on the sofa and tugged her down to join him. "She's the one who called it off. She's been offered a job in Chicago."

"I'm sorry. Are you okay?"

He chuckled. "I'm fine. It was time to end it—past time. I've known for months but haven't wanted to pull the plug. We were together a long time."

She thought he looked sad. Sad, but not devastated. *Maybe there's hope.* "Is there anything I can do?"

"You're doing it. I'd hate to go stag to this ball."

He drove them to the downtown hotel where the ball was being held and Nina felt like a princess when he pulled into the valet parking lane. He held her hand as they walked to the ballroom and introduced her to the people already seated at their table, all from his station. The food was forgettable, but filling enough to stop her stomach growling. The conversation was fun, and Nina enjoyed watching Seamus tease and interact with his co-workers, including a female paramedic he treated much like the other guys. She was fascinated by this side of him, entranced by the good-natured banter flying around the table. *He loves these people and it seems like he loves his job.* She remembered hearing him talk about his dreams to become a firefighter all through high school, his impatience at his parents' insistence he go to college first.

"So, Seamus, how's the application process going?" The speaker was Lisa Baca, Jon's wife. "Have you sent it in yet?"

Nina frowned at him, wondering what she could be referring to. He wasn't trying to get a new job and move away, was he?

He reached for her hand under the table. "I'm applying to the Arson Investigation team." He turned to Lisa. "I sent it in this week. Fingers crossed." He shrugged, as if it didn't matter one way or another. Nina suspected it mattered quite a lot.

"I didn't know you wanted to do that. You'll get it."

He let go of her hand and set his arm along the back of her chair. "Thanks. I've been wanting to apply ever since I joined the department. This is the first year I'm eligible." He shrugged again. "I'll keep applying if I don't get it this year. Eventually they'll take me, if only to get me to stop applying. I majored in fire science in college, though, so my chances are pretty decent, I think."

She'd had no idea he was so driven.

Lisa stood and held her hand out to her husband. "Well, I came to dance, sir. Your daughter will demand my constant attention the second we get home, so we need to make the most of this evening."

Nina smiled as she watched the couple take to the floor. Jon was an enthusiastic dancer, swinging his wife as they waltzed.

"What do you say, Nina?" Seamus stood and pulled her to her feet. "Shall we?"

She nodded and followed him to the dance floor. She stepped into his arms willingly; she'd been looking forward to this all night. She loved to dance and had missed it since her divorce. David had been a wonderful dancer and had taught her much of what she knew but being held by him had never thrilled her as much as being swept into Seamus's arms. He was so warm and solid. She wanted to nuzzle against his chest, but knew it wasn't the time nor place. "Your friends are great."

He chuckled. "Yeah. We spend a lot of time together, probably more than most other professions, so it's important to be tight with each other." He surprised her with a swift turn; his dancing would certainly never win any awards. "They're all wondering about you. I'm sure I'm going to have a bunch of questions to answer when I see them Monday at the station."

She looked up into his face. "And what are you going to tell them?"

He pulled her a bit closer. "I think that depends on you." At her questioning frown, he brushed her hair behind her ear. "It shouldn't come as any surprise that I'm having a hard time pretending to be 'just friends' with you. I need to know if you might ever be interested in more than friendship with me."

"You mean launching myself at you and basically forcing you to kiss me wasn't clear enough?"

He chuckled and pulled her close again. "You are so wrong about my willingness to kiss you."

"Oh?"

"Yeah."

Chapter Twelve

Seamus

"Is this better?"

"Yes. Those shoes were clearly designed by males who want to keep my gender subjugated and weak."

He glanced over to where her high heels lay discarded under their table. "Bastards." He whispered the words against her fragrant hair. She was so short the top of her head only came up to his chin, but he found he didn't mind in the slightest. Her small, slim body felt perfect against his. "You don't think guys invented high heels because they make your legs look smokin' hot?"

"No. I think men invented high heels so women can't run away from them."

He chuckled and pulled her close as they swayed slowly to the music. "As long as you don't run away from me. This reminds me of high school dances."

"How so?"

"All the girls have ditched their shoes and most of the people are wasted. I hope Jon doesn't plan to drive home."

"Lisa said she was driving. She's nursing the baby, so she didn't drink."

"Good." Seamus had been careful to limit his own alcohol intake during the evening; a first date wasn't the time to get sloshed. He glanced down in time to catch her yawn. "Why don't we get out of here?"

She smiled sleepily and took his hand to walk back to their table. He watched her slip her sandals on while he said goodbye to his friends.

She was quiet on the way back to her house and he appreciated how they didn't always have to talk. He pulled into her driveway and walked around to open her door. They'd danced and talked with his friends for hours, but now he was ready for a few moments alone with her. He'd told her about breaking up with Sloane, and he wondered where that left them. He hoped she was willing to explore a romantic relationship, but found himself unsure about how to broach the topic. He walked beside her, then stopped as she turned to him at the front door.

"Do you want to come inside? We could have a glass of wine." Her green eyes were luminous in the dim porch light.

He didn't know what to do with his hands. "I better not." He settled for stuffing them in his tuxedo pockets.

"Oh. Okay." She sounded disappointed as she searched in her small evening bag for her keys.

"Hey." He retrieved one hand and cupped her cheek. "I want to go inside with you, Nina, but it's probably best if we take this slow." He brushed his thumb across her full lips. He did want to follow her in, but knew he'd be far too tempted to move their relationship in the direction of her bedroom at light speed. "You're special and I'm on the rebound."

"Ah. I guess that's true." She covered his hand with her own. "I certainly don't want to be your rebound booty call."

He burst out laughing, relieved when she joined him. The image of this brilliant, beautiful woman as the object of such a casual, unimportant relationship was unfathomable. He stared into her eyes, aware he'd never felt these emotions for any other woman: this pull, this need—much more than sexual, although that was definitely there. He acknowledged it even as panic coursed through his body. *This is real. This is it. Oh, God. I gotta get out of here.* But first, he needed—not wanted—needed to kiss her. Laughter faded as the heat intensified between them. He knew she felt the same pull as her lips parted ever so slightly and her tongue slipped out to wet them. He dipped his head and pressed his mouth to hers, inhaling the warmth of her wine-scented breath. She sighed into his mouth and stepped closer, her hand sliding up his arm to his shoulder. He had to taste her more fully, so he allowed his tongue to lick softly, quickly, along her bottom lip, but retreated before she could grant full access to her mouth. *Keep it light. Slow down.* He changed his angle and softened his mouth as they both settled for sweetness rather than full-on passion, which simmered just below the surface. There would be time for that later, when he had some distance from his recent break-up, when they'd both had more time to process Neal's death. He gently pulled away and rested his forehead against hers. "Wow."

"Yeah. This is a whole lot better than the last time you kissed me on my front porch."

"Oh, really? Was I that bad a kisser back in high school?"

She smiled and shook her head. "It was my first kiss, so I'm no judge. I liked it. But you ran away last time like I had the plague. I assumed you were unimpressed."

He realized he'd hurt her all those years ago and it caused a physical cramp in his stomach. "You're wrong. I was too impressed, and I liked it way too much." He brushed his lips against hers softly. "I'm sorry, Nina. I was an idiot back then. Neal had strictly forbidden me to make a move on you, and I knew he'd be pissed if he found out I'd touched you." He clearly remembered cupping her small, soft breast as their long-ago kiss had gone on longer than he'd expected.

"Neal? You mean you...Seamus, did you *want* to ask me out back then?"

He smiled crookedly. "I did, but Neal refused to even think about it. He knew I wasn't good enough for you, Nina. He was right. You deserved someone special, and I wasn't that person back then. I like to think I've matured slightly in the years since." He stroked his fingers across the silky skin of her neck. "I wonder what Neal thinks of this now?"

"I miss him too. But we're old enough to make our own decisions." She stood on tip-toe and kissed him. "Besides, I think he's looking down and smiling. He'd want us to be happy. And you make me happy, Seamus."

***

"Dude! I thought you were gonna take your sister! You dog! Why didn't you tell me you'd asked Nina? You sure didn't waste any time! Impressive." Jon slid into his chair next to Seamus, ready for the morning station meeting.

Seamus didn't look up from the paperwork he was filling out. "I've known Nina since we were kids. I asked her before Sloane and I broke up and we went as friends." He saw the disbelief on his friend's face out of the corner of his eye and sighed. "At least that's how it started."

"No shit? Huh." Jon opened the manila folder he'd brought and began filling in his own overtime sheet. "Well, that's cool. Lisa liked her a lot. It would be great if you didn't screw this up. Whatever it is."

He smirked but didn't look up. "I'll see what I can do."

"So, are you gonna ask her out again?"

Seamus turned his head to spear Jon with his stony gaze. "Seriously, Jon? None of your goddamn business, buddy." He turned back to his paperwork for a few minutes as the awkward silence stretched between them. "Sorry. Of course I am; I'm not stupid. I spend nearly every evening over there with her and her kids when I'm not here."

"She has kids? As in plural? She doesn't look old enough."

"She's not. Not really. She's my age, but she was married to some older, asshole professor who insisted they adopt two little girls from Uganda, then he left her for some other woman he knocked up. Now Nina's a single mom with six-year-old twins."

"Dude, a ready-made family. That's intense."

"Whoa! Slow down! We've only gone out once." He swallowed, trying to force the panic down his throat. *I'm not ready for this!*

"Sure, sure. But you and her...I dunno, man. It just seemed different than with Sloane."

Seamus nodded and turned back to his time sheet, but his head was swimming. It was different—better, but scarier because it was so real. He knew he wanted to be with Nina, knew he wanted to help her as she dealt with all the aftermath of her brother's death, but what about after that? What about after everything was settled and they knew who had murdered Neal? Would they still want to be together? And what about the girls? He was only twenty-six years old, for crying out loud! He wasn't ready to be a father! But he thought of their little faces, so cute and similar, and knew they were part of it. He remembered when he couldn't tell them apart and now shook his head slightly in wonder. They were so different in his mind now...he would never mistake them again. He loved spending time with them, reading to them or listening as they read, playing board games, watching silly programs on television. It had started out simply as a way to help Nina, but it had morphed into something more. *I'm already in too deep. I don't ever want to back out. Oh, God.* Part of him was terrified, but part of him was ridiculously happy and excited to see what this new relationship with Nina could be and what it meant for their future.

The captain entered at that moment and Seamus forced his attention back to the realities of helping run a fire station. He and Jon pulled kitchen duty again, and a quick check of the fridge and pantry revealed it was time for the weekly Costco trip. They made their list and the menu for the next two evening meals, then headed out. Seamus had always preferred kitchen duty, but he'd never attacked it with such fervor as in the past few weeks. He'd found himself surfing the Web, looking for new recipes to try out, always thinking about recreating them for Nina and the girls. He'd discovered he could get Lily to eat meat if it was in smaller pieces and spread throughout a casserole or something similar. She would pick it out if it was more than a bite-size chunk, but she *would* eat her vegetables without prompting. Iris, on the other hand, would eat meat, but picked at her veggies unenthusiastically. She also had an odd aversion to anything red: strawberries, tomatoes, cherries, beets, etc. Well, he agreed with her on the beets, which he thought tasted like dirt. She would eat tomatoes only if they were pureed in a sauce. *God, those two are a trip!* He'd managed to get them to be more helpful around the house, as well. They now helped with the dishes every night and picked up their room before bath time. His mother had always insisted her kids—all six of them—carry their share of the household duties, and Seamus figured it had been more important than he'd realized back when he was bitching about having to clean his room. He'd never struggled with the mundane realities of adulthood as many of his friends who had never even done their own laundry before leaving home. He realized Nina had probably been trying to coddle them a bit since they were orphans and she felt sorry for them. He had no such compunctions, however, and treated them like any other kid.

"Which one, bro?"

"What?" He shook himself out of his reverie to see Jon holding up two packages of ground beef. He squinted at the labels. "The one on the left."

"This one's cheaper." He motioned to the package on the right.

Seamus shook his head and grabbed the one he wanted from Jon's hand. "Yeah, but this one's 98% lean, which means it's healthier and less of it cooks off as fat."

Jon looked at the remaining package and shrugged. "Huh. Okay." He tossed the meat back into the refrigerated case. "So, have the police figured out who murdered Neal yet?"

Seamus pushed the orange cart into the cheese aisle and reached for the sliced cheddar. "Not yet. They dragged Nina and me downtown for questioning, though. My sister-in-law talked to Nina, but some other detective questioned me. I felt like a criminal by the time he was done. The guy was a real ball-buster."

"You're not a suspect, are you?" Jon asked in disbelief.

Seamus glanced at him, eyebrows raised. "I think I was, at least until my alibi checked out." He'd found the beer receipt in the trash and a check of his phone records had proved he'd been at home all night.

"Holy shit!"

"I know, right? It was a real kick in the ass. But they cleared both Nina and me, finally. Now I don't know what or who they're looking at."

"Man." Jon shook his head. "Who would want to kill a guy like Neal? Did he have a lot of money?"

Seamus shook his head. "Nah, I think everything he had was tied up in his business."

"Cuz isn't money usually the reason people get killed? That or sex. Do you think maybe his fiancée found out he was having an affair or something?"

"Neal wasn't the type of guy to cheat on a woman. I know that for a fact."

"Hey, sorry, man. It's just that it's almost always the husband or wife." He shrugged apologetically. "I've never met his fiancée, so I don't know."

"It's okay." Seamus blew out a breath. Although he'd never really liked Kira and wasn't sure he trusted her, he didn't think she'd killed Neal. As he'd said, Neal had no money to speak of, and if she'd wanted out of the relationship, there was nothing to stop her from leaving. But someone had killed him. Someone had loaded him full of ketamine, shot him in the head, and then left his office, locking the door behind them. They'd even fabricated a suicide note. Seamus wasn't a detective, but even he could see Neal's murder had been meticulously planned and executed. But why? Why kill him and try to make it look like a suicide? All the details made it clear it was someone who knew Neal and knew his habits, someone who had access to him at RiskCom. But contemplating who had murdered his best friend was giving him a headache, and he had most of a forty-eight-hour shift to go. "Look, let's get this shopping done and head back to the station, okay?"

"Sure, sure. No problem."

***

Nina

He wanted to ask me out all the way back in high school. Nina couldn't get the thought out of her head, hugging the delicious secret to herself, examining it from every angle. *He would have asked me out if Neal had let him.* She wondered if she'd be angry with her brother if he were still alive, but thought it unlikely. Neal had always been protective of her, and she knew Seamus hadn't been the sort of guy any brother would want their sister to date. But Seamus had grown up and left his profligate ways behind. She smiled to herself as she imagined him teasing her for using big professor words like 'profligate.' Her smile faded a bit as she thought about what Neal would think of their budding relationship now. *Would you be happy for me, Neal? Or would you be difficult about me dating your best friend? God, I miss you! I'm so freaking mad at you for dying! How could you let yourself get murdered? We were supposed to go to each other's weddings and watch our kids grow up together!* She knew her anger was irrational, but it was still there, simmering under the surface while she got on with life, trying to make a happy home for her girls, who'd been through so much upheaval in their short lives. Her counselor—she'd kept her promise to make an appointment, even after they discovered Neal was murdered—had assured her the anger was a normal part of the grieving process and to expect to struggle with it for at least a few months. *But I'm tired of struggling. I'm tired of everything being so damned difficult. I just want to forget about it all and spend time with my girls and Seamus.* But it was impossible to forget the events of the past several weeks, to forget what had brought Seamus back into her life. *How can something so amazing, so unbelievable, come out of something so awful?*

"So? How was the ball? Did you get home before the clock struck midnight? Or did you and your delicious fireman drink champagne from your glass slippers until the wee hours of the morning?" Barb leaned against the doorjamb of the office door.

Nina chuckled and gestured to the chair in front of her desk. "Let's see. The ball was lovely. I did not get home before midnight, and Seamus and I definitely didn't drink champagne from my shoes. I mean, we would have, but they're sandals, and the champagne kept dripping out."

"You should have gone with the pumps." She cocked an eyebrow at Nina. "Is that it? Please tell me there's more to the story."

Nina leaned back and smiled as she crossed her arms. "He broke up with his girlfriend."

Barb raised her eyebrows. "Before or after the ball?"

"Before."

"And?"

"He kissed me when he took me home."

Barb clapped her hands excitedly. "Yay! I knew the Brazilian wax and sexy thong would come in handy!"

Nina shook her head and laughed. "It was only a kiss, Barb. Then he went home."

"Hmm. Well, that's disappointing. At least tell me you're going out with him again."

Nina tried, but failed to hold in the grin. "We have a date tomorrow night."

"You go, girl! Where is he taking you?"

Nina shrugged. "He didn't say. We'll probably go to dinner. Maybe we'll see a movie afterward."

"Ah, the classic date. Well, it's a start. What's the plan for after the movie?"

"I don't know. Coffee, maybe?"

Barb rolled her eyes. "This is why you need me, Nina. I'm talking about what you're going to do with the kidlets while you and Seamus have some time alone. You know, alone time?" She raised her eyebrows suggestively.

"Wow, Barb. It's only our second date. I'm not going to sleep with him yet."

"Fine. Spoilsport. But you have to promise me to

220

dish up all the juicy details when it does happen. Please? I don't have a guy in my life right now and I need the vicarious romance."

"Sorry to disappoint, but I have no intention of sharing any details of my sex life with you."

"Ugh." She stood and walked to the office door. "You're no fun."

"Bye, Barb." Nina waved as her friend left the office, then turned her attention back to her lecture notes. But the Gilded Age couldn't hold her attention when images of Seamus insisted on intruding. *I'm actually dating Seamus DeLuca. I've dreamed of this for so many years.* But would he disappear from her life once the police had found Neal's killer? She was angry that Seamus had been viewed as a possible suspect for a short time, but knew they had to consider everyone, even herself. Chris had finally told her both of their alibis had checked out. *Who could have done it?* Who had managed to get Neal in his office, somehow administered a fatal dose of ketamine, then shot him in the head, attempting to make it look like a suicide? It had to be someone who knew him and had access to the office. The list of suspects was fairly short: Kira, Gordy, Neal's secretary, or one of their other employees. Or could Neal have let one of his other friends in that night? Maybe someone called him and convinced him to meet them at RiskCom. *Ugh! It's so frustrating to not know!* She needed to let it go, to let the police do their job and stop obsessing over it. *Yeah. Easier said than done.*

She managed to focus long enough to get the basics of her lecture in her head—although she doubted she could liven up the boring topic of social change and railroad magnates in the late nineteenth century enough to make college freshmen care in the slightest. *I just need to get to the Roaring Twenties, then I can make it more interesting.* She taught her afternoon classes and only noticed one student fall completely asleep, so she counted it as a win. She had barely returned to her office when her cell phone rang.

"Nina? It's Mom. Can you talk for a few minutes?"

She sighed, knowing it was never simply a few minutes with her mother. "Sure, Mom. What's up?"

"Well, I just got off the phone with the insurance company and I don't know what they're trying to tell me."

"What insurance company? Mom, I don't know what you're talking about." Why would her mother think Nina could help with insurance?

"Neal's life insurance, sweetheart. I was looking through all the paperwork Kira brought over and ran across his life insurance policies."

"Okay. What's the problem?"

"Well, I can't seem to make heads or tails out of what they were telling me and your father isn't ready to deal with it yet. Could you stop by this evening and take a look at it?"

She rolled her eyes, grateful her mother couldn't see. "Sure. I'll stop by after I pick up the girls, okay?"

"Oh, that will be wonderful! Why don't you and the girls stay for dinner? You could ask Seamus too, if you want."

"He's working tonight, but the girls and I will take you up on the offer." Her mother was a wonderful cook and Nina was happy to skip kitchen duties for the evening. She'd gotten spoiled with Seamus cooking so often. Who would have dreamed he would turn out to be so domestic? He was awesome with the girls as well—better than David had ever been. "I've got to go, Mom, but I'll see you tonight, okay? Yeah, I love you too. Bye."

She took a deep breath and opened her laptop, prepared to work on a new article for a historical journal she'd pitched an idea to a few months before. She hadn't done more than glance at her outline before her cellphone rang again. *I'm not answering. I need to get some work done!* But it might be Seamus, and she would happily take the time to talk to him. Her stomach fluttered ridiculously as she reached for her phone. But instead of Seamus's handsome face on her screen, Gordy's number—no image—showed. Nina drew back her hand and waited for it to go to voice mail. *I do not want to talk to him right now.* Guilt swamped her, but she hated talking on the phone on her best days; this didn't quite qualify as one of them. Besides, Gordy drove her crazy and she had no idea why. She waited until the voicemail notification appeared on the screen, then listened, hoping the message didn't require any action on her part.

"Hi, Nina. This is Gordy. I was, uh, I was wondering if we could get together sometime soon? Maybe we could grab dinner or something? I'd really like to talk to you about Neal's part of the

business. I've got a lot of decisions to make and, well, I hate to push, but I need to talk to you about buying out Neal's share of the company. Anyway, if you could give me a call back, that would be great. Thanks."

Nina rubbed her fingers into her temples, trying to massage away the headache that had begun building when her mother called. *Crap. I have to call him back. Better get it over with.* She sighed and hit the call back button.

"Hey, Gordy. Sorry I missed your call. I had to step out of my office for a minute." She winced at the white lie.

"Oh, no problem. So, do you think we could get together sometime soon to talk about the business? Is there any chance you're free tonight?"

Bless you, Mom, for calling first! "Oh, sorry. I'm going to my parents' house tonight." She didn't want to commit to an entire evening with him, either. "What about this afternoon? Could we meet for coffee somewhere?" She would much rather get this over with, even if it meant falling behind on her article.

He hesitated for a moment. "Um, sure. Why don't we meet at the Starbucks across from the university? I could be there in about half an hour."

She readily agreed and hung up, determined to write for twenty minutes until she needed to leave to walk to the coffee shop.

He was already there and waved from a corner table. She ordered a dirty chai latte and went to join him. He wore a white button-up shirt with the sleeves rolled up and his tie loosened. She'd always thought him rather good-looking, in a nerdy sort of way, but she'd never been remotely attracted to him. He'd asked her out several times during college when they'd met during holidays, but she'd—thankfully—been dating Ben by then and didn't have to find another excuse. *It just goes to show that looks aren't everything. Something about his personality rubs me the wrong way.*

"Nina, hi!" He waved to her and gestured to the brownie he'd obviously bought for her.

She nodded unenthusiastically and waited for her beverage before joining him, grateful for the brief reprieve. She finally sat across from him but shook her head at the brownie and pushed it back toward him, finding it presumptuous to assume she would want a sweet. "So, what is it you need from me, Gordy?" She knew she sounded borderline bitchy but was out of patience with him.

His eyes widened as he gauged her cranky mood and she could practically see him backpedaling. "Oh, I really just wanted to check in and see how you were doing." He reached his hand to cover hers and patted it awkwardly. "I mean, I do need to talk about the company, but that can wait if you're not ready to deal with it."

She could see the impatience bubbling below the surface of his apparent good humor and she wondered what was so important. "It's fine. I'm sorry. It's been a frustrating day, that's all. I know you need to move on with the company; Neal would have wanted it to succeed, so I'll do whatever I can." There was no sense in causing unnecessary delays in the business her brother had given so

225

much of his time and attention to build.

Gordy smiled and she thought again how handsome he was. "Thanks, Nina. Yeah, I'm hoping to buy out Neal's half of the company. Right now, I can't do much more than pay the bills and sign the payroll checks. I'd like to find out what bank holds the note for his loan and pay it off. Then I'd like to talk to your parents about buying out his share of the business. Do you, uh, know if he had any files or paperwork at his apartment? Did Kira give anything to you? I've looked through his office, but his loan information doesn't seem to be there."

He doesn't know I loaned Neal the money. Interesting. So, he doesn't know I have controlling interest in RiskCom. I wonder why Neal never told him? Was he embarrassed because he had to take a loan from his sister? Probably. Well, I don't feel like telling Gordy now. "Um, you know, she did give me some of Neal's stuff, but I haven't looked through it yet."

"It's probably boring financial records. Why don't I come by and pick it up tomorrow? That way you won't have to bother going through it."

Wow. His presumption never stops. Because I'm a history professor he assumes I have no idea how to understand finances? "I minored in business, Gordy." She'd wanted to make sure she had a backup plan in case history didn't work out. Intricate accounting spreadsheets might be beyond her immediate grasp, but she knew the basics of how to run a business. "I think I can keep up."

"Oh, of course. I didn't mean...well, that is I don't want you to have to deal with all the company stuff so soon. But great. So, you'll let me know when you find out about the loan? And perhaps then we can discuss getting your parents to sell Neal's half of the company."

She smiled and sipped her chai. "Sure. I'm seeing them tonight and I'll be sure to mention it." Her parents had nothing to do with it since she had controlling interest until the loan was paid in full. Neal had died before he could finish paying it off. But Gordy didn't need to know any of that.

Chapter Thirteen

Nina

"What do you say, Lily?"

"I'm sorry I don't like your meatloaf, Gramma."

Nina's father snickered at the far end of the table while Nina rolled her eyes and shook her head. "No, sweetheart. What do you say when you wish to be excused?"

"Oh." The little girl sat up straight and assumed an angelic expression. "Please may I be excused, Gramma?"

"Well, of course, dear," Nina's mother said, nonplussed at the innocent disdain toward her famous meatloaf. She adored the two girls, but couldn't seem to remember Lily wouldn't eat meat, especially an entire slab of it.

"Please may I be excused too?" Iris wasn't about to be left behind, plus, she'd eaten half her meatloaf, although none of her peas.

While the girls retreated to the living room to play with the special toys their grandparents kept for them, Nina helped her mother clear the table. When they were done, and each adult had a cup of decaf in front of them, Nina asked her mother to explain the reason for the visit.

"Well, sweet Kira brought over Neal's portable filing cabinet and I got to looking through it to see if he had any credit cards that needed to be paid or anything like that. He did, but that's not what confused me."

For the love of all that's holy, would you get to the point? "So, what did confuse you, Mom?"

"Well now, I found a file folder marked 'Life Insurance.' And it seems like Neal had bought himself some life insurance policies."

"Okay. That seems pretty normal, especially since he was self-employed."

"So, I called to see how much and who the beneficiary was. And what do you think?"

"I don't know, Mom." *Patience, Nina.* She already knew she was the beneficiary, but it seemed wise to let her mother spin her tale the way she wanted. Neal had asked her to keep the loan a secret, not wanting the plethora of unwanted advice his mother would have felt compelled to give if she knew about it.

"Well, it's you, Nina. You're the beneficiary."

"Okay. That makes sense since I loaned him some money to start up the company. If you'll give me the information, I'll call them in the next few days and see about making a claim." She had little interest in even thinking about her brother's life insurance policies this soon after his death.

"Of course, but that's not all. The insurance man

said there was another policy, but I couldn't get a straight answer out of him about it, except that it seems to be Kira who is the beneficiary. But why on earth would Neal buy life insurance for her when they weren't even married yet? And then the insurance man kept on about death certificates and the like. I don't know what to think."

"He bought life insurance for Kira? That's unusual. Maybe he bought it recently because they were planning to get married soon?"

"Well, I don't know. Here." Mrs. Braden stood and crossed to the sideboard, where she retrieved a manila file folder. "This is all the information. Maybe you can get a straight answer from the insurance company. I couldn't make heads or tails of it and your father doesn't want to talk about it."

She flashed her father a look of understanding, then shoved the file in her bag and promised her mother she'd take care of it. She visited for a few more minutes, then used the excuse of needing to get the girls home for a bath to escape.

Iris fell asleep on the way home and wouldn't wake up enough to walk, so Nina juggled her bag and the rag doll form of her child as she followed Lily through the garage to the utility room door. She hadn't planned to be out so late and the porch lights weren't on as she pulled into the garage, making the house darker and creepier than she liked. She had to set Iris down to fish for her keys. She shoved the door open and Lily skipped inside while Nina bent to scoop the sleepy Iris up again. She fumbled for the light switch, wondering if there were some way to set the lights on an automatic timer so she wouldn't have to come home in the dark. Maybe Seamus would know how to set up something like that. She dropped her purse on the counter by the door and carried Iris through the dark kitchen into the family room, intent on laying her on the couch while she got Lily headed to the bath.

"Momma, what happened?" Lily stood frozen amidst the shambles of the family room. Furniture was overturned, papers and books were spread across the floor, interspersed with broken glass and stuffing from the couch cushions.

Nina wrenched her head around, taking in the damage and the shattered glass door that led to the backyard. Her adrenaline kicked into overdrive as fear raced through her body. "Lily! Come here!"

Her daughter came, alerted by the panic in her mother's voice. "Momma? Why are you yelling? I'm scared." She attached herself to Nina's leg like a barnacle.

"I know, sweetie. We need to go back out to the car. Now." She reached for Lily's hand and disentangled her enough so she could walk. She shifted Iris's dead weight higher on her shoulder and steered Lily back to the garage door. "Get in the car." She swiftly opened the back door of the SUV and shooed Lily in, then placed Iris in her car seat. *Shit. My phone.* She'd left it in her bag on the counter by the garage door. The last thing she wanted to do was go back inside where a burglary had clearly occurred. What if they were still there? What if they were in the back of the house and decided to come out when they heard Nina returning. What if they had guns? But she needed her phone to call the police, so she raced back into the house and grabbed her bag with trembling hands. She barely remembered to hit the garage door opener button before she backed out and tore down the street. The girls—both awake now—cried softly in the backseat, terrified at their mother's odd behavior. *What do I do? Who do I call? Police, of course.* She pulled to the curb at the end of the street and pressed 9-1-1 with cold, shaking hands. Once assured they were on their way, she dialed Seamus, knowing good and well he couldn't race home to be with her, but needing to hear his voice.

"Hey, this is Seamus. I can't come to the phone right now because I'm obviously insanely busy doing important stuff. But leave a message and I'll get back to you."

Disappointment swamped her. "Seamus, it's Nina. I'm so sorry to bother you and I realize you're probably out on a call, but I…God, Seamus. I came home tonight, and someone broke into my house. I'm freaking out. I'm fine—we're all fine. The police are on the way. I…I just need to hear your voice." She sniffed and took a deep breath. "Okay. It's okay. Just…please call me when you get this message." She hung up and stared at the phone in her hands for a moment before scrolling through her contacts and hitting the button.

"This is Hart."

Yes. A real person I know, at least a little. "Chris, it's Nina. I'm sorry to bother you at home, but I've had a break-in at my house. We're fine and I called the police. I…I'm sorry. I shouldn't have called."

"Where are you? Are you still in the house?"

Nina shook her head, then realized Chris couldn't see her. "No. We're in the car down the street from the house. I'm waiting for the police."

"Okay. Stay there. Are the girls with you?"

"Yes." She sniffed again as tears streaked down her face. "They're in the backseat. They're scared, though. We all are."

"I know, hon. Listen. I'll be there in a few minutes, okay? Just hang on. Don't go back to the house. Wait for me and the police. Promise?"

"Yeah. Promise." She hung up and fished in the console for a tissue. *Pull yourself together, Nina. You're scaring the girls.* She mopped her face, then crawled into the back to sit between the car seats, thankful, for once, she was petite. "Iris, Lily, I know you're scared, but everything is going to be all right. Someone broke into our house, but the police are on the way. I also called my friend Chris, who's a detective; she's Seamus's sister-in-law. She's going to come and help us figure this all out, okay?"

They quieted into sniffles and Nina figured it was the best she could hope for at the moment. She held their little hands as they waited for the police.

Chris arrived first, pulling her car to the curb in front of Nina's. Chris got out of the passenger side and Nina saw Hugh was with her. She extricated herself from between the car seats and met them at the front of her SUV.

Chris took one look at Nina and pulled her into her arms. "It's okay. You did the right thing. The police are nearly here, and we'll go take a look and make sure the house is empty." She rubbed her back as Nina clung tightly.

A patrol unit pulled up and Chris gently disengaged, sending Hugh a unspoken request. "Nina, I need you to wait here with Hugh until I come back, Okay?"

"Hey, Nina, why don't you introduce me to your daughters? I came along to help keep them distracted while you deal with the break-in." Hugh placed his hand on her shoulder and steered her toward the SUV while Chris strode away to join the patrol unit.

Nina looked up into Hugh's face and smiled gratefully. She'd met Seamus's oldest brother a few times, of course, over the years, but he was almost ten years older than Seamus, so they'd interacted very little. "Sure. Thanks." She opened the back door and peered in. The girls had stopped crying, but both had traces of tears streaking down their brown cheeks. "Girls, this is Hugh. He's Seamus's brother and Janey's uncle. This is Lily, and this is Iris." She pointed to each in turn.

"Where's Seamus?" Lily addressed the question to Hugh.

"Well, he's at work, sweetheart, but I know he'll be here as soon as he can." He squatted down to talk to them and Nina could see he had an instant rapport. He asked them questions about their school and about their favorite games while Nina paced and checked her watch every two minutes.

Fifteen minutes later, Chris jogged back to them and motioned for both Nina and Hugh to join her near the front of the SUV. "The house is empty, Nina—no sign of the intruder."

234

"Oh, thank goodness. So, it's safe to go back?" She had no idea what she would do about the broken glass door, but—

"Um, I don't think that's a good idea, Nina. Besides it being an absolute wreck in there, we feel it would be better for you to stay with someone for a few nights."

Nina's stomach clenched. "What are you not telling me, Chris?"

"Okay, listen." She drew her farther away from the car. "I don't want the girls to overhear, but you deserve the truth. The level of violence and destruction in your house has me worried. It seems a little too personal and I think it would be a good idea for you to stay elsewhere."

"Oh, my God." Her thoughts raced, but she was unable to process any of them. "I guess I could call my parents."

Chris met Hugh's eyes again, eyebrows raised slightly. He nodded briefly. "Actually, I was thinking you and the girls could stay with us tonight. There's no reason to upset your parents. We've got plenty of room."

And you carry a gun. It must be serious if she's willing to take us in personally. "I'm officially freaking out, Chris."

Chris hugged her again briefly. "I know, but I think this is for the best, just until we can figure out who did this. It will take at least a day for the police to process your house and then there's a lot of cleaning up in your future. I'd like you to stay with Hugh and me tonight and then we can talk about the next few nights. Okay? It's going to be all right,

Nina, I promise."

She followed them to their house and sat in the kitchen, drinking a cup of hot tea laced liberally with whiskey, while Hugh showed the girls to the playroom. Both were wide awake, but Nina knew they'd crash soon. Chris assured her they had plenty of spare pajamas they kept for Janey and the girls were more than welcome to wear them. She also promised to find a t-shirt for Nina to sleep in. She was on her second cup of tea, finally feeling warmth creep back into her extremities, when Hugh returned to the kitchen.

"They're fine," he assured Nina. "They found Janey's dress-up clothes and are having a fashion show with Bob." The girls had met Hugh's golden retriever when they got to the house and had fallen instantly in love with the friendly dog.

"Thank you both." She wrapped her hands around the mug and stared into the brown liquid. "I don't understand, Chris. You think someone broke into my house to do what? To kill me? Are you sure it wasn't simply a burglary" She'd thought of nothing else since Chris had told her she couldn't go back to her house.

Chris shook her head as she brought Hugh a cup of tea. "Not necessarily. We're not sure of anything yet, but the level of damage seemed...personal, somehow."

"What do you mean?"

"Well, I've seen burglaries where the house has been tossed, but there was something else at yours. The cushions were all cut, as well as the mattresses. Some of the walls were even gouged. It exhibited some serious anger, and I'm concerned whoever broke in didn't find what they were looking for. I don't want them to come back when you and the girls are there."

Nina nodded mutely. She cleared her throat, but her cell phone rang before she could speak. "It's Seamus. Excuse me."

"Nina? Where are you? Are you okay? What about Lily and Iris?"

She blinked back the tears that began the second she heard his voice. "We're all fine. We're at Chris and Hugh's house. The police won't let me go back to my house yet."

"Okay. Tell me what happened, hon. What was taken?"

"I don't know. It was all wrecked and Lily just ran inside, and what if the guy had still been there?" She lost it, unable to talk through her sobs. She'd held it in as long as she could.

Hugh gently took the phone from her and stepped out of the room as Chris rose and found a box of tissues.

Nina grabbed a handful and stood to pace, angry with herself for falling apart. "I'm sorry, Chris. I don't know why I'm crying."

"Don't apologize. You've had a shock and you need time to process."

Hugh returned and handed the phone back to Nina. "He wants to talk to you."

She accepted it and turned away from them. "Hey."

"Hey. Listen, hon. I can't get off work until Thursday morning, but I need you to stay with Chris and Hugh, okay? I'll be staying with you after that and you can go back to your house. God, Nina."

"I'm scared, Seamus."

"I know. I'll be there as soon as I can. Chris and Hugh won't let anything happen to you or the girls."

"I know." She sniffed and chuckled wryly. "This kinda sucks, you know?"

"Yeah. I'll see you Thursday morning."

She hung up and turned to see Chris and Hugh watching her; Hugh stood behind his wife, his hands on her shoulders. "Thanks. Sorry about that." She waved her hand vaguely. "I heard his voice and…"

"And kind of freaked out. Come on." Chris held her hand out. "I bet you could use a hot shower. Hugh will get the girls ready for bed." She led her up the stairs as she spoke. "We can put them in the twin bed in the play room, but the guest room has a queen-sized bed if you want them with you."

Nina nodded. "I would, thanks. I need to have them close tonight."

"Of course."

Nina could see Chris was brimming with questions about the phone call from Seamus and the rather obvious relationship implied by it, but she refrained from asking, something Nina was enormously grateful for. She wasn't ready to go public with it—whatever it was. And she couldn't handle anything else tonight.

Chris found her a t-shirt and a pair of shorts to sleep in, then showed her where to find everything she needed in the bathroom. Within a few minutes, Nina was standing under a steaming hot stream of water, letting it wash away some of the tension of the night. *Okay, take a minute to calm down. Yeah, it was scary and awful to come home to a break-in, but you and the girls are safe. Chris and Hugh won't let anything, or anyone get to you. I wish Seamus were here, though.*

By the time she returned to the kitchen, Hugh had managed to drag the girls away from the fashion show and fixed them each a small peanut butter and jelly sandwich along with a glass of milk. Nina waved away his offer to make one for her.

"Thanks, though, Hugh. Lily didn't eat much at dinner."

"I don't like meatloaf." Lily spoke around a mouthful of bread. Bob, still wearing a scarf around his head, sat on the floor between the girls' chairs, waiting patiently for a bite of sandwich.

"Hugh cut the crusts off, Momma." Iris whispered the words as Nina slid into the chair next to her.

"I see that." She'd learned she might as well cut off their crusts, since neither would eat them anyway.

Hugh winked at her as he refilled Lily's glass.

When they'd finished their snack, Nina instructed them to take their plates to the sink, then followed them upstairs where Chris was laying out pajamas for them. They were thrilled to find out they got to sleep with their mother and happily crawled into the big bed beside Nina. They were asleep in minutes. Nina thought she'd be awake for hours, but the comforting warmth of their little bodies lulled her to sleep in less than ten minutes.

***

Seamus

"Damn it!" His voice echoed through the cavernous garage, which housed the two engines, the paramedic unit, and the captain's SUV. He'd stepped out of the station for a few precious moments of privacy while he called Nina. Seamus shoved his phone in his back pocket and ran his hands through his hair while contemplating kicking the tires on the closest engine. *Nah. I'd probably break a toe, and everyone would give me shit about it. Goddammit. I need to be with Nina.* But he couldn't take off mid-shift without something more serious than a residential break-in; it would take a death in the family at the very least.

"Hey, everything okay out here?" Shella peered around the edge of the engine.

He huffed out a harsh sigh and nodded. "You drew the short straw, huh?"

She chuckled and shook her head. "I volunteered. I figured it might be girl problems and I'm a girl, so…" She shrugged. "Did you have a fight with your new girlfriend?"

He rolled his eyes. He'd told Jon about the break-up with Sloane; he should have known it would spread around the station like wildfire. "No, no fight. But there was a break-in at her house tonight and apparently the intruders trashed the place."

"Oh, my God! But she's okay, right? Does she have a place to stay?"

"Yeah, my sister-in-law, Chris—she's a cop, you know—took Nina and the girls home with her. I'll stay with her as soon as I get off Thursday. Shit. My brother said Chris is worried about the level of violence involved and doesn't want Nina to be alone."

Shella frowned and crossed her arms over her chest. "God, I had no idea! Listen, let us know what we can do, okay?"

"Thanks. Yeah, I will. God, how am I supposed to concentrate on work?" He eyed the tires again.

"It sucks, but she's safe tonight. And you're a professional, so you'll do your job, like always." She walked over to him and rubbed his shoulders. "It's going to be okay, Seamus. Did you say 'girls'? Does your new girlfriend have kids?"

He smirked down at her. "I did, and she does. But she's not my girlfriend, Shella. Not yet, anyway."

She waved his objection away. "Kids, huh? Wow. How old?"

"They're six—twins. Lily and Iris. What's that look for?" He narrowed his eyes at the insufferable expression on her face.

She laughed. "Nothing. I'm just amazed at the thought of you with kids."

"Shut up." Before he could say any more, the high-pitched beep of the station alert sounded and words began to scroll past on the electric sign posted above the door. Seamus and Shella automatically turned and headed to the computer screen monitor attached to the wall near the door.

"Engine 14, Ladder 12, EMS 5. Multiple vehicle

accident, Southbound I-25 at Lead/Coal. Delta response. Time out 21:23."

The message repeated, but Seamus and Shella had already left at a run. Shella ran toward the EMS truck while Seamus grabbed his gear and threw himself on board Engine 14. Both huge trucks pulled out of the garage in less than a minute, sirens blaring. The EMS unit had left in under thirty seconds. A delta response indicated a serious accident with life-threatening injuries and every single firefighter on duty at the station was mentally preparing for what they were about to face. It took nearly five minutes to reach the accident scene with the huge engines, but Seamus knew Shella and Brandon were already there, rendering whatever aid they could until the rest of the crew and the ambulances arrived. The police had cleared the traffic to allow the engines access to the scene and the truck finally pulled to a screeching halt about fifty feet in front of a mangled mass of metal that used to be at least two different cars, from what Seamus could see.

"Holy shit!" Jon breathed as he jumped down to the asphalt.

A police officer met them. "We've got a DOA in vehicle one—that's the red Prius—and one victim trapped in the black Honda. You'll need the jaws."

Seamus turned to grab the Jaws of Life from the truck and jogged with them to the remains of the black Honda. He and Jon worked together to free the male victim who sat, unconscious, in the driver's seat. As they managed to pry the door open, a paramedic team from another station stepped up to assess the man's condition before Seamus and Jon attempted to extricate him from the vehicle.

"Pulse is thready, breath stable. He's got a compound fracture of the lower left leg."

"Okay. Jon?" Seamus jerked his chin toward the car, signaling for Jon to take the lead and grab the guy's upper body.

"Hold on!" One of the paramedics stepped forward. "Let me get a collar on him before you pull him all the way out."

Seamus and Jon halted, Jon holding the man's torso while the paramedic fastened a brace around his neck, then backed away so they could finish pulling the unconscious man from the vehicle. Seamus was as gentle as possible as he reached for the legs, but the right one was jammed under the dashboard and wouldn't budge.

"All right. Hold on, Jon. I need to grab a crow bar." He ran to where he'd laid the bars and grabbed the one he thought would fit best. Within a minute, he had the man's other leg free and he and Jon carried him a safe distance from the vehicle so the paramedics could work on him. He'd lost a lot of blood and Seamus hoped he would live.

"Baca! DeLuca! Over here!" Brandon Davis was gesturing from the mangled Prius.

If they hadn't been told what type of car it was, Seamus wouldn't have been able to tell, so twisted and wrapped around the black Honda it was. They ran to join the paramedic. "What do you need?"

"We've got an infant in the backseat, status unknown. I need you to get the door open or the window or something."

Seamus peered through the cracked glass and saw a tiny baby in a car seat. *Ah, shit. I hate when it's kids.* There was no visible blood, but he knew that didn't mean the child was unharmed. "Let's get the ART." He jogged to the truck as he spoke to retrieve the glass removal tool. He and Jon worked carefully so as not to spray any of the broken pieces of tempered glass on the child. Jon pulled the remaining glass away and Seamus reached inside to cut the car seat from the seatbelt restraints, then hefted the child and car seat out the window and set it on the pavement.

Brandon began to work on the infant. "I've got a heartbeat and breath sounds. Let's get him to an ambulance." He stood and carried the infant—carrier and all—to a waiting ambulance.

Seamus and Jon then turned to the grim task of removing the female's body—likely the baby's mother—from the front seat. They didn't speak as they worked, except to signal to each other what they needed. The woman's face was covered by the airbag and the steering wheel was almost completely embedded in her chest. They had both long since grown used to dealing with such horrors on a daily basis, but the tragedy of it hit both of them.

"Fuck." Jon whispered the expletive as they closed the doors of the ambulance, which would take the body to the morgue.

"Yeah." Seamus agreed. The tow trucks had arrived and there was nothing more they could do, so they trudged back to Engine 14, hearts heavy. It was nearly midnight by the time they returned to the station, so they grabbed a snack and a bottle of water, then headed to the showers. Seamus wanted to text Nina and check in with her, but he hoped she was asleep, so he refrained. It took an hour, but he finally fell asleep and managed to get almost six hours. The next day was quiet; they only had two short calls, neither of which required both engines, so Seamus and Jon only had to go on one of them. He would have preferred a busy day; boredom was a terrible thing when he was frantic with worry about Nina and the girls. He tossed and turned most of the second night, then finally threw his covers off at 4:30 a.m. and headed to the workout room. He put in an hour with the weights and another half hour on the treadmill, then showered and prepared pancakes for the crew, although he wasn't scheduled for breakfast duty. He needed to stay busy, and while measuring flour and eggs couldn't totally keep his mind off Nina, it was better than staring at the ceiling above his bunk.

Nina's car wasn't at Hugh and Chris's house when he arrived, and he figured she was dropping the girls at school. She'd texted to let him know she was taking the day off to deal with the clean-up at her house. Hugh answered his knock and led him to the kitchen, where he helped himself to a cup of coffee and sat down to wait for her.

"Chris drove with her to drop the girls off at school." Hugh sipped his coffee and stared at his brother over the rim of his mug.

"What?" Seamus thought he knew, but he was going to make his brother ask.

"Nothing." He shrugged. "I'm just wondering

what   Sloane   thinks   about   your new…friendship…with Nina."

"Gee, *Dad,* it's really none of your damn business."

Hugh merely smiled and calmly continued to sip his coffee.

"Sloane and I broke up last week," Seamus said with a sigh. "I'm not *that* big of an asshole, you know."

"Oh, I know. I'm not sure you do, though." He sipped again. "Nina's a strong woman. Maybe not as gorgeous as Sloane, but…"

"Don't make me punch you, Hugh. You're trying to bait me, but I'm not in the mood. Nina is special and you need to shut up about her." He was too tired to deal with Hugh's older brother shit today.

"Okay. Good. You want some breakfast? I made French toast for the girls." He chuckled. "God, they're cute."

"They are that. I'm making inroads with Iris, finally. I'll pass on the French toast. Thanks, but I couldn't sleep, so I made pancakes for the station." He stood as he heard the SUV pull into the driveway. He tried to wait for her in the kitchen but couldn't. He met her in the middle of the living room and she walked straight into his arms. He laid his head atop hers and breathed in the heady, yet comforting fragrance of her hair. Out of the corner of his eye he saw Chris smile briefly, then exit the room quickly, giving them some blessed privacy. He pulled back finally and held her beautiful face in his hands, noting the dark circles beneath her eyes.

"Are you okay?"

She nodded and reached up to run her hand over his rough, unshaven jaw. "I am now."

He couldn't help himself; he bent his head and kissed her softly, sweetly. It didn't matter that Hugh and Chris were probably watching from the kitchen. He leaned his forehead against hers, eyes closed, and sighed. "I'm so sorry I couldn't be here earlier."

"It doesn't matter. I know you can't get off work for something as dumb as my house being burglarized. I don't know why I'm so affected by it. It happens to everyone."

"Don't downplay it, Nina. It's not dumb, and you have every right to feel violated or whatever." He brushed his thumb over her soft lips. "How are the girls?"

"Confused, but otherwise fine."

A quiet cough from behind him interrupted their privacy. "Why don't we get over to Nina's house so we can begin the clean up?" Hugh asked from the doorway.

Seamus refused to jump apart guiltily; he had nothing to hide or be ashamed of, and his family better get used to it. He turned but kept an arm around Nina's shoulders. "We?"

Hugh nodded. "I have a crew meeting us there, so we can fix the door at the very least. We'll see what else needs done."

"Thanks. Some of the firefighters are coming by in a while to help clean up." He looked down at Nina. "Are you ready?"

She nodded. "Thank you all so much. I know that doesn't begin to cover it, but—"

"We're happy to help, Nina. It's not a problem." Hugh ushered them all out the front door and to their separate vehicles.

Nina handed Seamus her keys as they walked hand-in-hand to her SUV. "Do you mind? Now that it's time to head over there, I'm freaking out again."

He squeezed her hand, then let it go to open the driver's side door. "I don't mind at all." They drove in silence, but he held her hand loosely across the console. Once at the house, Nina unlocked the front door and led the party inside. The formal living room was largely untouched, but the den and kitchen area were trashed, with every book pulled from the shelf, torn pages and papers littering the floor. The couch cushions had been slashed and the stuffing covered the tables like mounds of snow. Seamus stepped carefully through the mess to examine the broken glass of the patio door, through which the intruders had gained access. It was a wooden framed single door with a solid glass insert—about the most insecure sort of door he could ever imagine as an outer door—and he would never have trusted it in his own home. Hugh was already scraping the remains away from the edges and measuring for a replacement piece of glass while Nina and Chris walked down the hall to check the bedrooms.

"Can you recommend a different type of door than this friggin' glass piece of shit?" Seamus gestured to the one Hugh was measuring and the double version of it on the other side of the fireplace. "Dumbest doors I've ever seen."

"They let the light in, though. This room would

be a cave without them. I'd recommend security screen doors to cover them and an alarm system."

"Can you put those in?"

"I can do the doors. I've got a guy who does alarms and owes me a favor. If Nina wants it, I can give him a call and get one installed pretty fast."

"I'll talk to her. I appreciate it, Hugh."

"No problem." He paused to answer his phone. "My crew is on their way."

Seamus left him measuring and went to find Nina and Chris. He paused to peer into the girls' room, surprised to see nothing was disturbed. *Weird, but good. They'd be upset if their toys and books had been damaged.* Nina's room was another story. It looked like a hurricane had swept though. Her slashed mattress was lying half on and half off the bed frame, the sheets and pillows ripped and strewn across the room. All her dresser drawers were empty, several broken into pieces. The contents of her walk-in closet lay in a heap on the floor. More books and papers coated nearly every surface. "Do you have any idea what they took?" Although how she would be able to tell in this mess, he had no idea.

She stood, hands on hips, surveying the wreckage. "Um, other than the two laptops—mine and Neal's—I'm not sure. They may have taken some of my jewelry, but it's going to be awhile before I can tell for sure."

"We can track your computer, Nina, as soon as they turn it on. I'm not sure about Neal's, but we'll give it a shot," Chris said as she took notes in a small notebook.

Seamus's friends showed up within the hour and joined Hugh's work crew in the cleanup efforts. Nina directed, telling them where to put things and brewing endless pots of coffee. She agreed to let Hugh call in his favor for the alarm system and install the security doors. He promised to have the doors done before they left for the day and told her the alarm system would be installed the following day.

"Thanks, Hugh." She ran her hands through her hair and sighed. "I'll call and cancel my classes for tomorrow. What's one more day, huh?"

"Don't do that." Seamus rubbed her tight shoulders. "I'll be here, and I can take care of it."

She groaned softly and tilted her head to allow him greater access. "Why should you have to spend your precious time off making sure my alarm gets installed? It's not your problem."

"I'm making it my problem. Stop whining." He tweaked her nose and went back to cleaning.

Chapter Fourteen

Nina

The hot water sluiced over her shoulders and she was grateful David had insisted on having the larger water heater installed when they bought the house two years before. She allowed herself to stand under the massaging jets for nearly fifteen minutes; only the promise of a waiting glass of wine eventually lured her out. Seamus had taken his shower hours earlier, while she had gone to pick the girls up from school. He'd been hot and sweaty from the manual labor he'd engaged in all day and had wanted to get cleaned up before dinner. The girls had been thrilled to see him, and even Iris had hugged him tightly. Both girls had taken advantage of Nina's physical and emotional exhaustion to lobby for pizza and she'd acquiesced easily, although no one had eaten much. The sight of the heavy security screens covering the back doors upset the girls, as did the torn cushions and other changes. The construction crew and firefighters had done their best, but it was

251

obvious something had happened. Seamus promised them he wasn't leaving, and it seemed to help settle them down somewhat. She toweled off and slipped into yoga pants and a light sweatshirt before joining him in the den.

"They're finally asleep." He handed her a glass of red wine as she sank into the sofa. They'd flipped the cushions, but she would need to purchase a new couch soon. "I couldn't get them to sleep in separate beds, though."

"Thanks." She accepted the glass and drank deeply—now wasn't the time for lady-like sips. "I don't blame them." She frowned as she realized how her comment may have sounded and rushed to explain. "We all slept together last night in the big bed in Chris and Hugh's guest room. They needed to be close to me."

"And you needed to be close to them. Come here." He pulled her closer and wrapped his free arm around her.

She went willingly and pulled the afghan off the back of the couch to cover her legs. "I'm so glad you're here. I know I wouldn't be able to sleep if you weren't. Thank you."

"My pleasure. I wouldn't be able to sleep, either, so it works for both of us."

"I really didn't need this on top of everything else right now." She chuckled then, surprising both of them.

"Care to share what you managed to find to laugh about?"

"Nothing, really. It's just that this break-in certainly made for a distraction from obsessing about Neal's murder, huh?"

"That's one way to look at it. I'm glad we already made a copy of the files from Neal's computer to give to Izzy. Do you think you lost much of your writing from your laptop?"

"I back it all up to a dropbox, so I'm sure it's fine. I don't want to think about it tonight." She yawned hugely. "My brain can't handle anything else."

"Chris called while you were in the shower. No news on your laptop or any of the jewelry you listed."

Once the top layer of debris had been cleaned up, Nina was able to find her jewelry box. Several pieces were missing, including a diamond tennis bracelet and her engagement and wedding ring set from David. "Hmm." She leaned against Seamus's warmth and drank the last bit of her wine. Her eyes refused to remain open and she was barely aware of him removing the glass from her hands before she fell asleep.

***

She woke to the enticing aroma of coffee and a warm hand brushing the hair out of her face.

"Morning, Sunshine."

She pried her eyes open to see Seamus grinning at her. But he held a mug of coffee, so she forgave him and sat up. "Thanks." She wrapped her hands around the hot cup and hunched over its life-giving magic. "What time is it?"

He sat next to her with his own mug. "Six thirty.

Sorry to wake you, but don't the girls have to be up soon?"

"Yeah. God, did we sleep on the couch all night again? This is becoming a habit. Did you get any sleep?"

"I got enough. You crashed, and I didn't want to wake you. Sleeping with you certainly wasn't a hardship, Nina."

She laughed and leaned against him. "This wasn't quite what I had in mind for our first time." *Oh, God, did I just say that? I don't want him to think...well, that I...shit.* "I mean, not that there will be...or that you want—"

He slung his arm around her shoulder and kissed the top of her head. "Of course I want, Nina. But I know that's not what you meant. If I have anything to say about it, there will definitely be a real first time. But we can talk about that later." He stood and pulled her to her feet. "Why don't you go get dressed and wake the girls? I'll scramble some eggs and make some toast."

***

"So, how bad is it?" Barb peeked around the door of Nina's office.

"Come in. It's pretty bad."

Barb handed her the paper cup she'd brought from the student union building. "Here. I figured you needed this. If they had the good sense to sell booze over there, I would have loaded it up. I can run to my office for the vodka I keep in my bottom drawer, if need be."

Nina laughed and accepted the cup. "Vodka in coffee? I'll pass. I'm not quite that desperate. Not yet."

"Yes, vodka in coffee. Haven't you ever had a White Russian?"

"Yes, but those are cold. Now, if you have a bottle of Bailey's in your office, we would be having a different conversation."

"Duly noted. I'll pick some up next time I'm at the grocery store." Barb raised her cup in accord. "Tell me about the house."

Nina sighed. "It was awful. They completely trashed my den, my office, and my bedroom. They stole two laptops and some jewelry, but not much else. I'm so mad!"

"Fuckers! I hope the cops catch them soon. Do you need help cleaning up?"

"Thanks, but Seamus brought a bunch of friends and his brother brought a construction crew. It's all done, except for buying new furniture and some wall repair. Seamus is there today while my new alarm system is installed." She hated the thought of living in fear behind security doors and alarms, but what else could she do? She had to keep her kids safe. "He's staying with us until...I guess until the police catch whoever did this."

Barb smiled. "He sounds like a good man. I can hardly wait to meet him. Sounds like you may need that sexy lingerie after all."

Nina remembered what Seamus had said earlier that morning: *If I have anything to say about it, there will definitely be a real first time.* He'd kissed her softly before she'd left for work and she'd wished they could shut the door, shut out the world, and prolong it, but the girls were watching, wide-eyed, and she had to get to work. "Maybe I will. I doubt I'll ever have the guts to wear them, but who knows?"

"Never doubt the power of lacy, skimpy underwear on a male of our species, Nina. Keep it in mind if he seems reluctant to take the plunge, so to speak."

"I'm fairly certain Seamus DeLuca has never been reluctant to 'take the plunge' in his life. And I'm definitely not some young, virginal maiden who's afraid of losing her virtue."

Barb smirked over the top of her coffee. "Are you sure you're not sitting in here writing romance novels instead of historical research papers?"

Nina laughed. "I'm not, but it sounds like a lot more fun. Seamus's sister-in-law, the one who just had a baby, writes romance novels."

"Really? What's her name? I love to read them. The hotter the better."

Nina bit her lip to keep from laughing at the thought of Barb, a tenured professor of Latin American history with many academic accolades, reading romance novels at night. "She writes under her maiden name, Melanie Blythe."

"I'll look her up." Barb stood. "Gotta go, sweetie. I'm glad Seamus is staying with you. I'd worry like crazy otherwise."

Nina glanced at the clock and cringed. She quickly gathered up her notes and left to teach her Western hero seminar. It was her favorite class, as it allowed her to use all her dissertation knowledge, plus most of the students were graduate level and took it seriously. They had a lively discussion about Billy the Kid and whether or not he could be considered heroic in any sense of the word, leaving Nina feeling rejuvenated and newly in love with her chosen career field. She didn't always feel that way after a 101-level lecture class. She stopped by the SUB for a quick sandwich to take back to her office with her and had to push aside the manila folder she'd shoved in her bag two evenings before in order to find her wallet. The break-in had completely erased the issue of Neal's life insurance from her mind.

Back in her office, the cellophane-wrapped sandwich lay forgotten on her desk as she dialed the number for the insurance company. The agent wouldn't release much information over the phone, but was willing to schedule an appointment with her later in the week. She would need to bring two forms of identification and a death certificate. He absolutely refused to talk about the other policy for which Kira was apparently the beneficiary but relented enough to allow Nina to invite Kira to the appointment, provided she also brought the proper forms of identification. Nina thought for a few moments, then placed a call to her mother.

"Mom, did you find any evidence in the papers Kira gave you that Neal had made a will?"

"I don't think so, dear. He was so young and had no children, so I think it very unlikely he would think of such a thing."

"Why would he think of life insurance then? It doesn't make sense to me. What about anything with an attorney's name on it?"

"I didn't see anything like that, but you're welcome to come over and look through the files."

"Thanks, Mom. I'll do that later this week. I'm a little busy right now with getting the alarm system set up."

"Oh? You're having an alarm installed at your house? Is anything wrong?"

Nina cringed as she realized the can of worms she'd opened. She'd been distracted and forgot she was trying to keep the break-in from her parents. *Why couldn't I keep my mouth shut?* But it was too late now. She had to confess or risk an outright lie to her mother, something she knew would come back and bite her later. "There was a break-in, Mom. Two nights ago while I was at your house for dinner."

"What? Why on earth didn't you call? My word, Nina! Your father and I would have come right over! What did they take? Are the girls all right? Oh, they must be scared to death!"

Nina pulled the cell phone away from her ear as her mother continued to rant. *This is why I didn't tell you, Mom. This is why I try to avoid telling you anything.* When her mother finally wound down, she forced herself to speak calmly. "They're fine. Nothing of theirs was taken or disturbed." She chose her words carefully, anxious to avoid telling her mother about the level of destruction at the house and how they'd spent two nights with Hugh and Chris. "They stole my laptop and some jewelry." She neglected to mention Neal's computer since her mother didn't know Kira had given it to her. Less was definitely more with Nancy Braden. "I should have had an alarm system installed when we moved in, that's all."

"Are you home now? Do you want me to come over and be with you while they're installing it?"

Crap. I don't want to tell her Seamus is staying there, for multiple reasons, not the least of which is her antiquated notion of a proper dating relationship. "I'm actually at work. Seamus had the day off, so he volunteered to go over and wait around while it's installed. Thanks, though."

"Well, if you're sure, dear. I'll make up a few casseroles for you to put in the freezer and bring them by later, all right? I'm sure you don't want to have to cook with all this going on."

"Mom, you really don't need to worry about that. It's sweet, but—"

"No buts! It's no problem at all. I'll put a few together and take them over. Dear Seamus can put them in the freezer."

She'd better call *Dear Seamus* and warn him that her mother was coming over.

***

"Your mom loves me, Nina, so stop worrying. It was fine. As soon as she left, I divided the big-ass casseroles she made into smaller, lunch-sized portions for you to take to work. I hope that's okay, but Lily wouldn't eat any of the stuff she brought. You do have a microwave at work, right? Because you now have approximately six months' worth of lunches in your garage freezer."

Nina laughed and hugged him tighter. He'd pulled her into his arms as soon as she stepped in the door. *I could get used to this: coming home to this man's arms every day. If wishes were horses...we'd all be kings.* "Cool. I'll save a fortune by not buying every day."

"Let me show you how the alarm works before we go pick up the girls."

He turned to the new keypad next to the garage door.

"In a minute." She pulled him back and stood on tip-toe to press her lips against his. She kissed him briefly and whispered against his mouth. "It's so rare that we have any time alone. Let's not waste it."

He pulled her tightly against him and angled his head to deepen their kiss, opening her mouth and stroking inside with his warm tongue. His hands drifted, one down to cup her bottom, the other under the hem of her blouse to caress the soft skin of her waist.

She pressed against him, reveling in the taste of his mouth and the feel of his hands as they worked their magic on her. She'd never been kissed so well or so thoroughly, and she wanted more. She slid her hand from his neck, down his sculpted chest, and under the edge of his t-shirt. His skin was smooth and hot, the muscles underneath hard.

He gentled the kiss, plucking at her lips for a moment before lifting his head. "Okay, Professor. Enough of that. For now." He framed her face with his hands. "You are so beautiful, Nina."

She smiled radiantly at him. "So are you. I love

touching you." She ran her hand across his tight abs.

He caught it and brought it to his lips. "You are playing with fire, girl. Let's take a look at your alarm, and then we'll go pick up the girls." He rubbed his thumb across her lips. "But I'd love to continue this later, when they're asleep."

"Me too." Electricity zinged through her body at the possibility of finally making love with him later that night.

***

Seamus

He put the finishing touches on the eggplant parmesan and slid it into the oven, hoping the girls would eat it. It was a gamble, but he thought he could sell it to Lily since there was no meat and it was covered in cheese; he also hoped to convince Iris that vegetables weren't all bad. He turned to the cutting board to finish slicing the cucumbers for the salad. He would put the tomatoes on the side, since Iris wouldn't eat them or anything they'd touched, but everyone else liked them. He focused on cooking, vainly attempting to block out the thoughts of what the night ahead might hold: making love with Nina. *But how can I possibly think of anything else?* She'd felt so good, so right in his arms earlier, and he'd been a hair's breadth from scooping her up and carrying her to her bedroom. *Later, idiot. You can wait.* He'd probably need to give Nina another tutorial on her alarm system, though, since neither of them had been terribly focused or interested in the aftermath of their passionate kiss. *She's one hell of a kisser; how was I supposed to care about a friggin' alarm system?*

"Homework is done and they're playing in their room," Nina said as she entered the kitchen. "How about a glass of wine?" She pulled a bottle from the wine rack. "I'm feeling like a nice Cabernet."

"Sounds good. The ETA for dinner is about thirty minutes." He accepted a glass of the deep ruby wine and sipped appreciatively. "Good choice."

"Since we have a few minutes of quiet, can I tell you about something?"

He frowned at her and reached across the tabletop for her hand. "Of course, hon. What's up?"

"I haven't had a chance to talk to you since the break-in—it kind of took over everything in my life and I didn't tell you about the life insurance."

"I assume you're talking about Neal?"

"Yes. My mom called the afternoon of the break-in because she couldn't get a straight answer from Neal's life insurance company. That's why I went over that night for dinner."

"And?"

"Neal took out a life insurance policy and named me the beneficiary. I knew about it, but I don't know how much it was—I have an appointment Friday to look into all the details. It seems he also took out another policy. Kira is the beneficiary."

"Hmm. That seems kinda weird. I mean, I don't know much about life insurance—I think I have some through the fire department and I think my parents are the beneficiaries—but it seems strange to take out a life insurance policy for your girlfriend. Maybe he just took it out when they got engaged?"

She shrugged. "Maybe. I tried to ask her about it this afternoon when I called to tell her about the appointment, but she didn't answer. I left a message, but she hasn't called back yet."

"Do you trust her?"

She narrowed her eyes at him. "That's not the first time you've sounded suspicious of her. What is it about her you don't like?"

He let go of her hand and stood to check on the eggplant parm. The cheese was barely starting to melt, and he knew it had a while to go. "It's not that I don't like her…I don't know. I guess I never quite bought their relationship. She didn't seem like she was as into him as he was into her." He shook his head as he clicked the oven light off. "That probably sounds stupid, but…"

"No, it doesn't." She crossed her arms as if cold. "I think you nailed it, Seamus. I haven't been able to articulate it clearly, but that's it. He was so in love with her, but I've never felt she reciprocated in the same way."

He smirked and bent over to kiss the tip of her nose. "So, same thing, but you used bigger words?"

"Bigger words?"

"Reciprocated. Articulate. You're adorable, Professor Smarty Pants." Part of her charm was the fact she didn't seem to realize how much smarter she was than nearly everyone around her. He should probably be intimidated to date a woman more intelligent than him, but he shrugged and decided to simply go with it. He'd always known she was smart, so why should it bother him now? Besides, he thoroughly enjoyed the way her face flushed in the wake of his comment.

"Whatever. Those don't seem like big words to me."

He smiled as he set the table. "That's because you spend your days reading and writing all that academic crap."

"That reminds me; have you ever read any of Mel's books?"

He laughed. "Her romance books? No, they're not really my style." He squatted in front of her and took one of her hands. "I'm going to confess something, Nina, and it might make you rethink this relationship. I don't really read for pleasure. I'm more into movies and sports. I'm never going to be able to have intellectual discussions with you."

She reached to cup her palm on his cheek. "I have plenty of intellectualism at work. I don't need it at home." She leaned forward to kiss him. "I'm not much of a football fan, though. You should know that going in."

"I've got three brothers to watch football with."

"Good."

"Good." He kissed her briefly, then stood. "You should read one of Mel's books, though. Finn says they're great, but he's biased. Why don't you go tell the girls to wash up? Dinner should be ready in a couple minutes."

***

"Are they asleep?" She looked up as he sat next to her on the sofa.

"Yeah, finally. They were fussier than usual." He accepted the glass of wine from her.

"Hmm. They ate well at dinner, though. Lily seemed to really like the eggplant. All the shit happening in our lives has probably finally caught up with them. A good night's sleep will most likely fix their fussiness."

"I hope so." He sipped the wine, then set it aside and reached to pull her feet into his lap.

"Are you going to rub my feet, Seamus?" She giggled as he stripped her sock off.

"I'm planning to start at your feet. Who knows where I'll end up?" He massaged her feet, working his way steadily up her ankles to her smooth calves. The muscles in her slender legs warmed under his strong fingers as he inched closer to the edge of her khaki shorts. He bent to kiss the inside of her right knee, smiling as she mewled her pleasure. "Any objections?"

"None at all," she whispered as she speared her hands through his hair.

He grinned and moved to kiss her lips, knowing he needed to take it slow and starting with her shorts was likely to bring this delicious interlude to much too swift a conclusion. He pushed her gently back to lay against the armrest and braced himself above her with one arm while the other hand slipped underneath the hem of her tank top. She wasn't wearing a bra, and his palm covered her small breast as she sighed into his mouth.

"Oh, Seamus. God, that feels so good."

"Yeah, it does." He removed his hand from under her shirt and reached to slip the strap from her shoulder, baring her to his hungry eyes. "So beautiful."

"Momma? Iris threw up."

Seamus looked into Nina's panicked eyes and swiftly drew her top up to cover her breast, thankful his back was to the hallway entrance and Lily couldn't see what they'd been doing.

Nina flew off the couch and ran to find Iris.

Seamus held his hand out to Lily, who looked to be on the verge of tears. "Come here, Squirt." He pulled her on his lap and cuddled her against his chest. "Your mom will take care of Iris. It's okay."

Lily sniffled against his shirt but wriggled until she found a comfortable position.

They remained that way, with Seamus softly rubbing her back as she fell asleep, until Nina returned.

"I got her cleaned up and tucked her in my bed. I'm sorry, Seamus."

He smiled crookedly at her over Lily's head. "Don't worry about it. I'll take a rain check. Should we try to get Lily back to bed?"

"Yeah. I'll take her." She stood and bent to retrieve her daughter.

"I got it." As Seamus shifted to lift Lily, the little girl sat up, opened her eyes, and barfed eggplant parmesan all over his chest.

"Oh, my God! I'm so sorry, Seamus!" Nina reached for the now-crying child.

He stood with Lily in his arms, attempting to keep the vomit pooling between him and the child rather than dripping to the floor. "Follow me to the shower." He managed to get to the guest bathroom without making too much of a mess and stepped over the rim of the tub. He held Lily out of the way until the water warmed, then stepped under the spray, clothes, child, pajamas, and all. He rinsed as much of the vomitus from her as possible, then stripped her sodden pajamas off and soaped her up quickly so she wouldn't smell sour. Lily continued to cry through the whole process. "Here." He handed the dripping child out to Nina, who wrapped her in a big towel and carried her out of the bathroom. Seamus drew off his vomit-covered shirt and dropped it on top of Lily's soggy pj's. His jeans and underwear followed, and he scrubbed his body, wondering if he'd ever get the disgusting smell out of his nostrils. He dried off and wrapped a towel around his waist before heading to the guest bedroom for a change of clothes.

"Oof!" Nina slammed into him and he reached out to grab her before she fell on her butt. "Sorry." She drew her hands away from his bare chest as if they were burned. "Um, Lily's still crying. She wants you. Would you mind lying next to her until she falls asleep?"

"Sure. Let me just grab some pants first."

"Of course. Sorry." She backed away from him.

She's nervous. Interesting. We were minutes away from making love and now she's nervous? "I'll be there in a minute." He watched as she spun on her heel and retreated to her bedroom. He ducked in to the guest room and dug a pair of sweatpants and a t-shirt out of his duffle bag. He

267

padded barefoot into Nina's room, where she was curled up on her king-sized bed with the girls. Iris was asleep and snuggled against Nina, but Lily lay by herself, crying quietly. She saw him and held out her arms, melting his heart. "Hey, Squirt. Come here." He lay on top of the comforter and pulled her close. "I've got you. Shh." He rubbed his hand over her back until her tears stopped and she fell into a restless sleep.

"Seamus," Nina whispered. "I don't even know what to say. I'm so—"

"Don't apologize again." He covered her hand and squeezed gently. "It's okay, Nina. Kids get sick, and I've certainly been thrown up on before, believe me."

She raised her eyebrows, clearly questioning this.

"Yeah. Fun fact: people in physical distress of one kind or another frequently lose their stomach contents all over the firefighter trying to help them." He refrained from adding that they frequently lost control of their bowels as well.

"Thank you. It's nice to have some help at times like this. Having two sick at the same time is a challenge. She looks like she's asleep." She gestured to Lily. "You could probably go back to the bed in the guest room."

And leave her to deal with both girls waking up sick later in the night? Not likely. He knew they'd undoubtedly throw up multiple times before they got the bug out of their little bodies. "You mind if I stay? I doubt they're done with the barfing quite yet."

"I'm sure you're right. I don't mind you staying at all." She smiled crookedly. "I finally got you into my bed."

He reached across the bed for her hand. "Now that I'm here, I may never leave, you know."

"Okay." She raised his hand to her lips and smoothed her soft lips over his fingers. "I'm not complaining."

He watched as she tucked his hand beneath her chin, her eyes drifting closed as her breathing evened out. She fell asleep with his hand still clutched between hers. *God, she's so amazing. And exhausted.* The purple smudges under her eyes had taken up permanent residence and he wondered when she'd last slept more than a few hours at a time. He swore he'd help her get through this—through the pain, loss, and fear—and back to her life, this time with him in it. Was it possible that less than a month ago she wasn't part of his life? He smiled and watched her sleep until his own eyes were heavy.

He'd barely fallen asleep when Iris began to stir and whimper. Nina had left the bedside lamp on, so he could see when she got up and took the child to the bathroom. Retching sounds soon followed. Nina carried the limp girl back to bed and Seamus figured Lily would follow suit soon. He felt her forehead, but it didn't seem like she was running a fever. Probably just a nasty stomach bug. It was nearly forty-five minutes later when Lily awoke and told him she needed to throw up again. Nina started to get up, but he told her he'd handle it. He carried Lily to the bathroom and waited while she lost the rest of her stomach contents and then dry-heaved miserably for a few minutes. He wet a washcloth and wiped it over her sweet little face. "You wanna rinse your mouth, Munchkin?"

She nodded and swished the water around her cheeks before spitting it into the sink. "I feel bad, Seamus."

"I know, Angel. You'll feel better tomorrow."

"Will you stay with me?"

"Of course. Let's get you back to bed." He tucked her back in and this time slid under the covers beside her.

Chapter Fifteen

Nina

The aroma of freshly brewed coffee enticed her from sleep. She wrenched her eyes open, cringing at their grittiness, and glanced at the pillow next to her. It was unoccupied, but still held the indentation of Seamus's head. Lily was sprawled across the other side of the bed, while Iris lay curled in a tight ball against Nina. They'd both thrown up once more during the night but had finally fallen into a sound sleep around three in the morning. Nina was exhausted, but was reluctant to call in to work yet again; she'd cancelled her classes so often in the past few weeks she worried she might be endangering her job. She didn't have tenure yet and sympathy for her brother's recent death would only go so far. She hoped her mother would be able to watch the girls, at least for the morning. She could skip her afternoon office hours without too much of a problem, but she really needed to teach her morning classes. She carefully slid out from under

271

the covers, trying not to wake either of the girls. The best thing for them after a long night of throwing up was sleep. She grabbed a sweatshirt against the early morning chill and slid her feet into her fuzzy slippers before following her nose to the kitchen.

Seamus was nowhere to be found, but a note was propped against the coffee maker.

Back in a few.
♡ *S*

She smiled as she reached into the cabinet for a mug. He'd been completely amazing during the night, taking full charge of Lily so she could concentrate on Iris, who seemed to be the sicker of the two. She cringed as she remembered Lily vomiting all over him. David would have screamed and handed her off; he'd been awful when the girls were ill, saying he couldn't watch them throw up without doing it himself, so Nina had better take care of them. Besides, he couldn't afford to catch whatever they had because he was needed at work. But it was fine for Nina to miss, of course. Her lip curled as she remembered how difficult living with him had been. *You sure can pick 'em, girl!* She'd been so overwhelmed by his attention at the beginning of their relationship—a popular, charismatic professor deigning to speak to lowly grad student/teaching assistant—she never saw how selfish he was. True, he was generous to a fault with his money, but in a careless, offhand manner. The one thing his girls needed was his time, but he rarely saved any for them and hadn't raised a single objection when she'd demanded full custody. By then he was so wrapped up in his new girlfriend and her pregnancy he couldn't be bothered with his two adopted children.

She grimaced as she remembered, then shrugged and pushed the unpleasant memories away. *He did you a favor. You have two amazing daughters thanks to him. Time to focus on the present, which includes a kind, funny, and incredibly sexy new man in your life.* She shivered as she remembered the moments on the sofa the previous evening. If Lily hadn't interrupted…she sipped her coffee, then turned as the back door opened.

"Hey." Seamus set the grocery bag on the counter and bent to kiss her. "I tried to be quiet. Sorry if I woke you."

She smiled and pulled him back for another kiss. "You didn't. Did we need groceries?"

He turned to the bag and unpacked several bottles of Pedialyte, ginger ale, and Gatorade. "Supplies for the patients. I wanted to get out before you left for work to pick up some stuff to get the girls back on their feet." He put the beverages in the refrigerator before pouring himself a cup of coffee and topping off hers.

"That's incredibly sweet. I need to call my mom to see if she can come over to watch the girls while I'm at work."

"No need to bother her. I'm staying with them today." He set his mug on the counter and reached for a frying pan. "You want some eggs?"

It hit her so suddenly she sucked in her breath,

shocked. *I love him.* She'd been *in* love with him since middle school, but this was different: *loving* versus *being in love.* She'd never felt anything like it for David, although she'd once thought she'd loved him. Compared to what she already felt for Seamus, it paled in comparison.

"Nina?"

She smiled and crossed the room to slip her arms around his waist. It was far too early in their relationship to tell him what she felt—it would likely terrify him. "Thank you."

He kissed the top of her head and laughed lightly. "It's just eggs, babe."

She snuggled deeper against him. It was *way* more than eggs. "Let me cook breakfast."

"I got this. You go grab a shower. Food will be up in ten minutes." He stepped away and swatted her lightly on her rear as she turned.

The girls were still asleep, so she moved as quietly as possible as she took her shower and got ready for work. She was still reeling from her realization. *I love Seamus DeLuca. Of course I do. How could I not? But could he ever love me back?* A vision of his previous girlfriend swam across her mind, an extremely unwelcome intruder in her reverie. *He broke up with her. He's with me now. Stop worrying and just enjoy it for as long as it lasts.* She squared her shoulders and leaned toward the mirror to apply lip gloss. *Tonight, I'll make sure we're not interrupted.*

He had her breakfast waiting when she returned to the kitchen and sat across from her while she ate. "I have to work tomorrow. It's a forty-eight-hour shift, so I'll be gone all weekend."

"It must be hard to work such long shifts. You do get to sleep there, right?"

"Sure, as long as we don't get a call." He shrugged. "It's not too bad. I actually prefer the forty-eights to the twenty-fours. With a twenty-four, it seems like you just get settled and it's time to go home. I also like having ninety-six hours off at a time."

"That would be nice. Listen, Seamus. I love having you stay here, but I know you must be ready to get back to your place, especially since we have the alarm system installed. It can't be easy to be around such chaos when you're used to a much quieter existence."

He reached for her hand across the table. "It's not chaotic around here, and I love it. If you want me to go, say the word. But I'd like to stay. What do you want, Nina?"

You. In so many ways, not all of which are physical. "I want you to stay." She couldn't look away from his smoky blue eyes.

He smiled and squeezed her hand. "Good. You know, we never did get a chance to have our date. You busy Monday night?"

"I think I can squeeze you into my busy social calendar. I'll have to cancel a couple of other hot dates, though."

He laughed and stood to carry her empty plate to the sink. "You're sure sassy this morning. Hot date, huh? Gives a guy reason to hope."

"A girl too." She met his gaze and raised her eyebrow in challenge.

He let out a low whistle, then looked over her head. "Good morning, Iris. How are you feeling?"

Nina turned to see Iris, her hair sticking straight up, her eyes dull and shadowed. She crossed the room and knelt in front of the little girl, her hand going automatically to her forehead to check for a fever. "Do you still feel sick?"

Iris nodded, but allowed Nina to guide her to a kitchen chair.

Seamus left the room and returned a moment later with one of the fluffy blankets from the sofa to wrap around the little girl. "You think you could drink a little something, Angel?"

Iris nodded unenthusiastically and pulled the blanket tighter.

Seamus poured her a small cup of ginger ale. "I'll go check on Lily."

Nina kissed the top of Iris's head and sat beside her. "I need to go in to work for a while today, hon, but Seamus is going to stay here with you and your sister."

"Okay. I don't feel good, Momma."

Nina's heart broke. "I know, sweetie, but you'll feel better soon. You've got a tummy bug, but it will run its course and you'll be back to normal."

"I don't want to throw up again."

"I know." Nina glanced at her watch as Seamus returned. "I have to go. Are you sure—"

"I'm positive." He kissed her briefly. "Lily is still out cold. We'll be fine, and I promise to call if we need anything. Go."

***

276

She had to rush to get to her morning class. She lectured in a fog, then stopped by the student union building for a latte with an extra shot. She needed all the help she could get today. Back in her office, she sipped while sorting through the enormous stack of mail and interdepartmental memos. Halfway through the stack she found a forgotten Post-It.

Call Kira re: insurance.

She ran her hands through her hair and sighed. *Crap. I forgot all about it.* She dug a little deeper and found the file folder containing the insurance information. She flipped through the pages, refreshing her memory, then picked up her phone. She figured she'd have to leave another message, but was pleasantly surprised when Kira answered.

"Oh, Nina. I, um, I'm just on my way out the door. Can I call you back later?"

Nina was running on too little sleep and she'd had enough of Kira's weird nervousness. "This will only take a second, actually. So, it turns out Neal had two different life insurance policies. I'm the beneficiary of one; you're the other. Did you know?"

"Life insurance? No, I had no idea."

Nina frowned and rubbed the bridge of her nose. Kira sounded sincere. "Okay. I called the insurance company a few days ago and they said we could go in together to make a claim. What's your schedule like for next week?"

"Do I have to go?"

Nina closed her eyes and attempted to keep her temper in check. Honestly, it was like dealing with a child. "Yes, Kira. You have to go. I need you to do this, so what days do you have off next week?"

"Wednesday."

"Good. I'll call the insurance company and see if they have anything available on Wednesday." She glanced up at the knock on her open office door. "I have to go, Kira. I'll text you the details, okay?" She hung up and turned to greet her visitor. "Hi, Chris. What brings you here?"

Chris sat across from Nina and handed her a paper cup. "Dirty Chai latte. Seamus said that's what you like."

"Thanks. How in the world could he remember something like that? I don't recall mentioning it to him."

Chris grinned and sipped her own coffee. "He likes you. A lot. DeLuca men can be formidable when they're in pursuit of a woman."

Nina frowned. "I've been in love with him since I was in middle school."

"Have you? You married someone else."

Nina sipped her chai before answering. "Yeah, well, we're all entitled to a stupid-ass mistake or two."

Chris nodded. "I hear that. I didn't marry mine, but…" She shrugged and glanced around the office. "Have you actually read all these books?"

Nina smiled. "Not cover to cover, but I've at least skimmed most of them. Reading is what I do."

"Better you than me, girl. Listen, Nina, I do have a reason for stopping by. I wanted to ask you about your ex-husband."

Nina frowned again. "David? What about him?"

"Was it a contentious divorce? You got the house and the kids, right? Does he have partial custody of the girls?"

Nina grimaced and set her cup aside. "No on all counts. I simply asked David one day if he was having an affair. He said yes and asked for a divorce. I wasn't terribly surprised. He has a very short attention span. He didn't want any sort of custody, although he is generous with his financial support. I couldn't begin to afford that house on my salary."

"Does he ever see the girls?"

"Occasionally. He mostly makes excuses for why he won't be able to see them. Why all the questions about David? Oh." She reached for her chai again. "You're thinking he was the one who broke in to my house, aren't you?"

"The possibility crossed my mind."

Nina shook her head. "It's not his style. Whoever trashed my place was extremely angry. David would simply ask if he wanted anything from the house. There's no way it was him."

Chris nodded. "I understand, but I'd still like to speak to him. I wanted to let you know first. Can you give me his cell phone number?"

Nina shrugged. "It's a waste of your time, but sure."

***

Seamus

"Come on, Lily-bug." Seamus scooped her from Nina's bed and cradled her gently against his shoulder. "You can't sleep all day. Iris has been up for nearly an hour." He carried her to the sofa and placed her at the opposite end from Iris, then tucked the big fluffy blanket around her legs before handing her the small sippy cup. "Try to drink some juice, okay?" It was Pedialyte, but he didn't think they needed to know.

Lily nodded sleepily but took the cup and drank.

"Seamus," Iris whimpered, "I'm gonna barf again."

He carried her quickly to the bathroom, grateful she made it to the toilet before vomiting. He cleaned her up and soon had her back on the sofa with more Pedialyte. "You two want to watch a movie?"

They both nodded unenthusiastically and merely shrugged at his first suggestion. *They must really feel crappy; they're usually extremely vocal about their cinematic choices.* He turned on the cartoon, then stripped the sheets off Nina's bed and threw them in the washing machine with plenty of bleach. His phone vibrated in his pocket and he figured Nina couldn't resist checking in already. To his surprise, his sister's name was at the top of the text message.

Izzy: Are you home?

Seamus: No. I'm still at Nina's. Why?

Izzy: I have the info you wanted from her brother's computer. Text me the address and I'll bring it by on my way to work.

Seamus: The girls are sick, so you better stay away, Preggo.

Izzy: Gosh, Mom, I think I'll risk it. Send the address.

Seamus rolled his eyes at her bossiness and sent Nina's address. He was putting the sheets in the dryer when she knocked on the door forty-five minutes later. "Mac is gonna skin me alive if you get this stomach bug," he said as he stepped aside for her to enter.

"No, he won't. Stop fussing." She pushed past him and headed to the living room. "Hey, girls. Seamus says you're sick, huh?" She knelt in front of them—slightly ungainly at six months pregnant—and set about doing the little motherly things he'd seen her do a million times with Janey: feeling their foreheads, tucking their blankets more securely around them before turning to her brother. "When was the last time they threw up?"

"Iris did about an hour ago, but Lily hasn't since last night."

"See if Nina has any saltines for Lily. Iris probably doesn't want any yet." She took their cups to the kitchen and refilled them with Pedialyte. "Keep the fluids going all day."

He took the sippy cups from her. "Will do, Dr. DeLuca. Why does no one remember I'm a trained

EMT?"

"When I need an arterial bleed stopped, I'll call you. And it's Dr. MacNeil now. When was the last time you had to deal with a sick kid?"

"About an hour ago. I've got this, Izzy." He loved his sister, but *honestly*. "You said you had the info from Neal's computer?"

"Fine." She rubbed her burgeoning belly absently as she frowned at him. "I can see you're going to be stubborn about this. At least promise to call me if you need anything, okay?"

He rolled his eyes again and chuckled. "Yeah, I promise."

She reached for the large tote bag she'd brought and pulled out her laptop. "Good. Go give those cups to the girls while I pull up the spreadsheets."

"Bossy much?" he muttered under his breath but did as she ordered. The twins were asleep, so he set their cups on the coffee table and returned to the kitchen.

"All right, here's what I've found." Izzy waited until he sat beside her, then angled the screen toward him. "All these spreadsheets show are the company's expenses and profits for the last few years. Everything looks pretty standard for a startup company. They had finally started to make a profit, but it wasn't much."

"So, there wasn't anything weird? Why would he insist Nina got the computer?"

Izzy shrugged. "I have no idea, but I did find something interesting." She pulled the computer back and clicked on one of the tabs at the bottom of the spreadsheet, then shifted the screen toward him again. "See this entry here?" She pointed to a number in the middle of one of the columns.

"Yeah." He squinted at it, but it seemed like any other number. "What does the little orange triangle mean?"

"That's a comment." She hovered over it. "Or it usually is. Neal, being a computer-savvy kind of guy, managed to change the code and turn it into a button." She clicked it. "It links to a file attached to the spreadsheet."

"What's in it?"

"I don't know. It's password protected."

Seamus sighed and stood. "Well, maybe Nina can figure it out when she gets home tonight. She figured out how to get into his laptop, so he probably set a password she'll know if he wanted her to see what's in this document. Thanks for doing this, Izzy."

"I'm happy to help. You'll tell Chris and Finn about this, right? They probably have experts who can open the document even if Nina can't. It could be something to do with why Neal was murdered."

He accepted the flash drive she placed in his palm and dropped it into the fruit bowl in the center of the table, amongst the apples. "Of course we'll tell them." She had such a knack for making him feel like a child. It could have something to do with the fact that she was nearly seven years older and had babysat him and Tony frequently when they were younger. "Please stop nagging, Iz. I'm begging you."

She stood and slipped her arm around his waist. "But I'm so good at it." She kissed his cheek and turned to pack up her computer. "All right. Sorry about the nagging and doubting your childcare abilities. You're doing a great job here, Seamus. I'm really proud of you."

"Yeah, yeah. Now get lost so I can finish my laundry. Be sure to wash your hands and take some vitamin C, okay? Maybe you won't catch what the girls have."

"Now who's nagging?" She winked as she passed. "See you Sunday at Mom and Dad's?"

"Not this week, unfortunately. I work all weekend."

"That's too bad. Say hi to Nina for me. Let me know when the girls feel better, so we can arrange a play date. Janey loves them."

"Me too. I'll call you as soon as they're up and around." It was true. He loved Nina's daughters—not liked or simply tolerated—but loved them. He loved Nina, of course. He'd loved her since they were kids, but he knew he was falling headlong toward something more. Once upon a time, the thought of being in love with any woman, much less one with two children, would have sent him speeding in the opposite direction, but he had no intention of going anywhere at the present. *I'm falling in love with Nina.* He closed his eyes. *No. I'm already there. Damn. That was fast.* Then he smiled.

The girls slept for another hour, during which he managed to get the clean sheets back on the bed and some chicken broth warmed up. Lily was ready for some crackers and broth when she awoke, but Iris would only sip ginger ale. They watched another movie, this time without falling asleep, and both managed to not vomit all afternoon. Seamus hoped the worst was over. He sat with them, reading a chapter from *Harry Potter*, when his phone buzzed.

"How are they?" Nina didn't bother with a greeting.

He smiled at her concern. "Fine. They stopped throwing up and Lily had some crackers and broth. Iris is still on juice and ginger ale, but maybe she'll try a few crackers after story time."

"Oh, thank God. I've been so worried. Listen, I've got a staff meeting this afternoon, but I'll be home right afterward. I'll pick up some Chinese or something on the way."

"That sounds great. You want to talk to Lily?" The little girl had crawled into his lap and was mouthing a plea to talk to her mother. He handed her the phone and stroked her hair while she told Nina about how she was feeling better, but Iris wasn't better yet. Iris calmly held her hand out for the phone and proceeded to inform Nina that she felt better but wasn't hungry. If Nina wanted to bring her a popsicle, she would probably eat it. Seamus bit his lip in amusement as he took the phone back. "Everything is fine here, so just relax and concentrate on work."

She sighed. "I know, but when my babies are sick it's all I can think about. I'll be home as soon as possible. I—"

"What?"

"Nothing. Thank you, Seamus. I'll see you tonight."

He frowned as he hung up, wondering what she

had been about to say.

"Can I have more crackers, Seamus?"

"Sure, Lily." He set her back in her spot and tucked the blanket around her legs. "You want more juice, Iris?"

The other girl nodded unenthusiastically.

By four o'clock that afternoon, both girls were feeling much better. Lily had eaten some toast and Iris had finally asked for a few crackers. He'd put them in a warm bath and changed them into fresh pajamas, which seemed to rejuvenate them both. He washed their sheets, hopeful they might spend the night in their own beds, so he and Nina could finally have a few hours to themselves. *If she's too tired to make love, I'll just be happy to hold her all night.* He hoped he could stick to his noble sentiments when he was lying next to Nina.

By five o'clock, they were all impatiently awaiting Nina's return. She'd told him she should be home by five thirty at the latest. The girls were bored with movies and books, so he found the cabinet where the board games were stored and set up Candy Land, hoping to keep them distracted until their mother arrived. At five thirty, he sent a text but although it said it was delivered, she apparently didn't read it. He figured her meeting had gone later than expected and tried to focus on the game. By five forty-five, he'd sent another two texts and turned his phone off and on again to make sure the error wasn't on his end. By six o'clock, he'd tried calling her three times and was starting to freak out. *Where are you, Nina? Goddammit! This isn't like her!* By six thirty, he'd given up all

286

semblance of not worrying and now paced, compulsively checking his phone, while the girls pretended to watch another cartoon. He was on the point of calling Finn when the doorbell rang. His stomach sank into his sneakers as he jogged to answer it. Chris, grim-faced, ushered him outside. Hugh was standing slightly behind her. "What happened? Where is she?" His words were a mere whisper from a suddenly parched throat.

"She's been taken to the ER—she's alive, Seamus." Chris reached to steady him as he slumped against the door.

"What the fuck happened?" he growled.

"I don't have all the details yet, but it seems she was assaulted in the parking lot behind her office. A co-worker scared off the assailant and called 9-1-1. Finn is taking her parents to the hospital and you can go with me. Hugh will stay with the twins."

Seamus scrubbed his hands over his face. "Oh, my God. Okay. She's alive? You swear to me she's alive?"

"I swear, Seamus. Now put on your game face and let's go tell the girls without scaring them to death, okay?"

He nodded and pushed himself away from the door. "Yeah, okay. Shit! How did this happen? Who was it?"

Chris grabbed him by the upper arms and shook him slightly. "Seamus! We can get into all that later. Right now we need to make sure Lily and Iris aren't terrified."

"Yeah. Sorry." He swallowed hard and led the way back into the house, where the girls waited, wide-eyed, on the couch. He tried to smile as he knelt before them. "Listen, girls. Your mom has been in an accident, but she's going to be fine." *Please, God, let it be true!* "Chris and I are going to go be with her at the hospital for a little while, but Hugh is going to stay with you until I get back, okay?"

Lily started to sob. Iris, with tears stealing down her cheeks, asked, "Will you call us as soon as you see her, Seamus? Please?"

"Of course. I'll call you as soon as I know anything. I promise." He stood and turned to his brother. "They've been sick, so take it easy with them. There's plenty of juice and stuff in the fridge. Crackers are on the counter."

"We'll be fine. Go to Nina."

Chapter Sixteen

Seamus

The ride to the hospital was eternal. Thankfully, Chris didn't feel the need to fill the empty silence with meaningless chatter and left him to stare out the passenger window uninterrupted. He'd questioned her again as soon as they got into the car, but she didn't know anything more than what she'd already told him. Nina had been assaulted in the parking lot and taken to the hospital via ambulance. Chris had no further details.

In the emergency room, they were informed that Nina was in surgery. Seamus almost passed out and had to sit in a nearby chair while Chris got the directions to the surgical waiting room. Mr. and Mrs. Braden had arrived, along with Finn, a few moments before, and sat white-faced and tense in the far corner.

"Oh, Seamus!" Mrs. Braden vaulted from her seat as he entered the room and pulled him into her arms.

289

He looked over her shoulder to Mr. Braden. "What have you heard?"

"Not a whole lot," the older man replied, his face haggard and gray with worry. "They took her into surgery straight from the ER. We haven't been able to see her or talk to a doctor yet."

Mrs. Braden clung to Seamus, sobbing softly, until Mr. Braden pulled her gently from his arms and guided her back to a seat along the wall of the waiting room. Seamus sat next to her, but was up again within a few minutes, too antsy to sit. Every second that ticked by without news about Nina sent another shaft of dread through his body. *Please, God, I'm begging you! Bring her through this! Bring her back to me. I need her...Lily and Iris...oh, God! Her children need her!* He paced in front of the window until Finn stopped him and placed an unwanted paper cup of black coffee in his hand.

"Come on." Finn led him across the waiting room and pushed him down into a seat. "Drink up. You need to be alert when Nina gets out of surgery. She's gonna need you to be strong."

Seamus nodded numbly and sipped the hot coffee, cringing at the bitter taste. He'd never enjoyed black coffee, but he drank it anyway. Finn had brought coffee for her parents also, a welcome momentary reprieve from the constant worry. He couldn't begin to fathom how they must be feeling; their son had been murdered and now their only daughter had been attacked and none of them had any idea whether she would live. How did this happen? Why? Who? Pure rage began to bubble up in him, but he knew he couldn't entertain it at the moment. He shoved it down, somewhere behind the fear, and crumpled his empty cup as he stood to pace again. He called Hugh to check in on the girls and was relieved to hear they were asleep; he had no news for them and didn't think he could manage to keep the fear out of his voice.

Nearly two hours later, a tired-looking doctor appeared in the doorway and asked for the family of Nina Braden. Seamus's heart nearly beat out of his chest as he stood behind her parents to hear what the doctor had to say.

"She's out of surgery and we were able to stop the internal bleeding."

"What was she bleeding from?" Mr. Braden interrupted the doctor. "I'm sorry, but we don't know anything except that she was attacked."

The doctor shook his head. "I don't have any details about the attack, but we repaired what appeared to be a knife wound in her upper left abdomen. We had to remove her spleen."

Mrs. Braden whimpered and began to cry quietly.

"Is she going to be okay?" Seamus voiced the question he knew they all needed to know.

The doctor raised his eyebrows and nodded slowly. "We're optimistic. She's pretty banged up, but she's young and should recover fully. She's going to spend another hour or so in the recovery room, but you can see her for a few minutes." He motioned for them to follow him through the double doors into the surgical ward.

Seamus walked with her family, praying no one would try to prevent him from seeing Nina. He wouldn't take no for an answer, of course, but he hated to make a scene. They were led through a twisting series of hallways, past dozens of curtained alcoves until the doctor stopped in front of one and pulled the curtain aside. A nurse stood at the side of a hospital bed, hanging various IV bags. Mrs. Braden let out a sorrowful sigh and rushed to the bed. When she moved, Seamus could see Nina for the first time. *Oh, shit. What the hell happened to her?* Her right eye was purple and swollen and there were cuts and scrapes all over her face. Her left arm lay atop the sheet, encased in a stiff-looking brace of some sort. His gut clenched in sympathy and he wove his way around her parents to the far side of the bed.

"Nina," the nurse said kindly. "Your parents and your—" She looked at Seamus questioningly.

"Boyfriend." He didn't look away from Nina's face as he spoke.

"And your boyfriend are here. Can you wake up for them, sweetheart?"

He touched her hand gently as she opened her good eye slightly. "Hey."

She closed her eye, then opened it again and mumbled something unintelligible.

"Nina, love, Dad and I are here."

She shifted her gaze toward her mother's voice. "Mom." The word was barely understandable.

"Keep talking to her. We want her to wake up a bit more before we move her to a room. I'll check back in a few minutes." The nurse closed the curtain behind her.

Seamus glanced around the small room, noting

the various monitors attached to Nina, taking comfort in the steady beep of her heart. He brushed his hand softly across hers while her mother chattered continuously. Nina drifted in and out for nearly an hour before the doctor finally returned and gave the order for her to be moved to a room. The nurse told them to find the cafeteria and have a cup of coffee for an hour while they got her settled.

Chris was still there when they returned to the waiting room. She volunteered to take the Bradens home so they could get some sleep before returning in the morning. Seamus assured them he would stay, since the nurse had promised one of them could sleep in the recliner in Nina's room. Once they'd left, he realized he was hungry and set out to find the cafeteria to see if it was still open. He was in luck and managed to get a halfway decent cheeseburger and a large Coke. The sugar and food went a long way toward reviving him. He called Hugh to make sure the girls were asleep and told his brother to call him the minute they woke up the next morning so he could reassure them that Nina was going to be all right. He finished his meal and tried to find his way to the section of the hospital where Nina had been moved. He'd never been inside the sprawling University of New Mexico Medical Center before, but it was a level one trauma hospital, and the logical place for the ambulance to take a victim who'd been stabbed, especially since it was right across the street from the university where Nina worked. He finally found her new room and entered to see the nurse from the surgical ward adjusting an oxygen tube under Nina's nose.

"It looks like your boyfriend found your new room, Nina."

Nina opened her good eye and smiled slightly, obviously much more awake than she had been in the recovery room. "Hi."

He made his way to her bedside and leaned down to kiss her forehead. "Hi yourself."

The nurse finished setting her up as another one entered. The two conferred briefly, then the first nurse bid Nina goodbye and left.

"My name is Alicia and I'll be taking care of you tonight." The new nurse bustled around the bed, checking the various machines and tubes as she spoke. "This is the call button, and I want you to press it if you need anything. You shouldn't be in any pain tonight because you're on some pretty hefty meds in your IV. We'll wean you off those tomorrow. Now, is this guy staying tonight or should I get rid of him?" She nodded toward Seamus, and he detected a steely determination underneath the apparent good humor.

"I'm staying." He met the nurse's gaze with his own rock-solid stubbornness.

"Where are the girls?" Nina asked.

He brushed her hair away from her forehead. "Chris and Hugh are with them. They're fine."

She nodded slightly and looked at Alicia. "He's staying."

"All right. That chair is a recliner, and I'll send a blanket in a bit. Get some rest, Nina. I'll be waking you up all through the night to check your vitals and such." She made a few notes on the white board hanging on the wall opposite Nina's bed and left.

"Seamus, what happened?"

He pulled the chair next to the bed and took her hand gently so as not to disturb the pulse oximeter on her finger. "Do you remember anything?"

She closed her eyes and frowned. "Yes. I remember being attacked as I walked to my car. Some guy grabbed me from behind. I should have been paying attention, but I was checking my phone for messages. I fought him, but he punched me, and I guess I blacked out." A single tear leaked from her good eye. "Seamus, did he…did he—"

"No! No, hon." He leaned in and kissed her softly. "One of your co-workers heard you scream and called 9-1-1. They chased the guy off. But he stabbed you, Nina. The doctors had to repair some internal damage and they had to take your spleen. But you're going to be fine."

She turned her head away. "I'm so tired."

"Okay." He kissed her forehead again. "Sleep, sweetheart. I'll be here when you wake up." He tucked her blankets carefully under her chin, then texted Hugh to see if the girls were still asleep. They were, so he reminded him to text as soon as they were awake in the morning. He watched until she fell asleep, then took the thin blanket an orderly had delivered and tried to find a comfortable position in the recliner. He stared at the blinking lights on the heart monitor and wondered why so many bad things were happening to Nina. First, her brother was murdered. Then, someone broke into her house and trashed the place. Now, she'd been attacked in the parking lot at the university. It was a whole lot of shit to happen to one person in a short amount of time. Was karma capable of being such a bitch, or was there something else going on? He couldn't fathom what, but it felt off.

The nurse was as good as her word and returned every hour to check on Nina, change IV bags, and draw blood. Seamus woke for the first few, but finally fell into a deep enough sleep to not be bothered by it. He woke for good when the doctor arrived for his morning rounds. Nina's incision looked good, according to him, and he said he was taking her off the IV pain meds and wanted her up and walking in the next hour or so.

"That seems pretty harsh," Seamus muttered as the doctor left. Nina looked better this morning, but shouldn't she spend at least one day resting?

"Not at all. The sooner she gets out of this bed, the faster she'll recover. Don't baby her," she scolded.

"Yeah, don't baby me," Nina whispered, but smiled faintly as she said it.

"Fine. I'll try to resist. How are you feeling this morning?"

"Better." She met his eyes and he realized she was referring to her refusal to talk the night before more than anything else.

"Good." He leaned down to kiss her softly. His phone buzzed in his pocket and he smiled as he read the text. "You want to talk to Lily and Iris?"

***

296

Nina

"I know, baby. I miss you too. Let me talk to Lily again, please." Nina reached for her apple juice and sipped while she waited for Iris to hand the phone to her sister. She winced slightly as pain shot up her arm, but at least it was only a bad sprain. The doctor had removed the brace earlier that morning, and Nina was glad to have use of both arms.

"When are you coming home, Momma?" Lily's voice was more subdued than usual.

"The doctor said maybe tomorrow." She was determined to make it happen. She'd been stuck in this hospital bed for four days, and she needed to be home with her girls. They'd been staying with her parents for the past few days, and their pleas for her to come home had increased with each passing day. "Lily, sweetie, I need you to eat for Grandma."

"But I don't like what she makes. I like what Seamus makes. Can he come get us?"

Nina smiled in sympathy. Her mother was a wonderful cook but could never remember that Lily didn't like meat. "He's at work, Lil. He'll be home with us tomorrow, and I'm sure he'll insist on cooking." He had stayed with her the first two nights, cramming his long body into the poor excuse for a recliner, refusing to leave her alone while she was sedated and on heavy painkillers. She'd recovered quite fast, however, after they'd removed her catheter and insisted she begin walking. Once the doctor had lowered her levels of IV pain medication and her head was clearer, she realized she was going to be okay, and self-pity wouldn't serve any useful purpose. Yes, she'd been attacked and stabbed, and they hadn't found the bastard who did it, but she wasn't raped or disfigured, so she needed to pick herself up and move on. First, she had to get out of this damned hospital and home to her babies. On her third day in the hospital—yesterday—she'd stood up, pulled Seamus's face down to hers, and kissed him. Then she'd told him she was fine, and he needed to go to work. He'd stared at her hard for a moment, then smiled wryly and called his station. He was scheduled until the following morning and planned to come directly to the hospital and—hopefully—take her home. She forced her thoughts back to her daughter. "I need you and Iris to be patient for one more day. Please go easy on your grandparents."

"Okay." Lily sounded borderline sulky, but Nina let it pass. "I miss you, Momma."

"I miss you too, Lil. Put Grandma back on, please." She spent a few more minutes assuring her mother she was well on the road to recovery and would definitely be home the following day, then hung up and set the phone—a new one, since her attacker had stolen her purse—on the tray table and reached for her juice again. She'd been moved to a soft diet the day before and the nurse had told her she would be given regular food today, and if she handled it well, the doctor would be more likely to release her the following day. *I'll do whatever it takes to get out of here, so bring on the gross hospital food.*

"Knock, knock."

Nina glanced up to see Chris standing in the

doorway. "Hi. Come in. What brings you to my temporary neck of the woods?"

Chris waved a large brown envelope as she approached the bed. "I was in the neighborhood and thought I'd drop by with a few photos. Would you mind taking a look?"

"Sure. It's a photo lineup, right?"

Chris flashed her a half-smile and reached into the envelope. She arranged a half-dozen photographs on the bedside tray, then pushed it away. "This is indeed a photo lineup. Are you up for it?"

"Of course." Nina pushed herself up, hissing as her incision pulled. She waved her hand dismissively as Chris frowned. "I'm fine. Let's do this."

Chris nodded with approval. "Okay. I'd like to hear your statement again first, if you don't mind."

Nina smiled wryly. Chris had shown up bright and early the morning after the attack to question her, much to Seamus's chagrin and disapproval. Nina had shushed him and answered Chris's questions to the best of her ability, but she hadn't been able to remember or concentrate well. "I don't mind. I was on some pretty hefty painkillers a few days ago. My head's a bit clearer now; at least I think it is."

"Good." Chris pulled a chair next to the bed and reached for her cell phone. "Do you mind if I record this?" As Nina shook her head, Chris pressed the red record button and pulled a small notebook from her blazer pocket. "All right, Nina. I'd like to hear what happened on Friday afternoon as you left work."

"Yeah. I left the office around five o'clock. The girls had been sick all night, and Seamus stayed home with them. I should have stayed home too, but I've missed so much work since Neal died…well, I was worried about losing my job." She chuckled ruefully. "I guess it doesn't matter anymore, huh?" She ran her hands through her hair, wincing as she brushed the tender spot on her scalp. "Anyway, I was texting as I walked to my car—I know, I know." She rolled her eyes at Chris's frown.

"Well, I beg to differ, sweetie." Chris gestured to Nina's blanketed form in the hospital bed. "The evidence suggests you aren't aware of how dangerous it is to walk through a parking lot distracted. Clearly, a PhD doesn't necessarily equal common sense."

Nina shrugged. "Yeah, well, you know. Don't be mean. So, I was walking toward my car when someone grabbed me from behind."

"Can you describe the person who grabbed you?"

"I never saw his face; at least I don't think I did." She frowned and rubbed her forehead. "I can't remember. It all happened so fast, Chris."

"I know, hon. You're doing great. I know this is hard, but you may know more than you think you know. Now, how do you know it was a man?"

"I guess I don't."

"You said 'I never saw *his* face.' Why did you say 'his'?"

Nina shut her eyes and tried to remember. "Hands. I remember his hands. He grabbed my wrist and I dropped my phone. I saw his hand and it was a man's hand."

"What color was his skin? Were there any tattoos?"

"Brown skin, no tattoos; at least I didn't see any."

"What shade of brown? Light or dark?"

Nina rubbed her forehead. "Kind of dark, but not black. I thought Hispanic at the time."

"And what do you think now?" Chris looked up from her note pad.

Nina dropped her hand and sighed. "I still think he was Hispanic. I'm pretty sure I saw black hair. He punched me in the head right after he grabbed me, though, so I wasn't really paying attention to details. Sorry."

"It's okay, Nina. You're doing great. Do you need to take a break?"

Nina laughed mirthlessly. "Yeah, I do need a break. I need about a month off from all the shit in my life. Maybe two."

"Well, if I can figure out who did this to you, maybe you can get some peace of mind, at least. What happened after he punched you in the head?"

"He stabbed me. Wait." She held her hand up as a memory, distant and undefined, swam up from the depths of her injured brain.

Chris froze, pen immobile on the pad, as she stared at Nina.

"He said something before he stabbed me. I didn't remember it before."

"Okay." Chris drew the word out. "What did he say?"

"Someone wants you gone, bitch."

Chris wrote as she spoke. "That is definitely significant. How sure are you about this memory?"

"I don't know. It just came to me when I was talking. Do you think I'm wrong? That I made it up?"

"No." Chris glanced up and stopped writing. "But if you really heard him say that, this wasn't a random mugging."

"*Shit.*" Nina muttered the curse as she wiped away a tear. She sniffed and pulled herself higher in the bed.

"Agreed. So, what do you remember after he stabbed you?"

"Pain. Then someone yelled, and the guy ran away. Everything got really fuzzy after that. I remember paramedics."

"Okay. You're doing really well, Nina. Can you take a look at the photos now?" Chris was already pulling the tray table back to the bed.

"Yeah." Nina leaned forward and examined the six photographs. She looked at them one by one, passing her gaze over the unfamiliar faces until she came to the fifth picture. "I know him."

Chris picked up the photo and read the information on the back. "Okay. What about the others? Do any of them look familiar?"

"No." Nina glanced over them again, but focused on the photo that had grabbed her attention. "But this man…"

"Is he the one who attacked you?"

Nina rubbed her temples. "I don't know, Chris. He looks so familiar, though. I know I've seen him." She shut her eyes and forced her mind back to the horrific moment she was grabbed in the faculty parking lot behind her building. What did she remember about the man? Her heart rate accelerated as she relived the terror of being attacked. The man had stayed well behind her, but she'd seen black hair out of the corner of her eye. Had she glimpsed his face? She must have, because this photo was ringing such a strong bell in her memory. "God, I just don't know."

Chris wrote a few more notes on her pad, then slipped the photo in the envelope with the rest. "Okay. We've got something to go on. I want you to rest and try to forget about this for a while. When do you get out of here?"

"Tomorrow, hopefully."

"Good. I know you'll feel a lot better once you're back home with your girls. And Seamus. He's still staying with you, right?" Her question sounded anything but casual.

Nina nodded, deciding to ignore the implication; she simply couldn't handle it right now. "He's been so amazing through all of this. I finally had to insist he go in to work."

Chris smiled. "I think people tend to underestimate Seamus. You're good for him, Nina. You believe in him."

"I love him." She chuckled nervously and glanced at Chris. "I haven't exactly told him, though, so I'd appreciate you keeping it to yourself."

"Sure. Mum's the word." She shoved her hands in her jeans pockets. "Is there anything you need?

Do you have enough to read? It's got to be dull lying in bed all day."

"I've got several books and my new laptop, so I'm not bored. But…" She shook her head at the silliness of what she'd been about to ask. "Never mind."

"What? Come on, Nina. Spill."

"It's stupid. I just wondered if maybe you have a lip gloss or something I could borrow. Seamus is coming in the morning and I finally get to take a shower later today and—"

Chris smiled kindly as she held up her hand to stop the flood of words. "I get it. All I have is a Chapstick right now, but I'll send some makeup later today."

"Really? That would be great, actually." She laughed self-consciously. "I feel a bit ragged."

"Not a problem. Get some rest."

The shower later in the afternoon was wonderful, and Nina felt like a new person as she slipped into the clean hospital gown. The doctor had seen her earlier and ordered her IV removed. If the oral medication managed her pain for the rest of the day and overnight, she would likely be released the next afternoon. Nina didn't care how bad the pain was— she was determined to go home. She tried convincing him to let her go immediately, but he stood firm.

"Tomorrow is soon enough, young lady. We'll see how you do tonight before I sign your release." He smiled absently at her, then finished updating her chart.

She realized he might be right when taking a

shower completely exhausted her. A brief nap revived her, however, and she was working on her article for *True West* magazine when Izzy appeared in the doorway.

"Are you up for visitors?"

Nina smiled and closed her laptop. "Of course. Come in. Hi, Cara."

Cara slid around her sister and came forward to hug Nina. "Hi. Chris said you could use some makeup, so we brought a few essentials." She held up a large tote bag.

"That looks like way more than lip gloss." Nina raised her eyebrows at the bulging bag.

Izzy smiled and leaned down to kiss her cheek. "Yeah, well, once we got started we were having so much fun we couldn't stop. We brought pajamas, a robe, makeup, and some clothes to wear home tomorrow. Chris said yours were probably taken as evidence."

"I hadn't even thought of that. Thanks. I really appreciate this. I would love to look a little nicer when Seamus comes by. This black eye makes me feel hideous."

Cara leaned in for a closer look. "It's not too bad. Nothing a little concealer can't handle."

"At least the swelling has gone down. I couldn't even see out of it the first couple days." She fingered the silky short robe Izzy had lain across the bed. "Do you mind if I change out of this hospital gown?"

Cara grinned and reached into the bag again. "I thought you might appreciate these." She held up a pair of lacy bikini briefs with a small, pink tag dangling from the edge.

"Oh, my God, yes! I've been going commando for days and it's driving me crazy. I swear I'll pay you back as soon as I get out of here."

Cara laughed as she scooped up the robe and pajamas from the bed. "I had a feeling. I'll follow you to the bathroom."

Nina threw the covers back and dangled her feet over the side of the bed as the nurse had told her; she certainly didn't want to pass out and risk further injury. She held her hand to her incision as she stood, sucking her breath in at the pain the movement caused.

"Are you okay?" Izzy was beside her, concern written across her features.

"I'm fine. It just smarts when I move." She made her way to the bathroom and changed into the soft fleece pants and warm pullover, then slipped the silky robe over it all. The thoughtfulness of the women—including Chris, who'd organized it— touched her deeply.

"It looks like it all fits fairly well," Cara said as Nina made her way to a chair in the room. "We raided Izzy's closet because she's the smallest. Or at least she used to be." Cara gestured toward Izzy's burgeoning belly.

Izzy smiled and touched her stomach in the way pregnant women often did.

Nina watched her and wondered what it would be like to carry a child. She'd never had the least desire to be pregnant, but watching Izzy rub her belly absently caused something new to flare to life deep inside Nina.

"We also brought some fuzzy socks and slippers." Cara reached into the bag yet again. "I know how cold it gets in hospitals." She handed them to Nina. "You ready for your makeover?"

"Bring it on. I'm feeling so wonderful right now I don't see how it could get much better."

Cara pulled the tray table over and began setting out various tubes, pots, and brushes. Within twenty minutes, the yellowish-purple skin around Nina's eye had been covered and her lips glistened a soft pink. While Cara had made up her face, Izzy brushed her hair and clipped it on top of her head with a barrette. She'd thought the shower was nice, but real pajamas and a little makeup made her feel like a million bucks. She enjoyed the conversation with Izzy and Cara as well, and looked forward to getting to know them better over the next few months. Nina yawned. It had been a busy day and she had no energy reserves; by the time the orderly appeared with her dinner, she was exhausted and wanted nothing more than to return to bed and sleep, but hated to make Izzy and Cara feel unwelcome.

"Well, we need to get going." Cara finished clearing the makeup items to make room for the meal tray. "Let us know if you need anything else, okay?"

"I will. Thanks so much. I can't tell you how much I appreciate it." Nina stifled another yawn.

"Let me help you back to bed." Izzy held out her hand and helped Nina to her feet. "It's amazing how tired just sitting in a chair can make you after surgery, huh?"

"Yeah. I had no idea." Nina sank gratefully into the bed as Cara slid the tray table closer.

"Eat. I know you'd rather just go to sleep, but you need to build your strength back."

"Are all you DeLucas so bossy?" She ended on another yawn.

"Yes, and stubborn to boot." Izzy flashed her a crooked smile as she took the plastic lids off the various bowls and cups on the food tray. "This looks terrible. Hurry up and get out of here so you don't starve to death."

Once they left, Nina attempted to eat all her dinner, but only made it halfway through her salad and beef stew before her eyes wouldn't stay open any longer.

Chapter Seventeen

Seamus

"Godammit!" Seamus ran his hands through his hair, then when that didn't alleviate his frustrations, he punched the door of his locker. "What the fuck is going on?"

Finn stood, hands in pockets, and watched his brother. He'd stopped by the fire station to tell Seamus about Nina remembering what her attacker had said the day before. Chris had called and asked him to deliver the news on his way to work while she went straight to the precinct to find more information on the suspect Nina had identified from the photo lineup. "I don't know, but I swear Chris and I will find out."

Seamus glanced at his watch, wincing at the pain the movement caused. *I sure hope I didn't break anything.* "I have another hour before my shift is over. Is she safe at the hospital?"

"Yes. We have a uniform outside her room. But there's no budget for a protective detail once she's released. She had an alarm system installed at her house, right?"

He stared at Finn, his jaw tight. "Yeah, she did. But what good is that going to do if the asshole who stabbed her shows up at her work again?"

"Listen, I know it sucks, but it's the best we can do right now. New Mexico is basically broke, you know. I haven't had even a cost of living raise in over three years."

"*Fuck.* Yeah, I know. Me neither. God, Finn! What am I going to do? How can I keep her safe?"

Finn clapped his brother on the shoulder. "Trust me; I know what you're going through. I'll do my best to figure out who's doing this."

Seamus wanted to shrug his hand off but knew that would be churlish. Finn did know what he was going through. His wife, Melanie, had been stalked and nearly killed by a crazy woman who'd become obsessed with Finn. "Yeah, okay. This is too much, you know? First Neal and now all this?" He narrowed his eyes at the sudden change he'd seen come over Finn's features. "Wait. You think this is connected, don't you?"

Finn shrugged. "It may be. We're not ruling it out."

"What about the break-in at her house? Is that connected also?"

"Possibly."

"Well, shit." He rubbed his sore knuckles absently. "You need to solve this, Finn. Fast. And I need to keep her safe."

"We will."

***

He gripped the flowers tightly as he showed his identification to the state police officer seated beside Nina's door. He heard voices as he pushed the door open and realized she already had company. The bed was empty; Nina and an unfamiliar man sat together in the two chairs near the window, chatting. Seamus narrowed his eyes. *Who the hell is this?*

"Seamus!" Nina interrupted the man and smiled radiantly.

That's better. "Hey, hon." He crossed the room in two quick strides and bent to kiss her. "You look beautiful today." She was wearing real pajamas and looked like she'd put lipstick on or something. Her black eye looked much better too. She glanced back at the stranger, and Seamus noticed the tightness around her mouth, which he knew indicated irritation.

"Thanks. Are those for me?" She gestured to the flowers.

"Oh, yeah. Here." He placed the bouquet in her lap and raised his eyebrows at the man seated next to her.

The man took the hint and stood, hand extended. "Hello. I'm David Schaeler."

Ah. The ex-husband. At last. No wonder Nina looks annoyed. He shook the proffered hand—perhaps a bit firmer than his usual handshake—and managed a tepid smile. "Seamus DeLuca." The guy was thin, with greying hair and glasses, and Seamus wanted to punch him in the face for bothering Nina

311

at the hospital.

"Hmm. I assume you and Nina are dating?" Schaeler glanced between Seamus and his ex-wife.

"We are." Seamus wasn't about to hide their relationship from anyone, especially the man who'd thrown away his wife and family.

The two men stared at each other for a long moment, each clearly assessing the other.

"It was nice of you to stop by." Seamus crossed his arms and rocked back on his heels, eager to get rid of him.

David raised his eyebrows, acknowledging the dismissal. "DeLuca? Any relation to the state police detective who stopped by to grill me at my office earlier this morning?"

"My brother."

"Well, isn't that cozy? Seems a bit, I don't know, *conflict of interest,* if you ask me."

"Nobody did."

"All right, boys! Let's dial it down, okay?" Nina stood quickly, hissing in pain, and stepped between them.

Seamus felt like a total shit for causing her discomfort. "Sorry, Nina." He took her hand and led her toward the bed. "I'll behave."

"Yeah, me too. Sorry. I need to be going anyway. I hope you'll tell the police I had nothing to do with any of this." David addressed his words to Nina as she pulled the blankets over her legs.

"I already did. Take care, David."

Seamus waited until the other man had left. "Well, he seems great."

Nina speared him with a look that made him feel

about five years old as she threw the covers off again. "I'm sick of being in bed. I only got in to get him to leave." She sat in the chair she'd vacated and flashed Seamus a crooked smile. "I was young and stupid. What can I say?"

He knelt in front of her and took her hand, raising it to his mouth. "I didn't mean to be such an ass. My track record certainly isn't a shining example of functional relationships, either."

She smiled and pulled him closer for a kiss. "Here's to new beginnings, then." She pulled back and cupped her hand on his cheek, still scruffy from several days' growth of beard. "Did you see the girls this morning?"

He kissed her hand again, then took the seat next to her. "Yeah. I stopped by your folks' house and took them to school. Your mom will pick them up and drop them by the house this afternoon— assuming they let you out of here."

"I hope so. The doctor hasn't been here yet."

He watched her carefully, noting the frown between her eyes. "You okay?"

She shrugged. "Besides the fact that I'm recovering from a stab wound? Yeah, I'm fine. It's just that David didn't even ask about the girls. He heard from Finn about the attack and rushed over here. I thought it was because he was concerned, but it was mostly to make sure I knew he wasn't involved." She shook her head and chuckled ruefully. "God, what did I ever see in him?"

He had no idea, but thought it would be wiser to let her speak without his input.

"I didn't know he was married when we first

started dating—I really didn't." She put her head into her hands. "But I figured it out pretty fast. I should have called it off—I know that now. I have no excuse."

"Hey." He reached for her hand and squeezed gently.

"You know, I think the reason I let him push me into adopting Lily and Iris was because I felt some sort of misplaced guilt over breaking up his marriage. Oh, God!" She jerked upright and stared at him in horror. "Please don't think I don't want them! I do! I love them! I just—"

"Hey," he said again, and moved to kneel in front of her. "I don't think that, Nina. I know how much you love them. Sweetheart, you can tell me anything, you know. It's not my job to judge you. It's my job to l—" He stood suddenly and rubbed the back of his neck, appalled at what he'd been about to say. He wasn't supposed to blurt out something so important like this, in a hospital room, with Nina in her pajamas recovering from being attacked. He was supposed to wait until they were on a date, with candles and flowers and romance. *Aw, screw it.* He turned and knelt in front of her again. "It's my job to love you, Nina." He smiled crookedly. "It's my self-appointed job. And maybe it's too soon, but I can't help it. The timing sucks, I know, but there it is. And I know your brother died, and someone is trying to kill you now, and I just broke up with my girlfriend and—"

"You're not really selling it, you know." She rubbed her thumb over his lips, halting the overflow of words, and tried to lean forward, but she'd

314

forgotten about her incision. "Ow. You mind coming up here?"

"Sorry." He stood and held his hand out to help her up.

She smiled up at him and looped her arms around his neck. "Stop apologizing and kiss me." She pulled his head down and raised her lips to his.

He tried to remember she'd been injured and was still delicate, but her mouth was intoxicating, and it had been days since he'd done more than brush her lips. He angled his head and slid his tongue into her softness, groaning in appreciation as she answered in kind.

"That's better." She spoke the words against his lips. "I happen to love you too, Seamus. Let's focus on that and not worry about the timing, okay?"

"Okay." He slid his arm around her waist, careful to avoid the area of her bandage.

"Well, I don't usually see this sort of thing when I stop by to check on my surgical patients. You must be feeling better, Ms. Braden."

Nina, to her credit, didn't jump away guiltily, and held on to Seamus so he couldn't either. "Hello, Dr. Knight. Yes, I am feeling much better. I'm ready to go home."

The doctor smiled and walked to the computer screen in the corner to check Nina's chart. "We'll see. Why don't you have a seat on the bed so I can take a look at your incision? Do you want your..." he gestured to Seamus, "*friend* to leave while I examine you?"

Seamus bristled and was about to speak, but Nina beat him to it.

"He can stay." She winked at him and gestured for him to sit. "He's my boyfriend and he's going to be taking care of me at home, so he should probably hear what you have to say."

"Good enough," the doctor said absently as he continued to type into the computer.

Seamus met Nina's amused glance as the doctor finished inputting information into Nina's chart.

"All right." The doctor turned on his stool. "Your blood work looks good, Ms. Braden. How's the pain from your incision?"

"Fine." She nodded brightly.

She's unbelievable. Seamus coughed into his fist as he stared at her.

She flashed him an evil frown, then rolled her eyes. "Actually, it's still pretty painful."

It was the doctor's turn to nod. "That's reasonable. I would be surprised if it didn't hurt at this point. You were stabbed, after all."

"Oh." She deflated visibly. "So, what does that mean? When can I go home?"

Now the older man smiled and stood to approach the bed. "Let's take a look at your incision." He waited while Nina pulled up her pajama top and rolled slightly to give him access to her wound. He gently removed the bandage and prodded the tender skin around the incision, causing Nina to hiss. He straightened and returned to the computer. "It's healing well. As long as you promise to follow my guidelines, I'll release you this afternoon. I know you'll miss these luxury accommodations, of course, but we have a waiting list."

Nina smiled. "I'll bet. Yes, I promise to follow

all your guidelines. I'm dying to get home to my daughters."

"Well, my first order is to have some help. You need lots of rest." He turned to look at Seamus. "You'll be staying with her?"

"Yeah. I'll make sure she gets plenty of rest."

"I don't want her cooking or cleaning or taking care of kids for at least two weeks."

"Of course not. I'll make sure she doesn't."

The doctor stood. "All right. I'll get your release papers started. You should be out of here soon after lunch. I'll see you in my office in ten days, Ms. Braden." He shook her hand, then turned to Seamus. "No sex until then."

"Got it." He nodded and shook the physician's outstretched hand. "Thank you for taking care of her, Dr. Knight. I'll make sure she takes it easy."

***

"What did the doctor say? You're supposed to be resting." He reached past her to take the pillowcase from her hand. "Good God, woman! I let you out of my sight for two minutes and you sneak off to strip your bed! Changing the sheets falls under the category of 'cleaning.' Let me do that. Sit!" He pointed to the pink velvet chair in the corner of her bedroom.

"Sorry. I didn't want to bother you and they smelled musty." She eased into the chair with a sigh of relief. "I figured I'd change them quickly before I took a nap. I never realized how much energy it takes."

He took over the chore, realizing that keeping her quiet and still for several days would be challenging. He tucked in a corner and turned to look at her, expecting a drawn, pale face. Instead, she glanced away quickly, a slight blush highlighting her cheeks. "Were you just checking out my ass?"

She turned back, her eyes now alight with humor. "Maybe I was. What are you going to do about it?"

He chuckled and finished making the bed. "Not a thing. It's a free country and I've checked yours out often enough." He held out his hand to help her up. "You want under the covers?"

She shook her head. "I'd rather lie on top with a blanket." She carefully lowered herself to the bed. "Will you stay with me for a few minutes? Please?"

He smiled and toed his shoes off. "Of course." He lifted the blanket he'd arranged over her and slid beneath, spooning against her slight figure. "Nina, love, how are you doing? I feel like we've barely had a chance to talk since this all happened."

She brought one of his hands up to her mouth and kissed the back of his fingers before tucking it under her chin. "I've been better. But knowing you love me is pretty amazing. I wish I could have skipped the whole being stabbed part, though. I'm so tired of being scared. What am I supposed to do with this new information that someone is trying to kill me? Should I hire a bodyguard? Never leave my house? What do I do, Seamus?"

"I don't know, love. How about for now you just sleep?"

She nodded again. "Will you stay here? Just until I fall asleep?"

"Of course."

***

Nina

"I don't understand. She already came in?" Nina doodled furiously on the notepad as she waited for the insurance agent to answer.

"Yes. Ms. Karlsson came in during the regularly scheduled appointment and took care of her part of the life insurance settlement."

Nina wondered if the judgment she heard in his voice was simply her imagination. "I'm sorry I missed our appointment; as I said, I've been in the hospital. I'm surprised Kira already went in, though. She hasn't mentioned it." She'd seen Kira several times during her hospital stay since she worked in the same hospital, although on a different floor, and had stopped by to visit a few times after her shift.

"When would you like to reschedule, Ms. Braden?"

Nina pulled her planner closer and flipped through the pages. "Do you have anything Monday afternoon?" It would be her first day back at work, but only a half-day.

"Two o'clock?"

She wrote the appointment down, then hung up and frowned as she pondered the information she'd received. *What is going on with Kira? Why didn't she wait for me, or at least tell me she already*

319

went? What was it Seamus said? He asked how well I really know her. I guess I don't know her well at all. She tried not to be pissed, but it was difficult. *She's in such an all-fired hurry to get her hands on Neal's life insurance money that she can't even wait until I get out of the hospital so we can go together? Whatever.* But what if it was more than that? Or rather, what if the life insurance money was more important to Kira than she'd admitted? Was it possible she'd known about the insurance policy all along and had killed Neal to get her hands on the money? *Don't be ridiculous! I couldn't possibly know someone who is a murderer. Chris and Finn must have it wrong. They must have missed something, and Neal was killed by some random person I've never met. It couldn't possibly be Kira. Could it?*

She slapped the pen down on the notepad and pushed her chair away from the kitchen table, needing to do something to get her mind off these insane theories her brain insisted on making up. Her hand went automatically to her side, although the pain from her surgery was almost completely gone. Seamus was sleeping. He'd come home straight from his shift and looked exhausted. He'd explained they'd had two nights in a row of multiple calls and little time for sleep. She'd kissed him and sent him straight to bed. It was nearly one o'clock now and she was hungry, so she scrounged around the kitchen and found the makings for grilled cheese sandwiches and tomato soup and set to work quietly. If Seamus woke, he'd insist on taking over, and she was sick to death of him waiting on her.

She'd been to the doctor the day before for her two-week check-up, and he'd cleared her to slowly resume normal activities, with the exception of driving, which would have to wait another couple weeks. She was more than ready to get on with her life and had made arrangements for her mother to keep the girls overnight, so she and Seamus could finally spend some time alone. They'd been sleeping together for weeks, but they'd never made love, and tonight was the night. *I will literally murder anyone who gets in our way tonight!* She cringed at the unthinking word choice. *I don't think I'll ever use that phrase quite so casually again.*

The soup was simmering, and the sandwiches were ready for the pan when the doorbell rang. She hurried to answer, irritated at the interruption.

"Hey, you're looking great." Gordy reached for the handle of the screen door as he spoke.

Nina sighed and told him to wait while she grabbed the key to unlock it. Seamus regularly lectured her about keeping it locked at all times when she was home. There had been no sign of a threat since she'd been released from the hospital, but he wasn't willing to take chances. "Come in, Gordy. I'm in the middle of fixing lunch." She locked the door behind him and led the way to the kitchen. She didn't bother telling him to be quiet, because she knew Seamus would never have slept through the doorbell.

"I won't stay long. I just wanted to stop by and see how you're doing. Here." He handed her a small, beautifully wrapped gift.

Every time I try to be annoyed with him, he does

something nice. Crap. He'd brought her flowers and a stuffed bear while she was in the hospital. "Gordy, you already brought me a present."

He smiled and pressed the box into her hands. "I know, but I wanted to bring you another one. It's just a little something to cheer you up during your recuperation. Open it."

"Fine." She rolled her eyes at his extravagance and slipped her finger under the seam of the paper. Inside was a small box of beautifully decorated chocolates from a local candy maker Nina had heard was quite expensive. "Thanks. They're too beautiful to eat."

He chuckled. "Nah, I figured you'd appreciate something delicious and decadent after all that hospital food." He turned at the cough behind them. "Oh, hey, DeLuca. I didn't know you'd be here."

Seamus entered the room, pulling his t-shirt over his head as he walked. Nina appreciated the glimpse of his muscular chest and abs and felt sure he'd waited to put his shirt on just to annoy Gordy. "Oh, I'm always here when I'm not at work. What brings you by?"

"I wanted to check on Nina and bring her a gift." His face had taken on a sour expression as Seamus helped himself to a bottle of water from the refrigerator and examined the chocolates Nina had placed on the granite bar separating the family room from the kitchen.

"Huh."

Nina bit the inside of her lip to keep from laughing at the two men. It was clear Seamus was jealous, but she had no idea what Gordy might be feeling. *Who would have dreamed that someone like Seamus DeLuca could ever be jealous about me?*

"Well, I can see you're busy." He glanced at the stove, then back at Seamus. "It's great Nina cooks for you, especially considering how recently she was in the hospital." He walked around the bar to hug Nina.

She watched Seamus's face suffuse with color at the taunt, and narrowed her eyes at him over Gordy's shoulder while mouthing the word *"don't."* She pulled back and smiled at Gordy. "Thanks for stopping by." She needed to get rid of him before the men came to blows.

"Of course. Please give me a call if you need anything. I'll stop by again soon."

She walked him to the door and wondered if he heard Seamus's whispered *"asshole"* as they passed. Probably.

When she returned to the kitchen, she found Seamus standing at the stove, spatula in hand and sandwiches in the frying pan. "Give me that." She pulled it from his hand and pointed to the chair he'd occupied before she left the room. "You're letting him get to you. I'm fine and I want to fix lunch myself. I'm pretty damn sick and tired of you waiting on me. I love you, but I'm done feeling helpless."

Seamus slipped his arms around her waist, resting his head atop hers as she attended to the sandwiches. "So feisty. All right, but please take it easy. I know you're feeling better, but I don't want you to push it. Promise?"

She smiled as she turned down the heat under the

pan. "I promise." She turned and twined her arms around his neck. "I saw my doctor yesterday and he gave me the go-ahead to resume normal activities. I'll start back to work on Monday—half days for a week or so—and no driving for another couple weeks. But otherwise, I'm good to go." She pulled his head down and lifted her lips to his, hoping he would understand her unspoken message.

He grinned against her mouth. "Well, that is excellent news, Ms. Braden. Good to go, huh?" He kissed her lazily as his hand slipped under the hem of her t-shirt and caressed the warm skin of her back.

Her pulse accelerated, as it always did when he touched her. She was tempted to suggest they forget lunch and drag him to the bedroom, but her mom was due to drop the girls off in a few hours and she wanted a full night with Seamus the first time they made love. She reluctantly pulled away from his addictive mouth and turned back to the sandwiches. "Yes, good to go. But the girls are due home soon."

He pushed her hair to the side and kissed her neck. "I wasn't hinting. Honest."

She set the spatula carefully on the granite countertop next to the burner and turned to stare up at him. "I was. I've arranged for my parents to keep the girls tonight, but I want to see them after school for a little while. I've made reservations for dinner, and then we have the rest of the night to ourselves. Is that all right with you?" She arched her eyebrows, pinning him with her gaze.

His eyes grew large and she heard him swallow. "Nina, love, of course I want that, but I want to

324

make sure you're fully healed first."

She'd been worried he wasn't interested for some reason, but could see from his expression he was simply concerned for her health. "I'm fine. Tonight, Seamus." She turned back to the stove and flipped the sandwiches.

***

"What time is our reservation?" Seamus reached across the console to lightly cover her hand.

"I made it for seven."

"It's only six fifteen now, so do you mind if we swing by my place, so I can pick up a few things?" They had spent a few hours with the girls, playing board games and helping them pack their overnight bags, before dropping them off with their grandparents for the night.

She turned her head to smile at him. "Of course not." She squeezed his hand and hoped they could move past the awkwardness that had surrounded them ever since she'd announced so boldly that *tonight was the night. What was I thinking?* Now both of them were nervous and jumpy and she regretted her statement. *I should have let it happen naturally. Stewing about it for hours was no fun. Now I just want to get it over with, so we can get back to normal.*

He exited the freeway, and a few minutes later pulled into the driveway of the small adobe house. "Casa DeLuca revisited." He killed the engine and hopped out to meet her at the front of the SUV. He took her hand and led her up the walkway to the small porch. "You can have the nickel tour tonight if you want."

"I do. I wasn't paying much attention during my previous visits." She followed him inside and paused to look around the living room, noting the polished hardwood floors and thick adobe walls. "It's charming. Do you know when it was built?" They'd passed a sign on the corner of his street that claimed this was the Historic Silver Hill Neighborhood, but she didn't know anything about it.

"Uh, no clue. It's old, though. The heat and plumbing suck, but my landlord is great." He shoved his hands in his jeans pockets and stared at the floor. "You want anything? A beer? A soda? You know, while I pack up some clothes?"

She bit her lip and shook her head. This was ridiculous. They were acting like a couple of inexperienced teenagers. It was time to take matters into her own hands and put them both out of their misery. "No thanks. Can I use your bathroom?"

"Of course." He led her down the narrow hall, past a surprisingly spacious kitchen. "I'll be in my bedroom. Take your time." He winced at what his words could imply and turned to his room, shaking his head.

She rolled her eyes at his retreating figure and stepped into the bathroom, closing the door firmly. *What now? How do I move us past this awkwardness?* She glanced around the room, noting the gleaming black and white tile. The whole duplex was adorable, and she appreciated how clean Seamus kept it, if a bit dreary and underdone in the decor department. She spied one of his fire department t-shirts slung over a towel bar and reached for it. It smelled like him, a mixture of spicy cologne and the scent that was all his own. She brought it to her nose and inhaled deeply. Then, without pausing to consider the wisdom of her sudden inspiration, she set it on the sink counter and reached for the hem of her own blouse.

Chapter Eighteen

Seamus

He stuffed a stack of clean boxer shorts on top of the t-shirts and zipped the duffle bag. Nina was still in the bathroom. *What could be keeping her?* A cold finger of fear prickled down his spine as he considered all the horrible things that could happen to her: she might have gotten dizzy and passed out, hitting her head on the sink and was now lying unconscious in a pool of...*get a fucking grip! She's fine and definitely wouldn't be amused by your mother-hen hovering.* He chuckled and ran his hands through his hair. *When did I become such an old woman?* "Nina?" He grabbed the duffle bag. "We should probably get going or we're going to miss our—" He turned around and froze.

"Reservation?" She raised one eyebrow. "Yeah, no doubt."

Holy. Shit. She leaned against the door frame of his bedroom, clad only in one of his fire department t-shirts, one shoulder bared due to the stretched-out neckline, the hem falling to her mid-thigh. He swallowed audibly, though his throat was suddenly bone dry.

She pushed away from the door and crossed the room, stopping directly in front of him. "I hope it's okay that I borrowed your shirt."

He opened his mouth to answer, but all he could manage was a dry rasp. He settled for a nod.

She smiled crookedly and stepped closer to loop her arms around his neck. "Let's not waste time on dinner. We have one night to ourselves, Seamus. I don't want to wait any longer."

How could she be so calm? His own heart was threatening to beat out of his chest as he reached a shaking hand to cup her cheek. "Nina, are you sure? I don't want to rush you into anything you're not ready for."

She covered his hand with hers. "You're not. I'm more than ready for this." She stood on tip-toe and pressed her lips against his softly. "It's finally our time, Seamus. I don't want to wait another minute."

Since he couldn't manage to form actual words, he opted for pulling her against him and kissing her deeply. Then he scooped her slight form into his arms and laid her gently on his bed. He stared down at her beautiful face and wondered what he'd done to deserve her. He had no answer, so he simply pulled his shirt over his head and joined her. He skimmed the t-shirt up to bare her stomach and let his hands caress her softness, his thumb brushing across the small scar left from her recent ordeal. He would give a lot for five minutes alone with the asshole who caused it. "Nina, are you sure you're up for this? Is it too soon?"

"I'm positive. Unless you don't want—"

He didn't let her finish her ridiculous statement; he pulled her atop him, curving his hand around her shapely bottom, pressing her against his rampant arousal. "I want." He pulled the shirt over her head and feasted his eyes on her bared breasts. "God, you're so beautiful."

It appeared her bravado had run out though; she couldn't seem to meet his eyes and her hands moved to cover her nakedness.

He smiled and caught her wrists, bringing them to his mouth. "Don't, love." But he pulled her down to lay against him, understanding her shyness. He knew he needed to be extra gentle this first time, but it would be a challenge. He also desperately needed to find a way to slow this down or it would be over far too soon. He moved her so they were lying side-by-side and let his hand slowly slide up her thigh, pausing at the edge of her panties. "Black lace?"

"Yeah. Do you have a problem with that?"

He grinned leaned in to kiss her. "Not at all. In fact, I think I've found a new favorite thing."

She laughed softly, causing his heart to soar. He was enchanted by her anew: her bravery inciting this encounter, her obvious enjoyment of him, her sheer joy, so evident on her beautiful face.

He slipped his fingers under the edge of the lace and she stopped laughing to suck in her breath. "Oh, Seamus," she said on an exhale.

He grinned lazily, feeling much more in control now. He hooked the edge of the scrap of lace and tugged. "I need you naked. Now."

He lost track of time as he explored her curves, learning what pleasured her most. It could have been minutes or hours later when he watched her come apart as he stroked her flesh, her face so exquisite in passion it took his breath away.

She regained her breath and reached for the button on his jeans. "My turn." With his help, she wrestled his jeans off and set about exploring, her slim fingers an exquisite torture on his distended flesh.

"Enough." He covered her hand and brought it to his mouth. "I need to be inside you." He spared a moment to reach into his nightstand drawer for a condom and tore the wrapper open with his teeth. He rolled it on with shaking hands and covered her body, positioning himself between her thighs. He paused and stared into her flushed face, recognizing the magnitude of this moment, this consummation of everything between them. "I love you, Nina."

She smiled up at him. "I love you too, Seamus."

He pushed forward, sliding into her gently, but firmly. He closed his eyes and willed his body to slow down. He wanted to pound into her until they exploded in ecstasy, but he knew that would have to wait until she was stronger. He settled for a steady rhythm, gritting his teeth as he strove for control. Her sighs and muted groans threatened to break it, and when he felt her tighten around his length, he lost the tenuous tether on sanity and thrust hard three, four times before he exploded, groaning her name and barely managing to catch himself before he collapsed on top of her. Instead, he lowered his weight slowly, pulling her with him to snuggle against his side, regrettably disengaging from her body. He took a moment to get his breath back, then kissed the top of her head. "Are you okay?"

She feathered her fingers lightly through his chest hair. "Better than okay. I'm feeling pretty damned good right now."

He laughed softly. "That was my goal. I hope I wasn't too rough. I was trying to be careful."

She levered herself to lay atop him. "I can hardly wait to see what it's like when you're not careful." She kissed him briefly. "I can take it, you know. I'm fine."

He framed her face with his rough palms. "We'll see. You have a tendency to push yourself, love."

She grinned and leaned in for another, deeper kiss. "Maybe, but it sure is fun right now." She wriggled against him.

He laughed with her as he shifted her to the bed. "I'll be right back." He retreated to the bathroom to clean up, then returned to the gorgeous woman in his bed. He stood, gazing down on her, and felt a renewed stirring of desire. *I'll never get enough of her.*

She reached her hand toward him. "Come here. I'm not nearly finished with you for the night."

He grinned and gladly joined her again, pulling her slim, smooth body to him. "Good, 'cuz I'm not even close to being done with you, Professor. I'm just getting started." He kissed her, letting his tongue tangle with hers for several long moments before sliding his mouth away and continue on an in-depth exploration of her flesh. "I didn't get to taste you before." He pulled a rosy nipple into his mouth and laved it with his tongue, then switched to the other. He spent several long moments worshipping her delicate breasts before kissing and licking his way down her smooth stomach, intent on his final goal. He gently slid her legs apart and settled between them, determined to bring her to pleasure again, this time with his mouth.

"Oh, God, Seamus!"

He paused to grin again, then set to work. She was incredibly responsive, and the taste of her exploding in passion was the best thing he'd ever experienced. He groaned and wrenched himself away to reach for another condom. He rolled over and pulled her to sit on top. "You set the pace, love."

She leaned forward to kiss him. "Don't hold back this time," she ordered.

He didn't; they were both soon groaning and straining toward completion. Nina came again before he let himself explode, flipping her over at the last moment so he could thrust more deeply. This time, he couldn't stop himself from collapsing on her body as he finished. "Sorry," he grunted. "Am I crushing you?"

"I love it. Stay right here." She smoothed her hands down his sweaty back to cup his buttocks and push him more firmly inside her. "Why did we wait so long to do this?"

"No clue." He eventually wrenched himself away so he could clean up, then returned to bed and pulled her close. They slept for an hour, then woke and decided to order a pizza. She donned his t-shirt again while they ate, and he found the sight of her sitting cross-legged on his bed, her hair still mussed from their love-making, incredibly erotic.

"What?" she asked as she reached for another slice. "Am I disgusting you with my ferocious appetite?"

He chuckled. "Nope. Not even close. I'm actually just trying to catch a glimpse of what that shirt is hiding."

She took a bite, then hitched the hem higher, exposing a hint of the soft down between her legs. She arched an eyebrow in challenge.

He fell back against the pillows and covered his eyes with his arm. "You're killing me."

She laughed. "Well, we can't have that. Sit up and eat. I'll behave." She waited until he'd sat up and took another bite. "For now."

He smiled in appreciation, then winced as he remembered something. "I forgot to tell you my good news." At her questioning look, he continued. "I got accepted to the arson academy."

"What?" She threw a crumpled napkin at him. "That's amazing! I can't believe you waited this long to tell me!"

"Sorry. I was exhausted when I got off my shift and totally forgot. And I've been a bit distracted since I woke up."

"Hmm. Well, I will make you pay for it later. When do you start?"

"In about a month." He grew serious and reached for her hand. "This means my hours will be a lot more normal from now on. I'll be able to be there for you and the girls every night."

She smiled and set her half-eaten pizza slice

back in the box. She pushed it aside and crawled across the bed to straddle him. "That's one of the many reasons I love you so much, Seamus. You take something you worked so hard for and turn it into a new way to care for us. You're an amazing man, Mr. DeLuca."

He tossed his slice into the box and slipped his arms around her. "Not really, but I do happen to love you a bunch. I love the girls too."

"I'm not really hungry anymore; at least not for pizza." She pushed him back against the pillows and began to kiss her way down his chest. "It's my turn to taste."

***

The pounding on his front door woke them early the next morning, startling him into a sitting position. "Stay here." He pulled on his jeans. "I'll see who it is." His heart beat faster than normal and he tried to tell himself it was impossible whoever was after Nina had tracked her down at his place, but he grabbed the baseball bat out of his hall closet anyway. He peered through the peep hole and grimaced as he saw Finn and Chris standing on his door step. He wrenched the door open. "Jesus, Finn. This better be important. How'd you know we were here?" He stood aside and ushered them inside.

"Because we're detectives, bro. It is important. Can you ask Nina to join us?"

"I'm here." She'd dressed in her clothes from the evening before and pulled her long hair into a messy ponytail. She handed Seamus a t-shirt—a clean one, not the one she'd so memorably worn the night before.

"Thanks." He pulled it on and took her hand and gently tugged her to sit beside him on the sofa. "So, what's up?" He could tell from Finn's demeanor that no one was dead, so he managed to relax slightly.

"We stopped by Neal's apartment earlier this morning to talk to Kira before she left for work. Were you aware that she collected on Neal's life insurance money a few days ago?"

"I was." Nina looked at Seamus with a small smile. "I didn't have a chance to tell you."

He nodded, frowning, and turned back to his brother. "Okay. Why does that concern us?"

"Because she wasn't there. In fact, it looks like she left in a hurry. It also turns out she hasn't been seen at the hospital for several days. Do you have any idea where she might go, Nina?"

"What? She's gone?" She sighed heavily. "I have no idea where she would go. Oh, my God! Does this mean it was her? Did she kill Neal? For the life insurance money? How much was it?"

"Two hundred thousand dollars," Chris said.

"Holy shit. That's a lot of life insurance." Seamus squeezed Nina's hand. "How much was the policy you were the beneficiary for?"

She shook her head. "I haven't had a chance to go the insurance office yet. I have no idea." She looked at the detectives. "You'll find her, won't you? She can't get away with this."

"We don't know whether or not she was the one who killed your brother." Chris held up her hand to forestall Nina's objection. "But I'll admit this doesn't look good. And we will find her, don't worry. Has she ever mentioned where she's from? Maybe where her family lives?"

Nina shook her head again. "Not that I recall." She shrugged apologetically. "I guess I never paid much attention if she talked about her background."

Chris stood, signaling their interview was at an end. "Don't worry. We'll find her. We wanted to let you know. I still think you should continue to be careful, but it looks like you may have less to worry about now, at least as far as your own safety is concerned."

"What about the guy who attacked her?" Seamus asked.

Chris sighed. "The man you identified in the photo lineup is a janitor at the university. He works in the student union building, which may be where you saw him. He has a solid alibi for the time of your attack: he was in jail on a DUI. Your attack may have been random after all."

Finn pushed to his feet. "Yeah, looks like you can relax a bit. Well, we'll get out of your hair and let you get back to—"

"Shut up, Finn." Seamus growled the words and narrowed his eyes at his brother.

Finn simply laughed and headed to the front door.

Chris flashed Nina an apologetic look and followed him out.

Seamus stood and ran his hand through his hair. "Sorry about my brother. He's an ass."

"It's fine," she said, waving her hand

distractedly. "Is this it? Is it over? I mean, once they find Kira?"

He held his hand out and pulled her next to him. "Maybe." He kissed her forehead. "But I still think you should be careful, hon, like Chris said. Let's take it a day at a time."

She smiled up at him. "Okay. You have nothing in your fridge, sir, so how about you take me out for breakfast before we pick up the girls?"

"I'd love to. Let me grab a shower first."

She wove her fingers though his belt loops. "Sounds great. Is there room for me?"

He grinned and scooped her up in his arms. "Let's find out."

***

Nina

"Thank you." She shut the back door of the car and waved to the Uber driver. Barb had picked her up for work that morning since Seamus was working, but she'd taken an Uber to the insurance office and another home. It had been good to get back to work, but now she was exhausted, and realized making the appointment for her first day back may have been a bit of a reach. She carefully locked the door behind her, but didn't feel she needed to set the alarm while she was inside. She always forgot and set it off by opening a door. *I'm tired of being such a nervous Nelly! I don't know why Kira tried to have me killed, but she's gone now. She got her money and took off. The police will find her sooner or later, and I'm sure I can stop being so vigilant. I must have been wrong about what the man said before he stabbed me.* It had been bothering her since Chris had told them the man she'd identified had an alibi. She knew trauma could mess with the mind; her memory, suspicious for showing up only well after the event, must be something her brain invented. *This is all so far from my area of expertise!* She was used to dealing with problems and issues that came up by heading to the library and digging into research. Everything in her professional world could be dealt with by hours spent with primary source documents unearthed from the archives. But this murder investigation and the threats against her were baffling. And exhausting. She tossed her bag on the table by the door and shrugged out of the light jacket she'd worn in the chilly morning air when she'd left for work. She grabbed her cell phone, though; she always had it close in case the girls needed to get in touch with her.

She'd received her own check from the insurance company, a staggering amount that would more than cover the cost of Neal's funeral and the outstanding debt. She knew she would need to deposit it soon, but she didn't want it and couldn't begin to deal with it now. *Later. I'm too tired to think about it now.*

She'd planned to take a short nap, but found she couldn't settle her mind enough to fall asleep. *Did Kira really kill Neal to get her hands on the life insurance money? Did she then try to make it look like a suicide? It seems so incredibly elaborate and*

far-fetched. She never came across as mercenary.
Nina had no answers, but couldn't manage to shake
off the questions swirling in her mind. They'd been
invading her thoughts all weekend since Finn and
Chris had interrupted her secret tryst with Seamus at
his apartment. She smiled wryly at her dramatic
term, but their time had been so special and that's
how she liked to remember it. He was scheduled to
work the next forty-eight hours, but they'd used
every spare moment over the weekend to make
love, needing to make up for lost time. They'd
taken the girls to swim at his parents' house on
Sunday afternoon and Izzy had brought Janey, so
the girls were in heaven. Nina had enjoyed visiting
with Izzy while Seamus and Mac swam with the
girls. Izzy had stated she wouldn't be caught dead in
a swimsuit as pregnant as she was, and Nina was
happy to lounge by the pool with her. It would be
one of the final swims of the season, and she
actually found it a bit cool already to be donning a
bikini.

Cara had shown up closer to the dinner hour and
the three had made plans for a girl's night out soon.
When Mel and Finn appeared, they told him they
were kidnapping Mel for a few hours away from the
baby and he could suck it if he didn't like it. He'd
simply laughed and handed little Ava to his mother,
who was eager to hold her new granddaughter.

"It'll do her good to get away for a couple hours.
I'll see if the guys want to come over and watch a
game and help me change diapers."

Nina smiled as she remembered the time with
Seamus's family. *I wonder if he realizes how lucky*

he is to have such a close-knit family? Her smile faded as she thought about her own family, never as close, and now heartbroken over the loss of Neal. She shrugged her shoulders, determined not to let the black mood have its way. She swung her legs over the edge of the bed and decided to spend some time picking up around the house. Nothing like a little housework to take her mind off things. It had gotten out of control during the time she'd been in the hospital and she was eager to whip it back into shape. Besides, maybe it would make her sleepy, so she could get back to her napping.

She picked up the family room, wondering how in the world the girls could leave so many pairs of shoes under the coffee table. Did they actually own that many? She clearly needed to weed some out as soon as possible and donate the extras to Goodwill. Thinking of how Seamus would approach it, she amended her idea: *I'll have the girls do it and clean their room while they're at it.*

She wasn't up to running the vacuum yet, so she settled for dusting, then moved on to the kitchen. Seamus had kept up with the dishes while she was recuperating, so there was little to do. The apples and tangerines in the fruit bowl in the middle of the kitchen table had shriveled, however, so she grabbed up the bowl and dumped the withered fruit in the garbage can. She stopped as the stainless-steel lid slammed shut—it had broken months ago and she needed to buy a new one soon—and reached to open it again. She'd glimpsed something odd, something which didn't belong in a fruit bowl, and re-opened the trash can to retrieve whatever it was one of the girls had left there. But as she wiped wet coffee grounds off the flash drive, she knew neither of the girls had left it. *What in the world?*

She retrieved her new laptop from her bedroom and plugged the small piece of plastic into the USB port. She double-clicked on the icon as soon as it appeared on her desktop. The directory showed a long list of Excel files, a video file, and one Word document. *These must be the files from Izzy. It's odd she didn't mention it Sunday when I saw her.* But Nina remembered how much had happened in the last few weeks and couldn't blame anyone for not remembering to mention a flash drive. *There probably isn't anything useful on it, anyway.*

She clicked open the Word doc and saw it was a note from Izzy:

Hey Seamus & Nina,
All the financials look legit. It appears the company turned a small profit last year and was on track for the same this year. I found the MP4 file embedded in one of the ledgers and extracted it. It's password protected, however, so I have no idea what's in it. Good luck! Hope this helps!
Izzy

Nina's heart pounded as she double-clicked the video file and was presented with a password prompt. After a half dozen attempts, she typed in 36NealzSe(retF!le24 and was astonished when the screen blinked and a still video shot, clearly of Neal, was displayed. She raised a shaking hand to move the mouse over the white triangle and clicked it.

"Hey, Sis."

Nina sucked in a breath as she gazed at Neal's face. *Oh, God! I miss you!* She wiped a tear away impatiently as she listened.

"So, I know you'll think I'm a worry-wart with conspiracy theory leanings, but hopefully you'll never have to watch this anyway." He laughed and scratched his cheek, the same way she'd seen him do so many times before. *"Anyhoo, I just figured I'd make this little video and bury it deep in my personal computer. I told Kira to make sure you get the laptop if anything ever happens to me."* He laughed again. *"God, that sounds so dramatic, huh? I'm not the type of guy anything would ever happen to, though. I'm just boring, old Neal Braden, after all."*

Nina reached for a paper napkin to staunch the flow of tears she couldn't contain.

"But here's the thing, Nina." He looked back over his shoulder, then leaned closer to the camera. *"Something is going on here at RiskCom. I'm not sure what, but it's not good. I think someone in the company may be selling us out. I've been hearing rumors that our flagship program isn't as secure as it's supposed to be."*

"Well, well, well. I guess he wasn't quite as stupid as I figured."

***

Nina shrieked and leapt to her feet, sending her chair skidding across the tile floor as she spun to face the intruder. "Gordy! How the hell did you get in my house?" She'd locked the door behind her; she remembered locking the door. She backed away from him, fear coursing through her body. There could be absolutely no good reason for him to be here like this.

He reached forward and pressed pause on the computer. "We're missing the best part." He straightened and turned to her, an exasperated expression on his face. "I have a key, Nina. I stole it from Neal the night I killed him. The stupid twit had them labeled. I slipped them off his key ring right before I shot him. No one ever noticed they were gone."

"You killed him? Why? He was your best friend!" She could barely hear her own voice over the pulse pounding in her ears.

"Yeah, well, we weren't actually that close any more. You know what? I'd like to hear what Neal knew before I tell you why I did it. Come sit down and let's watch the rest of the video. It's pretty shitty production value, but what can you expect from such a low budget affair?"

"Get the fuck out of my house, Gordy!" She reached behind her, fumbling on the counter for her cell phone, which she'd set there earlier.

"Later." He pulled a small, yet lethal-looking hand gun from his pocket. "Now, I said come over here so we can watch the rest of this video. And you can leave your cell phone right where it is. You won't be needing it."

She shivered at the coldness in his voice, wondering how he'd kept this side of himself hidden for so long. She shook her head, glancing at the time displayed on the oven clock, desperate to know if her mother would be dropping the girls off soon. They weren't due for nearly an hour. *Oh, thank God! I don't want them anywhere near here until Gordy's gone.* She was terrified for herself, of course, but couldn't bear the thought of anything happening to her children. "Are you going to kill me too?"

"Definitely. Don't worry, though. I'll make it look like your intruder came back and I'll be gone long before your kids get home. I'm not a monster, Nina."

She refrained from commenting, knowing anything she said would only get her killed faster. She thought frantically, desperately trying to think of anything she could do to save herself. *I don't keep a gun in the house. Even if I did, I'd never get to it before he shot me. Oh, God, I don't want to die! I want to live and watch my daughters grow up. I want to grow old with Seamus.*

"Now, come sit down so we can watch the rest of this captivating video together." He bent to pick up the chair she'd knocked over and gestured with the gun for her to sit. "Don't make me tell you again, Nina."

"No." She crossed her arms and spat the words at him. "I'm not going to do anything you say. Why should I? If you're going to kill me, then just fucking do it! I don't want to hear any more." She wasn't being fatalistic; she realized Gordy wanted to enact some sort of soliloquy like the criminals always did at the end of a television mystery. But she had no desire to listen, and she hoped she could make him angry enough to drop his guard for a moment. *And what the hell will I do if he does?* She had no clue, but she prayed she'd know when the time was right.

His mouth hardened at her defiance. He lunged forward and grabbed her arm, yanking her to the chair. He pressed the barrel of the gun hard into her cheek; she knew there would be a nasty bruise later. "But I want you to listen and I want to watch the rest of the video, so sit the fuck down and I might not insist on having a little fun before I shoot you." He let his eyes drift to the front of her shirt and linger on her breasts.

Her blood ran cold at the thought of him touching her. *Oh, God, anything but that!* She sat. He'd found a sure-fire way to quell her rebellion.

Gordy pressed play again and Neal's voice filled the room.

"—but I can't be sure of anything yet. I hope I'm wrong. I wanted you to know, however, in case something happens to me. You can go to the police, but whatever you do, don't mention any of my suspicions to Gordy. I don't have any proof, but something's definitely up with him. He's always been the one to look for shortcuts, and I think he's gambling again. I don't trust him, Nina." He paused to rub his cheek again. *"Well, I've rambled on long enough, especially considering no one will*

ever see this. Hopefully. Hey, I love ya, sis! Take care!"

Neal leaned forward, and his face blurred and filled the screen for a moment. The video ended, and the screen went black.

"I knew he didn't trust me. Fucker." Gordy slammed the laptop shut and threw himself into the chair next to Nina's, keeping the gun trained on her. "He was a pretty smart guy; I'll give him that." He set the gun on the table in front of him and ran his hands through his hair.

Nina's eyes darted to the weapon.

Gordy met her gaze with a smirk. "Go ahead. I know you're thinking about it."

Nina crossed her arms and sneered at him. "Fuck off."

He chuckled. "Such a mouth! I used to think you were so sweet. You always acted like you were too good for me, even back in college. Then you married that old-ass professor. But Neal told me he was rich." He smiled at her knowingly. "I guess we're not so different, are we, Nina?"

She looked away from his insufferable face. *Please, God, give me a way out of this!*

"Neal always hassled me about my gambling, but a guy's got to have a way to let off some steam. My poker habit has gotten expensive lately, however, and a few months ago I was approached by a couple of Chinese gentlemen who made me an offer I couldn't refuse." He laughed at his own joke. "They wanted to purchase the code for our Proteus program. They thought they could reverse engineer it and turn it into some sort of master key to hack into the government or some shit. I didn't care. They offered me a load of cash to give them the code. So I did. But then Neal got nosey, and it was either him or me. I chose me."

"Who are you to decide your life is more valuable than someone else's? Than my brother's?" Her voice shook as she whispered the words, not expecting an answer, but needing to ask.

Gordy stared at her, a small frown between his brows. He was saved from answering by the doorbell.

Hope flared briefly in Nina's chest.

"Are you expecting someone?"

She shook her head.

The hope was quickly extinguished by Gordy's next words. "We'll ignore it, then. It's probably FedEx or something."

But the doorbell rang again, followed by a female voice. "Nina? Are you home? It's Cara."

"Who's Cara?" Gordy leapt from his chair and growled the question in her ear, the gun jammed against her neck.

"She's just a friend of mine," she whimpered. She had no intention of giving him more information than was absolutely necessary.

He stood, pulling her to her feet. "Get rid of her. Answer the door but tell her you're sick or something. I don't care, but she needs to leave. I'll kill her if she doesn't. You don't want that on your conscience, do you?"

She walked to the door, her legs trembling so hard she feared she'd fall. Gordy followed closely behind, the gun pressed into her back. He took up a position to the side of the double front door, just inside the living room, where he couldn't be seen as long as she didn't open the door wide. She wanted to give Cara a hint but had no idea how to do it without endangering the other woman. She couldn't risk it; she'd have to act as normal as possible. She opened the door a crack and peered out.

"Nina? Hi! I stopped by on my way home from work to drop off some clothes one of the girls left at my parents' house last night." She held up a small, plastic grocery bag. Nina could see the brightly flowered print through the plastic: the flowered shorts Iris had worn over her swimming suit. Cara reached for the handle of the security screen door, but found it locked. "You mind if I come in?"

"Oh, um…actually, I'm not feeling well. I guess I pushed myself too hard my first day back to work. Why don't you just leave the bag on the porch? I'll, uh, get it later."

Cara frowned, her hand frozen on the screen door. "O—kay." Her eyes darted to Nina's, frowning. "Is everything all right?" She tried to peer into the house behind Nina.

Nina stepped forward to block her view. "Everything's fine. I'm sure I'll be better by Thursday for our girls' night. I know how much *Chris* is looking forward to it." She stressed the name ever-so-slightly. It was the only hint she could think of that Gordy wouldn't understand. She realized the probability of Cara getting it was slim, however.

Cara stared at her for a long moment before she finally nodded. "Yeah. Okay. Well, I'll just leave this here." She bent to place the bag on the door mat. "Call me later? Get some rest." She turned and strode down the walkway to her car.

Nina breathed a sigh of relief and closed the door.

"Lock it."

She flipped the lock then turned to him. "What now?"

"Wait." He turned to look out the front window between the slats of the shade. "I need to make sure she leaves." A moment later he turned back to her. "She's gone. Let's return to the kitchen." He gestured with the gun for her to precede him.

As Nina walked in front of him, she wondered if perhaps she could get him to talk more. He'd seemed eager to tell her why he killed Neal, and she was desperate to give Cara enough time to call the police, on the off-chance she'd understood Nina's veiled hint. She desperately held on to the gossamer thread of hope. "How did you do it?"

"Do what? Oh, you mean how did I pull off such a brilliant murder? The police totally bought the whole suicide thing for quite a while." He resumed his seat and motioned for her to sit. "I planned it meticulously. I took the gun from Neal's apartment a few months ago. I knew he kept it in his closet, but I also knew he never checked it. He said he hated it and only bought it because there'd been some break-ins in their neighborhood. I got the ketamine from a veterinarian friend of mine who knows not to ask questions. I snagged your key after I killed him—I had a feeling it might be necessary. I figured Neal would have told you about his suspicions. I used it to get in after Kira told me she gave you Neal's laptop. Dumb bitch!"

"Was she involved? Did you plan this together?"

He laughed harshly. "With Kira? No. She's too stupid for words. She might be a total slut—" He broke off at the surprised look on her face. "You mean you didn't know?" He continued to laugh. "Yeah, she's quite the little gold digger. She'll sleep with anyone she thinks she can get a few bucks from. I stopped screwing her almost a year ago." He appeared contemplative for a moment. "I don't think Neal knew. Huh."

Poor Neal! He was so in love with Kira. I hope he never knew what she was really like.

"Anyway, I made a bit of a mess looking for his laptop, so I decided I better make it look like a burglary. Sorry about that." He grinned in a way that let her know he wasn't sorry at all. "But it gave me the idea for the mugging in the parking lot behind your office. That almost worked. You just can't get good help these days. So, I decided I'd better—"

A loud rapping on the kitchen window interrupted his disgusting monologue and they both looked up suddenly. Cara's shocked face peered in as she yelled, "Hey!"

Nina knew this was the moment—the only chance she'd likely get—and she acted without hesitation. She grabbed the heavy, yellow Fiesta ware fruit bowl she'd so recently emptied and swung it at Gordy's head as hard as she could. He saw it coming at the last second, but didn't have time to duck. Instead, his sudden turn presented his face to the bowl, which slammed into his nose. Blood spurted violently over the table and Nina, as Gordy fell backward out of his chair and collapsed, unconscious, while the bowl broke into several large pieces around him. Nina scrabbled over him for the gun.

"Unlock the goddamn door!" Cara screeched as she pounded on the security screen, which had been so recently installed after the break-in.

Nina stepped over Gordy's splayed legs to flip the lock and let Cara in.

She pushed past Nina to stare down at Gordy. "What the hell is going on? Who is that?" She glanced from the body on the floor to Nina. "Shit, girl! Give me that!" She took the gun from Nina's shaking hands.

"Did I kill him?" Nina's voice was calm, but she couldn't stop the trembling in her hands and legs.

"Hopefully." Cara reached for her cell phone and dialed 9-1-1. She told them she had interrupted a home invasion and they needed to send police, paramedics, and an ambulance. Then she called Finn. "Okay." She hung up and turned to Nina. "Sit down and give me the quick version before they get here."

By the time Nina finished her story, they heard sirens approaching. Gordy hadn't awakened and she feared she might truly have killed him. She didn't want to be responsible for his death; she wanted him to live and go to jail for the rest of his life. Cara kept the gun trained on him anyway. Once the sirens sounded near, Cara laid the gun on the counter, far away from Gordy, saying she didn't want to be shot when the police came in.

The ambulance was close behind the police and Nina was relieved to learn Gordy was still alive. The paramedics were treating her for shock when Finn and Chris arrived. She had barely finished giving her statement to the police when Seamus burst in.

"Nina!"

She stood and ran to him, pushing a paramedic out of the way. The only place she wanted to be in that moment was in his arms. As he pulled her close, she finally gave way to the tears that had been threatening to burst forth all afternoon.

He led her to the sofa and wrapped her in a blanket, holding her while Finn told him what had happened. "Where is he? Where's Gordy?" Seamus bit the words out.

"On his way to the hospital. Don't worry; he's not going anywhere. Nina clocked him good with a bowl of some sort," Finn said.

"My Fiesta ware fruit bowl." She sat up and reached for a tissue on the side table. "I broke my beautiful Fiesta ware fruit bowl on his fucking face."

Seamus pulled her back against him and kissed the top of her head. "Good job, hon. I'll buy you another fruit bowl, I swear. God, it was him all along?"

"Apparently," Chris said, entering the room. She handed a bottle of water to Nina. "I got hold of your mom. She's going to keep the girls until you're ready for them. She said she'll keep them all night, if necessary."

Nina nodded and opened the water. "When can I clean up the kitchen? And I need a shower in the worst way." She stared down at her silky blouse, now spattered with Gordy's blood.

"I'll clean up the kitchen as soon as they let me," Cara said. "You don't need to worry about that."

"Thanks, sis," Seamus said. He turned to Nina. "We can go get the girls as soon as everything is finished here. I know you want them close."

"I do." She capped the water bottle and looked up at him. "But I want you here too. Please stay."

"Always."

Epilogue

Seamus

"You sure it's warm enough for you?" He reached for her hand, which was ice cold.

"It's fine. It's so gorgeous; I don't want to go back inside yet."

They stood on the beach, gazing out on Tomales Bay, an hour and a half north of San Francisco. Nina was on spring break and they'd decided to take a short vacation, just the two of them. Her parents had taken the girls to Disneyland, and Seamus and Nina had grabbed the opportunity to leave town as well for a few days. The months since Gordy's arrest had been stressful and they needed to get away. He'd been arraigned and was being held without bail until his murder trial, but Chris told them he had also been charged with treason and would likely stand trial for those federal charges first. Treason carried a possible death sentence, so the likely life sentence for his murder trial in New Mexico would be moot. *It serves him right, but shit!*

A death sentence? Seamus shivered at the thought and pulled Nina close. He didn't want to think about betrayal, murder, and death here in this beautiful place.

Kira had surprised them all by turning up on Nina's front porch two days after Gordy's arrest. Finn and Chris had discovered the life insurance check ripped into tiny pieces in Kira's trash can.

"I didn't want his money," she explained over coffee. *"I had no idea he took out an insurance policy; he never told me."*

"But why did you leave so suddenly? We thought—"

"I know, believe me. The police showed up at my mother's house in Poughkeepsie with guns drawn. I just needed to get away. It was all too much, and I couldn't take it anymore." She broke into sobs and buried her face in her hands.

Seamus exchanged a bewildered glance with Nina as she awkwardly patted Kira on the back.

"I still don't understand why you left, Kira. You ripped up the insurance check. Why?"

Kira lifted her tear-stained face, mascara streaming from her eyes. "Because I don't deserve it. I cheated on Neal! I was having an affair! That's the kind of person I am!"

"Hey, don't be so hard on yourself. We all make mistakes. I wish you'd chosen someone other than Gordy though."

"Gordy? Gordon Sanderson? Why would you think I had an affair with him? Oh, my God! Did he tell you that?"

Nina nodded, apparently dumbfounded.

"He wishes! He came on to me soon after Neal and I started dating, but I would never sleep with my boyfriend's best friend. Correction: supposed best friend." She shrugged. "I met Dan at the hospital. He's a surgeon." She stood and carried her mug to the sink. "I'm in love with him. I was going to tell Neal, but it was so hard. I might not have loved him anymore, but I certainly didn't want to hurt him. When he died, I thought he'd found out about Dan and killed himself." She poured the dregs of her coffee down the drain and turned to them, fresh tears streaking through the black makeup. "I'm so sorry."

Seamus had expected Nina to rail against her, but she'd blown him away by gathering Kira in her arms and holding her as she cried. When would he stop being surprised by the depth of Nina's heart?

He had finished the arson academy a few weeks before Izzy had her baby, a boy she and Mac named Benjamin David. He was beginning to settle into his new job, and although he missed the camaraderie of the station, he loved the new work and the more normal hours that went along with it. Being home with Nina and the girls nearly every evening was awesome, and he was eager to make the situation permanent.

"I can't believe you found this place." Nina slipped her arm around his waist. "It's perfect."

He'd asked around at the office and had liked the sound of this out-of-the-way resort situated right on the water. Their room had a small kitchenette and a patio they'd been enjoying in the cool evenings, sipping wine they bought at local wineries in Sonoma and Napa while watching the sun set over the waters of the bay. It was still early enough in the season that the resort was sparsely populated, and both were enjoying the peace and quiet. "I'm glad you approve. Does this look like a good spot?" They'd come down to the beach with a picnic dinner of local oysters, fresh sourdough bread, cheese made on a nearby farm, and a chilled bottle of sparkling white wine they'd found earlier in the day.

She nodded and spread the blanket she carried on the sand. "I don't want to leave tomorrow."

He grinned at her. "Me neither. I do miss the girls, though. I hope they like the sweatshirts we found for them."

"Of course they will." She twisted the wires from the wine and popped the cork. "Here." She handed him a glass of the bubbly wine. They'd borrowed the glasses and other utensils from the cupboard in their room.

He took the wine and sipped. Then he cleared his throat. "Nina, I want to ask you something." He'd planned this a hundred different ways and hadn't been satisfied with any of them. It had to be perfect; Nina deserved no less. He'd almost asked a half dozen times but couldn't quite get the words out. Now they were on their last night and he was out of time.

She paused mid-sip and gazed at him. "Okay."

He set his glass on the blanket and reached into his pocket for the small pouch, which had been burning a hole there all week. His hand got stuck. His attempts to dislodge it caused his glass to tip over on the uneven ground, spilling wine all over his jeans. *Shit*. He finally wrestled his hand from his pocket and tried to open the drawstring pouch. The strings had tangled, of course, and he cursed as he struggled to undo what chaos theory said couldn't be undone.

"May I help?"

"Nope. I got it." He didn't have it. "Damn it, Nina." He chuckled ruefully. "This was supposed to be perfect. I'm sorry."

She arched her delicate eyebrows. "What was supposed to be perfect?"

"This proposal. I've been trying to find the perfect moment all week to ask you to marry me, but now we're out of time and I can't manage to get these *effing* strings undone!" His fingers had become useless sausages, fumbling with the tiny silken threads.

She smiled and reached for the small bag. "Let me try." She took the bag and had the knot undone in a few seconds. "Small fingers." She winked and returned the pouch. "Carry on."

He smiled and rolled his eyes. "Yes, ma'am." He pulled her to her feet and lowered himself to one knee.

"The whole nine yards, huh?"

"Of course." He cleared his throat. He had no idea why he was so nervous. He'd basically moved in to her house, after all; they were living as a married couple already. "Nina Braden, I love you with all my heart. I love your daughters like they're my own. Would you make me the happiest man alive and do me the honor of marrying me? I promise to spend the rest of my life trying to make you happy."

She smiled as a tear tracked down her cheek. Then she knelt in front of him and leaned forward to kiss him. "I love you with all my heart and soul, Seamus. I always have. Can I see the ring?"

"Oh, yeah." But he dropped it in the sand and buried it when he lunged for the tiny piece of jewelry. They spent nearly three minutes scrabbling around, sifting sand through their fingers.

"Ah ha!" Nina held it up triumphantly, blowing sand from the crevices.

Seamus peered at it. "No, that's not it. Keep looking." But he was laughing, the ridiculousness of the situation finally winning.

"Sweet. I get two." She handed the ring to him. "Put it on."

He grinned and took her hand, fitting the diamond solitaire on her slim finger. "You haven't answered me yet."

"I didn't? Oh," she said with a laugh. "I guess I didn't. Of course I'll marry you."

"Whew. Great." He pulled her close and kissed her soundly. "I'm glad that's out of the way. Sorry I muffed it up so badly."

She laughed and pulled his head back for another kiss. "It was certainly unique. Why were you so nervous?"

"I don't know." He stared into her luminous green eyes, willing her to understand. "But it's the most important question I've ever asked, and I

360

wanted it to be perfect. You deserve the best, Nina."

"So do you." She grinned and looped her arms around his neck. "Would it be indelicate to ask when you want us to get married?"

"I'd marry you tonight if I could. You name the day and I'll be there."

"Hmm. I don't want a big wedding unless you do." She glanced up at him through her lashes. When he shook his head, she continued. "How about right after school lets out for the summer? I'm not teaching a first session summer class, so I'll have time. Getting stabbed used up all my sick days, but I should be able to take a week of vacation around then."

"Sounds good to me. Listen, Nina. We could probably have the reception in my parents' backyard. Finn and Mel did that, and it was really nice. Do you, uh, mind if we have the ceremony in church, though? My mom is pretty traditional."

She smiled. "I don't mind. Do I need to become Catholic before then?"

"You'd do that? I know you've always been Protestant."

"It's important to you. Besides, I haven't gone to church in years."

"Well, I don't make it to mass nearly as often as my mother would like." He kissed her again and tucked a fly-away strand of hair behind her ear. "What do you say we eat this picnic before the oysters desert us and head back to the ocean? I don't think I spilled all the wine."

"I'm starving, so I say yes. Besides, oysters are an aphrodisiac. Did you know?"

"I had no idea." But his grin told her he was lying. He pulled her across the blanket and fell back, causing her to sprawl across his chest. "I really don't think we need an aphrodisiac, do you?"

She arched her eyebrows and smirked. "Prove it."

He loved her feisty spirit. "You got it." He rolled, pulling her body under his and lowered his mouth to hers. She tasted of the fruity wine and he swept his tongue in to taste her more deeply. He found the edge of her sweatshirt and pushed his hand underneath to cup her breast, teasing the nipple until it was a hard bud. He kissed and caressed her for several long minutes, then rolled away. "That's all for now, you naughty minx. I don't want to get arrested for having sex on a public beach." He rooted inside the picnic basket. "Let's eat these oysters, then I'll take you back to our room and see how well they work."

The End

Acknowledgements

Special thanks to Lacey, who spent so many hours—many of them in the hot tub—helping me talk through the plot and decide who Neal's killer really was. Thanks also to my amazing writing group, Maslow's Ding Dong. You guys rock and continue to keep me honest and humble.

As always, I must give a shout out to my editor extraordinaire, Toni Rakestraw, who polishes and shines and pushes me to be a better writer. Thanks also to the whole team at Limitless Publishing for the opportunity they've provided, and the enormous amount of care and work that goes into each and every book.

About the Author

Amy Reece lives in New Mexico with her incredible husband and two ridiculous mutts, Greta and Sodapop. When she's not writing, she's teaching high school English and social studies or maybe wandering through a thrift store in search of the next lucky teapot for her vast collection. She is an unrepentant bookaholic and has overflowing bookshelves in nearly every room of her house. Her favorite authors include J.R.R. Tolkien, J.K. Rowling, and C.S. Lewis–must have something to do with initials! She loves to travel and is hoping to need many research trips for future writing projects.

Did you enjoy this book? If so, please, please, please leave a short, but stellar review on amazon and/or GoodReads. I would really appreciate it!

If you want to cyber-stalk me, here are some helpful links:

Good Reads:
https://www.goodreads.com/author/show/13884337.Amy_Reece

Amazon author page:
https://www.amazon.com/Amy-Reece/e/B00WDG12RO

Facebook Fan Page:
https://www.facebook.com/areeceauthor

Twitter Fan Page:
https://twitter.com/AReeceAuthor

Website:
https://www.amyreeceauthor.com/

Blog:
https://amyreece.wordpress.com/